PRAISE
FOR JONATHAN SHAW

"Finally, after twenty-plus years of coaxing, cajoling, pleading and basic needling on my part, my ol' scallywag brother Jonathan Shaw has put his pen to paper, dragging and drudging up virulent and violent hallucinations from his not-so-cute brainscape. Been waiting too long for this. So have you, whoever you are, believe me. If you don't yet know him, you will. If you didn't want to, too bad. Once he's in, he's in. Jonathan Shaw's words, work, life, lives, deaths, rants, rage, hilarity and taste rank with the best of 'em. If Hubert Selby Jr., Charles Bukowski, Ernest Hemingway, Jack Kerouac, William Burroughs, Neil Cassidy, Dr. Hunter S. Thompson, the Marquis de Sade, Antonio Carlos Jobim, Joao Gilberto, Edward Teach, Charley Parker, Iggy Pop, Louis-Ferdinand Celine, R. Crumb, Robert Williams, Joe Coleman, Dashiell Hammett, E.M. Cioran and all of the Three Stooges had all been involved in some greasy, shameful whorehouse orgy, Jonathan Shaw would surely be its diabolical reprobate spawn."—***Johnny Depp***

"Although known primarily for his work as a famed tattoo artist, Shaw is also a talented writer whose latest book, *Scab Vendor*, draws on his own life, vacillating between first person and third person to tell his story in this sprawling, experimental autobiography. . . The comparisons to Charles Bukowski are obvious, but *Scab Vendor* reminded me more of Hubert Selby Jr. and Henry Miller in terms of tone and style. . . .

Interspersed with vignettes from Shaw's life (and) foggy memories of a chaotic childhood ("other kids got [the] Hardy Boys. . . I got Hieronymus Bosch"), *Scab Vendor* [is] a whirlpool of drugs and alcohol. The gritty, gutter prose is sharpened by Shaw's gift for dialogue and sharp insight. This tale is one of shame, humility, and wonder at how it all happened." —***Publishers Weekly***

"The grunge of Bukowski. . . The teeth-grinding momentum of the Beats."—***Kirkus Reviews***

"Jonathan Shaw is the next Bukowski."—***Rolling Stone***

"{Shaw is} a hunk of shit fish-asshole cunt-sucker!"—***Charles Bukowski***

"Is he bitter? Oh, just a tad."—***R. Crumb***

"Compelling and hot as a sticky summer night that won't let you sleep." —***New York Times Book Review***

"Jonathan Shaw's writing is one hell of a wild ride through the bizarre netherworld of his own damaged consciousness. His experiences are real and his language and insights kinetic and brutal. This is what the French would call "littérature maudit," and Shaw's writing certifies him as a subversive and criminal inhabitant of the world of human expression." —***Jim Jarmusch***

"Jonathan Shaw is a decorated veteran of the drug war whose deviance is only exceeded by his clever ability to weave his own sickness into a true classic of American literature. He is Oscar Wilde and Charlie Manson tattooing a portrait of Dorian Gray on the white underbelly of a society desperately in need of this type of fearless storytelling." —***Marilyn Manson***

"Jonathan Shaw has been a Zelig-like figure in American underground culture for the past forty years."—***Esquire***

". . . {Jonathan Shaw is} a real writer. . ."—***Henry Rollins***

"Jonathan Shaw has made it through the eye-of-the-needle into our lives. This kind of rite of passage gives his perspectives a sense of the physical world that he creates for us. To immerse ourselves in this bare-bones attitude is what a novel is supposed to do for the reader. Lucky us."—**Debbie Harry, Blondie**

"Jonathan Shaw's passionate descriptions of the surreal, paranoid jungle he inhabits capture the haunting poetry of his soul."
—**Hubert Selby Jr., author of Requiem for a Dream and Last Exit to Brooklyn**

"Shaw's writing reinvents and promotes life. Be prepared to see yourself in the pages of *Narcisa*, the essence of your own poor humanity, weak and vulnerable and unprepared—and to see at the same time your own strengths, whatever your circumstances."
—**Paulo Lins, author of City of God**

"Required reading. One of my favorite writers."
—**Lydia Lunch, author of Paradoxia**

"Jonathan Shaw has had his passport stamped in hell so many times he could get his mail there. . . Written in blood, his writing takes us places most people never come back from. . . Vile as junkie-cum, beautiful as a dead drunk's bible, *Scab Vendor* will keep you clawing at the pages. . ."
—**Jerry Stahl, author of Permanent Midnight**

"{Jonathan Shaw's Narcisa is a} compelling novel that grips you right from the beginning."—**VICE**

"Shaw's poetic collage lays bare the poetry of the streets and probes the shadowy corners of the soul with fearless candor."—**Jillian Lauren, New York Times bestselling author of Some Girls**

"Shaw's life is nothing short of movie fodder."—**LA Weekly**

"Shaw (leaves an) aesthetic legacy." —**NY Observer**

"Literate and compelling. . . "
—*Harlan Ellison, Grammy Award-winning author
of* **Strange Wine**

"Shaw has lived many lives, but in many ways writing about his vast and varied experiences is just the beginning of a new odyssey."—*Agronaut*

"Jonathan Shaw has blazed a new literary trail, and ripped a new asshole in consensus reality along the way."
—*Carlo McCormick, author of* **Trespass**

"Jonathan Shaw is a revelation. The pen may be mightier than the sword, but Shaw's work is an IED on paper."
—*Dan Fante, author of* **Chump Change** *and* **86'd**

"Dazzling!"
—*Harold Schechter, author of* **Deviant** *and* **Man-Eater**

"Amazing writing."—*Kat Von D*

"An example of human indestructibility that is hard to surpass."
—*Eugene Hutz, Gogol Bordello*

"A writer of immense passion and soul, Jonathan Shaw has the courage to vivisect his own soul."
—*Joe Coleman, author of* **Cosmic Retribution**

"Few have dipped so deeply or functioned so extensively in the cultural underbelly of our world than Jonathan Shaw. . . He is a virtuoso."
—*Robert Williams, author of* **Slang Aesthetics**

"Jonathan Shaw is a true old-school storyteller with a criminal mind and heart who's lived what he writes. Welcome to Hell."
—*Bonge, Hells Angels*

"Jonathan Shaw is a Renaissance Lowlife. Openhearted prose. . . Pure magic."
—*Larry "Ratso" Sloman, author of* **The Secret Life of Houdini**

"An agonized cri de coeur . . . Shades of Dante, of Baudelaire, of Bukowski, of Celine. . . "—**Tom Nolan, author of Three Chords for Beauty's Sake**

"Nightmarish talent. . . wedged between outlaw and genius. . . serious street cred."—**N.Y. Press**

"Jonathan Shaw is a myth: an American anti-hero whose wild exploits are folklore in underground circles the world over."—**Huck**

"Bruised, brilliant and unapologetically raw."—**Gonzo Today**

"Jonathan Shaw is an American classic. . . a barbarian intellectual and optimistic cynic. . . "—**Juxtapoz**

"{Shaw's writing follows} in the great tradition of cultural criminals like Genet, Rimbaud, Artaud through the Beats."—**Paper**

"Shaw is an acknowledged master craftsman."—**Seconds**

"*Narcisa* reads like a long-lost literary classic by Kerouac, Burroughs, Miller, Fante, Bukowski."—**CVLT Nation**

"A cult classic. . . Oozes delicious dysfunction. . . Gritty and raw as an open wound. . . Never before has an author explored {codependency} with such honest integrity. . . "—**Beverly Hills Courier**

"In line with the best of Fante, Bukowski and Kerouac. . . Uppercuts for each sentence. . . Powerful, furious, brilliant."
—**Librairie Quai des Brumes, France**

"Magnificently narrated by Shaw, *Narcisa* presents a violent and dazzling Rio de Janeiro as its ghostly, otherworldly stage."
—**El Fanzine, Mexico**

"Intense as hallucinations from the flames of Hell, Shaw's writing transcends the dark melancholy of a devastated Paradise."
—**Reporte Indigo, Mexico**

"{*Narcisa*} will bring tears to reader's eyes."
—***Folha de São Paulo, Brazil***

"Narcisa' is the confession of a hungry ghost, the insatiable, the unloved core of humanity's deepest sorrow. This beautifully written, brutally honest tale speaks to the wounded and weary child within each of us."
—***Noah Levine, author of* Dharma Punx *and* Against the Stream**

"An intoxicating classic of subversive writing. Stains your soul with pitch black tar."—***Dengue Magazine, Brazil***

"Shaw is an iconoclastic stranger in the literary nest."—***Life and Style***

"Very vibrant, very important art."—***Men's Journal***

"Jonathan Shaw is a notorious innovator and creator."—***Ponyboy***
". . . A resoundingly successful debut {by a} counter-culture icon. . . "
—***Inquisitr***

"Shaw is a true philosophical, transcendent soul."—***Citizine***

"Absolutely intoxicating. . . Bukowski on acid. . . Dark and hypnotic."
—***Powell's Books***

"Your jaw will drop, your mind will be blown."—***Crusher magazine***

"A sordid tale. . . Fascinating and toxic. . . "—***Grazia, France***

"Jonathan Shaw is a modern pirate, the last filibuster of the underground."—***Lenta, Russia***

". . . An explosive, intoxicating novel. Oral, electric, crazy. *Narcisa* seduces."—***Hall des Livres, France***

"Jonathan Shaw is an authentic 'beatnik'. . . The real-life model for Johnny Depp's Captain Jack the Pirate. . . Heir to Kerouac and Bukowski, with a strong Brazilian cultural orientation."
—***O Globo magazine, Brazil***

"Written in a frenetic, addictive style not suitable for all audiences,

HOMEWARD BOUND

HOMEWARD BOUND

CONFESSIONS OF A TATTOO ARTIST

-BOOK 2

A self-portrait by **Jonathan Shaw**

TURNER

Turner Publishing Company
Nashville, Tennessee
New York, New York

www.turnerpublishing.com

Scab Vendor: Confessions of a Tattoo Artist

Cover artwork: Jonathan Shaw and Miguel Angel Maese
Cover design: Maddie Cothren
Book design: Glen Edelstein
Author's Photo: Larnce Gold

Library of Congress Cataloging-in-Publication Data Available Upon Request

9781684421367

Printed in the United States of America
16 17 18 19 20 9 8 7 6 5 4 3 2 1

FOR MY MOTHER, DORIS DOWLING, WHO WAS ALWAYS THERE. AND
FOR MY BELOVED PARTNER GENEVIEVE ALTAMIRANO, WHOSE LOVE
ARRIVED ON THE WINGS OF A HUMMINGBIRD, TEACHING ME EACH DAY
TO BE A BETTER MAN.

AUTHOR'S NOTE

You might know the name Jonathan Shaw as belonging to the first tattoo artist to ever appear on *The Tonight Show with David Letterman*. Or maybe you've seen my unlikely likeness depicted by Pulitzer Prize-winning artist Art Spiegelman on the cover of the *The New Yorker*. You might know me as the son of legendary Swing-era bandleader Artie Shaw—or maybe the tattooed thug giving Clint Eastwood beef in the movie *Tightrope*.

You may have seen the magazine I founded back in the early '90s, International Tattoo Art, at your local newsstand. Or you might have read my novel, *Narcisa: Our Lady of Ashes*, published by Johnny Depp's HarperCollins imprint, or my recent visual archeological dig into the history of tattoo art, *Vintage Tattoo Flash*, on Powerhouse Books.

You may have already read *Scab Vendor - Confessions of a Tattoo Artist*, the first volume of this ongoing memoir series. Or maybe you only remember the name Jonathan Shaw as the infamous "Tattoo Artist to the Stars" who made headline news for being indicted by a New York City Grand Jury and charged with 89 felony counts of illegal weapons possession.

Or . . . maybe you've never heard of me at all. I'm going to assume that's the most likely scenerio and - at my publisher's suggestion - write a few short words of introduction about myself, and this book:

For decades I was a journeyman tattoo artist. Eventually, I became a world-famous "celebrity tattooist." Over the course of that long, surreal career, I became known as one of the most infamous and influential tattoo men on the planet. My growing client list included cops, criminals and captains of Industry, along with many famous names. Names like Johnny Depp, The Cure, The Velvet Underground, The Pogues, The Ramones, Marilyn Manson, Jim Jarmusch, Joe Coleman, Johnny Winter, Kate Moss, and the notorious Great Train Robber, Ronald Biggs—not to mention Tupac Shakur and all his bitches. Even Vanilla Ice was lining up for an appointment - much to my embarrassment - but hey, it was the 90s, right? Strangely, I'm still one of the most well-known names in the tattoo profession today—despite having retired over 15 years ago from an industry with an absurdly short memory— an industry I was unwittingly instrumental in pioneering.

So, what to say about this book?

The long, cockeyed evolution of this second installment to my multi-volume *Scab Vendor* memoir saga has more to do with the long, cockeyed evolution of the long, cockeyed life that spawned it than with any high-falutin literary aspirations. All of the crazy shit contained herein is basically fertilizer for this humble chronicle of a life. My life. The good, the bad, and the ugly. Continuing the narrative from the point in time where the first volume, *Scab Vendor*, left off, *Homeward Bound* spans roughly the second decade of this bizarre, stranger-than-fiction existence – my late teens and early twenties. The rest, as they say, is history. History, which will be covered in subsequent volumes, God willing.

That said, Homeward Bound is very much a sequel to the previous volume. While the overall storyline of this book can easily be enjoyed as a stand-alone work in its own right, there are certain references in its pages to specific characters, places, and events that will be more fully understood and appreciated having first read Scab Vendor. Either way, whether you've already read Scab Vendor and liked it enough to continue the long, strange trip with me here, or if you're just getting on the train at this particular stop, I thank you for your interest in my dubious contribution to the world of literary expression.

For what it's worth, I believe that, as human beings, we all come hard-wired with an inherent need to share our strength, weakness, pain, passion, despair, hope, love, hate and general personal stories with others of our kind, in order to help one another navigate our common human experience. In that sense, storytelling can be seen as a powerful evolutionary tool. And, like tattooing, it seems to be one of the most ancient compulsions of the human psyche.

Like most American school kids of the 50s and 60s, I was weaned as a reader on the adventures of Tom Sawyer and Huckleberry Finn. Those kids were my first real literary heroes. As a restless, unsatisfied 15 year old eager to escape the deadly curse of my unhappy home of origin, I came across the following phrase by Henry Miller: "I hated the place I was born in; I will hate it till my dying day. My earliest impulse was to break loose from the home, from the city I detested, from the country and its citizens with whom I found nothing in common." Reading those words, I immediately felt a deep and powerful sense of identification, and, like Miller, I knew I needed to get the hell out.

Not having the slightest idea how to get the hell out or where to get the hell out to, all throughout my troubled teenage years, I became a walking question mark, an open wound searching for a band aid - until I discovered alcohol, and later heroin and other hard drugs. Those magical substances became the emotional remedies that I was in desperate need of. As a kinder, softer alternative to suicide, they kept the lid on my restless existential discontent for a number of years - until the cure became worse than the dis-ease they treated and eventually opening the gates of Hell.

Then, one hot, miserable strung-out summer evening, wandering the sleazy nocturnal back streets off Hollywood boulevard, I stumbled upon a copy of Jack Kerouac's On The Road at an all-night book and news stand. I must have been around 16 at the time, and I was strung out like acancer patient. I'd never heard of Kerouac, but the book's title called out to me, shining through the darkness of my addiction like a burning spear of hope. Desperate as a drowning man grasping a life preserver, I snatched the book off the rack and stuffed it in my pocket. In the following days, I tore through its pages. Reading of Kerouac's adventures on the road in a more hopeful unspoiled America that still existed, and his travels in an exotic, adventurous, somewhat dangerous Mexico I longed to explore drove me to a life-changing decision. In short order, I kicked dope, "borrowed" a few bucks from my long-suffering mother, packed an overnight bag, and, like some post-apocalyptic junkie Tom Sawyer, stuck my thumb out on the highway, and never looked back.

This book is essentially a memoir of those early days on the road in Mexico and South America.

Sadly, many of the things, places and populations described in these pages no longer exist as they were experienced by an intrepid young hobo in those crucial life-affirming times - if they even still exist at all anymore. Consumed by a pernicious plague of globalization and that heartless greed-fueled cultural holocaust politely referred to as "gentrification," the kind of worlds once available to the experience of the adventurous traveler have since been largely paved over by politically-correct beige steamrollers of mediocrity and ugliness. This book speaks of a time in the not-so-distant past; a time before McDonald's, KFC and Subway; a time before Smartphones for stupid people - a time when the road less traveled still offered a kaleidoscopic totality of marvelous experience to the hungry soul seeking a glimpse of the sublime.

So, dear reader, I invite you to dig in and read all about it. In the words of my esteemed predecessor, Hunter S. Thompson, "buy the ticket, take the ride." I sincerely hope you will enjoy taking the ride half as much as I've enjoyed surviving it.

Jonathan Shaw
Veracruz, Mexico, 2018

HOMEWARD BOUND

'There!' he said to the soul. 'Stay there!'

Stay there. Stay in the flesh. Stay in the limbs and lips and in the belly. Stay in the breast and womb. Stay there, O Soul, where you belong.

Stay in the dark limbs of negroes. Stay in the body of the prostitute. Stay in the sick flesh of the syphilitic. Stay in the marsh where the calamus grows. Stay there, Soul, where you belong.

The Open Road. The great home of the Soul is the open road. Not heaven, not paradise. Not 'above.' Not even 'within.' The soul is neither 'above' nor 'within.' It is a wayfarer down the open road.

Not by meditating. Not by fasting. Not by exploring heaven after heaven, inwardly, in the manner of the great mystics. Not by exaltation. Not by ecstasy. Not by any of these ways does the soul come into her own.

Only by taking the open road.

Not through charity. Not through sacrifice. Not even through love. Not through good works. Not through these does the soul accomplish herself.

Only through the journey down the open road.

The journey itself, down the open road. Exposed to full contact. On two slow feet. Meeting whatever comes down the open road. In company with those that drift in the same measure along the same way. Toward no goal.

Always the open road.

—D. H. Lawrence

1. NEW BEGINNINGS

Veracruz, Mexico, 2002. Slashes of dusty Mexican sunlight crisscross the shabby little hotel room by the old port. Mariachi music from a downstairs cantina pounds at the ancient Spanish-tiled floor. Above a steady din of traffic from an open window, a ship's horn booms long, low, and steady. Cigano—aka Jonathan Shaw—sits lost in silent concentration as his buzzing tattoo needles chart a steady path across his client's skin.

"So what happened after you left California, Jonathan Shaw?" The Brazilian kid looks up at him, an animated human question mark. "You must have many stories, no? You were telling me that you've written a lot about your travels in Mexico and Brazil. How old were you then?"

The tattoo man looks up from the maze of his work and shrugs.

"It was a long time ago, Jaco. Back in the mid-seventies. I was just a kid then, around your age, I guess. I started out in my late teens, early twenties, and from there I never looked back. . . . " He sets his tattoo machine down on the shiny blue wooden table. With a deep sigh, he falls silent and stares out the window, time-traveling back to another time and place, another life.

JOURNAL ENTRY—Hollywood:

Finally kicked a massive two-year heroin jones. The rest is up to me now. This time I'm not going back to the junk. My fucking life is on the line. I know it now, and for once I actually give a shit. Gotta beat it out of town fast, before I find some fucking excuse to start up again. Still feeling pretty shaky, but fuck it, I've made the Big Decision and I gotta follow through, or else. Next stop, Mexico. No turning back. I'm finally getting out of this stifling little shit-puddle of sorrows, once and for all. Going out on the road to live the life I got back. Been clean a whole week now, still feeble as a slug, but feeling strangely hopeful too. Sat up all night, rereading Kerouac, my mind traveling over all the possibilities. So much to see and do and live. So many places to go and see and be. Couldn't even sleep, high on the glow of new revelations and adventures, the first real hope I've felt in years. Watching the dawn's dingy gray light sneaking in the dirty old window, sitting in this cramped little room, surrounded by the irrelevant rubble of years of stupid junkie despair, for the first time in forever I suddenly felt free. Only a week ago, I wanted to snuff out my life like a smelly old thrift-store candle, and now I can't wait to get out of this sordid little roach hole and live again. They say all life is suffering, so maybe I'm not so subnormal in all my overabundant introspection and pain. Maybe it's just the changes I had to go through to wake up to this new day. Now, there finally seems to be sense to all the sadness and madness and badness, and I know I can go on from here and wherever I end up is cool. Just need to get out into the world again and make connection with the days as they form and take shape, a day at a time. All the misery I've put myself through here is forgiven. The flowers and trees need to suffer to grow and blossom and die, in order to be reborn somewhere else from their seeds scattered to the winds. People are no different. All the pain and suffering was only my resistance to change. But change is the spark and sparkle of life. It's all I've got now, all I ever had, this holy life, holy experience, holy needle, holy trap, holy day, holy night, holy love of holy life and death and pain. Holy despair. And I'm wholly ready and willing now, longing to go on and feel all the bruises of it all wholly; to know and love the pain and the sting, to embrace it wholly and fully; even the nonsense, the inertia and the dying, because without it all, there's no first light, no all-night-life-loving-silly-high hopes, no tomorrows, no dreams, no friends, no days, no nights. No nothing. No growth without pain. And I want to learn to take as much of the pain as I can, to fully know the totality of it all with eyes wide open to the holy beauty and the holy ugly; open to the truth, these ugly, drugged-up, droopy eyes opening faster and faster as I get closer and closer to going out on the long holy road, where I will crack open my brain like a walnut and eat its meat, and take another form, see another color, learn another language, dance another dance, love another love, dream another dream, find another expression through all the pain and the pleasure, through the alone and the together, find the joy of another day, and just be high on that. And even in despair, in down-dirty-ugly-self-hating-self-pity-nauseous-gag-love-wail-castration-heartburn-salad, fuck it, I say. No problem. Just get the essentials down into a little travel bag of tricks, and pick up what I need as I go, a few more splinters and scars and wounds and bruises and batterings and beatings along the way, fuck it, I say, it's okay. That's life, not inertia, not just pain or bliss either, but to always know that when the changes worm their way in there, right down into the very soul where life is reconstructed, it's all as it must be, because this whole crazy circus of life is woven together into a multicolored straitjacket-tapestry of pain and awakening, again and again, and there's just no good reason to be dead now. This much I know. Through all the impossibility and struggle, I just have to live on and get through it all with as much class and style as I can and show the fuckers what ever I find. I will never have to go through this shit again. Just hang on. Find the grace to look to the stars. Be a star-fucker, man, and dare to make a hundred dollar bet with the goddamn devil, and WIN, goddammit, win.

"So yeah," he sighs. "What happened after I split home. . . . Well shit, that's a *really* long story, brother."

The tattoo man looks up, his mind still sifting through yellowed pages of his old journals. "That's basically what I been trying to piece together here, goin' through all these old diaries and writing about it."

He reaches across the table. He opens a notebook filled with rambling memoir notes, and begins reading aloud.

❍   ❍   ❍

As I burned up the roads of Central and South America in a frantic effort to escape its ironclad grip, the Curse stayed right on my tail.

Months stretched into years as I fled the living nightmare of my past. But the longer and farther I ran, the closer it always seemed to get to catching up.

o   o   o

Don't get me wrong. There were plenty of good times, times when I really thought I was free. But the past was never behind me at all. It was always right there with me: hiding, toying with me in a baffling game of cat-and-mouse, forever watching and waiting—patiently ensconced in the last place I'd ever suspect: right behind my eyes. Like a parasite that takes over the will and life of its host, the Curse was fully alive and functioning, all along, operating in my mind's deepest recesses, clouding my perceptions, making all my decisions, and charting the course of my life.

All my high-flying dreams of travel, adventure, and romance were hopeful, colorful distractions, of course. But I really had no idea I was attempting the impossible as I set out on that prolonged flailing retard marathon—a doomed attempted psychic jailbreak, which would only serve to lead me back to the rancid core of myself: my past, my memories, my traumas—the insidious bondage of Self.

My desperate unconscious quest for escape from the inescapable would take me to truly bizarre extremes as my frenetic geographic acrobatics propelled me across the planet like a crooked nuthouse top. But, like a top, I would always run out of momentum and topple over again. Again, and again, and again.

o   o   o

Lulled into a contemplative state by the steady hum of traffic outside the window, Cigano sets his notebook down, shaking his head.

"Yeah, man. Looking back over my life today, I was like a fuggin' dog running around in circles, trying to catch its own tail. Well, in my case, trying to run *away* from my tail." He snorts. "But try telling something like that to a shell-shocked kid whose only survival skills were rooted in massive doses of drugs, booze, denial, resentment, and self-pity. I was always laying the blame for all my problems on other people, other places and circumstances, always searching for some convenient outside excuse for all my self-made inner torment."

He looks up at his young listener and sighs. "Fuck, man, even when I meant well—and I really *did* mean well most of the time—I just couldn't ever manage to get it right. Einstein said it, bro, that ya can't solve a problem with the same mentality that created the fuggin' problem in th' first place. But I was so blinded by my own ass-backward thought process, I just couldn't see that the only real source of all my trials and tribulations, the one fuggin' common denominator, was always *me*."

"So what happened? What changed for you?"

"What changed?" Cigano laughs. "Good fuggin' question, man. In a word, me. I started changing. Inside. They say your past will be your future if ya don't change. Well, I guess I finally just got beat down enough to finally see what had been right in front of me all along. I'll tell ya, man, it was a bitter pill. Before I started crawling out of that alcoholic cesspool of self-deception, my whole life was just one long, hard road to nowhere. And every step of the way, I honestly believed I was going somewhere. I mean, yeah, I was movin' around all over the place geographically, sure. I lived like that for decades, traveling all over the fuggin' planet. But *inside*, the only place that really counts, I was just running around in the same old fucked-up little loop. . . . "

Taking a deep breath, he reaches over, picks up his notebook, and begins to read out loud again.

2. GREAT ADVENTURES

By the time I set out to Mexico, I'd already read Kerouac's *On the Road* so many times that it was a part of me. And it all sprang to life in living color the minute I finally made the decision to just get up and go. I soon came to realize that's exactly how it was always meant to be, that the long Gypsy road to nowhere was my one true destiny. I'd just been waiting to step off a rancid junkie treadmill to go out and live it.

Standing at the freeway ramp, I took a long final look at my home: a sad, smoggy little wasteland of lost souls. I hopped into the first car that stopped and rolled off, leaving Los Angeles and the fading nightmare rubble of my life there behind.

As the car picked up speed, a familiar wave of euphoria hit me, reminding me of my first big adventure on a bus ride into Hollywood with Paul Magad, back when I was a stoned-out starry-eyed kid. And now, another end, another new beginning. Another big adventure.

JOURNAL ENTRY—Somewhere in California:

*Suffering turns to joy with the blaring awakening of a new day.
I know the burden and uplift of this new life are mine to bear alone.*

May I bear them well on the long road ahead. Just as plantman tends to his crop, abundant, holy, and reverent, like a fat, glistening black mama with child, born anew this day, I am my own child now, my own madman and circuit electrician, my own master, zookeeper, wiseman, pilot, slavedriver, and pimp. The dream is finally a reality, and the truth is coming up like a hairy windless pet ape silver-confetti umbilical attachment—part of the equipment. I was trying so hard to say all these things that I forgot the whole skeleton on which to hang my little rags of life-poetry, like tattered, colored banners waving in restless night nowhere breeze. I lost sight of the one true purpose, the truth, the love, the lust, the life, and before I knew it I'd lost the language of soul-feel-bebop-expression; lost it, goddammit, like some fool gone nuts cuz he dropped his 14-karat gold ring on the beach one fine sunny day, and shit-fuck, he didn't even feel the sun on his neck anymore as he hunched over like a crippled baboon, crawling along the line of eternity-watery-churning-sparkle-darkness-forever. I just lost touch with it all, till I woke up one blaring sunrise Sunday, perplexed as a schoolboy staring baffled at the Eternal Now, speaking in unholy tongues of Cal Worthington living-dead America vision. I carry this fear along with me like a fetus in a baggie wherever I go now, my insanity, the bloody curse of my existence. But I've got the key to the highway burning in my hand today, along with a whole mixed bag of charity, hope, faith, fear, death, love, speculation, confusion, euphoria, and despair. My vision blinded so long by the grinning skull of self-destruction, life is all around me again, in strange, abundant fruit-offerings, like a tree, or a silent night's wind, a shooting star. And I'm gonna latch on to the dreams fast as I can catch 'em, boy, hot damn! They burn and sizzle in my grasping hand, like whizzing skyrockets, too fast for my little frog-faced reality to hold onto. But the burn is another awakening today as my hands reach out, bloody and blistered, grabbing for more, skirting a razor's edge in a breathless alarm-clock emergency race to keep up with it all. And it's all right here, in virgin momentum moments of serenity, when pain and suffering are just words for hopes and dreams and lives unlived, so tangible and real to me here and now as I sit in the back seat of an anonymous jalopy, wind whipping through hair, radio full blast, a long, lost highway stretching out grand and mysterious ahead, the only times to remember and be a dreamer forever, and I do believe I just might make it now.

As Cigano reads on, details of that crucial day surf the waves of his memory, conjuring the image of a beat-up old black Lincoln Continental with Oklahoma plates.

○   ○   ○

A hitchhiker scrambles to the stopped car. A massive semi-rig screams past as he reaches for a pitted chrome door handle.

○   ○   ○

Sweating like a convict, I dove into the back seat. A grizzly old bearded hillbilly in a battered cowboy hat gunned the motor. I looked out at the highway as the big car took off and picked up speed. As I settled back, scribbling in my journal, an abstract dialogue was raging up front between a pair of weathered rednecks. Sharing a bottle of Old Crow, they even looked like old crows. Carnies, I gathered from their bizarre speech patterns. The old Continental was a dusty pirate spaceship shuttling me into another dimension. I even began to wonder if Paul hadn't maybe slipped a hit of acid into my coffee back at the donut shop as a parting gesture, a psychedelic going-away present or something. As the miles rolled by, though, I knew he hadn't. This new life was just very weird. How not, after being bound up like a shrink-wrapped mummy in a dirty gray heroin coma for so long?

Hank Williams's "Lost Highway" played on the car radio. The two old geezers seemed oblivious to my presence as they railed at each other in that garbled Benzedrine twang. Finally, the one in the passenger seat passed the bottle back. I took a deep pull.

Feeling better, waking up to the world with each passing mile, I was coming back to life with a sense of blessed relief, ease, and comfort. And I welcomed it with an ancient instinctual fervor. The road was my only destination and my only home now, my real and rightful home of choice, the only place I belonged: The road of dreams. The uncertain. The mysterious. The playful. The unknown. I settled back in the seat. With a warm Gypsy wind blowing through my hair, I fell into a long, deep, dreamless sleep.

Hours later, the car skidded to a stop, threadbare tires kicking up a dust cloud at a barren crossroads in the middle of the desert. I got out and stood by the side of the road, feeling a hot wave of overwhelming silence. I watched the ragged hillbilly space pilots drive off without a pause in their alien speedfreak patois.

Engulfed in that vast oven of nothingness, I looked up and down the long shimmering stretch of empty blacktop. Spotting some low-lying buildings in the distance, I shuffled off in their direction. Why did the junkie cross the road?

The air was hot as rattlesnake piss. The burning afternoon sunlight felt odd on my pale skin as I staggered ahead like a soft white lab rat suddenly released into the wild. The lyrics to a familiar song echoed in my ear, *any world that I'm welcome to, is better than the one I come from,* as a pair of massive eighteen-wheelers streamed past like phantom meteors in the eerie dreamscape. I held the Key to the Highway burning in my hand like a box of starburst secrets, unfolding into a mad, mysterious network of secret puzzle codes. And I knew that, from now on, my very life would depend on learning to navigate the surreal maze of new reality unfolding around me.

Coming to a deserted railroad-switching yard, I spotted a group of hobos sitting in the shade of sleeping boxcars. They waved and pointed to a hole in a chain-link fence. As I slipped through, one of the tattered road-dogs gestured for me to sit. Taking my place in their dusty semicircle, I downed a pull from their bottle of sweet wino brew and sat back, immersed in their colorful tales of trains and trucks and mystical cities of the night. The bottle went around, and I listened with the rapt attention of an initiate to some crucial new life-saving creed.

Fortified by the wine and that warm dose of hobo camaraderie, I took my leave and trudged off down the eternal typewriter ribbon of two-lane blacktop again, waiting for another ride. A burning desert sun was setting at my back, shifting sands welcoming me into a sprawling empire of dust. I looked down at my boots as I walked, as if they had been plodding along that endless asphalt limbo forever, waiting for me to join them. A lone tumbleweed clawed its way across the ground, a drunken ghost of the lengthening shadows. I stopped and stared up at a huge burning red disk rising over the twilight horizon, grinning in silent triumph. Nobody would ever see this monumental moonrise but me!

My heart caught in my throat. "There's never been a moon like this before," I whispered.

Off in the distance, coyotes yipped and howled an eerie reply. Standing still as the phantom cactus shapes dotting the roadside, I listened to those mad, feral calls. Then I started yipping and howling: a lone coyote echo shadow figure with a satchel and a pair of dusty boots, standing by an endless black ribbon of road in the middle of a vast desert on a lonesome planet, under an infinite cosmic explosion of darkening sky. I was nothing and nobody now. Nothing but a wandering, nameless shadow with a fiery lunatic sunset at its back and an insane magnificent moonrise looming before me. A stunning pallet of purples, pinks, and impossible pastel reds tugged at my senses, reminding me of the wonderful Maxfield Parrish paintings I'd always loved as a kid.

I reached into my pocket and took a final swig from my half-pint of Bourbon. I tossed the empty bottle into the desert. It landed with a hollow invisible *thunk* in the dark sand, and I broke out in a wave of mad laughter, a cackling, plodding shadow echo, yipping and howling into the vast desert night. A dry hot wind licked at my feet as a pair of dust devils danced at the side of the road like drunken Gypsy spirits.

Like a caged bird taking flight for the first time, I'd started out a little cockeyed. But as I flew off into those wild unknown winds, the things I saw, heard, smelled, tasted, and lived those first days were all pieces of a magical new jigsaw puzzle, subtly, inexorably revealing its mysterious substance to my shell-shocked senses.

My only travel companions now were the Spirits. Liquor bolstered my resolve and courage, taking the edge off any lingering doubts and fears. Still half-kicking a long, debilitating heroin habit, slowly, weakly crawling out of that interminable foggy limbo, I sensed I was being reborn out there in the middle of nowhere. Raw and vulnerable as a newborn baby bunny all alone in the world for the very first time, I slowly surrendered to a mystifying new thrill ride vortex. Deep in my core, I knew it would be my only home from now on. Escape. Travel. The Run. The long, crooked Gypsy road to nowhere.

I never once regretted my decision to leave everything behind. I never looked back or even wondered why. Moving forward, easing into the world again, a mile at a time, I simply surrendered myself to the unfolding journey, turning my fate over to the wild, boozy, unknown road ahead, the Great Mother of all adventures, hopes, and dreams.

And, all along the way, the benevolent spirits of alcohol bonded my soul to the path, just as naturally and spontaneously as I'd once given my life to the dark, solitary nightmare realm of heroin.

o   o   o

As the tattoo man reads on, a prehistoric reptilian eye clicks like a camera shutter in his memory. He conjures an image of a Gila monster sitting on a high rock, sliding its jet-black tongue out in a silent, slow-motion slash across the face of time. He envisions a battered blue pickup stopped at a desert roadside. A young man climbs in back, and the vehicle starts off down a narrow, dusty stretch of two-lane blacktop. He can see his own youthful face grinning into the warm desert wind as a small green sign flashes past, engraving the moment onto his consciousness forever.

MEXICO SIXTY MILES

"I knew I'd been born for life on the run," he reads. "And how not, growing up a feral child on the edge of the desert and the churning blue Pacific, a deep, watery mass of imagination between the Mexican border and the vaporous, blurry frontiers of a feverish young mind?

"The new life unfolding before me trembled in my hungry eyes like a sparkling sea of jewels, details flickering in a ghostly procession of light and shadow, in and out of time and space, through merging dimensions of new realities, all blending together with the ever-present psychic rhythms of dark, angry, pounding delirium visions."

3. CROSSING OVER

"CHANGE OF SCENE HAS NO EFFECT UPON UNCONSCIOUS CONFLICTS."

—EDMUND BERGLER, MD

A few days later, the tattoo man is sitting in his hotel room alone again, reading through his old journals, taking detailed notes.

JOURNAL ENTRY—NOGALES, MEXICO:

Crossed the border in the back of a rusty pickup with a gang of wild-eyed Mexican cowboys. The driver passed a bottle of tequila back, and we drank it as we rode into town like a pack of old-time gunslingers. Under a flurry of smiles and backslaps, I hopped off by a run down bus station. I prowled the dusty sidewalks of Nogales for hours, feeling happy to be alive and following my nose. Wandering past a row of sad-faced little hookers, it dawned on me I haven't had a fuck since Lincoln discovered electricity or whatever. That's what that fucking dog food will do to you, turn you into a dickless little human hamster on a gray heroin hamster wheel. Looking around for a cheap room, I merged into the crowds on a big commercial avenue, real noisy, grinding gears of dilapidated old buses spewing massive black fumes, mariachi music blaring from distorted loudspeakers, announcing sales and discounts, indecipherable deals and imperative advertisements, talking, yelling, imploring, all

> *at once, in a wild, apocalyptic clamor of machine-gun Spanish, beat-up old taxis blasting horns to the tune of "La Cucaracha." Olive-skinned Marlboro Men with bushy mustaches and cowboy hats. I wandered on in a daze, digging the chaotic sidewalks packed with shoppers, vendors, beggars, scrawny stray dogs, and gaudy old beefy-faced whores, a dizzy rush of motion and frantic, sensuous life. Hot damn! Mexico!*

A soft knock at the door interrupts the tattoo man's reading. He looks up as Jaco, the Brazilian kid, walks in.

"Hey, man!" Cigano looks up from his notebook, grinning. "I been reading through some of my old travel journals, trying to jump-start the memories. I just started writing some more about those first months in Mexico back in the day." He flips through some pages. "Want me to read ya some of this new stuff?"

Jaco pulls up a chair, smiling like a kid at Christmas.

❍   ❍   ❍

Border town. Dust. Heat. Noise. A squat brown teenage girl. Round face, dark bovine eyes. Concepcíon leans against a wall like she's been standing there forever, part of the scenery. Oblivious to the clamorous, smoky taco air and blaring cantinas reeking of piss, stale beer, and unseen chaos, she stands like a cheap tourist trinket, a little ten-peso statue of Hope. The greasy old street corner is her workplace. And Concepcíon is open for business, in worn high heels and a tight-fitting, sparkly black miniskirt. Shrouded in a shiny red nylon blouse, girlish breasts imprisoned like a pair of mangos in an oversized padded wire bra, Concepcíon blows another big pink chewing-gum bubble, thinking about last night's *telenovela*.

She's hoping she can earn enough to leave her post early for the hot, dusty bus ride to the distant *colonia* on the outskirts. Her mind is already on the room she shares there with four other country girls as she replays last night's drama in her thoughts.

Her musings are interrupted by an attractive young *güero* carrying a little satchel. Approaching her corner, he seems like a traveler, maybe a *gabacho*, a *gringo*. A *gabacho* would be very good, she muses. They rarely haggle over price or complain when their time is up. Sometimes they pay for another twenty minutes in the small air-conditioned hotel room and even give her a tip for her services, a *propina,* when they're finished. Concepcíon is thinking she'll reach out and tug at his sleeve as he walks by. Often they are timid and shy, the *gabachos,* as if they are ashamed to pay for *sexo.* They are strange men, but sometimes they make her laugh. Concepcíon likes to laugh.

As the young traveler passes in front of her, though, something stays her girlish hand. There's something strange about this one, she senses, something she doesn't care to touch. Something sad. Something dark. Something that makes her think of *santísima Muerte.*

Concepcíon makes a rapid sign of the cross over herself to protect her soul from whatever evil spirits accompany the handsome young *güero.* Her thoughts return to the adventures and intrigues of her *telenovela* as the odd stranger turns the corner and disappears.

o   o   o

Reading on, Cigano pictures himself standing at a street vendor's stall on a crowded border-town sidewalk, trying on a brown straw cowboy hat. It fits. Spying his image in a little hand mirror, the young traveler knows he needs to blend in here, to disappear into the flow of anonymous cowboy hats bobbing down the busy *avenida.* He must learn to merge with the mad, bustling stream of life in this new place: a blessed refuge, where his memory is momentarily absent, where he is no longer Jono. This is the time and place where he will erase his past and dream himself a new one. This hat will serve him as a reminder of everything he is not.

"Cuánto vale?" he asks the man in broken Spanish. The man says twenty. Young Jonathan grins and hands him sixteen. *Órale!* The man shrugs, smiling back in a flash of gold teeth as he takes the money.

Feeling triumphant after this first bargain in his new incarnation, Jonathan slips back into the crowded stream of the avenue, feeling the singular new joy of finally fitting in somewhere. He smiles to himself: a shifty little smirk, as if he has just gotten away with something, successfully evaded some nasty old law. Maybe he has. He can't define it, but he knows he has somehow beaten the game again.

He strides down the busy *avenida,* absorbing the euphoric smells and sounds of freedom. He stops to contemplate an enticing display of food at a lunch counter. Steaming trays of beans, rice, sauces, fragrant meats, and greasy stuffed *poblano* chiles dripping with melted cheese; a scent of garlic, barbecued meat, and spices beckons from within. Yeah, this is the place to sit and have his first real meal in ages. His mouth waters like a dog. As he steps inside the little eatery, a cooked goat's head seems to glare at him sideways from a bubbling stainless steel tray. He takes a seat at a table with a flowery plastic tablecloth. A stocky woman with rough Indian features bustles over with a menu.

As Cigano reads on, the woman's face stands out in his memory, a smiling vision of a young traveler pointing to a menu.

"Por favor, los chiles rellenos . . . ?"

The waitress squints at the young *gabacho* with open curiosity, trying to decipher his meaning. He points at the menu again, struggling to pronounce the unfamiliar words, one laborious syllable at a time. *"Chil-ly Re-len-os."*

She gets it. *"Ah, ! Chee-lay-rrrey-yay-nos!"*

"Chee-lay-rrrey-yay-nos!" he repeats, a proud parrot. *"Sí!"*

"Ahora sí!" She nods. *"Órale!"*

"Órale!" He smiles back, satisfied with his first informal Spanish lesson. *Órale!* He repeats the word to himself, grinning, not quite sure of the meaning of what he's just said. *Órale,* a word he's picked up somehow; a common expression everyone seems to be using all the time. It will do, he guesses, till he can learn what the fuck it means. For now he doesn't much care. And neither does anybody else, it seems.

As the tattoo man reads on, the woman's round face graces his fondest memories with a proud Mexican smile, displaying a spectacular row of gleaming gold teeth.

"I sat waiting for my food," he reads, "looking out over the busy Mexican rhythms of the street. I felt instantly at home and comfortable there, in a way I'd never known. I suddenly realized that all my life until that good and simple moment, I'd been held hostage in an unhappy, bastard culture not my own."

He turns the page and continues reading.

"Minutes later, the waitress returned carrying a big wooden tray. She set the meal in front of me, a plate at a time. Refried beans. Chunky yellow rice. Fried poblano chiles stuffed with cheese and delicious shredded meat in a rich, greasy red sauce. Steaming tortillas wrapped in a colorful cotton towel. Homemade salsa. Fresh onions and radishes, and little green lime halves.

I devoured the food, washing it down with a big brown liter bottle of strong brown Mexican beer. A subtle epiphany was taking hold with each bite going down my throat, bonding me with the land, the people, the sounds, smells, and frequency of Mexico. Finally, I leaned back, burped, and lit a cheap unfiltered cigarette," he reads.

"The paper tasted sweet as I sat there, smoking and staring out the window. Home at last. I grinned. I had finally found my rightful place in the world, and life seemed very good."

4. HOTEL CINE

After lunch, I wandered the streets of Nogales till I came to a stately looking old hotel the place had obviously seen better days. A weary phantom lurking across from the ancient downtown railway station, its dirty wedding-cake Victorian façade looked like a holdover from some weird Mexican *Belle Époque*. After a week on the road, a cool shower, four walls, and a roof over my head were all the luxury I craved. And all I'd have to do was walk across the street in the morning for the long train ride south.

The aptly named Hotel Cine was attached to a cavernous old-time movie palace. Threadbare families and their frazzled luggage crowded a run down lobby doubling as both reception desk and box office. Perched like scruffy parrots on dusty leather seats under battered, mismatched crystal chandeliers, the people seemed to have been sitting there forever. A surreal lineup of gaudy, aging prostitutes leaning against a peeling filigreed plaster wall completed the tableaux. The whole setup reeked of the absurd.

Breathing in a ghostly aura of days gone by, I ventured across a timeworn art-deco carpet to where a skinny old clerk sat behind a weathered marble counter. As he took my money—about a dollar in Mexican pesos—one of the ancient whores detached from the wall. She shuffled over and took a room key from the man. Gesturing for me to follow, she led me down a dark aisle at the side of the theatre.

Her ample behind shifted back and forth like a pair of pit bull puppies wrestling in a pillowcase as my eyes adjusted to the hoary, dream-like space. Men sat in the dark, some alone, others with wizened whores. Travelers waiting for a train to nowhere. A bizarre Mexican Twilight Zone of hotel guests who'd gone to an afternoon matinee and never left. Up on a giant movie screen, an old film was playing.

A feeling of déjà vu percolated in the center of me. The words *A long time ago* flashed across my mind as the titles of an old American film filled the tattered screen. *THE HIDEOUS SUN DEMON.* Jumbled, distorted Spanish dialogue blared in the darkness as the woman led me up a narrow flight of gum-spotted cement stairs, through a deserted balcony, and down a tiled hallway lined with worn wooden doors. Finally she stopped and opened one.

I peered inside. Single bed. Starched white sheet with faded blue lettering: *HOTEL CINE.* No window. A dark cubicle with a seatless toilet doubled as a shower stall. All good for the price.

I stepped inside. Thankfully, she didn't follow.

"Gracias," I mumbled, closing the door behind me.

The walls and bed frame shook, vibrating to the movie as I sat down on the bed. The springs bit through the thin mattress into my tailbone as I kicked off my boots and fell back on a crisp little slab of a pillow. Fatigue descended like a greasy shroud as I dropped down into watery chambers of sleep.

The sounds from the theater were blasting into my dreams. I could feel myself slowly morphing into a grotesque mutant creature. Its weird, alien life-force was permeating my bone marrow, reshaping my DNA in vibrating patterns of mutation. . . *mutation.* . . *mutation.* . . . As the word bounced around in my head, I could hear the old familiar phrase whispering in the background. . . . *A long time ago.*

A long time ago. . . . Suddenly, the walls of the dream sprung a leak, and fetid brown water came gushing in. *Fuck!* In a flash, I was awake. I looked around the tiny room in panic as a series of horrible cramps clenched at my guts. I struggled to sit up. I couldn't move!

Dear Lord! Paralyzed in pain, a fierce lightning bolt struck my entrails. I doubled over on the bed in waves of deep, stabbing agony. My stomach was grumbling like a dying garbage truck as an underwater earthquake rumbled up from my bowels, exploding in a series of blustering farts! I staggered to the toilet, and a raging sewer spray gushed from my ass, stinking like a truckload of dead porcupines.

Montezuma's Revenge! *How did I ever miss reading **that** fucking page in* Mexico and Central America on Three Dollars a Day? *Sweet Jesus!* If I'd thought kicking heroin was bad, this was like jumping from the frying pan into the flaming toilets of Hell! Drenched in toxic sweat, my skin went slick and gray as the timeworn concrete floor. Fever burned through my aching carcass, covering me like a clammy diarrhea blanket. Pounding tremors of delirium engulfed my brain, rocking my body back and forth on the toilet.

Helpless, I slid to the floor and rested my burning skin on the hard, cool surface. My guts churned like a cement mixer as another cataclysmic wave of flatulence propelled me back to the toilet. Grasping the shit-spattered yellow rim like a life preserver, I retched from the depths of my tortured soul. I shuddered like a dying marlin as my entrails rumbled, forcing more gushing streams of waste through me. Where did so much fucking vomit come from? I was a helpless, miserable, dying vessel of rancid animal dung. Tears rolled down my face in waves of foul, molten lava, burning, transforming, marking, altering, and mutating my very essence. Finally I passed out on the floor, drowning in delirious nightmare fever visions.

ø   ø   ø

Cigano turns the page and reads on, describing a surreal underwater vision of thick dark sewage, sludge, and feces.

With each word, the lens of his mind's eye descends farther down through the watery murk. From a parched desert landscape comes a distant, pounding rhythm, followed by an annoying quacking sound. The dreamer stares at a goat's head floating in a boiling shit stew of greasy, bacteria-infested beans. The goat seems to watch him.

"Is this Hell?" he beseeches those sad, dead, accusing eyeballs. "Oh, God, help me, I'm in Hell!" he cries, and then he's sitting naked on a toilet in that eerie desert underworld, surrounded by weird misshapen cacti. Melting Salvador Dali clocks fold over themselves like rancid tacos. He rocks back and forth on the bowl, straining to squeeze another gushing stream of poison from his churning guts. A quacking sound grows near. Louder. Closer, until the insistent noise is vibrating right beneath him! He leaps off the toilet and looks down to see his childhood rubber ducky splashing around in the filthy water, swimming back and forth in grotesque, demented little swirls, quacking, quacking.

The dreamer lets out a long, piercing scream. He begins to gag. Choking, drowning in his own toxic bile, he pukes in gushing spasms till he's dry-heaving. Tears roll down his cheeks. He struggles for breath as a cluster of blood-red-painted fingernails gurgles up out of his gullet. They dribble down his chin into the dark, noxious toilet water, floating like dead roaches in cryptic, hieroglyphic patterns around the frantic, animated quacking rubber duck.

His brain flashes up a distant memory. *"Bastard! Ya son of a bitch! I shoulda killed you a long time ago, ya dirty bastard!"* His mother is slurring her words, hefting the heavy pistol in her elegant porcelain hand. A long red-tipped finger grips the trigger as she stands pointing the gun at little Jono's father. Her face is contorted into an ugly mask of hate, screeching and glowering. *"How does it feel now, ya bastard?"*

A baby stares out from behind playpen bars. *Bastard! Bastard! Bastard!* The angry words echo in the dreamer's mind, blending with distant sounds of pounding machinery. It all reminds him of something vague and far away, something from a long time ago, as his mother pulls the trigger. **POW!** A sound of thunder pounds in his head as he sees his father jump behind a sofa. His mother fires again. **POW!** From behind bars, a baby watches its parents, a pair of actors in an old horror movie. The baby's father rises up from behind the sofa like a snarling swamp monster. He grabs the pistol clicking in its mother's hand. He slaps her across the face, hard, again and again. **SWAPP!!** Again. **SWAPP!!** Again. **SWAPP!**

The pounding machinery grows louder as a big ruddy knockwurst hand leaps out of the toilet, grabbing at his face. "Oh shit! What th' fuck?" Jonathan cries.

He struggles to flush it away, but the handle turns to putty and breaks off. The ghastly phantom appendage is clawing at the air like a mad spider. He turns to run. He trips and falls to the ground, gasping for breath. Burning desert sands blow over him as he struggles to crawl away. As he clutches at the earth, it turns into a soft, muddy funnel of quick-sand, opening up and swallowing him, and then he's slipping, sliding, down, down, down, into a dark, throbbing pit of tangled, pounding machinery.

Caught like a fly in an ice cube, eyes frozen open in horror, Jonathan stares in impotent dread at a tattered movie screen. Familiar black-and-white images flutter before his eyes: a scene from *The Lost Weekend.* A man is lying strapped on a hospital bed, shaking with DTs. A white-clad orderly stands over him, speaking with a cynical smirk.

"Delirium is a disease of the night." The words blend with the raging mechanical chaos. *Delirium is a disease of the night. . . the night. . . the night. . . night. . . night. . . .*

The film cuts to another scene, the man drinking in a saloon, talking to a young prostitute played by Jonathan's mother. She points a long, elegant finger at him, speaking with a mischievous wink, as her red fingernails flash before his eyes: "Beware the Jabberwock, my son." *Beware the Jabberwock. . . the Jabberwock. . . Jabberwock. . . Jabberwock. . . wock. . . wock. . . .* As the words echo in his brain, his mother's face freezes on the screen and cracks down the middle. The dreamer watches on in sinking dread as the image shatters into a thousand tiny shards of broken mirror glass.

An ascending din of pounding machines and angry voices rises in volume, engulfing the vision in a cacophony of shouting, cursing, and banging hammering metal. The sounds grow louder and louder as a dark reptilian shadow descends over him. He tries to scream, but he has no mouth.

૦   ૦   ૦

The tattoo man takes a deep breath and reads on. "I stayed holed up for days in that little room, wrestling with demons of the Curse. My head was reeling in a boiling shit stew of hallucinations and nightmares as old movies blasted through the walls in a surreal, distorted soundtrack. Godzilla was tearing my brain to shreds, even as some other, more devastating unseen presence seemed to gnaw at my bones from within. I could feel it inside me, distorting, transforming, twisting, and reshaping my human apparatus into some weird new mutant being. It was pure agony, even worse than kicking dope.

"After that radical, violent passage," he continues, "something seemed to have permanently altered in me, as if on a molecular level, like one of those old shape-shifting movie monsters. Lying all alone in a tiny Mexican hotel room, I realized I'd been changed, somehow. Transmuted, rewired, renewed. As hellish, nightmarish visions ushered in a new life, I finally emerged like a chrysalis, born into a different, altered reality in which I would never be the same."

With a weary sigh, Cigano sets his notebook down on the table. Closing his eyes, he pictures himself as a young traveler standing before a timeworn hotel bathroom mirror.

Some color has returned to the gaunt, unfamiliar face as young Jonathan squints into the cloudy glass. "It's still me," he mumbles. "I think. . . . " His voice sounds different—distant, and strangely disembodied. He has a sense it's not really his own image at all, staring back at him through the looking glass.

"Through the looking glass," the young traveler whispers, feeling a funny sense of something he can't quite remember. Shaking his head, he snorts at the cumbersome, useless language of his people, his culture, his past. A strange, clumsy verbal nonsense he has no more use for anymore than for this greasy little shit-reeking room.

Looking down at his boots, he realizes he's fully clothed, though he can't remember getting dressed. He picks up a roll of toilet paper and stares at it. He blows his nose, wads the paper, and tosses it into the toilet. It bounces off the rim and lands at the base. He blinks, noticing a pile of long red fingernails littering the bathroom floor. . . . Or maybe they're just dead roaches.

He turns to his little travel bag sitting on the bed like a sleeping cat. He slings it over his shoulder and moves to the door. The movie theater is quiet now. Was it all just a long, bad dream? He can still hear faint echoes of distant machinery pounding behind him. His hand hesitates on the doorknob. He turns and takes one last bewildered look at the empty room. . . . *Key to de highway. Believe it's time to go.*

He spits on the floor. "*Chinga su madre*, Montezuma!"

His voice sounds distinctly different, echoing in his ear like the words of some invisible Mexican stranger as he steps out the door and slams it shut behind him.

5. ON THE ROAD

Cigano clears his throat and reads on.

"I sprinted across the street to the bustling old railroad station and boarded an ancient locomotive headed south. Traveling through the vast, barren Sonoran Desert, time whooshed by in a flood of details, weaving into my senses as the train rattled and clattered its way deep into the bosom of Mexico.

"My only idea of a destination was a fuzzy little red star on a tattered road map folded in my back pocket—a distant southern seaport called Veracruz. My vague plan was to find work on a ship there and earn my passage to Rio—ten thousand miles away, but only inches on a map. That ancient mystery train would be my definitive gateway to another world, a lazy sensory riot of sounds, smells, and sights, like an old *film noir* movie sprung to life."

The tattoo man turns a page, describing a dusty train car plodding through a stark lunar landscape. Dark-eyed Indian children stare listlessly out the cloudy windows at an endless expanse of barren desert. Threadbare *campesinos* sit resting on bulging bundles of burlap-covered merchandise from the rural backlands.

A young traveler edges past a group of olive-clad teenage soldiers. Standing, passing a marijuana cigarette at the end of the car, they regard him with disinterest as he moves by. Young Jonathan drifts on down the aisle like a ghost. Swirling dust molecules float in a smoky sepia light, shifting and morphing into images of people and things as Cigano reads on.

A stout, barefoot Indian woman with long jet-black braids stands out in the living collage, a flurry of colorful, handwoven fabrics weaving between his words.

○   ○   ○

I made my way down the wobbly train corridor, feeling like a giddy sailor. Everything seemed to be moving in an unearthly slow-motion ballet, as if the car had its own mysterious laws of time, space, and gravity; another reality, separate from the stark, blurry landscape moving past outside the dust-caked glass of its few unbroken windows.

A scruffy gray goat wandered the aisle. It stopped beside a teenage girl with a face like the *Virgen de Guadalupe* as she sat staring out the window, breast-feeding a tiny brown baby. Bundles of clucking chickens, their feet tied together like feathery prisoners, crammed the overhead racks as the train clattered on through deserts and upward into towering crystalline mountains.

With every passing mile, I was awakening from a long, debilitating nightmare. Nearing the Tropic of Cancer, the climate became hotter and more humid, bursting with steamy new tropical sensations. Breathing in the healing essence of that marvelous new world after lying like a rotten banana in a windowless little room hallucinating with fever, everything felt vital, marvelous, and real: an intricate, moving Caravaggio painting of sepia lights and shadows bathed in a dusky, dreamlike patina.

I took a seat beside a balding little man in a frayed suit jacket. My smiling neighbor was holding a wooden cage with two green parrots. I watched as he made funny faces at the birds, coaxing them to speak. His pencil-thin mustache jumped like a drunken caterpillar as he repeated a word, over and over, in a high-pitched, cartoonish voice.

"*Pendejo . . . Pendejo.*" One of the parrots cocked its head.

The man kept at it. "*Pendejo.*"

Finally, the bird squawked "*pen-de-jooo!*" followed by a loud, boisterous whistle.

The little man's eyes lit up, a grin stretching across his face like a rubber band. He looked up to make sure I was enjoying the show. But my attention was on the parrot's crisp little cartoon voice as my own lips slowly began to move, silently mouthing the word.

Then I spoke. *"Pen-DAY-hoe!"*

The odd little fellow shot me a curious glance, and the second bird whistled boldly, congratulating me on another impromptu Spanish lesson.

○   ○   ○

Disembarking from the train in Guadalajara. I spent the next months hitchhiking around Central Mexico. Moving from town to town, a wandering phantom hobo shadow, I was slowly learning and assimilating the language and culture of my adopted land. In a quiet fishing village on the Pacific Coast, I settled into a humble grass hut by the sea. Cooking and eating whatever fish I could catch, I was enjoying the fruits of a quiet, simple life at last.

There were few people there, but for once I wasn't restless or lonely. Enjoying the quiet and solitude with only the birds, fish, insects, and crawling lizards of the tropics for company, I felt as far from the stark, arid deserts of northern Mexico as from the drab, soulless spiritual desert of Los Angeles. That place I'd once called home seemed a strange and distant planet, a universe away from the blessed stretch of deserted beach before me. Staring out over the windswept tropical vista, I felt completely comfortable in my skin.

I realized things had changed radically for me over the months of my travels. I still wrote in my journal every day, searching for words to describe the details of my new existence. But mostly I just lived, basking in the experience, one quiet moment at a time. Life was becoming very slow, measured in moments, as I felt myself in a state of grace, rescued from the wreckage of heroin addiction and washed up on a peaceful new shore—just as I'd always dreamed of in groggy dope stupors. I took great comfort in the knowledge that I'd never have to go back. How could I? I wasn't the same person who'd left just a few months before. Traveling had changed me, and all I wanted now was to just keep going.

○   ○   ○

After that peaceful sojourn by the sea, I headed out on the road again. And what a road! Some of the remote country paths I traveled had extraordinary names—like one crazy passage, aptly named *La Espinoza del Diablo*. The Devil's Backbone.

The highways of Mexico were always colored with a poetic life-and-death aura. That constant proximity to death made even the smallest detail of daily life feel vital and precious. Mexicans seemed to understand the concept of mortality on a crucial level, largely unknown to their sheltered, overfed Yankee neighbors.

The cheap long-distance Mexican buses were colorfully decorated old American school buses. Big racks on top were stacked with luggage, livestock, and even people. Sometimes, you had to squeeze in with a hundred other passengers, another dozen sitting on the roof, some hanging like monkeys from the side, even a few brave souls standing on the rear bumper. The drivers would gladly stop for anyone, anywhere along the barren country routes. To make up for the time lost by frequent stops, they drove the beat-up old collectives like racecars. Those daring kamikaze pilots were expert at mad, suicidal maneuvers, passing slow-moving trucks on blind curves at breakneck speeds, disregarding all principles of common sense or gravity.

But the Mexican bus driver always conducted himself with a reassuring, unflustered coolness. All across the country, those fearless, dignified long-distance bus jockeys commanded a respect worthy of airline pilots. Some even had their own co-pilots, teenage boys who shifted gears or steered around perilous curves for them at absurd speeds as they leaned back to light a cigarette or eat.

Mexicans, I would learn, have a tremendous faith in God—and in their valiant, daredevil bus drivers.

o   o   o

Recalling having written about one especially hair-raising trip, Cigano flips through his pages of notes. Finding what he's looking for, he grins. Folding the page back, he reads on.

o   o   o

I cringed as another handmade cross memorial whizzed past the dusty window. A sound of grinding gears jolted my ears as the bus swerved around the sharp mountain curves. Guts frozen, I stared out over the cliff's jagged edge and down a steep ravine, into the unknown.

Straining to see the rusty wreckage of other buses and trucks that hadn't survived the journey, I made the sign of the cross, steeling my weary, hungover nerves for the fatal moment when that giant rattling metal coffin would hurtle off the steep dirt path and out into space.

Rosaries, crucifixes, and crude roadside shrines seemed to be everywhere I looked. A prisoner in that mad, racing roulette wheel of life and death, I squirmed in the hard metal seat, sweating, choking on dusty air that tasted of the dirt of that impossible land, the flavor of a roadside grave. My ass was a tortured pincushion of discomfort as the chauffeur wrestled with the huge steering wheel like some demented midget orchestra conductor, conjuring up a demonic racket of grinding gears and exhausted machinery.

I glanced up at a hand-painted sign above the cockpit, surrounded by a blinking carnival of gaudy religious icons and colorful talismans. Staring at the words in mounting horror, I pieced the sentence together in Spanish.

PLEASE GOD, BE MY EYES, FOR I AM BLIND.

Sweating like a condemned man, I fumbled for a smoke, staring out the window at the steep precipice with no railing. Lighting up with trembling fingers, a terrible sickness invaded my soul. Feeling helpless as a bag of slugs, I contemplated the end. My eyes darted like mad houseflies between the driver, the cliff, and my fellow passengers as the bus sped forward, inches from the edge of the deadly gorge. I could hear its bald tires squealing like the tortured spirits of a thousand murdered rats.

Wishing my mother had taught me how to pray, I looked up at the pulsing Christmas lights, flailing around in my brain for whatever holy-sounding words I could muster. My harried desperation prayers must have floated up to His Omnipotent ears sounding something like: *Oh say can you see, our father full of grace, sweet Jesus, row, row, row your boat gently through the shadow of death, I pledge allegiance to the Lord forever, amen, oh man, oh shit fuck, please, God help me!*

I looked around at people's faces, taking dubious comfort in the fact that at least I wasn't alone. I didn't want to die alone. I was in a very weird movie, fast-forwarding madly as the scenery whipped past, faster and faster. As I felt Death approaching, my ears popped with a distant echo of pounding things. Time and space took on a strange rubbery feel, *Gumby and Pokey, Black Holes, the Man in the Moon, Potato Famine,* and I felt myself detaching from my body, my brain shuffling through a slideshow of surreal images and thoughts. *Scientology, Wolfman Jack, Easter eggs, blood transfusions.*

An ancient Indian sitting beside me seemed to sense my anxiety. With the mystical grace of a wise native shaman, he produced a bottle and passed it over. I took the cloudy green *pulque* and drank, feeling a fine carbonated tingle as the slimy unrefined cactus spirits soothed my nerves. I nodded at my neighbor. The old man smiled back. The rough elixir warmed my gut with a new wave of courage and good cheer as the kind spirits of the cactus wove their carefree spells in my blood.

I grinned and passed the bottle back. Feeling an overwhelming bond with the benevolent stranger and everybody else on that mad, clattering deathmobile, my heart swelled with pride. I was prepared to die now, together with those good, simple, God-fearing people.

A soft amber light bathed us in a warm glow as I sat back, grinning, making funny faces at an Indian child whose head popped up from behind the seat before me like a funhouse Jack-in-the-box. A shimmering, kaleidoscopic vision of the Virgin of Guadalupe presided over all from its playful frame of winking, blinking Christmas lights.

6. PARADISE LOST

My days on the road flashed by like a fuzzy slideshow. Weeks merged into months as I inched my way across Mexico, always dreaming of the mysterious, distant port of Veracruz.

But now, I was in no great hurry to get to any particular destination. Time had become irrelevant. Nothing mattered to me anymore but the sights, shapes, smells, and sounds of the road—a phantom parade of images and impressions, quietly exploding in magnificent daily bursts of reality, burning into my mind's retina like old-time photographs developing in a shadowy darkroom and emerging as memories and experiences: an ethereal spider-web road map taking stealthy form as I traveled through the dreamlike jungles and cities of a strange and magical land.

In Mexico City, I spent a hectic week in a long, delirious tequila daze, stumbling around like a befuddled ghost in the shadows of that apocalyptic volcano-ringed third-world megalopolis.

One afternoon, at a downtown taco stand, I met a guy with longish hair. He was well dressed and didn't look Mexican, but he didn't look like a gringo hippie either. As I stood eating beside him, he smiled and inquired where I was from. Ashamed of my unlucky nationality like a rotting corpse in the closet, I quickly changed the subject. He was from

Brazil, he told me, making his way back home by land after trying to get into the States and being turned away at the border. We talked a while and agreed to meet the next day to hitch a ride to Acapulco together.

After traveling all alone for months, I was glad to have some company on the road. And he spoke better Spanish than I did.

The ride was pleasant as the scenery rolled by and I picked my new friend's brains about Rio de Janeiro. But nothing he told me about his home could have lived up to my fantastic expectations. Often, one's mental image of places is far superior to their reality. I had to protect my dreams, so I let it go.

Arriving in Acapulco, we wandered the streets for hours. The only reference I had there was the address of a hard-drinking Mexican model friend of my old girlfriend Ellen Janov. As we walked up to the fancy beachfront condo where the girl lived, I hesitated, wondering if she even knew of poor Ellen's overdose. I didn't really look forward to showing up like the Grim Reaper to break such tragic news to a virtual stranger. But it was a moot point: the chick wasn't home. According to a snooty doorman, she was out of town, working abroad.

After that, we couldn't find a decent place to stay anywhere near the water. Everything was overpriced and obscenely Americanized.

Acapulco turned out to be a real letdown, a tourist trap infested with gringos. I cringed at their obnoxious high-pitched drunken screeches. The Mexican tourists were even worse: gaudy upper-class buffoons in ugly pastel beachwear. Those creepy gringo clones were like surreal caricatures of the archetypical Ugly American, a frightening cultural role model for an emerging, post-modern globalized nightmare world. The beaches were a sandy nether-realm of obese Mexican families who obviously watched too much American television. No wonder I liked heroin so much, I mused as we strolled the beachfront, remembering how it always smoothed out the rough edges for me. But, even at its most hideously surreal, I preferred to swallow the big Reality Sandwich whole now, chasing it down only with tequila.

As we stood by the seaside, watching the lumbering droves of *turistas* milling around in the sand like beery-eyed, sun-damaged zombies, I wondered out loud how a perfect tropical paradise like that could have become so perverted. My Brazilian friend just shrugged and smiled, saying there were plenty of tourists in Rio too, especially around *Carnaval.*

He was used to it, he said as we wandered away from the fabled sands of Acapulco, looking for a place to stay.

We ended up in a run down working-class area by the bus station, the underbelly of that big, glitzy tourist hell. After a couple of aimless days of overpriced meals under the predatory gaze of sinister hustlers lurking in the shadows of the whitewashed palms, I was feeling restless again. And, as much as I'd enjoyed the Brazilian's company, I missed traveling solo. When he suggested we hitchhike down the coast to where there were cheaper, less-populated coastal villages, I told him I needed to move on alone. He didn't seem to get it. He looked kind of sad, but what could I say? The road was my only friend, and I wanted her all to myself again.

As I walked along the highway waiting for a ride, I contemplated how, over my months in Mexico, I'd begun thinking and even dreaming in Spanish. Not having been able to converse much with people at first, except at the most primitive level, I became starkly aware of how much I'd always used words just for the sake of idle talk, rather than to express important ideas. Since slipping into that magical solitary zone of constant motion, freed of the burden of past and future, I was fast losing the ability to express myself with any language at all.

No more staring at a cumbersome old typewriter, haggling with myself over meaningless abstract words. I grinned, remembering old Bukowski telling me to just go out and get a fucking life. And he'd been dead right. Fat lot of good an avalanche of words had ever done me. The only thing that had ever made a difference in my short, unhappy life had been my actions—decisive ones, like getting out of Hollywood before I ended up dead there like all the others.

The only connection I had with my old life at all anymore was through writing; poor, gutless little words and haunted memories. The past felt like a dream. Maybe that's the only reason I kept scribbling in my journals, despite a long self-imposed verbal silence—simply to not let go of that one final weak vestige of Self.

JOURNAL ENTRY—ACAPULCO:

Troubled sleep in a musty little hotel room. Beside me, the Brazilian snores to wake the dead. The ghosts are already awake here, anyway, and they're keeping me up too. Haunted by dreams of Ellen, I sit up on the bed, writing, trying to placate the unruly memories. "There's fifty discotheques in Caracas," she'd told me, one of the last times I saw her alive. How strange. Did she know somehow that I'd end up there someday? From the depths of delirious tequila dreams, I can hear her saying "follow me there." I never did follow her. But I remember being with her in another dream, back in Los Angeles, right after she died. In that one, I was on my way to South America, crawling through seedy Mexican cantinas after her memory—the closest I ever got to really knowing her. Well, the beer sure tasted good on those hot dusty desert nights alone, dear Ellen. Yeah, I enjoyed it. That's the kind of slob I am. Nothing lies beyond human depravity: not murder, rape, torture, madness, or necrophilia. And, like you, my sweet Ellen, it's all the same to me, dead or alive. I watch through marble mortal eyes as the dream technicians scrape my brains off the walls of sleep. Going crazy, the only way to become sane. Your blackness I continue to invade daily, my dearly departed. Please forgive the intrusion, but I'm a shiny-red cockroach-clad psycho-punk with nowhere else to go. Boozing it up in this Mexican carnival of psychic carnage, I can't look up, can't look away from these annoying little ant-farm dreams, love-feel instinct sting of madness, as karma creeps through dream sweeps by the Brain Police. Don't look up or you're dead. Don't look up, I say, as she crawls your way. Pass us another drink, pal, and we'll go visit the giraffes at the bottom of the sea. Might as well be there, another funny city, she can't follow us there, can she? Won't remember in the morning. Hand us another bowl of maggots, won't you, please? There's a good fellow. Ah, the rotting fruits of my lethargic labors of love.

As I burned up the road like an invisible beggar's shadow, trying to flee the tragedies of my past, I realized that even before I'd left home I'd already been long gone. Ellen was dead, and I hadn't even cried. I, too, had become a ghost. Heroin does that to you. I could see the whole devastating process so clearly now. By the time I'd split, Paul was the only close friend I'd had left. And as the road unfolded, I felt increasingly grateful to him for having saved my miserable junkie life the day of my own near-fatal overdose.

The further away I moved from the scene of those frightful crimes against myself, the more I seemed to awaken from a long bad dream. I began to really understand that I'd gotten myself strung out because of some terrible unknown darkness in me, a living Curse I could only hope to unravel over time and distance. But the clearer my memory got, the weirder it became, too. More and more, I found myself drinking uncontrollably, in a futile attempt to blot out the pain attached to my unfolding awareness. And as my mind surfed the turbulent waves of raving drunken blackouts, I vomited the poison of my soul into my journals, scribbling away as if possessed, and awakening the next day with no recollection of what I'd even written.

JOURNAL ENTRY—ACAPULCO:

Sunrise warning: greasy fingers and a barbecue-charred tongue, surveying the wreckage of another night of heavy boozing and general despair. Come off your horse, whoever you are, and bear me away, falling, falling uphill. So goddamn sick of your face in the mirror every night, Jono, you goddamn fool. Where were you when I didn't need you, sitting up in some goddamn cantina, standing naked in the graveyard, chewing your existential nursery rhymes? The division between us and God is so strong that I can't even look at a bloody Mayan pyramid. Not till I'm falling down the stairs in some crummy junkie hotel. You can have your Howard Johnson churches, America. You can keep your phony antiquity, too. I'll change my own water from now on, if it's all the same to you. Maybe we can do lunch sometime, feast on the carcass of your stale heathen pretensions. How I loathe you, America, you fuck, you phony cesspool of pus-sucking lies. How does one demented little nation dare to impose its twisted, self-righteous puritanical will on the rest of the world? I'm clever enough to break your father's pipe and smoke your fucking slippers, send smoke signals to your sexless cunts in their whitewashed tombstone down the block. Ding-dong, the witch is dead. Long live the stench. Look, you weren't supposed to be reading this, Ellen, put it down now. I'm just looking out for my own ass here, baby, so you go on and look out for yours in the goddamn afterlife. Ah, hell, get me a gun. I'm shooting my way out of this crazy dream. Get me a postage stamp, and I'll mail myself home in an envelope, like the triumphant return of some 2nd class Parcel Post Prodigal Son. I can just hear the old lady screaming, "God, no more of this junk mail," as she and her pitiful conspirator gather around their placid man-made air-con nightmare soup for cocktails. Fuck 'em. I'll stay right here till I rot, Ellen. I'm a fucking zombie too now, honey; yeah, when the sun goes down, I go through the transformation, just can't help myself. The lights of downtown

Acapulco blink and wink at me through another dusty window escape hatch, and I'm gone. Plaster-faced cigarette butt eyes aglow, I descend the sixty-nine stairs, get on my outlaw stallion, and go. I'll be in some other creep-show dream in no time, looking for a girl who has no face. Hey, we all live underwater, didja know that? Ellen is her name, unctuous, striving hair flying. "Go off and die with the rest, it's for the best!" they told her. Now she's starving, and her face is a very bad mess. Too bad for you, too, you fuck! Don't you know you loved her eyes once? I can still remember hoping she didn't call when I was there. It's too much, darling, I can't make the scene anymore; you're making my cat flip out. Oh, he looks all right, but what you don't know is he's just sitting there, purring, waiting for us to extinguish ourselves, so he can grab our souls. What kinda second-rate grave is that for a couple of healthy American kids? My mind is creeping out of its bottle again. Don't stop the musty stuff. It keeps me out of the junkyard. The Cat People are waiting, must I remind you? My life is a crime of passion, no more trees to climb. Some idiot set fire to my forest the night you died, and now I'm forsaken. It might have been me, the dolt with the matches, in a drunken nicotine-fit stupor. My dream of eternal drunken cantina vigils comes true, but I'd rather not have another drink of tequila, rather not face that sad hangover routine again. "No no no," he cries, "never again!" No wonder all the mannequins seemed to laugh and dance for him at night—such an amusing fairy tale, the boy who cried pussy. It must have gotten tiresome for my old dead friends. How I hate you, you dirty fucks! How dare you get tired of the movie and die off on me? Bastards! And after I put on such a great show for you all! You think I tired myself out like that for nothing, you fuckers? All that random speculation, the aimless days and nights, fucking your sisters, your lovers, your mothers, and you weren't even watching! Go to hell, you dogs! I wasn't kidding. I really am a goddamn flea circus or something, Ellen, ah, my dear Ellen, what things did you tell me so long ago, and what did it all mean? Why am I here, and why are you not? Why are you the one that keeps coming back to me, the only one I trust, like some sleazy skid row exterminating angel? I feel like a necrophiliac when I think of you with such tenderness, you are so close to me in such a morbid way, really not dead at all. Hearing your unbearable tears in the night is like holding on to some greasy gray cumbersome thing. I think you understood all this way before me. We are surely very close, still. Listen to me now, with your poor, sad, ghostly feet, squashed, prostituted, dead feet. The eternal Lady of Spain, how she holds you to herself; the twenty-nine gold charm dreams on her wrist told of your suffering, so shamefully. And her eyes of steel-blue skies, freedom, lust, agony, and revenge, you and her together now in my dreams, so shameful, so true, just as the pasty cactus mash alcohol makings of the mysterious pulque cannot hide her scars in eternal hallways of quiet screams. Shit, I couldn't even wish you a happy birthday after you died, just told you in another dream that I was still crazy and lost as ever, and blah blah. It's gonna come back to me someday, like I won't believe, man, and I couldn't even call you back, I don't even remember which dream I'm thinking about anymore, O God, what have I done? It's a different story. It's about a bunch of goats eating a field of cannibals or something, and I'm just sitting in this rancid little hotel room, waiting for when those workers out on the street get that big ditch dug. I'm gonna go over and sit in the shade and smoke cigarettes, ya don't think I'm busting my spine like a broken chopstick for a lousy twenty pesos. No, I'll just sit and watch and drink, and if anyone says a word about me being a lousy freeloader, I'll just yell your name, O Lady of Spain. Yeah, when they finish digging that cruddy old ditch, I'm gonna jump right in and beg them to fill it up. Now, if I could just habla español, *I'd con my way right into the fucking Promised Land or Hell, whichever comes first.*

The darkest manifestations of my progressive alcoholic madness always seemed to come out in those drunken writing jags. At the same time, though, as my days on the road unfolded like mysterious alien flowers, I was also getting closer to some little lost ghost of a child in myself. And the people I met along the way seemed to reflect that innocent, childlike quality back to me.

Mexicans were the most authentic people I'd ever known—noble, honest, and pure; generous, simple, and un-neurotic, in a way I'd never seen before. Day by day, my eyes were being forced open to the important things in life. As I grew increasingly comfortable with the simple daily routines of survival on the road, I found myself thinking less than ever about where I came from. That world and its people were dead to me. After Ellen's death, I'd given up on having friends.

All I had left of a past anymore were some scattered, quickly fading memories. And, as the road became my world, replacing everybody and everything that went before, I could barely even remember my dead friends' faces. They had finally become like abstract cartoon characters to me—fuzzy, one-dimensional beings in some old comic book I'd once read, a long time ago.

Walking along the highway, I thought back to a letter I'd found waiting at the post office General Delivery window in Mexico City. It was from Richard O'Connell, telling me of another friend's fatal overdose. Reading it was like reading a newspaper piece about the passing of some distant stranger. I hadn't felt a thing. My heart was closed to them all now. I'd slammed that door shut for good.

In the surreal, solitary fantasy realm of Mexico, people and things of the past only existed for me at all anymore in mindless, booze-fueled writing excursions and pounding fever dreams.

◎   ◎   ◎

Cigano stops and looks at Jaco. "I didn't have a clue then, but I'd already crossed some blurry, invisible line into full-blown alcoholism."

He sighs. "Shit, man. Bottle in hand, I'd twisted my fuggin' mentality into such a habitual obsession for lopsided reasoning, I just couldn't see what th' hell was happening to me, that all I'd really done when I left home was swap a fucking heroin habit for a big, long, booze-driven destruction derby. Same shit, different flies. So the joke was on me. And, like any good card-carrying alkie, I was always the last one to get the fuggin' punch line."

With a weary grunt, the tattoo man flips a page and reads on.

7. UPS AND DOWNS

After standing at the side of the highway on the outskirts of Acapulco for hours, I climbed on top of the first truck that stopped.

With the wind in my face again, the blessed details of the land filled my heart with that special feel of freewheeling liberation, motion, and life. All I cared about was being all alone in my solitary little adventure movie again, free from the illusionary comforts of human society. I'd had so many friends back home, and where were they all now? Dead in the fucking ground. Never again, I vowed, would I let myself get close to people.

The truck dropped me off near a remote fishing village a good way down the Pacific Coast, where a family of humble fishermen sold cheap food and beer. My new home was just a hammock strung between two palm trees on a long, empty stretch of beach. After the pre-fab, plastic horrors of Acapulco, that tranquil spot at the edge of a sprawling coconut grove was my own private tropical paradise.

I spent the next few weeks there, sitting at a wooden table in the shade reading and writing, and swimming in the sparkling blue waves. I even curtailed my drinking to a few late-afternoon beers.

Lulled into a soporific dream state by the warm, salty sea breezes and gentle waves, I enjoyed long, dreamless sleep with the watery spirits of night. Waking at dawn to watch the sunrise, I knew this was the only way to live.

When a fierce Pacific storm came blustering in across the sea one morning, I finally packed my bag and walked back through the jungle to the highway, feeling unusually keen and focused. The pressures of time and space had relented at last, slowing the pounding shouts in my head to a comfortable murmur. The road was my religion, my comfort, my only drug of choice. And, like any other drug, I craved more.

Having become expert at living on next to nothing, I mostly traveled by hitching rides on trucks. I often slept out under the stars beside the highway, rather than squander my limited funds on buses and hotels. I normally cooked my own meals in a little frying pan I carried. Even in the cities, I spent little, eating at the working-class public *mercados* and staying only in the cheapest transient hotels. I never once asked my mother to send money. It was as if anything from home was tainted. I didn't want any part of it, preferring to stretch my meager cash reserve till I could get to Veracruz and ship out.

Living on less than a dollar a day brought me into close contact with the people of the land, where I learned that communication was far more essential to survival than all the money in the world. I mostly stayed in small rural villages, where the people were honest, simple, and generous of spirit. Even in the most backward, poverty-ravaged backlands, I was awed by the kindness of those humble folk, who fed me and put me up in their simple country shacks with no thought of asking anything in return.

Mexicans were a hospitable, generous people—nothing like the greedy, paranoid, self-centered Americans I'd grown up with in that overfed spiritual ghetto. I couldn't wait to learn enough Spanish to pass for anything *but* a gringo. The longer I lived in Mexico, the more I felt the deep shame and disgrace of being from a place where everything was made of plastic—including people's souls. Living among Mexicans, I came to deeply understand why the whole world thought Americans were so stupid. They were.

Like a weary gunslinger, I rolled into Puerto Escondido one day, just after dark. The entire village was overrun with shaggy-haired gringo backpackers wandering the narrow dirt paths like lost chickens.

After a few turns around the dusty little beach town, I wandered back out into the night. Shaking my head in disgust, I trudged off down the bleak coastal highway. Not a single truck passed. I'd already walked a few kilometers by the time I realized I was stuck in the middle of nowhere, far from Escondido, and nothing up ahead. Determined to put as much distance as possible between myself and the unruly plague of loathsome gringos back there, I staggered onward, sweating and muttering to myself in the dark.

Finally I came to a small bridge. I followed a little dirt trail down into the jungle, searching for a spot to lay my weary blanket. I stopped to drink from a stream beneath the highway, then waded in for a cool moonlit swim. Feeling renewed, I hiked on downstream, eventually wandering through a sleeping village of simple straw-roofed dwellings. Mules tied to posts. Chickens clucking in the dark. A few pigs wallowing in muddy potholes. No sign of human activity.

Dogs began barking as I hurried past in the dead of night, feeling like a furtive vampire. Finally coming to a sprawling coconut grove by the sea, I stumbled over palm fronds and coco husks in the dark. I could hear crashing waves as I spotted a deserted hut on a stretch of savage, tropical coastline. No dogs, no pigs, no chickens. Nothing. I went in, laid my blanket on the hard dirt floor, and fell asleep to the sound of the pounding surf.

At dawn, I hiked back to the village and bought some eggs, tomatoes, and onions to cook my breakfast. I spent the next several days camped out right there, swimming in the ocean and bathing in the river at dusk. The only people I ever saw were some fishermen, who would stop at day's end to offer me first choice of their catch. There was nothing to drink but coconut water. I didn't care. Hiking all the way to the village for booze I couldn't afford seemed a stupid idea. I was doing fine without a drink. I wondered how long it would last.

о   о   о

After a week, I felt the restless urge again. Trudging out to the two-lane highway, I quickly caught another ride heading south. It was late afternoon by the time I got dropped off at a barren crossroads. I stood out there till after dark, waiting for another ride. Nobody stopped. I decided to lay my blanket down by the highway and get an early start the next morning. But the playful spirits of the road had other plans: I was awakened in the middle of the night by distant music.

I got up and walked along the roadside, following the sounds. Approaching a nearby town, I saw that the whole place had been converted into a giant carnival *fiesta*, with a Ferris wheel, brass bands and games, and what seemed like every drunken *campesino* in Mexico and their families. Nothing to do but join the party.

I spent the rest of the night drinking with some crazy *vatos* from a traveling circus, playing with their mangy lions and tigers and flea-bitten monkeys. I consumed way too much cheap mescal. Old Indian ladies with gasoline tins, gourd bowls, and coconut shells were hawking the stuff like evil soda pop. As we drank like Romans till dawn, my new *compañeros* exhorted its supposed hallucinogenic properties. By the time I'd swallowed enough of that deadly brew to possibly trip on, I was way too fucked-up to remember much.

I came to the next morning with the piercing shriek of a rooster crowing in my ear like some hideous medieval demon. I pried my sweaty carcass like a painful scab from a canvas cot on someone's porch, looking around in cotton-mouthed bewilderment.

The circus was gone. The *fiesta* was over. Head pounding, sweating under an angry tropical sun, I staggered back out to the highway, feeling like some beat-up thrift-store Jesus with a crown of barbed-wire thorns. Piecing together painful details of the night's festivities, I vowed once again to never take another drink.

I had to assure the next truck driver who stopped that I wasn't carrying any *mota*. His concern reminded me of the *Federales* I'd seen manning roadblocks across Mexico, where they supposedly confiscated vehicles if even one passenger was caught with a single joint. With my short greased-back hair and Pancho Villa mustache, I looked nothing like those grubby pot-smoking hippies back in Escondido. My chest swelled with relief as the trucker smiled and told me he was going all the way to the capital, and yes, I could ride up on top.

As I climbed aboard, I remembered some gringos warning me not to hitchhike to Oaxaca. It would be twelve hours of hell, they'd cautioned, skirting hairpin mountain curves on a bumpy, dangerous dirt road. *"Take the plane, ma-an,"* they'd whined. *"It takes less than an hour, and it only costs like ten bucks."* Those well-meaning weekend warriors didn't know ten bucks was enough for me to survive on for weeks. I had to make my money last till I could get to Veracruz and find work on a ship. With their annoying gringo chatter ringing in my memory, I grinned as the truck started off.

My cocky, self-satisfied smile soon faded as I found myself clinging to the wobbly cargo rack, bouncing around on top like a nervous cat. My shell-shocked, hungover guts churned with rancid bile as the truck sped through the hot jungle terrain and began a steep ascent. Soon we were rattling and clattering up a towering mountain rising high into a dense, murky fog. Then it started getting cold. Within minutes I was a shivering, frozen chicken. My brains throbbed in a miserable stew of confusion as the merciless mountain trail twisted around and around like the nine circles of Hell.

With growing dread, I realized the road wasn't even wide enough for two vehicles going in opposite directions to pass! Onward we hurtled at breakneck speeds, around serpentine curves skirting a thousand-foot precipice with no guardrail. Cringing in dry-mouthed terror, I pictured another big truck charging around one of those blind hairpin bends at the same reckless velocity. Visions of death tugged at my bowels like a gang of angry dwarves as I peered down into the cold, foggy darkness below, wishing to Christ and all the saints that I'd heeded the wise gringos' warnings.

I was about to climb down, jump off the moving truck, and start walking back, when I heard a strange little voice behind my head: *"Relax, kid. You'll make it."*

I looked around and felt the phantom presence of a comforting Gypsy hand on my brain. Taking a deep breath of cool, pine-scented mountain air, I sat back again, looking out over the scenery. Just then, the fog broke, revealing the most breathtakingly panoramic vista I'd ever beheld. The sea stretched out before me, far and blue as infinity. I could swear I saw the earth's curve on the horizon. Up ahead, the road wound around another tortuous blind curve. Mercifully, the truck began slowing as it lumbered up the mountain. To the left, a giant rocky cliff towered above us. On the right, a gaping, bottomless pit.

Before I could start to panic again, I looked up into the bluest sky on earth, filled with the kind of magnificent, billowy clouds you only see from airplane windows. Or from Heaven.

Fuck it. I was ready to die. I lay back again, staring up at those grand celestial shapes, grateful for my ghostly Gypsy traveling companion's reassuring company. All in all, it turned out to be a pretty enjoyable ride.

8. OAXACA

I arrived in the capital city of Oaxaca well after dark. With a few tacos and beers from a roadside stand in my belly, I walked around till I found a cheap room by the sleeping downtown *mercado*. Exhausted, I went right to bed.

In the morning, I got up early and explored the chaotic indigenous *Centro* till way past dark. Checking out every fascinating path and back-alley labyrinth, my heart rejoiced at the raw poetry of life bursting all around me. I got back to the hotel late. Reeling with psychic overload, I fell into a deep untroubled sleep.

The next day, I stayed in the cramped little room all day long, resting and writing in my journal. As I fumbled for the words to describe all the marvelous things I'd seen and people I'd met, my efforts felt especially poor and primitive. The words were weak, toothless little creatures.

Finally, after dark, I tossed my notebook across the room and dressed. A hyperactive junkie craving another sensory fix, I needed to walk those magical streets again. Maybe someday I'd find the time and focus to write, I mused. Maybe when I was older, wiser, more experienced. Maybe then I'd be able to express the things I was feeling and living today. Or maybe not. Shit! I sighed in disgust as I looked at my little notebooks littering the floor. I'd probably just forget it all over time. Either way, I knew I'd begun to lose my taste for writing, once and for all. I preferred to just be with the people of the land now, living the vital experiences of that poetic daily existence.

I wandered the streets in a daze, thinking how I hadn't spoken English for so long, I'd almost forgotten how. As I stood at a corner *taqueria*, drinking a beer and listening to the gentle singsong conversations of the Mexican night, I realized that even my thoughts were coming in Spanish now. As rudimentary as my command of the language still was, it was the only one I felt at home with anymore: the simple, comfortable music of daily existence, a soundtrack to my life in a far better world than the boring, predictable sinkhole I came from.

The Indians of Oaxaca never seemed to talk much, either. I sensed that they had some sort of crazy telepathy going on. I watched them as they peered at each other in silent huddles around the marketplace, communicating quite efficiently, apparently, without the burden of words. Navigating the crowded, narrow streets around the old *mercado*, half drunk on beer, I marveled at those noble, mysterious folks. In the presence of their magical, ethereal aura, I realized that the most depressing thing about where I came from was the fact that a dull language of the intellect had replaced the essential spirit of life.

I remembered reading about indigenous shamans telling Artaud how the Great Spirit had completely abandoned the white man. I knew for a fact that Americans had long lost that crucial connection. My people just let the fucking TV do their thinking for them. Maybe that's why I was always so unhappy, so restless and ill-at-ease there.

Since seeing the obscene hordes of gringos sunning their inflated pink beer-bellies on the beaches of Acapulco, I commonly made a point of steering clear of tourist places. The only foreigners I ever ran across at all were the occasional hippie backpackers—bleary-eyed dread-locked *turistas* with their huarache sandals and gaudy colorful ponchos instead of Bermuda shorts, Hawaiian shirts, and cameras. These new Age of Aquarius Ugly Americans smoked pot and gobbled down magic mushrooms in place of beers and margaritas with little umbrellas. But to me they were all the same. I felt no kinship with the graceless, weed-addled, pink-faced budget tourists I'd see stumbling around like confused children. Whenever I saw those ungainly backpackers coming, I'd duck down a side street or disappear into a crowd, desperate to avoid them.

The longer I was away from America, the more I came to see my countrymen as a race of ugly, mean-spirited, mercenary cowboys. But I knew the gluttonous gringos I shunned were really just a microcosm of people in general. Human beings were all the same shit everywhere. There were mercenary Mexicans too, of course. I thought of the shady rip-off artists hanging around the gringos in Acapulco, like fruit flies hovering over a pile of rotten fruit. Still, the most obnoxious predators always seemed to thrive in places infested with foreigners.

Rich jet-set tourists or budget hippie backpackers, it didn't make any difference to me. Americans and their pompous, overfed European ilk just seemed to bring out the worst in people wherever they went. They sure brought out the worst in me. The mere sight of them triggered fits of seething resentment and blinding intolerance in me; probably because they were nasty reminders of my own loathsome past—unwelcome reflections of everything I really despised in myself, my own festering roots of whiny gringo entitlement.

Weirdly, though, I never saw myself as a gringo. More like a refugee, the proverbial man without a country.

I knew that Mexico was the only place I'd ever belonged, and I was fiercely possessive of it. I wanted my self-centered, solitary little adventure movie all to myself. In true alcoholic form, separation from my memories and my roots had become my creed as I fought to dodge my own hated self-image in an endless house of mirrors.

Wandering the quiet cobblestone streets of Oaxaca that day, I felt myself bombarded by haunting echoes of my mother's obnoxious, maudlin, drunken ramblings, forever dwelling on her glamorous life in Italy, back when she'd been young, happy, and carefree. I could almost hear her incessant whining, pissing and moaning about how much she regretted ever coming back to America. And I cringed to see a shadow of that same festering dissatisfaction in myself.

Still, there was no escaping the fact that I knew exactly how the old lady must have felt. Perhaps it was in her restless Gypsy blood, or maybe just her alcoholism, that relentless inbred Curse we both carried like an insidious deadly virus, a bitter seed of unsatisfied, irritable discontent. But I swore I'd never make the same mistakes she had. I wouldn't go back. Ever!

○   ○   ○

"So what made you finally return to America, Jonathan Shaw?" Jaco interrupts his reading.

The tattoo man lets out a weary groan. He closes the notebook and looks up at his young confessor, feeling a little awkward. He scratches his head, staring out the window in silence.

Finally he faces the kid and sighs. "I dunno, man. I guess I just got to a point where I finally felt an urge to connect with my fucked-up roots somehow. When I first went back, I really didn't know why. I guess it boils down to what I wrote there, about trying to outrun yourself in a house of mirrors. Cuz that's all this life is, I think, just a big reflection of what's inside you. Wherever ya go, man, there you still are, right?"

Jaco nods, saying nothing, waiting for him to go on.

Cigano shrugs. "I dunno, man. Makes me think of my last visits with th' old lady. It's funny. My whole life, I could never stand to be around her, y'know? I mean, I loved her, she was my mother and all. But for most of my life I just couldn't be in the same room with her for ten minutes without getting into a big screaming battle over some stupid shit. We were always like oil and water, me and Doris Dowling."

"That's very sad." Jaco rubs his chin, like a baffled psychiatrist.

"Yeah, man." He shrugs. "It was pretty bad. And I guess I just got to feel the weight of that. Like I said, after I sobered up and left New York, I went back to California, wanting to spend some time with her. I'd already been trying to make peace with the old lady for a while, in a half-assed way, even before I got sober. But after I quit drinking, I really wanted to take it to the next level. I guess I felt a need to open up all the old wounds, to clean and disinfect the whole nasty mess, once and for all. So I started going around to see her. I knew I had to try and make things right, somehow. I just wanted to find forgiveness and healing with her, before it got to be too late, y'know?"

Jaco nods.

The tattoo man lights a cigarette and sighs out a long gray plume of smoke. "She was really getting on in the years last time I saw her, an old lady, drinking like a fuggin' bottomless pit. Last few times I was over there, man, she was putting away like a quart of vodka every day, along with God knows how many pills, and whatever else, chain-smoking all day and night, just a long, slow-motion suicide, y'know?"

He snorts. "And her husband, Len Kaufman; Jesus, man, ya shoulda seen the old scarecrow! He looked like some kinda harried old white-haired ghost, runnin' back and forth to th' supermarket and th' drugstore, doling out booze and pills to her like the fuggin' Angel of Death. I mean, how long can that kinda shit go on, right? So I figured I'd better stick around and spend some time with my mother, try to make my peace with her, before she finally drank herself to death."

"That must have been painful for you," Jaco muses.

"It was pretty uncomfortable at first, yeah." Cigano shakes his head. "Fuck! Just walking into that fuggin' house was like opening up some creepy old Pandora's box. I really wasn't loving the idea of being there at all, believe me. Especially being newly sober. God, did I want a drink in those first few months! It was like pullin' teeth." He sighs.

"But I'd just go over and sit with her, and we'd talk. The funny thing was, after being such a raging, violent, poisonous freak-demon all her life, th' old lady had suddenly become real mellow."

"What do you think happened? What changed her?"

"That's the big question, man. I guess a part of it was that I'd changed a lot myself. I really *wanted* to forgive her for being such a nut job when I was a kid. And that desire for forgiveness had a profound effect on my perceptions. It's funny how as soon as ya start to see things from a different angle, how fast all the people around you seem to shape up." He smiles.

"But you said she was mellow. She must have become much different from the mother you describe in some of your stories."

"Yeah, man!" Cigano's eyes light up, as if realizing something for the first time. "She really *did* change. Big-time. I guess ya gotta know the alcoholic mind to really get that kinda shit. It was like she'd always been trying to control her drinking, y'know? But she could never just straight up admit she was an alcoholic, that she *needed* to drink. So she always blamed all her misery on everybody else. I think that's what mostly made her so pissed-off all her life. The frustration. Fuck, there's nothing more miser-able than an alkie who can't get enough booze, always trying to ration their doses and maintain some kinda respectable front. It's pure torture, believe me. Not that I ever really felt much of a need to moderate. . . . "

He shakes his head and laughs. "Out of my many character flaws, feeling the need to please other people by controlling my drinking was never an issue. I never gave a shit what anyone thought. But the old lady, I dunno, man, she was from another generation, I guess. She couldn't let on that she had a 'drinking problem,' y'know, and that made her so miserable, I think, always having to maintain a mask of respectability, that whole bullshit façade."

"So why do you think that became less important for her?"

"Well, I guess she finally just got to the point where she was like *'fuck it, so I drink, so sue me,'* y'know? She just didn't care anymore what people thought. Probably because she'd already driven everybody away. Everyone but her husband, the textbook enabler. That's when she just pulled the plug outta the jug and took to her bed, boozing it up around the clock. She could just lie there in her twilight years and guzzle as much as she'd always wanted to, but never could cuz she didn't want people saying she was a drunk. As if it had ever been any big secret." He guffaws. "But ya wanna know the weirdest part?"

"What's that, Jonathan Shaw?"

"Once the old lady started drinking all the time, she suddenly became the *sweetest* thing. I mean, really nice! It was like night and day, the way she went from the raging hell-monster I grew up with to this sweet, harmless little old lady."

He smiles fondly. "I'd go over and visit with her, and we'd just sit around and talk for hours. And we ended up having some really good times together, bonding after all those years. It was amazing. I guess we both knew she wasn't gonna be around much longer, so it was kind of a nice way to say good-bye, making peace with each other. It was really healing for me, I'll tell ya, after a lifetime of hating her."

"I'm glad you had a chance to finally mend that relationship before your mother passed away, Jonathan Shaw."

Cigano rubs his chin and sighs. "Yeah, well, she's still alive, technically. . . . I dunno if I'll ever see her again, though. She's pretty far gone, y'know, mentally, like she'll just slip in and out of reality, dreaming all these weird dreams, and then she doesn't even know if she dreamed the stuff, or if it really happened. Anyway, I'm just glad I got to spend some good times with her at last, so we could both finally have some closure."

The tattoo man smiles sadly, thinking back on his last visits with his mother.

9. A MOTHER'S LOVE

Doris takes a Marlboro Red from the pack. She holds it up with a frail, shaky hand. "Give me a light, darling."

Cigano reaches over and lights her cigarette, glancing at his mother's wrinkled, booze-ravaged profile. Her ratty snot-stained bathrobe is riddled with cigarette burns.

She sits back, blearily regarding her son across the kitchen table, drinking her lunch from a tall plastic tumbler. Just enough orange juice to give the vodka a little color.

"Don't you weep for me when I'm gone, Jono." Her voice is a soft, blurry slur. "I've had a very exciting life, you know. My years in Italy matured me in a way I didn't realize I needed at the time. Ah, the arrogance of youth!"

A dreamy smile crosses her face. "Ah, but I loved Italy. I was a big star over there, you know, and I adored living in Europe. I was a very good actress. I made *Bitter Rice* when I was just a girl. It's a classic, you know. They put me on an Italian postage stamp for being in it." She takes another swig. "I was so in love with Raf Vallone, my leading man. And he loved me back. Till he got bored with me. He went after another young girl and married her. He just got bored with me. It hurt. I was still in love with him when I married your father. . . . Well, they were good years. Very exciting. Ah, I've lived a full life. I think Vallone was the only man I ever really loved. . . . "

She stops and notices her son staring at her. "Oh, I loved Len, of course," she adds with a sheepish grin, "but in a different way. He'd bore the shit out of me, but he was good to me. . . . Artie, oh God, your father was absolutely terrible! Nobody liked him much, you know."

"People still don't like him very much." Cigano laughs. "Not that he has much contact with people anymore. The poor guy's pretty hard to like. I can see my own worst traits in him sometimes. I have to work real hard so I don't end up like that. I don't wanna be anything like the man. But there's always a potential for it, DNA and all. . . . "

"Don't worry, darling, you're nothing like Artie at all. God! He was always such a prick!"

Cigano smiles. "I think I musta been a lot more like him before I sobered up. Selfish, self-centered. I guess I wound up with the worst of both of you. So now I just try to shoot for the best of you both. Cuz there's good in him. And I know you always loved me, even when you were nuts. I guess I always knew it, somewhere inside. But Artie, he never loved me. I doubt he ever really loved anybody. I don't think he ever wanted to put up with raising a kid, so he just split. . . . He never even tried to see me when I was little, did he? He says he did. He still blames it all on you, says you wouldn't let him see me, but I don't buy it. I mean, if he really wanted to, he woulda found a way. . . . "

"No! Never! I *wanted* him to love you, Jono. But he didn't."

"I know you could never get along with him. You never had a kind word to say about him when I was a kid. That was kinda fucked-up. But still, he coulda tried, too. Bastard never even tried. He coulda tried a little harder. Argh, whatever, I was better off without him. . . . "

"He never loved you, Jono. That man never loved anyone in his life. The only thing he ever cared for was his music. And then he quit playing."

"Well, I guess you're right about that, Ma." Cigano smiles. "I really believe he's incapable of caring about another human being. He musta got hurt real bad as a kid, too. We all did, I guess, one way or another, we got screwed up when we were kids. It musta been hard for you, too, with your father, a drunk Gypsy crook. All the violence and craziness. He musta been hell to grow up with."

"No, that's all just Grandma's talk. My father wasn't bad to me at all. Never! He loved me. I was loved. I was his princess, and it gave me strength, a lot of strength. Being loved that much when you're a child is a very ego-boosting thing. My father absolutely *adored* me. And I was always his favorite, there was no question. He loved the others, but not like he loved me. And that was very strengthening."

He stares at his mother as she takes another drink. Her voice drops to a dreamlike whisper as she goes on. Cigano leans closer, straining to hear every word, like an archeologist examining a fragile artifact.

"Well, he loved me," she mumbles, "and then he lost me, by his ego. He was so egotistical, he couldn't give. He never knew how to give. But he loved me, all right. Oh, yes! He *married* me, for God's sake, didn't he?"

Cigano stares across the table. . . *Whoa! She was just talking about her father, and now she's got him mixed up with Artie! What the fuck is she talking about? Does she even know what she's saying?*

"Getting married to me," she rambles on, "it was a commitment to something. Oh yes. He loved me, but he got bored. Just bored. . . . "

Bored. She just said the same thing about her old lover in Italy, that he got bored. Cigano scratches his head. *Is that who she's talking about? Or is she talking about Artie? Or her father? Does she even know? She's got 'em all jumbled together.* He pictures her raging at the dinner table when he was a kid, hearing a ghostly echo of her angry drunken tirades. *"Men! You're all the same! Bastards!"*

"He never accepted himself. He doesn't know it. He never knew it. He was so wrapped up in himself. I suppose we all were, in our youth. . . . " She seems to lose her train of thought.

She reaches over and takes a long drink, as if to fill the space between her blurry musings, then goes on. "Ha, but my years in Italy were the best! I was so at home there. I was bilingual, you know, completely fluent in Italian, and I made great pictures there. . . . But I got homesick."

"Homesick? How come?"

"Well, this was my country. It's my home. . . . "

"That's funny." He shrugs. "I never felt that way about this country. I found a home on the road in Latin America. Whenever I come up here, I still feel like a foreigner. But when I'm in South America or Mexico, I always feel right at home. It's like Italy was for you, I guess. But you came back, and I never did. Not really. I mean, I worked in New York all those years, but I always felt out of place. I *still* feel like an immigrant here.

It's weird. I guess I've just never been real comfortable in America. The whole culture just feels alien to me. I think my spiritual home has always been Brazil. I was lucky to find it. Most people don't. They just stay wherever they're from all their lives, cuz that's what they think they're supposed to do. But sometimes people are born where they don't belong. I think I just needed to go out and find my own place. And ya really *can't* go home again. You change. And then if you're lucky, ya find your real home."

"Well, that's exactly what Italy was for me."

"Maybe that's what always made you so unhappy, Ma," he ventures. "Coming home. Like you thought you *had* to, like you felt some sort of responsibility to be here, and you could never really accept it because Italy was always calling you back. But something told you ya had to stay here and do the right thing, or whatever. . . . "

His mother nods and takes another drink.

"But maybe it *wasn't* the right thing," he goes on, "because you were never happy here. I wonder about that. You never fit in here either. You always complained about being a 'suburban PTA matron,' remember?" He laughs. "You really *hated* it. Your spirit was much too big for all that bullshit. But you stayed, and then maybe you felt like you'd sorta betrayed yourself in some way, cause you'd had such a great time in Italy."

She smiles. "You're right, Jono! I never felt aligned with this country. And I *did* become a suburban matron! God!"

"But you didn't wanna be, Ma. You never fit in here, just like me. Connie did the same thing, I think. She tried to fit in. Sometimes I think that's what killed her. . . . Ya think she married Ivan Tors for security, like for his money?"

"Oh, yes. Definitely!"

He takes a deep breath and sighs. "So, she betrayed herself, her dreams. For cash and prizes. Shit. And then one day she woke up to it, and she took her life. Jeez, poor Connie. She must have felt so trapped." He winces. "Those three kids, and that idiot Ivan, that big house. She didn't really want any of it. Maybe she longed to be back in Italy where she was happy too. She musta been miserable here, and her life just went bad. I guess she couldn't see any other way out. . . . "

"My God!" Doris shakes her head violently. She falls silent, as if searching for the right words to make the ugly memories stop. She downs half of the vodka in one gulp.

Finally, she begins to speak again, slowly, deliberately. "She could've just divorced the bastard and gone back to Italy! My sister never loved that man! How *could* she? She married Ivan for the money, of course she did. I don't think she even liked her kids very much. Three boys. Monsters. They were like a pack of wild monkeys. . . .   But Connie always loved you!"

"I know, Ma. And I loved her so much when I was a kid."

Doris smiles. "She loved you from the time you were born. She used to push me away from your carriage when you were a baby, you know. She always thought you were a great artist. Oh, Jesus, Connie!" She shakes her head and finishes off her drink. "Well, she gave herself to a matronly life, and had children with a man she didn't respect."

She sighs. "And then she was so bored. Yes. She certainly married him for money. Of course she did. We were so poor, and we always lacked security, growing up. We were very, very poor when we were young. God, we lived in such poverty!" She grimaces. "What is there about the smell and taste of cabbage that reminds me to this day of the odor of feces? Ugh! The poverty was absolutely devastating. . . . "

o   o   o

With his mother's voice reverberating in his memory, Cigano searches through his bag and pulls out another pile of old papers. "Here it is." He looks up at Jaco.

"What's that, Jonathan Shaw?"

"Another one of those old stories my uncle wrote. Man. Uncle Robert wrote so many tragic little slices of life, but he never finished anything. Too painful, probably. God knows, I went through the same kinda writing block most of my life."

He shakes his head with a sad smile, mumbling to himself. "So now maybe it's up to me to put the pieces together here, so they can all finally go off and rest in peace somewhere."

Return To The City
—BY ROBERT SMITH

We were on the subway late at night; my mother, myself, my little sister, Doris, my baby brother, Richard, and my twin sister, Connie. All of us were sleepy and barely able to keep awake. The train was deserted. I don't know how old I was, but I was pretty small. I sat opposite the others. I felt embarrassed, ashamed of them; ashamed of being part of the group. We had all these heavy cardboard boxes with us, strewn over the seats and on the floor. We were returning from some place on Long Island, probably Rockaway. That's where the "Shanty Irish" like us lived. My mother wore a black coat and a black hat. Everyone looked sad. I think we were all scared because there'd been a funeral and my Pop was in jail and we'd just been evicted again. I remember the stop on 103rd and Broadway, and how we all had to move boxes, getting ready before the train entered the station. It was quite late and there weren't many people on the street. We made a trek over to Amsterdam. I had to go back and make a second trip for a box left behind. On Amsterdam, near the corner, in front of the Old Ladies' Home, we piled all the boxes on the sidewalk near a fence. My mother told us to stay there and wait; she'd be back in a little while. We were all scared as we waited on the corner there. No one seemed to pass, and we kept on looking and looking for Mother. She'd been gone a long time. Doris, three years younger than Connie, and me, began to cry. She kept saying "Where's Momma?" I was furious with her and told her to shut up.

Mother returned, finally. It seemed she was much brisker. She had a black purse. There was something a lot better about her. "All right, children. I found us a place."

I think we all felt more animated. I did, at least. The address sticks in my mind. Thirty-three Manhattan Avenue. It seemed large and pretty nice compared to the dump we'd just left, where we'd all had to sleep together on a bare mattress on the floor. This place was even furnished. I can envision myself lugging those boxes up the stairs, the metal rim on the edge of each step. It was two rooms, I believe, in the front. There was a bed on one side of the room; a sofa on the other, and another bed. Near the window was an upholstered chair. I climbed into bed, just a sheet cause it was hot. I slept with Connie. After a while, something woke me up. I was frightened. My sister Doris was in my mother's arms, crying. They were sitting next to the window. My mother was trying to quiet her.

I said, "What's the matter?"

"Nothing, it's all right," said my mother. "Go back to sleep."

Connie was up too. She said, "There's a lot of bedbugs."

Doris's empty bed was nearby. There was a good deal of light in the room, the lamp-post being right outside the window.

"Where?" I asked, sitting up.

Connie pointed toward little Doris's bed.

"Go back to sleep, Robert," my mother said. "It's nothing."

She said it in a funny way, as though she didn't mean it. Just something to say. It made me worried. I leaned forward and looked at Doris's bed. A large black shadow, a kind of gleaming stain made by some black liquid was spread over the center of the white sheet. There was something peculiar about it, and I looked closer. It seemed to be moving. It took a while to register, but with a sense of horror I realized that it was a huge mass of bedbugs. I leaped out of bed, loathing everything about the place. My mother and two sisters sat up by one window. I sat alone at the other window. I felt a great distance from the three of them. I knew I could never sleep there again, and somehow I knew that there was no money to go anyplace else.

I looked out the window for the rest of the night. The deserted street corner, the lampposts remain vividly clear in my mind. I remember it getting light and becoming morning. It was a long night and the dark becoming grayer and lighter seemed exciting and wonderful. I'd never seen the dawn arrive before.

10. A GLORIOUS FRIENDSHIP

"Yeah, man." Cigano looks up at Jaco and sighs. "No wonder Doris and Connie were both so eager to whore out their very souls. Anything for the promise of security! What a fuggin' mess. . . ."

○   ○   ○

"Connie was in therapy for a long time," Doris rambles on, "and she always told people that yes, she married Ivan for money. Ivan was having financial trouble at the time she killed herself, you know, and when she realized there wasn't any money, and they were going to have to sell their big house and live on a budget, well, she woke up and said *Jesus, what have I done with my life?*" It's very sad. Cesare Pavese was in love with her, but she left him because he couldn't offer her stability. And then he killed himself. God! Pavese was a genius, a true artist, and Connie always cared for him. But poverty was so awful. . . . "

"Maybe that's why I never was a big fan of wealth." Cigano grimaces. "You know that, Ma. As long as there's enough money to get by, I don't really care about having more. I never wanted to be like all those Beverly Hills fat cats, with their big cars and big, empty houses. I guess I sorta learned to hate rich people from when I was little. I saw what the desire for cash and prizes did to all you people."

"Yes, you did. You'd always hear our arguments."

"Yeah, I can still remember the fights. Not the words, I can't remember that. But I remember all the yelling when I was little. And I didn't like it. It scared me, and I thought if that's what being rich is all about, who needs it? I just wanted to get away. I didn't need much money to go where I wanted. I lived in the slums of Mexico and South America, and I always felt right at home there. It's funny." He chuckles. "You ran away from poverty, and I ran right into it."

"You certainly did, Jono."

"And we were both looking for th' same thing."

"Right. Peace."

"Yep. Peace." He smiles. "And I think we've both finally found it now, after a hard life. You in your way, me in mine. We got peace today, Ma. And nobody can ever take that away. Cause we fought for it. We suffered and bled and we hurt. But we're okay now, right?"

"Well, you're okay. I'm still an alcoholic. . . . I was born one."

"Well, maybe I was born for it too. Who knows? I'd still be drinking today if I thought I could get away with it, but it just got to hurt too much: I had to let it go. Believe me, if I could still get any comfort from it, I'd be right there drinking with you. I always loved it. But it got so bad for me, I had to have a drink in the morning. My hands would shake, and then I'd take that first coupla shots, and everything would be all right. For a while. . . . "

"You inherited that." Doris frowns. "Oh yes, Papa was an alcoholic. He got it from his people, the Gypsies. They were all alcoholics, you know. Inherited. They've discovered drinking is inherited, you know. I inherited it from my pop. Pop was an alcoholic, and he never tried to quit. But he adored me. That's where it all started. You never knew him. He died right after you were born. He came to see you at the hospital when you were just a baby. He put his hand out, and you grabbed on to his finger with your little hand and just hung on. You wouldn't let go! After that, he died, so you never knew him."

"I've always thought I got it on both sides." Cigano shrugs. "Artie's got that alcoholic personality too, y'know, all the typical alcoholic character traits, self-centered, narcissistic, cranky, perfectionistic, unsatisfied. But he never drank. I kinda suspect that's what his real problem is. If I ever met anyone who needed booze to lighten up, that man really could *use* a few drinks." He laughs.

"He's just so damn irritable all the time, and he doesn't even have anything to take the edge off, poor soul. At least we always knew how to feel better. Drinking was never really my problem. It was the solution to all my problems. Till it stopped working, and then it got so bad, I had to quit. But for years, it gave me so much relief. Artie could never get that. He was always miserable, from what he tells me about his life. So I guess he's the real tragic one. I think a latent alcoholic without a drink has gotta be the most miserable person in the world."

He sighs, thinking how much easier it is to talk to his mother after all these years, now that he's finally sober, and she's finally happily drunk.

"Yes, Jono. Your father was always afraid of drinking."

"Yeah, but he was attracted to it in a weird way, too, right? I think most of the people around him were alkies, or junkies. All his friends, the guys he played with, most of his wives. That's a strange thing. I wonder where he got that. . . . "

"He probably inherited it."

"We all get what we get." He shrugs. "I feel pretty lucky."

"Yes, you are. You managed to stop in time."

"Most people I knew couldn't. I couldn't, either, for most of my life. Then, one day, I dunno, something just shifted. I can't really explain it."

"I was always an alcoholic, Jono. . . I *am* an alcoholic."

"We all are, this whole damn family. Except Grandma."

"Grandma always loved you, you know, Jono. She adored you from the day you were born. She thought you were very special. Well, she knew you were alcoholic, too, just like my Pop. She could see what she called the Curse in your eyes, she used to say. But she loved you anyway. She always thought you were a genius, a very special talent."

"Really?" He smiles.

"She said that all the time. I should have told you more often. She thought you were a genius. And you are. I've always told you that."

"Well, Artie's a genius, twisted as he is." He grins. "Maybe I got *something* good from him."

"Oh, yes, very much so. He knew everything." She pauses and looks at her son. "You go and visit him sometimes, don't you?"

"Yeah. He's still a big know-it-all, probably hasn't changed much."

"Such an ego!" She snorts.

"He's pretty opinionated, all right." Cigano laughs. "He knows so much about everything under the sun, but he's really his own worst enemy with that." He shrugs. "Sometimes, too much knowledge can make a person arrogant, ignorant, closed-minded. . . . "

"I'll say! People didn't like him much. He wanted that. He always thought he was better and smarter than anybody else. Enormous ego."

"Maybe that's where I get my own arrogant streak from. I still struggle with it. I always thought I was smarter than most people too."

"Well, you *are*, darling." She gives him a mischievous wink. "I'll tell you a secret." Her voice falls to a theatrical whisper. "So am I!"

"That's gotten me in a lot of trouble." Cigano scoffs. "It's miserable being intelligent sometimes. Cuz you know you're sharper than most people, so you get to feeling superior. But then you sorta hate yourself for it, and you end up feeling alienated, cuz you can't just be like everybody else. That's one of the reasons I took so many drugs, I think. To dumb myself down. I always wanted to fit in. I don't give a shit anymore. I'm glad I'm different now. But I try really hard to not be arrogant, like Artie, cuz it just sets you apart from everyone. It's a shitty way to live."

"The man was absolutely hateful to people."

"Well, I think deep inside he musta really hated himself. Maybe because he didn't have a father. That's probably why it was so hard for him to be one. He just didn't know how. His father wasn't good to him, and then he split, so that was Artie's model. I've tried so hard to forgive the guy for doing the same to me, but it hasn't been easy. He's just so *mean* to me all the time. I've tried to understand and forgive, but it takes a long time to get over something like that."

He sighs. "I can't afford to hate him, though. I've done plenty of messed-up stuff too. You know I've got a son in South America I've never even seen since he was born. Jesus! He must be almost twenty by now, a grown man. I know I'm gonna have to try to find him and his mother and make some kind of amends for never being there. I can't expect to be forgiven for being a lousy father if I'm not willing to forgive Artie. Not forget, but forgive, cuz I just feel better when I don't have to carry all those old grudges. I think that's what made me so miserable for so long. It's probably one of the reasons I drank and took so many drugs, cuz I just hated everybody and everything, and I didn't even know why. I guess I mostly hated myself, deep inside. So I've had to face all that and try to let it go, one grudge at a time."

"My God, Jono! You've become quite wise in your old age!" She laughs. "Wisdom. Ha! That's all Artie ever wanted, you know, more than the fame or the money, or any of it. That's why he kept his head buried in a book. He was so smart, brilliant mind, but he couldn't feel. So he never got wise. Never. You've really upstaged him, you know."

"Well, I never set out to 'upstage' anyone, Ma!" Cigano guffaws. "God forbid. All I ever wanted from him was some little sign of acceptance."

She beams at her son. "You don't need his acceptance, Jono. You've become a good man. And you've found a wisdom born of living and suffering. That must drive him absolutely mad! God, what an ego!"

"Maybe that's why he's so standoffish with me." Cigano shrugs. "His ego. Like ya said, Ma, he just can't stand to be outdone. The fact that I have people I care about. I think he's pissed-off cuz I told him I wanna go find my son and try to get to know the kid, y'know, show some kinda interest. When I told him I was going back to Brazil to see him, he actually said to me, 'Why do ya wanna do something like that? It's too late! He's already formed. He's a stranger!'"

He sucks his teeth. "I told him I didn't see it that way, and it really pissed him off. But I think he's really so against it cuz, deep inside, he's embarrassed—ashamed, even. Cuz that's what he could never do for me, just be there and show me he cared about me. He just couldn't do it. He was always too self-centered. I think it sticks in his gut that I wanna try to get to know this kid. He told me if I went down there to meet my son, I could forget about ever talking to him again. The guy really doesn't *want* me to do any better than he did! Jesus!"

"No, he doesn't, Jono."

Cigano shakes his head. "I've forgiven him th' best I can, but now he wants me to co-sign his self-centered bullshit by making the same mistakes he made! Screw that! Sometimes, I think the old bastard's even started to go deaf just so he won't have to listen to anything I tell him. And now he's even going blind, too!"

"He was always blind, Jono. The man is an emotional cripple."

He laughs. "God forgive me, but I wonder if th' poor guy's losing his sight just so he won't have to read the book I'm writing. I know it sounds crazy, but, jeez, it's just so ironic. I mean, the man's read thousands of books in his life, but he hasn't got the slightest interest in reading one by his own son."

"Well, it's his loss, Jono. You don't need his approval. You never needed anything from any of us. You just went your own way."

"Yeah." Cigano laughs. "I guess I did. I think that's what saved my life, when I split and went out on the road. It gave me a real sense of belonging to the human race, put me in touch with my humanity. I guess Artie never really had that. He just got famous, and it separated him from the world. He started to look down on people and hate everyone, and then he just went off and became a hermit."

"Well, you were right to take off at a young age, Jono." Doris smiles. "You were always a survivor. Boy, you were tough! Just like my Pop! He was a full-blooded Romany Gypsy. He could never stay in one place either. And you knew there was nothing for you here, so you went out and lived like a Gypsy too, traveling the world all those years. My God!"

"Thank God for that." Cigano smiles. "The road was my real home. I was always looking for a home, I guess, and I finally found one. But it wasn't about any particular place. I just wanted to move around. Guess it's in my blood, like ya said. I'm trying to write about it now, to find a way to be at peace with it all. I'm still pretty happy just living out of a suitcase these days. I really don't care about a home anymore. I've lived in so many different places, but I never felt comfortable anywhere, so I guess I'm okay just being a Gypsy. Ya know they call me 'Cigano' in Brazil. . . ."

"Cigano? That's a pretty name."

"It's Portuguese for Gypsy. Anyway, I've calmed down a lot. Not all the way, but I do have quiet moments now. Before getting sober, I never had a quiet day. My mind was always racing ahead a thousand miles a minute, and I just couldn't keep up with it. I could never seem to run fast enough to outrun my own fuggin' brain. But it's starting to slow down a little now, so I don't gotta run so fast to keep up anymore. That's been a real blessing."

"Yes, it is, Jono. I'm very proud of you." She beams.

"Thanks, Ma. I'm proud of you too!"

"My beamish boy!" She smiles. "You're very sturdy. And you're *much* calmer. I can see a *big* difference, Jono. You're doing good!"

"Well, I'm no saint." He laughs. "But at least I'm not at war with myself all the time now. I was in a battle all my life, y'know. I guess I just got tired and gave up. It's a big load off my back, believe me."

As if to underscore Cigano's words, Len glides into the kitchen, silent as a ghost. Cigano smiles, and the old ghost smiles back.

Doris falls silent. No words are exchanged as Len hands his wife a couple of pills and "freshens up" her vodka. Cigano knows it's part of an old ritual: The Three "V"s: Valium, Vicodin, and vodka. Good to the last drop. Cigano grins sadly as his stepfather fades away, a haggard old gray shadow.

"Yes." Doris sighs. "We were always fighters. Connie and I really had to fight our way out of the ghetto. . . . "

"I remember when we went over to her house that night, the night she. . . . " He hesitates and looks at his mother.

She waves a hand. "Oh, I've made my peace with it, Jono. I was devastated when I lost Connie. She was my other half. But I've found peace with it, in my own odd way. I've had a pretty good life." She looks him in the eyes. "Don't you ever weep for me when I'm gone, Jono. Len loves me, and I've loved him for forty years. I know you never liked him, but you must understand one thing: We've loved each other a long time. And he's been very good to me. He's done everything he can to keep me happy. That's very good. I get bored with him sometimes, but that's just me. It's in our blood, Jono. Gypsies. We get bored easily."

"Yeah, we do, Ma." Cigano smiles. "And sometimes we get lost. And we get hurt. But I'm real grateful, I really am, for your patience and love when I was a kid. I know you did the best ya could. You were just confused and lost, too. But I understand your pain now. I was lost most of my life, too."

"Yes, you were, Jono. But you're getting better all the time."

"Thank God."

"No! Never mind God. You can thank yourself. Because you fought. You fought very hard. There was a long period when you didn't know who you were. And you fought. You always were a fighter, even as a baby. My God! You always had to be your own person. You weren't happy much. And you hated me a lot. But I never gave up on you. I was just there. I always loved you. You'd be rotten, it didn't matter, couldn't stop my love for you. Nothing could. Not your father, not Len, not the drugs, nothing!"

Cigano looks across the table at his mother, feeling a sudden warm surge of love for the woman he's despised so bitterly all his life. At first it feels a little uncomfortable, unfamiliar, weird. He stares at her in wonder, as if meeting this intriguing, charming old lady for the very first time.

"There are men that make war on their sons." She fixes him with a serious look. "You had some of that with Artie. And you always hated Len. I suppose he wasn't much of a role model. He was intimidated by you, by your intensity. Even as a child, you were so dark. Troubled. Nobody could get near you! But I wouldn't give up. You were the light of my life. And when we finally became friends in the last few years, it was glorious."

o   o   o

Ah, my years in Italy were the best. But I got homesick. This is my country, my home. With his mother's voice echoing in his mind, Cigano glances across the table at his young friend and shrugs. Suddenly he feels very old.

He picks up his notebook and turns a page. As he reads on, he pictures himself as a kid, sitting in his mother's den, tearing through old issues of *National Geographic*. The child's eyes sparkle with wonder, dreaming of exotic, faraway lands.

11. A VERY INTERESTING LIFE

—DUTCH PROVERB

Oaxaca turned out to be a fairly large city. I spent countless days there just wandering the crowded back streets around the sprawling downtown *mercado*. It was unlike anywhere else I'd ever been. The whole place was like one big hyperactive flea market, the way I'd always pictured places like Marrakesh and Hong Kong. I could walk those teeming passages for hours without once seeing a tourist.

When not out exploring, I rested up in my room. The hotel was pretty comfortable, especially for less than twenty cents a night. But there was no bathroom in my room, and they kept a pack of hogs in the public showers at the end of the hall. There was a big crack in the thin wooden wall by my bed, affording a panoramic view into the next room, where portly, naked Mexicans did unspeakable things in the night. After a few days of that, I moved to another room with its own little private water closet. It cost an extra ten cents, but I gladly coughed up the difference, just to not have to brave the fierce porkers down the hall. My new bathroom was one of those cramped little deals where you had to sit on the toilet to shower, but I was used to that kind of setup. And it beat bathing with a gang of gigantic pigs.

Right outside the hotel, there was an incredible variety of eateries. I'd never seen so many good things to eat in one place. The food was cheap, too, even cheaper than cooking for myself. I would buy three ripe black avocados, some juicy red tomatoes, and a bunch of fresh limes and cilantro—enough to mash up a big bowl of guacamole—for just a few pesos. I'd eat it with a hot meal from one of the many busy market stalls, where hundreds of little stands stood, back to back, under long, open-air tents. A plate of steaming *chiles rellenos* stuffed with spicy meat, cheese, dried fruits, nuts, and spices, in a mouth-watering spicy-chocolate *mole* sauce, with another big plate of rice and beans, all cost under twenty cents. After Oaxaca, I often found myself wishing everyplace else was as abundant as its amazing *mercado*—especially when I'd wander into some little bug speck on the map, hungry and tired, to find a cloud of flies swarming over a couple of half-rotten tomatoes and a limp brown wad of lettuce.

The big market day in Oaxaca was Saturday. On weekends, it seemed half the region's population gathered there to buy, bargain, sell, trade, barter, steal, look, inspect, fondle, and generally engage in every form of commercial exchange known to man. On my first day, I sold a cheap Instamatic camera for five times what I'd paid for it in LA. I rewarded myself with a new handmade leather travel bag to replace my beat-up old plastic thrift-store valise. The new kit would have cost a fortune back home. A small luxury, but since it was my only home, it seemed important.

There were so many great things to buy there, but I had to be content with looking. Even if I could afford all that stuff, where the hell would I ever put it? That's the trouble with bags and extra pockets on the road. You get rid of all the useless crap in them, and they're still always full somehow. And as you acquire more things, you never stop needing to find new places to keep them. Before you know it, you're all bogged down like those silly gringo backpackers I'd see stumbling around with the cumbersome burden of their ridiculous consumer culture strapped to their backs, like shaggy pink-faced pack mules.

The longer I lived on the road, the more it seemed the best thing would be to get rid of all my stupid belongings and just move on with nothing, like a wandering Buddhist monk. When you've got nothing, there's nothing to lose or carry around anymore.

And so it was with the past. But I just couldn't seem to ever be rid of all the heavy baggage of my memories. I couldn't take that final step mentally, somehow. Maybe because I unconsciously equated it with death: something to fear and respect as the one non-variable element in the mad jigsaw puzzle of life. And the more I saw of the world, the more I found myself thinking about death. It was always in the air in Mexico, an ever-present mystical shadow. I couldn't know what lay beyond that mysterious door, but my spirit knew, I was sure. It felt strange to be living so intensely after seeing so much death, destruction, and misery in my short, confusing life. But you can't go around with your pockets or your head full of shit all the time. I knew something was calling the cards, and I intuitively sensed it wasn't me.

o   o   o

As the tattoo man reads on, he flashes back to another cloudy day in Los Angeles. A cold Pacific fog hangs in the air of his memory. Cigano is wearing a thick sweater and a motorcycle jacket. His mother sits up in bed, lighting a cigarette as he walks into the stuffy room. He steps over, looking down at her, feeling too large for the airless little space.

"There's my beamish boy!" Her eyes light up. "My, but you're looking so *sturdy*, Jono! Pass me the ashtray, darling." She points to a large, overflowing crystal Tiffany ashtray on her dresser.

He reaches over, dumps the foul contents into the wastebasket, and hands it to her. She sets it on the quilt and takes a long swig of vodka from the pink plastic tumbler on her bedside table. She looks so small and frail that it seems the tumbler is sucking her spirit out into it.

"I've been dreaming a lot," she slurs in a woozy, medicated drawl.

He smiles down at her. "What do ya dream about, Ma?"

"It's like an ongoing dream, honey. . . . " She pauses, looking baffled. "I'm in a foreign place, and I'm searching for you. We meet, and you take me to a tavern. We meet your friends there, and they're all involved in drugs. The police come and arrest them. I go and bail them out. . . . That's all I remember. Sometimes, I don't know, I think it's real, that it's actually happening. Then I wake up, and I say something to Len, and he says 'What are you talking about?' and I carry on this whole story, and he says 'What are you talking about?' again. Then I realize it's my dream. Very lucid, I really think I'm there! I wake up thinking I'm still there."

She falls silent, with a faraway look.

As Cigano stands by the bed, shifting from foot to foot, she looks up at him and smiles. "Ah, I know now, yes! We're together, in a foreign country. The police arrest you, and I come down to bail you out. You call the jailer a faggot. He's very angry, and you're really on a roll. You can't be stopped! When you're on a roll, Jono, you're *really* on a roll!" She laughs. "But you were always smart. You were good, and you were always ahead of the game. But you got busted this time, I think for dope. I bail you out, and you're cursing everybody all over the place. When you're on a roll, boy, there's no stopping you! We drive around. You introduce me to your friends, and they all like me."

"I remember my friends always loved you when I was a kid. I could never get along with you, but my friends thought you were great."

"Well, never mind, darling, you love me now, and I love you, which is not so common. Children tend to hate their parents in their teens. We never did that. We always respected each other. That's really quite special."

He smiles at her, not bothering to correct her boozy recollections. What purpose would it serve?

"So, you're writing a book?" she asks. "And you're going away again tomorrow? Where to this time? Mexico? Brazil?"

"Yep." Cigano nods vaguely, feeling a shadow of that old feeling of distrust. Secrecy. Still there. Old habits die hard.

"Wow! Brazil's a beautiful country! What's that famous statue there in Rio? The big statue of Christ? So beautiful."

She gets a faraway look in her eyes and sighs. "I don't pray anymore. Do you ever pray?"

"Well, yeah." Cigano looks at her, surprised, feeling oddly defensive again. "I do. I mean it's not like getting on my knees or going to church or anything like that, but I pray a lot, yeah. I just kinda talk to the universe, and if there's a God out there, I talk to him and say: 'Hey, God, if you're there, can you help me do right and see me through another day without a drink?' I just talk to God in my thoughts. I send them out, and they come back with good things. But it's not like conventional prayers in the church or anything. I guess it's more like trying to make a conscious contact with something else, something bigger, wiser, stronger than myself."

"I don't believe in God," Doris snaps. "I believe in evolution. I don't believe there's any God. No. I believe in science. I don't believe in God. No."

"That's okay." He smiles. "I don't think God needs anyone to believe in him. Or it. To me, God is like this all-powerful energy force. Creative, intelligent, healing energy, the life-force, whatever ya wanna call it. It's there in everything. God's the air you breathe, the spirit that moves your physical existence. . . . "

"Mm-hmm. What made you feel that way? It must be a very sustaining belief."

"Well, I just came to believe there's gotta be something besides just me, my little life. That can't be everything. I used to assume it was, but that's just ignorance. I mean, there's a whole universe out there. There's a lot going on beyond our limited perceptions. People living and dying. Spirits talking to us, listening to us, watching, tormenting, protecting us, whatever. I really don't know what's going on. I just know there's a lot of stuff beyond my perception, a lot more going on than what I can see or touch or taste. Human vision is real primitive, y'know. But this thing called God, to me it's like this higher intelligent order of things that sees all, knows all. And it's everywhere, all the time. No limitations, no beginnings, no ends. Everything is perfect. In God's eyes, everything is good. God is love. Energy. Creative energy. Yeah. Ya can't touch it with your hands, can't see it with your eyes, can't explain it with logic, but it's always there. You can feel it, sometimes, if ya get real quiet, real still. And you always just kinda know it, feel it. In here." He touches his hand to his chest.

"Yes, I see what you mean, Jono." She stops, shaking her head. "But I don't believe in any God! No! I believe in science. Evolution."

"Well, if ya believe in science, you can't touch that or explain it either. Electricity. Ya can't see it, but ya know it's there. And you sure do rely on it. You just expect the lights to go on when you hit the switch, right? Ya never wonder if it's gonna work or not. Ya just *know* it works. That's kinda how prayer works, I think. In this world. . . . But I believe there's a lot of other worlds out there that we don't know nothing about. . . . "

"You think so?"

"Sure I do. Otherwise, why would we even be here?" He shrugs. "There's no accidents. I think the universe is extremely intelligent."

"No! Not if we're the highest form of creation."

"Well, I certainly don't think that's the case." He guffaws.

"Oh, absolutely!" Doris exclaims. Just then, she has a terrible coughing attack. "Oh God," she gasps. "Hand me the water, darling."

He passes her the bottle of Evian on the table.

When her hacking subsides, he smiles and goes on. "We're only the highest form of creation that we *know* about, Ma. But we're so fuggin' primitive, we can't even *see* the higher forms, even though they can probably see us."

"No." She looks at him, and goes on in a weird, dreamy drawl. "They'll come, Jono. They are coming. We're evolving. And as we evolve, we gain more insight into ourselves. So far, we're the highest form of creation that we know of. What's next. . . . "

"Nobody knows what's next. Strange things. Nobody knows."

"Well, you've had a fascinating life, Jono. You went out looking for it. And you've found something. But I don't believe in God." She shakes her head. "No. I believe in people."

"Well, that's how God speaks to us, mostly, I think." He smiles. "Through people, our interactions and relationships with other people."

"Yes, I think so, too, Jono, but I don't believe in a God, a supreme deity. No. I think from the age of reason, about ten, I stopped believing in it, in God. I don't know that there is one."

"Well, me neither, Ma. But I don't know there isn't a God, either. Really, I don't know much about anything. That's the real truth. The older I get, the less I really know about things like that."

"The older I get, the smarter I become. I'm nearly eighty years old, you know, so I'm pretty smart by now. You're smart too. And I'm glad you're religious."

"I wouldn't call myself religious, Ma." He laughs. "I just try to keep an open mind about things. I know I don't have the answers. That's not religious, that's just curious."

"No, but you believe in a higher being. . . . "

"Well, yeah, that I do." He shrugs, feeling that odd defensive stab again. "I just believe there's something that guides me and teaches me, and it can't just be me alone. Cuz too many crazy things have happened in my life. Things that I couldn't possibly produce by my own unaided will. I've experienced too many amazing coincidences to believe my little shit-brained intellect is the spearhead of evolution." He guffaws. "Seriously, Ma. There's gotta be something much more than what we can see or touch or define."

He falls silent, closing his eyes, asking that mysterious "something" for guidance.

Finally, he looks up and smiles. "I think the answer is inside, Ma. I believe this God thing lives inside us. That's why people look for it in quiet states of prayer and meditation. It seems to come to me best through my writing, contemplation, creative expression. That's where I can really feel it. Intuition. That's why I think the religions are lying to people. I'm not into all that organized religion. I think it's a kinda mind control for the masses. God's not some pissed-off old guy with a beard sitting in a big chair up in the sky, judging everybody. Not to me. That's all bullshit. God's right here." He points to his chest. "Inside. There's a spirit in here where God lives. So when we die, we don't cease to exist, the spirit just moves on. . . . "

"Oh yes, I do believe that!" Her eyes light up. "When I was part of the early LSD research experiments at UCLA, I saw it. Saw it all! It was quite marvelous, really. I can certainly understand why people claim to have religious experiences. I guess I did, too, when I was on LSD. And then, when Grandma died. She died here, you know, right in this bed. Well, you were in Brazil then, but when she died, I was right here with her, and there was such a look of *wonder* that came over her face, the moment she passed, as if to say, 'Oh! Look how *marvelous* it all is. . . . '"

Cigano thinks back to a day in New York, when his mother asked him to walk her to St. Patrick's. He remembers standing beside the altar while she lit candles for her poor suicidal nephew, Jono's cousin Malcolm.

As she talks, he can almost smell the incense. He pictures the dozens of little candles blazing in the darkened sanctuary, like a blast furnace in some giant factory of prayers.

"There was no fear or pain in her eyes when she went," Doris whispers. "Just this wonderful look of childlike wonder. . . . I used to talk easily to God, you know, when I was a child. But I was brought up as a Catholic, which is a very severe religion."

"Severe's an understatement, Ma. The church is all about control. Brainwashing the masses. That's why I'm not down with religion. I think the Catholic Church has turned more people *away* from God than all the atrocities of mankind put together. . . . "

"You've become quite wise, Jono." She beams at him. "And you're so sturdy! My God! Whatever it is you're doing now, you just keep on doing it. And don't you ever weep for me when I'm gone. . . . " She reaches for the plastic tumbler. "I've had a very interesting life."

Cigano smiles sadly, fighting back a lifetime supply of tears.

12. A HEART TATTOO

A ship's horn sounds outside the window, breaking the spell.

Cigano rubs his eyes and looks up at Jaco. "Yeah, man." He sighs. "The old lady's a real piece of work, God love her."

A wry smile creeps into his eyes. "She even got me to give her a big old tattoo one day."

"Really?" Jaco raises his eyebrows.

"Yeah, man." He thinks back to the time, a few years before she took to her bed with a bottle, when his mother came to New York on one of her short yearly visits. She'd been staying at some fancy Midtown hotel, and going to the theatre, wandering around buying cheap trinkets in Times Square, like a tourist in the city of her youth.

"I put an old-school traditional heart with a banner on her arm." He grins. "With 'MOM' in big bold letters. That's what she wanted, an old-time sailor tattoo. It was just the right thing for the old lady."

Jaco smiles. "She must have been really proud of that."

"Oh, yeah! She sure was!" Cigano laughs. "After getting tattooed, she asked me to give her a ride back to her hotel on my motorcycle. She was almost eighty years old, drunk as a fiddler's bitch, freshly inked, and hanging on the back of this greasy old Triumph I used to ride. Fuck! Some balls! She's never stopped talking about that day. . . . "

He smiles as his mind travels back to his mother's kitchen.

◦   ◦   ◦

"Remember when you gave me this?" Doris grins, rolling up the sleeve of her bathrobe, showing the large, colorful heart tattooed on her scrawny arm.

"How could I ever forget, Ma?" He laughs.

She beams. "I waited all my life for you to accept me, Jono. And you finally did. It took a long time, but finally we became friends. That was really, truly glorious. You came to love me at last. O frabjous day! Callooh! Callay!!" She giggles, reciting the words from the Jabberwock poem she used to read him when he was a child. "Ah, my beamish boy! And now I have you tattooed on me."

"You really blew my mind, getting that tattoo." Cigano smiles fondly. "Ya didn't even flinch."

"Yes. Well, I'm a tough old bird, Jono. You always admired my strength, and my individuality, which was always very strong. I didn't march in the same parade as most. You struck out on your own, too. But you always knew I was there. Your individuality was much advised by me." She looks at him with a tender smile.

He nods and stays silent.

"Anyhow, we've finally learned to love each other. But boy, you fought me. For years, we couldn't even speak, much less see each other. You just had to do it all yourself. And I wanted you to. You grew strong in your own person. You were unsure a lot, and you quit a lot. But I was always there. You hated me a lot, too. Sometimes I paid no attention to you at all, none. I was just there. If you ever needed me, you always knew I was there, and I would do anything for you. But you had to be on your own. I recognized that early, so I let you go. I didn't cling. And here we are now. We love each other. You admired my strength, and I admired your will. Even when it turned you against me and you hated me, I wouldn't give up the love I felt for you. And you always knew it was there. There was nothing you could do, nothing that could turn me against you. And you had your moments, boy, running around with the Manson family, shooting heroin, getting arrested. Didn't matter, didn't matter. . . . "

Doris stops talking, as if she's expended her lifetime allotment of words. She drains the glass and looks across the table at her son with a bleary, bewildered expression of tenderness.

Finally she speaks again, in a familiar little singsong voice, like the one that used to read him fairy tales. "Didn't matter, didn't matter." She recites from the Mad Hatter in *Alice in Wonderland*. "At present I'm afraid I'm as mad as any hatter, so I'll keep it to myself, 'cause my opinion doesn't matter. Remember that one, Jono?" She giggles.

"How could I forget, Ma?" He grins.

"And then the Jabberwock came! Oh yes! I used to read you those stories. You always looked so wide-eyed. Ha! 'The vorpal blade went snicker-snack! He left it dead, and with its head, he went galumphing back! And hath thou slain the Jabberwock?' Yes!" She goes on in a dreamy voice, looking her Beamish Boy up and down. "I do believe you finally *have* slain the Jabberwock, Jono!"

"Well, it's a big fucker to slay, Ma. But I'm working on it, one day at a time."

"Yes! And then there was Tweedledee and Tweedledum. Fell off the barstool. And all the king's men and horses couldn't put Humpty Dumpty together again. That was from an old jazz riff. My Pop loved jazz. He was always falling off barstools. 'But, I'm afraid at the moment, I'm mad as any hatter. Doesn't matter, doesn't matter'. . . . "

He stares at his mother with a mix of wonder and sadness.

"I think I'd like to go back to bed now, darling." Doris giggles tipsily, her eyes glazing over as the pills kick in. "My goodness, I'm suddenly feeling very drowsy. Doesn't matter, doesn't matter. . . . "

Cigano stands and helps her up from her chair. As he walks her into her bedroom, she staggers and almost falls over. He catches her, holding her steady.

His mother feels incredibly light. Like a ghost.

13. SOUTHERN WINDS

In Oaxaca, I spent the long lazy afternoons exploring the busy downtown *mercados*. Lost in a sea of buzzing activity, I walked the streets like a kid at a carnival.

One big section of the huge, sprawling marketplace sold an amazing array of beautiful handmade indigenous crafts. But the bulk of commerce was devoted to everything else: livestock, auto parts, farm equipment, tools, clothing, household items, meat, and produce. It was all on display in the musty rows of cavernous old market buildings, each one a full city block long.

On weekends, truckloads of indigenous people would swarm into the city center from the outlying *pueblos*, displaying their exotic goods on the sidewalks, wherever they could claim a few inches of space. By midmorning, the frantic commerce spilled out onto the streets all around the crowded indoor markets and tents.

The human traffic in that mad, buzzing insect hive of humanity was so intense, it could take twenty minutes to walk a block. It was pure chaos: people yelling, shouting, hawking, vending, pushing, shoving, cussing, and clawing at each other like packs of heat-crazed hyenas. Feeling like a rat in a hyperactive human maze, it got to where I could barely move an inch in any direction without knocking someone down and walking over their flailing body. The afternoon would degenerate into a desperate, savage free-for-all open-air barroom brawl of fallen pedestrians: people cursing and pounding at my ankles with their fists as my foot descended onto their faces. Just as I'd begin to progress a few inches again, some big sweaty cowboy would come barreling through the crowd, shoving me over like a rag doll onto a pile of sparkling red tomatoes. Impossible to avoid squishing one with my elbow, I struggled to rise to my feet as a crazed, toothless hag slapped at my back, calling me a son of a cow, spitting and cursing like a wild-eyed harpy. Her angry shouts and raspy insults faded into the din as I was carried off in that surging river of struggling bodies. It was like being in an ant farm or something.

And, out of that ungodly human feeding frenzy, the good people of Oaxaca would thrive and survive, getting paid, fed, and supplied to live for another week on the blessed green earth of that bittersweet, magical land.

ʘ   ʘ   ʘ

After a few weeks in that magical city, feeling the age-old restless itch, I took a local bus out to the main highway and stuck out my thumb.

The first truck took me all the way to the Isthmus of Tehuantepec, where tall Zapotec women strutted around in their colorful indigenous garb, like proud Gypsy princesses.

It was late at night by the time I got dropped off in the middle of nowhere, miles from any town. I was walking along the dark, empty road, wondering what to do next, when a bus came creeping up—the first vehicle I'd seen in an hour. It stopped beside me. The door opened, and the driver gestured for me to get in. I told him I didn't have any money. He just smiled and shook his finger, telling me I could ride for free. I offered to sit up top with the cargo, but he wouldn't hear of it. He even insisted on buying me a meal at the next village, and he wouldn't take no for an answer.

There it was again, I mused, that wonderful Mexican magnanimity, as we sat eating at an all-night taco stand, drinking beer and exchanging stories of the road. That's just how people were in Mexico: big-hearted, generous of spirit, and kind to strangers. There would surely be a special place in Heaven reserved for them, I thought as I wandered the quiet, dark streets of another faceless, nameless little town, looking for a place to stay.

I walked around the sleeping village without finding a room. Finally, I ended up spending the night in jail—and without even getting arrested, for once. Over the months of my travels, I'd learned that in smaller towns where there's no hotel, passing migrants were sometimes allowed to stay overnight in municipal buildings—usually police stations. After a few friendly words with the local *arcalde's* wife, I was in. I slept fitfully in the little cell—even though the barred door stayed open all night.

When the *Jefe* arrived in the morning, he turned out to be a smiling old boozer with a bushy white Pancho Villa mustache. He looked more like the janitor than the chief of police. One of the other cops laughingly told me the jail hadn't been used for years, other than for the boss and his cronies to sleep off their hangovers. After a few jovial beers with them, I set out again.

It was late afternoon by the time I got my next ride heading south. I fell asleep up top as the big truck lumbered off into a warm sunset. I woke up hours later, surprised to find myself shivering under a frozen blanket of cold unblinking stars.

I spent the rest of the steep uphill voyage wide awake, shaking like a wet Chihuahua. Just when I thought I couldn't take the biting cold for another minute, we rumbled into the remote mountain hamlet of San Cristóbal de Las Casas in the dead of night.

Stiff and chilled to the bones, I climbed down from my frigid perch. I wandered the empty cobblestone streets, looking for a place to stay. Icy mountain winds tore at my exhausted flesh like a thousand tiny whips. When I'd left Tehuantepec that morning, it had been a humid ninety-five degrees under cloudy tropical skies. Now there I was, high in the mountains of Chiapas, staggering around like a wayward beggar.

Finally I found a small hotel. The room was so cold, I could see my breath in the bed. I couldn't wrap enough blankets around myself to get warm. But the luck of the Gypsies was on me again. I learned from a sleepy clerk that I could use the hotel's amazing steam baths with hot and cold showers, just across a dark courtyard. I spent the rest of the night thawing out in that poor man's spa, for less than a dollar—lodging included.

Situated just miles from the Guatemalan border, the stately old colonial enclave of San Cristóbal lay hidden in a high mountain valley.

Clean, quiet, and old-worldly, it was a vision from another time—more like a quaint Swiss village in the Alps than a weird antique time warp rising from the steamy tropical jungles of southern Mexico.

As in Oaxaca, the population was mostly indigenous. A friendly vendor at the downtown *mercado* told me the city took its name after a Spanish monk who was famous for his passionate appeals to the Crown on behalf of the Indian populace, who were treated like beasts of burden by the local gentry.

As I wandered around the next afternoon, it looked as if the dirt-poor, landless indigenous people's plight hadn't improved much since colonial times. Whole families of stone-faced peasants in traditional native garb clustered around the main square like hungry dogs. Many more sat huddled in the shadows of an impassive baroque cathedral, begging. Conversely, most of the surrounding homes were built of luxurious stone, with solid red tile roofs and smoking chimneys. Scores of elaborate, gold-guilded colonial churches loomed over the city, while the people of the land lived in abject poverty.

Walking back out to the highway, anxious to move on to warmer climes, I passed through a squalid shantytown where undernourished Indian children played in the dirt, naked to the elements as so many scrawny chickens. So much for the Church. Thinking about that noxious wave of unrestrained genocide known as colonization, its indelible scars were everywhere I looked.

I climbed atop the first truck that stopped, feeling at once relieved and deeply ashamed for belonging to the human race.

ɔ   ɔ   ɔ

A cold wind ripped at my skin as we descended from the mountainous heights. Sitting up top, shivering like a beached flounder, I wrapped up in my blanket and laid back, staring up at the sky. As night fell, stars littered the dark heavens like snowflakes as the tops of tall pine trees whizzed by in the frosty air.

Finally, we began a steep descent. I could feel my ears pop as the truck began winding its way downhill and the climate got steadily warmer. After a while I shed my blanket and sat up again, marveling at the dramatic changes in terrain. In under an hour, we'd gone from frigid alpine forests, past sprawling eucalyptus groves, and down into the steamy tropical jungles of Chiapas.

The highway was suddenly surrounded by dense vegetation and wild primeval rain forest. Giant rock cliffs covered in vines and creepers jutted out over the road, surrounded by jagged palms, banana plants, and waterfalls. At intervals, the road became nothing more than a narrow dirt path, cutting through remote little jungle outposts. Distant marimba music blended with the eerie shrieks and whistles of great tropical parrots. Monkeys screeched in the darkness like heat-mad phantoms. It felt like I was riding through some old Humphrey Bogart adventure movie.

Creeping along one of the narrow dirt turnoffs, the trucker turned off into a village of straw-roofed huts, and stopped. A local *fiesta* had taken over the whole place. There was a marimba band and costumed indigenous dancers wearing colorful handmade animal masks. After treating me to a delicious meal of fresh lamb *birria*, the driver pointed to the festivities with a childlike grin. *"Vámonos?"* Of course.

We walked around for an hour, sharing *caguamas* with some local farmers and laughing like kids at an amusement park. Like so many places in Mexico, that nameless jungle enclave and its people were pure magic.

Back on the road, I sat up front with the driver the rest of the trip. We talked all night long, finally reaching our destination just before dawn. Brothers for life now, we shook hands and he drove off, shouting a cheerful *adios, mi hermano!* from the window.

I stood beside the highway in a comfortable blanket of quiet tranquility, taking in the ancient Mayan ruins of Palenque sprawling across the jungle floor. Breathing in the sounds and smells of the tropics at first light, my bones felt renewed by the life-giving heat and humidity.

As the sun rose like a giant red ball of fire silhouetted against the mysterious, looming indigenous structures, I trudged out to a massive stone pyramid. Everything was enveloped in a mist of serene, pristine silence. After hours shouting back and forth over a noisy diesel engine, I felt as if I was ascending into Heaven as I climbed to the top of the Tomb of the Inscriptions. Standing at the exact spot where mass human sacrifices had once been conducted to appease the bloodthirsty Mayan gods of old, I pictured their empire sliding into decline, just as my own bloated culture was self-destructing from within.

To underscore my musings, busloads of tourists began to arrive in a noxious wave of pastel-colored ugliness, spilling their unsightly passengers onto the grounds like a troop of evil clowns. By midmorning, the grounds were hot and crowded and noisy. Reluctantly, I climbed down from the pyramid. It was even worse at the bottom as more buses pulled up, discharging their obnoxious human cargo.

Covered in sweat, I ran off into the jungle and enjoyed a cool, refreshing shower under a shady crystalline waterfall. Then I hiked back to the road—dodging the magnificent ruins this time. I couldn't bear to see them infested with tourists. I wanted to preserve that sacred place in my memory, just as I'd first seen it, unsullied by the ugly droves of bumbling morons swarming, gawking, clamoring, and squawking, with their cameras and snacks and screeching brats. Still, I felt honored to have gotten a glimpse of that cadaverous ancient civilization, just as it must have looked before the Conquest. And that's how I would always remember Palenque.

Without looking back, I stuck my thumb out, slouching into the warm southern winds of another long, magical day on the road.

14. CHETUMAL

The next ride took me all the way to the Caribbean coast. On the outskirts of the village of Tulum, I camped out in a deserted coconut grove, where untouched Mayan ruins hidden in thick tropical vegetation loomed over a savage deserted coastline.

This time there wasn't another human being in sight. No tour buses, no noise; only miles of peace, quiet, and blessed solitude. For the next week I lived all alone there by the sea, like a poor man's Robinson Crusoe. Sober as a monk, I subsisted only on an abundance of coconuts littering the ground, drinking their sweet water and extracting the nourishing meat with my machete, until I couldn't stand to look at another one.

Finally giving in to hunger, one afternoon I hiked along a narrow jungle path to the local straw-roofed grocery. There, I was greeted by several chubby live iguanas, hanging upside down from the rafters, their prehistoric claws bound with string like tiny prisoners of war.

A toothless old *campesino* gestured to the squirming green monsters, smacking his lips. *"Son bien ricas, señor! Muy buenas para tu cena,"* he assured me.

After a week eating nothing but raw coconut meat, I was almost tempted. But in the end, I passed on the exotic captive reptiles and settled for some boring eggs, onions, and tomatoes. I trudged back to the deserted coconut grove and cooked my dinner over an open fire overlooking the ocean at sunset.

I sat eating to the sound of breakers. As darkness engulfed the sea, a massive full moon rose up over the sparkling coastline, blazing on the horizon like a giant silver dollar. Later, I wandered along an empty stretch of beach beside crashing phosphorescent waves.

Coming to the base of the deserted ruins, I clambered up through dense tropical overgrowth covering a huge vine-encrusted Mayan pyramid. The entire edifice was coated in slippery green moss that rounded its massive stone steps and corners. Being in that vast complex of abandoned monoliths in the middle of the jungle, listening to the eerie howls and screeches of stampeding monkeys with childlike faces and crazy long tails as they scampered madly about in the moonlight, was a revelation.

Standing atop those palatial ruins, I felt as if I'd stumbled into a time and place totally alien to the complexities of the modern world. In that magical moment, I knew what that ancient compound must have been like thousands of years ago, when the desolate structures had been at the center of a thriving, advanced civilization.

All gone now, I mused. Nothing but relics, a forgotten graveyard of lost archaeological residue. The remains of a sprawling noble empire laid to waste by shiploads of brutal European invaders, come like a swarm of human locusts to spread their bloody Catholic doctrine.

I watched in awe as a meteor shower poured down over the ocean in a cascade of silent fiery jewels. It had never dawned on me that there were so many stars in the sky.

That night, I dreamed of my dead cousin Malcolm staring into the heavens through the mad, illuminated eyes of his tragic hero, Vincent van Gogh.

○　○　○

After a quiet week alone by the sea, the highway was calling to me again. Soon as I stuck out my thumb, I got another long ride. The big truck rumbled off, down an endless stretch of shimmering blacktop cutting straight through the jungle like a tunnel. A dizzying procession of foxes, iguanas, and armadillos wandered into the road. Lulled by the steady hum of the sputtering diesel engine, I squeezed myself in between a cluster of massive steel beams on the back and quickly fell asleep.

I awakened, hours later, just as the lumbering rig groaned to a stop on the outskirts of the sleepy Caribbean city of Chetumal.

The spooky old pirate town faced a choppy ocean bay on Mexico's southern border with British Honduras—the fabled "Gateway to Central America." My heart swelled as I climbed down onto the steaming asphalt.

As the truck rolled off with a great blast of horns blaring "*La*

Cucaracha," I stood by the road, listening to the insect-twittering jungle air. Breathing in a sweet, septic watery weight of the tropics. I could feel the call of faraway lands whispering across the dirty green water.

I walked along the dusty road till I spotted a deserted hut at the water's edge. I stopped as a pair of fishermen in weather-battered straw hats approached, lugging bulging wicker baskets. I bought some fresh green tiger shrimp and cooked them on an open fire in the weedy yard overlooking the bay. After lunch, I hung the colorful hand-woven hammock I'd bought at a roadside prison cooperative near Oaxaca, where convicts sold their handicrafts for food money.

Lulled into a lazy stupor by the muggy sea breeze, I lounged in that yard for the next several days, relaxing my travel-weary bones.

Strung up like a mummy between two sturdy coconut palms, I finally cracked the thick paperback Dostoyevsky book I'd been carrying with me since fleeing Los Angeles.

JOURNAL ENTRY—Chetumal, Mexico:

I close my eyes, sitting by the stagnant waters of time, and I see a scratchy image of Artaud hanging on the wall of my mind. It's like a close-up of some weird Dostoyevsky character: a man waiting in a food line, leaning against the columns of cold old Mother Russia. Old weary Moscow morning, another threadbare winter day, a man waiting at the end of a long line of cripples and beggars and madmen; old ladies with shopping bags stuffed with mildew and dust of history. He's standing in that dirty old cold line, just waiting his turn. That's why Dostoyevsky was such a great writer—a god who created crazy little characters who worried and fretted and regretted and lived and died. But this isn't some neutral or even benevolent interventionist god. No, this is a Man-God at work, full of sadness, misery, and loss. Set before a firing squad that snapped him out of it or into wherever the Holy Mother visions come from, where his comrades fell to the ground in shock and terror, he just stood up and wandered away, back to his world of miserable, magical characters. And when his gambling ran sour or the vodka money was gone and he was down and out and defeated, he had to suffer through it all over again; but always working those mad illuminated characters of his through their tragic little paces, whew, and he just kept on writing, no matter what. That was a writer! That was a man!

Chetumal was a lethargic world's-end seaport with a musty ghostlike aura. With free lodging on the outskirts, it seemed the perfect spot to rest up for a while. In my new makeshift home, the jungle came right up to the water's edge. The sea changed from a sparkling emerald green in the morning to a choppy dirty brown in the afternoon. The air was hot and humid, but there was always a cooling wind blowing in off the bay. Ensconced in as peaceful a place as I'd ever known, I spent my days there lying in the hammock, dozing, daydreaming, writing, and reading Dostoyevsky's *The Idiot.*

At night, it would get so cool by the water that I had to wrap up in a blanket—also to fend off the nightly invasion of bloodthirsty mosquitoes. They would zero in around dusk, a battalion of tiny vampires, leaving bites over every inch of my body. After scratching my hands and feet raw, finally I went to a local *farmacia* and gave myself a quick malaria shot. Doctors were scarce in that part of the country, but you could buy cheap medicines and plastic syringes over the counter. And shooting up a dose of bug juice wasn't brain surgery for an old junkie *veterano.*

After a few days of blessed rest, I pried myself out of the hammock and wandered into town, where I strolled the sleepy docks, looking for work. There were only a few small ships in port, but I made it a daily routine, just for the pleasure of basking in the languid air of that charming seaside time warp.

The old deco-style buildings facing the bay had obviously seen many tropical cyclones. Some of them had window glass half an inch thick. I dreamed of returning someday with a purpose. Reading Dostoyevsky, I pictured myself writing a book there, fueled by the weight of obscure history, exotic tropical mysteries, and the mute poetry of the rusty old architecture.

Afternoons, at *siesta* time, I'd sit in a scruffy plaza by the deserted seawall, reading, writing, drinking beer, and eating fresh shrimp by the water's edge. Sometimes I'd join a casual soccer game with a gang of local kids. They didn't know a word of English, other than the usual *"focka jooo modda."* I would reply with snappy comebacks in my now near-fluent Spanish, and we'd all cackle like fools. Better friends I'd never had.

After a week living out of the abandoned house, one day I spotted a massive tarantula crawling right toward me across the yard. That got me out of my hammock, fast. There's always some fucking thing, I mused, shaking my head.

My arms covered in goose bumps, I packed my bag in a hurry and beat it, without a backward glance. Some things you never get over. I rode a rickety local bus into town, thinking for the first time in years of my earliest childhood terror.

15. NO DIRECTION HOME

From time to time, I'd find the odd letter waiting at Post Office General Delivery windows in places where I stayed long enough to get mail—mostly in response to the many letters and postcards I'd sent from different places along the road. Over the early months of my travels, I'd written home a lot. Somehow, I found it easier to communicate with my people after leaving them behind. Maybe that old saying was true, that distance made the heart grow fonder.

In Chetumal, I found several letters waiting for me at the local *lista de correios*. There was news from Paul Magad, Richard O'Connell, and a few other friends who were still alive. But reading their words after all my time away was depressing. Nonetheless, I was delighted to find a long letter from my mother—mostly for the hundred-dollar bill folded into the pages. I was far from "homesick," though, as the old lady speculated. Give me another five or ten years on the road, I mused, and maybe I might have a thought of visiting that toxic shithole again. My only home now was wherever I landed. Thomas Wolfe really nailed it when he said you couldn't go home again. There were just too many better places to be. Mexico had proved that to me, once and for all. I'd missed out for too long on life: a luxurious banquet of possibilities, from lobster tails to pheasant under glass, with the occasional shit sandwich thrown in just to keep you guessing. But until taking to the road, I'd always settled for a stale potato chip or two, before running out the door of oblivion. I had to make up for lost time now.

As far as "missing my friends," as my mother's letter implied, I knew better. The significance of friendships wasn't in their history for me, anymore, or even how long they lasted, so much as in their intensity and their impact on my soul. That's where I always found the unforgettable moments, unexplainable happenings, and incomparable interactions with others—not by carrying around a cumbersome load of obsolete, sentimental memories. I wouldn't make the same mistake the old lady had when she came back from Italy, settling for a mediocre life of low-grade, grumbling misery. Fuck that. I wasn't looking back.

As I sat beside the seawall reading my friends' letters, their language seemed so weak and irrelevant that hearing from them was more disturbing than comforting. Most of them were still strung out like lab rats. Their words were pathetic, infested with the same old useless excuses and regrets I'd heard from myself a hundred times before: long-winded litanies of uselessness, oozing futility, bitterness, and that familiar, cloying junkie self-pity.

Jerome Ali's missive rambled on about how he was going to get straight and start a new life "soon." Poor old Paul even congratulated me for getting out of town, and O'Connell said he'd been so inspired by my example that he was planning to do the same thing "real soon" too. But I knew that that ephemeral junkie "soon" would surely never come for the poor, deluded devils. They were all full of shit.

As their words buzzed in my head like mosquitoes, their weak pipe dreams awakened a mixture of contempt and pity in me; bitter reminders of my own rancid junkie failings. Why bother writing back? They'd probably all be dead before my letters arrived. And even if I wanted to, how could I ever begin to describe the unique adventures that made up this overwhelming new totality of experience? How could I possibly find words to transmit all the magical sights, sounds, and smells, to describe all the people I'd met and the places I'd been? How could I even begin to write about any of it?

In that moment, I understood what old Bukowski had meant when he'd told me that Art was in the living, the experience—not in the rendering of some musty, drab little literary trophy. Poetry was the world I lived in now. It was life, not some redundant, pretentious verbal expression. Art existed for me in the simple poetic details of everyday experience: an art of living, not a pile of useless, abstract descriptions. That's why I'd never be an artist, I realized, other than to simply pursue my dreams with as much class and courage as I could.

Reading my old friends' letters was another grim reminder of how I'd been caught in the same dark whirlpool they were all in now. And, like them, I hadn't cared. I'd been far too sick to imagine a way out—until it became my only chance to survive. I'd shrugged off a deadly malady, awakened from a long, dull heroin coma, and that's all that mattered anymore. I didn't want to look back or think about the people I'd left behind. It was just too painful.

"Fuck this shit. . . . " I muttered as I stacked all their letters together. With tears in my eyes, I tore them to shreds, one by one. I held them out over the choppy green waters of the Caribbean and watched the wind take them. The scraps of tiny words sat floating on the surface of the bay like a flock of defeated butterflies.

I suppose I must have feared that if I'd kept them, all those thoughts and memories might jinx me, somehow, breaking the spell of the abundant new reality I'd conjured from the dust of defeat. I still had so much to learn and see and do, there simply wasn't time to think of the past. It was scary enough just being alive in the world without a home or a destination. But I knew I'd be better off dead if I didn't keep going somehow.

I walked away from the deserted seawall that day with a sneaky little smile on my face and a heart trembling with hope, feeling, once again, the seductive siren call of the mysterious, unknown Gypsy road to nowhere.

16. A FRIEND TO THE CHILDREN

A bus rumbles around the corner, rattling the windows of the hotel room. Cigano is laboring over a section of Jaco's massive full-body tattoo. Finally, his young client breaks a long, painful silence.

"I was thinking about what you were reading yesterday, Jonathan Shaw. It's incredible how vivid your memories are of your travels, that you can remember it all so well. . . . "

The tattoo man looks up and peels off the rubber gloves.

"Well, I wish I could claim a photographic memory or some shit." He lights a cigarette and sighs through a cloud of smoke. "Truth is, I probably wouldn't remember any of it if I hadn't been keeping all those journals. I did a lotta writing in Mexico. Much as I wanted to get away from it and just live life, I s'pose I still felt a need to put stuff down on paper. Guess it's finally coming in handy now."

He reaches over, picks up a battered blue notebook. He squints as he leafs through it, as if trying to decipher a stranger's writing.

JOURNAL ENTRY—CHETUMAL, MEXICO:

A dreamlike vision of a murky green bay at the mouth of a winding jungle river keeps me rooted to a long, lethargic spell of nothingness here. Chetumal was supposed to be the Gateway to Central America, via British Honduras, but there's no ships going anywhere from here, so the only gateway is by land. Everyone tells me I've got to go to Veracruz if I'm looking for work on a ship. So be it, but I'm not feeling in any hurry to leave just now. Something about this place makes it hard to break out of this murky lethargy and move on. Sitting in limbo, smoking weed, and looking out over the water, it's hard to get motivated. If I had money to live by, I'd probably just stay on in this obscure little dream zone forever, lost in the languid air of a song of the Caribbean, forgotten by time, hammock swinging in the breeze, a cat hollering on a tin roof. Sitting by the little taco stand across the street this afternoon, I savored the final pages of The Idiot. *Siesta time, nobody on the street, this wiry little guy comes over and sits down beside me. He's Mexican, a young cat, strange, funny, happy, and zealous. We talk. Somehow, we understand each other enough to trust each other's eyes. His name is Silvestre. He's interested in my book, he tells me, says he wants to learn English. Books are his friends, he says, and he believes in some magical life force, something I think I kind of understand. There's a gentle gleam of kindness in his shiny black eyes. As we're talking, a young boy comes up, maybe eight years old. The kid smiles. You could fit a 10-peso coin between his rotten front teeth. Both the kid's legs are crippled with polio. Silvestre starts talking to him and shows him good spirit. This is good. He has just made a crippled kid's life a little better. I would like to be like this Silvestre, I think, because of that simple gesture of brotherhood, his subtle, miraculous camaraderie to a crippled boy. We talked some more and I gave him the book I'd just finished. I told him he would learn English, and he smiled. We shook hands and he got on a bus back to his village, some place called Bacalar by a big lagoon in the middle of the jungle. As he rode off, I sensed he'd wanted something more from me. I couldn't put my finger on it, but it felt like he needed my help somehow. It was just a feeling, though. There was nothing I could do.*

*JOURNAL ENTRY—*Chetumal:

I started out on the road today, trying to get as far as Mérida, Yucatán, on the way to Veracruz. I ended up getting stuck in Bacalar, of all places. Not a single car on that road, not a truck, nothing. The sun was going down, so I gave up and built a fire and slept by this big spooky lagoon. I had weird dreams. Then, stumbling around in the pre-dawn darkness for a piss, I kicked my bag into the water by accident. I had to spend some time sorting everything out and getting it dry, so I went in for a swim. Later, I waited by the road with my thumb out. I drank a lukewarm Orange Crush from a thick glass bottle, standing in the shade and talking with some local kids. Finally, a truck stopped and I got in. I never even went to look up Silvestre in Bacalar. He'd given me his address, but I didn't want to impose. Later, I would feel stupid for that "not wanting to impose" thing—my lousy old gringo programming. I've really come to understand—not without some guilt—that there is no hospitality better than Mexican hospitality. People are different here. The lonesome traveler can easily go astray by hanging onto a fucked-up old Americano ego. I really want to let it go, but it seems to stick to my soul like the gummy glue in the Chetumal post office. The truck was only going about halfway to Mérida, so I waved the guy on and sat by the road in the middle of the jungle again, trying to get another ride. All the traffic was headed the other way, though, back toward Chetumal, so I just gave up, walked across the road, and caught a ride back here. Another hazy week passes, and I don't see Silvestre. I think of him sometimes, which is strange because I hardly know the guy. No! I do know him, goddammit, just like I knew Malcolm and all the other beautiful, trapped, moribund spirits I couldn't help in my stinking life. Yes, I do feel guilt. I can circle the world like a flaming jalapeño pepper ass-rocket, but I can't ever outrun the guilt and shame of my past. Shit!

*JOURNAL ENTRY—*C*HETUMAL:*

I'm walking down the street with a couple of crazy Mexican kids I met, when, bang, I bump right into Silvestre. He's with his mother. We stop and greet each other and he introduces us. My new friends greet the old lady politely, hola, Señora, mucho gusto, blah blah, and then we all part ways again, just like that, just a few unlikely bodies stopped for a few moments on a sleepy downtown street corner. But there was something reserved in Silvestre this time. Something of the mad childlike zeal and good spirit of our first meeting was held back in him, and in myself, too, I guess. I didn't think much of it, just that he was with his old mother and I was with these crazy Mexican Gypsy types, and it's a different time and a different place. I wondered if he'd ever learned enough English to read the book I'd given him, then I just forgot it. Shortly after that random encounter, I met a beautiful Italian chick. She paid for two bus tickets to Mérida. We stayed together for days there, fucking and honeymooning like movie stars in her fancy hotel room by the Zócalo, eating grilled prawns from the room service, talking and drinking champagne. I told her of my travels, and she wanted to go with me, and I said yeah, sure, why not? I was supposed to be on my way to Veracruz, but I figured it could wait. Easy to get sidetracked with so many places to stop along the way. That's the beauty of this crazy life: it doesn't matter where you go, or even if you ever get there at all, because the road is its own destination. After a couple of days, she invited me to go with her to a little beach town on the Oaxaca coast. It was tempting. In the end, I opted for the solitary road again. I knew it was that selfish old spirit of solitude and adventure calling me back, a dark dead-man junkie longing for all the time I've spent alone in my life. It was kind of scary to realize I've actually grown to like it, like a defeated lab monkey liking its cage. But that same dark, futile spirit is also what keeps calling me back to dreams of faraway ports like Rio and other places that only exist in my lonesome travel fantasies. And so my beautiful Italiana went on to her "Place in the Sun," as she called it, and, instead of moving on to Veracruz as I'd planned, I just came back to Chetumal again. After she was gone, I even felt sort of glad to be on my own again. New events followed with some other wild Mexican kids I met here. We wandered around town and joined forces with these crazy Reggae musicians from British Honduras who were playing at a local fiesta. We smoked their strong weed. They were good and righteous mystical souls. Their esoteric metaphysical Rastafari language riffs were flying way over my head, but I started to learn about music and the spirit world and the river of crazy karma and destiny. It was good. A few days later, I meet up with this other young Mexican named Antonio. We hang out, smoking the smoke and living the lazy pirate life. Antonio and I are walking along the seawall one day, going nowhere, when I see the little crippled boy again. He's sitting on the sidewalk in front of the park, looking at me as we walk by. I'm used to being stared at, that's just Mexico, but I recognized him from before and thought of my friend Silvestre who is a friend to the children. I wanted to give the kid something, but something stopped me. I wanted to give him something more than a few pesos, wanted to give him something real, something better, the way Silvestre had done. And, wanting to be like Silvestre, I smiled. The kid's face broke into a broad smile. Suddenly those two little smiles seemed to float away from two random bodies suspended in eternity; they broke free for an instant and mingled in some distant dimension where smiles mingle, as if to say "it's okay, no matter how fucked-up it all seems, it's only destiny and karma, and we're just a couple of smiles mingled here for this good and happy moment, and this moment is alive right now, and it's all perfect and right." And that was it. I felt proud and happy as I walked away, not ashamed at all anymore that I had a few pesos in my pocket and that little crippled boy had none. It didn't matter. The moment was real and alive for us both. I felt good to have given him a real and valuable human smile. But it's hard for me to say now, hard for me to think with this earthly mind, where confusion reigns. All the little signs fall together, and it all seems clear, perfect even, as though contrived by some great cosmic Master Planner. Right after seeing the crippled kid, I spotted Silvestre walking by the fish market. He came over and spoke of many things. I didn't understand it all, but I liked him again. I could see the good in him so clearly, the simple, innocent honesty of somebody's way, but as he talked, I could tell Silvestre was not happy. Suddenly, I saw Death in his eyes; the same clear eyes I'd seen and trusted before, those eyes so full of truth and simplicity and kindness, I saw the Fear and the Death in them. But my own eyes refused to see. Like looking into a burning tropical sun, they just closed right up. It was too harsh and too scary to see Silvestre like that. I just stood there in mute horror as an avalanche of dark, ranting, paranoid words tumbled from his mouth, like falling leaves from a dying tree, heralding a long, cold, ugly, barren winter.

17. BORDERLINE

"THE BORDER BETWEEN THE REAL AND THE UNREAL IS NOT FIXED, BUT JUST MARKS THE LAST PLACE WHERE RIVAL GANGS OF SHAMANS FOUGHT EACH OTHER TO A STANDSTILL."

—ROBERT ANTON WILSON

Leafing through his old journal, Cigano's mind conjures a face; a long-forgotten ghost, whining in the depths of his memory. Silvestre.

*"I no got it de pasaporte! I wan' go United E'state. When I see ju before, I wan' e'say ju, hey, le's go travel to there, but I no got de pasaporte because de fock e'sheet military. No es bueno para mi. I no like it de pinche military. I wan' go 'way for e'study on de e'school in Merida for no gotta go de military, but is no good. They no wan' me in de e'school. My peoples don't wan' me in de home no more too! They e'say me I am The Idiot! Mexico very bad place for me. E'school no wan' me. They e'say I am The Idiot!! I am **NO** The Idiot!!! My mother no wan' me. I wan' my mother but she no wan' me! Now is bery bad for me thees place, an' all de time I e'smoke de cigarette an' I drink! I drink and I e'smoke de cigarro. Before, I no e'smoke and I no drink. Now is bery much bad for me! Chetumal de bad place for me. I wan' go Estados Unidos. I want go with ju de Belize. No good for me here. De policia don' like me here. They say I am The Idiot! They put me inside de jail for four day. I no got nothing for eat inside there. I no wan' go de jail! **NO!** Is bery bad place for me. I no wan' de policia. Where is it ju hotel? I wan' le's go to there. De peoples no wan' me, no like me here. I wan' go for ju hotel. De policia no good for me. They say I loco. They say I am The Idiot. . . . "*

JOURNAL ENTRY—Chetumal:

As Silvestre ranted on, my thoughts turned to Malcolm. Guilt had me in a headlock. I felt I was responsible. I'd given Silvestre that goddamn book, just like I'd given Malcolm the acid before he killed himself. Why had I given it to him? What hell had I wrought on another person this time? Ugly shades of the truth, the karma, the shame of my soul, were closing in on me in flashes of morbid terror. I wanted to melt into the big gaping cracks in the weedy sidewalk and never come up again. I'm not strong enough to see this kind of human disaster again, I'm not equipped to make any sense of it or do any good with it. What could I say or do? Finally, Antonio started talking about something else, and we went to cop some weed. I could see he couldn't understand poor Silvestre at all. Silvestre was making him nervous. Silvestre was indeed acting strange, but he was still my friend. So the three of us went and scored, then we split to the park to go smoke the mota. But after Silvestre took a couple of hits, it set off a fierce new wave of paranoia.

"Cuidado! De policia coming! Vamos! These mota, she bery bad for my brains. I don' like it thees thing, no! Vamos!"

With the ghostly words ringing in his inner ear, Cigano continues scanning the yellowed pages of his old journal, remembering.

JOURNAL ENTRY—Chetumal:

It must have been the first time the poor devil smoked pot. I started talking to him, trying to steer him out of his downward spiral. I told him to hold his head up and breathe and stop being scared, but he just kept raving about the cops and the Army and the jail, and how he'd not seen his mother in four days. It was murder. Rather than helping him out of the hole, I was getting sucked in with him. I began to think of Malcolm again. Before long, I was a guilty, paranoid basket case myself. Antonio got up and split. I didn't blame him. It had been getting weirder ever since we'd lit that joint. I was all done in. Finally, I wandered off to take a piss and didn't come back. Silvestre was on his own. I never saw him again. And I think of Silvestre and Malcolm and Chris and Ellen and Bruce, Stephen, Roger and all the others, and I think of what this world has done to them all in one quick turn of the screw. So many questions, as the skeletons and evil clowns come bubbling up to haunt me. The thing with Silvestre was another horror show, just like Malcolm. I don't like to see the casualties of this life. It's a very bad business when a bright light like Silvestre is snuffed out. But he's not the first, and he won't be the last to eat shit along this long, crazy road we all travel. To survive is a great work of the heart, and not an easy one. When Lights Out comes for me, I'll hit the fucking switch myself, and it will be a righteous affair! We are all masters of our own fate, and when the lights go out it's because we turned them out ourselves, or maybe pissed-off somebody standing next to the switch. I'm not sure just why this is, or even if there are any whys about it, but I'm pretty damn certain we are all personally responsible for our own survival. Hence, No Fate. But I can only speak for myself, and it's hard to tell about that too sometimes. Anyway, what's the use? Stoned.

JOURNAL ENTRY—Cʜᴇᴛᴜᴍᴀʟ:

It's Good Friday, Semana Santa, Holy Week, and, holy shit, I've been in Chetumal a whole month now. The air molecules move around the room slowly—the calm before an inevitable shitstorm that's coming. This whole place is gonna go bat-shit-bug-house-loony-toons-nut-crackers crazy soon, I can feel it in the air as my hammock swings in the breeze and a cat hollers on the scratchy tin roof next door. Everything is still and quiet here. Another afternoon of suspended animation by the humid green water. Six o'clock now, and the sun is going down over the jungle. As my little hotel room grows dark, I listen to the distant rumble of life outside. Suddenly, the battered wooden doors downstairs crash open and the lobby fills with voices raised up to the heavens, in defiance of the great approaching starry net of eternity. Today's not just any day, I know as I listen to the loud chatter rumbling down below like approaching thunder. It is Semana Santa, time for another week-long Mexican religious piss-fest, a perfect occasion for Holy vows and holy cows, drunken bravado and broken bottles, music, noise, and vida loca; time for another carnival blow of celebration shattered against the walls of forever, with blessed forgetfulness in the morning. A National State of Hangover will be declared. Como no? So it must be! I rise up from my hammock, knowing the fiesta will go all night long. I must get ready to go out and join the mayhem. I can already hear it outside. The music down by the seawall calls to me, calls to us all, in this sleepy port on the edge of nowhere, and we'll all be drawn to it like flaming moths. Como no? People will arrive by bus, truck, boat, bicycle, moped, burro. They will crawl right up out of the steaming jungle rot to be where other people are drinking and shouting and jumping up and down like deranged monkeys, for the next drunken week of this Most Holy Semana Santa. I stumble over and slap some tepid tap water onto my face and pull on my boots. Yowza!

JOURNAL ENTRY—CHETUMAL:

Ten o'clock at night and the party has been going for hours; a strong, noble Caribbean beat with a soulful saxophone wailing out beat-down staccato riffs. The churning, unstoppable Mexican river of sound grows in intensity as the night rumbles forward like a wailing ghost train through the jungle. A singer is up on the bandstand, belting out a '50s rock n roll number in Spanish, and the crowd dances and surges around like a tide trapped between rocks. Soon the net will break, I'm thinking. Sure enough, the robotic, drunken dancing grinds to a halt at the center of the crowd. Bodies start to fall out of line, people running forward to cluster around two men who are fighting. Then there are ten. Then twenty. Thirty. Forty. Now it's a full-scale riot, and the cops are swinging their clubs above the surging chaos like sweaty, machete-wielding campesinos *in a cane field. The people grow thicker around the confusion, like an infestation of hungry insects, and the mad Mexican noise machine churns on. People in the middle of the crowd look baffled as they move around in fading little robot dance steps. They know something's happening, but not quite what. A shot is fired. Then another. A well-dressed young man politely excuses himself from his pretty date. As soon as he's reasonably out of sight, he runs like a mad dog to jump into the fray. By the time he reaches the apex, it's over. He stands watching the diminishing tension like a baffled phantom of night. In the morning, it will all be back to normal. I wander off, looking for a quiet place to sit and drink and smoke another joint. I like the idea of these festive crowds of drunken mass revelry much more than I care for the actual sweaty, clamoring Beast of the Crowd. Sitting all alone on a park bench at the edge of the fiesta, getting drunk and smoking another fat joint, I think about time and space. The stoic, tin-roofed wooden houses on the*

*waterfront, with their vacant, battered, wood-shuttered windows
that have seen hurricanes and stillness, they speak to me; these are
the things that make me want to jump behind the dreary façade
of illusion on this lonely blue planet. Some kind of joker is surely
playing with my destiny.*

*JOURNAL ENTRY—*Chetumal:

*Last week was a flashing, drunken blur. This week was a long,
hungover nightmare. Overstayed my visa, goddammit, and I don't have
enough money to pay the fine, so now I can't get out of Mexico legally.
A boat left for Nicaragua today and I almost got a job onboard, but
they wouldn't take me on without a valid Mexican visa. I learned
from some guys on the dock that I could get a brand-new visa for cheap
from a guy at the local Immigration office, no questions asked. Then
I can just walk across the border into British Honduras and travel
on from there. The guy running the boat told me they would definitely
throw me in jail if I tried to leave without a Mexican exit stamp, so
I guess this is it. Late afternoon, I strolled into the Immigration office
in a dilapidated little storefront by the port, and handed my last few
pesos to a jolly old Señor behind a desk. I waited in the plaza across
the street with a cigarette and a beer while he typed up the new visa,
good for 180 days. Now, with a little good luck and a happy smile,
I can cross the border on foot, take my chances in British Honduras,
then maybe make my way through to Brazil by land or sea, whichever
comes first. Maybe I can get a ship in Central America. If not, I can
always keep going overland, or just turn around, come back to Mexico,
and try shipping out from Veracruz—my original plan. Sitting in the
park waiting, I watched an old drunk arguing with a fresh-faced young
policeman. I don't know what it's about, but I can see from the cop's
firm grip on the old man's arm that he's being taken in. They're both
yelling as the cop tries to drag him away, but the old geezer grabs ahold
of a bench and hangs on for dear life. The policia tugs and yanks and
pulls, but not too roughly, as if he's afraid the old man's arm will come
off in his hand if he pulls too hard. The old drunk isn't giving an inch.
If the constable wants to take him in, he's going to have to work up a
sweat. Finally, the cop throws up his hands and turns his back on the
ancient offender. I see him shrug disgustedly, as if to say "it's too hot
for this shit," which indeed it is. The old man stumbles off to another*

end of the plaza and slumps down on another bench, muttering old man's mutterings to the stagnant air. The cop heads for a spot in the shade and pulls his cap down low, shaking his head and muttering policeman's mutterings to the dirty green sea. Simple, and everyone's happy in the end, just as it should be. Mexico is a civilized country. Tomorrow, I cross the border into British Honduras.

JOURNAL ENTRY—Corozal Town, British Honduras:

End-of-the-world obsolete British Colonial time warp, just across the border from Chetumal. Crisp-faced Negro Immigration man in crisp tan British uniform stamps my passport with an efficient BAM, *then a quick bus ride to this hurricane-beaten little border town, and holy culture shock as reality shifts from Mexico to the lazy, lowdown wooden tin-roofed shacks of the Caribbean.* BAM. *Just like that. Wild-eyed Negroes, shiny faces black as sea lions, barking in crazy pidgin English slang, easy and cool as the night. Eternal backwater hustlers lean against a weedy old wooden fence outside the pool hall, smoking big spliffs and watching a giant Caribbean moon rise up in the sky like a bare light bulb hanging from the ceiling of the gods. There's a sweaty crap game going on upstairs, and you can get that fine strong ganja in the back room. You can drink dark Belikin beers and listen to crucial lazy reggae on the jukebox, and dance the night away with wild-eyed laughing African princesses. The wind is blowing strong behind you over the little wooden docks as you walk down a dark dirt path into the night. The only sounds are the boats splashing on the windswept water, and the palm fronds clacking above. Music is drifting in and out with the steady warm Caribbean breeze. You look up into the molten darkness and the sky is a silent riot of stars. Onward, they say.*

18. EL MUTANTE

JOURNAL ENTRY—Corozal Town, British Honduras:

Living in third-world countries, you can easily see how much power the bad old American Dream has. The many expressions of its greasy octopus reach are all the more absurd in the context of different cultures. Take a small Central American backwater like this. You sit in a crowded, humid little tin-roof cinema, watching a movie about a guy who burns the Mafia for a million bucks. After the lights come on, they all get out of the hot, sweaty sardine can and run like mad dogs around the corner to consume gallons of Coca-Cola—an institution undoubtedly as powerful as the Mafia, and far worse in contributing to the overall destruction of mankind. The money Coca-Cola takes out of a country the size of Mexico in a year could feed every starving person on the planet for the rest of his life. And where does all that cash go? I shudder to think. In Mexico, Chiclets are sold in great abundance by armies of nagging, ragged street urchins. People who are really hungry, having such easy access to Chiclets, could probably just eat the fucking things. All the better to pretend they're not starving to death, by swallowing a gay assortment of multicolored little plastic wads. What else can an economically oppressed people do after the overpowering voice of Big Brother short-circuits whatever brain cells they have left? This is what I call real cultural decadence.

The tattoo man looks up from the yellowed page, smiling at the memories. "Just came across a whole bunch of freaked out stuff I wrote in Central America, right before I first came up here to Veracruz."

JOURNAL ENTRY—PUERTO CORTÉS, HONDURAS:

Split Corozal Town for the stinky, overcrowded capital of Belize City, where open sewers run in vast brown rivers of shit beside every street. It smelled like everyone in the place had crapped in their pants at once. My first day there, I actually saw a mad swarm of catfish battling each other for a fresh turd, ejected through a pipe made of tin cans from a shack teetering over one of those rancid "canals." After a week spent drinking cheap rum in funky wooden dockside dives with mad-eyed Negroes, I couldn't even smell the looming stench anymore. I'd become a local. Then, finally, I got work on a ship! The rusty old bucket was only going as far as Honduras, Nicaragua, and some nearby islands before returning back to the mainland, but I felt like a full-fledged swashbuckling pirate captain as we sailed out of the septic brown waters of the Belize City harbor. Ah, but the grand swashbuckling high didn't last for long. After the captain gave me the wheel and showed me how to keep a steady course, I got drunk on his big bottle of rum and ended up steering the damn ship around in circles all night while El Capitan slept. They booted me off at the next port, of course. Now I'm stuck in this godforsaken place. Well, at least I'm somewhere, and I did arrive here by ship. So now I've finally been to sea—technically, anyway. Waiting around in limbo, listening to classical music on the little transistor radio I bought in Belize to celebrate my first big adventure at sea, I'm nearly broke again, sitting in candlelight darkness of a cheap little hotel room by the port, my lonely pants hanging from a nail by the window (the same pants I wore when they took me to jail for a week in Belize City—but that's another story). Outside, it's pouring a hot, clammy tropical rain. The whole world is underwater tonight, empty and hopeless and wet—a forlorn feeling, resigned and happy-sad, like when the ship pulled into this moldy, faceless port at first light, and I wanted to slit my throat, seeing the dead industrial wasteland of docks and the horrible, foggy green hills and meadows of Honduras. Alone here for days now, I've grown accustomed to this place, even kind of comfortable. But those hills behind the port still make me feel all empty and bad when I look out past the ships and see them there, knowing those hideous hills will be there after I'm dead and gone. Worm food. I hate those creepy, vacuous hills of Hell, all grave-rot green, peaceful and horrible, like massive mossy tombstones looming across the bay. It's late at night now and I'm sitting in my room by the railroad tracks, across from the docks full of ships, big booming monsters from faraway China and Londontown. It's raining hard now, and I'm content with this happy-sad feeling, classical music playing on my little radio. I don't need any lively Latino ritmo tonight. Don't wanna get drunk and dance in the street with wild-eyed negritas, just a candlelit radio playing sad-static sounds in an endless night of rain.

JOURNAL ENTRY—Puerto Cortés, Honduras:

Two maids came in to change my lonely sheets while I was sitting here writing. One was making the bed, the other one just standing around, staring at nothing, doing nothing, and PICKING HER NOSE, right in front of me! Neither of them said a goddamn word, but I'm certain that when they got out into the hall they must have snickered and whispered about something in my room; the cigarette butts on the floor, the empty bottle, my Panama hat, some damn thing. Paranoia. I know I'm a freak of nature here, and they all know it too. Everywhere I go, there's staring, staring, they're always staring at me, like they'd never seen a stranger's face before. You can feel the heads turning behind you to stare and gawk and gossip as you walk past. What is it with these chicken-faced donkey-fuckers? Another hangover in a tragic little end-of-the-line port town, another hole in space where the Holy Church is the people's straitjacket. Everywhere I go, I see pictures of the goddamn Pope. That's a big problem if you want to get laid. Or maybe it's just a long, terrible feeling of frustration after not having a woman for so long. But these local chicas don't move me at all, with their fat, listless, chicharon chomping asses. I just want to get drunk at night and indulge in sad, morbid fantasies, dreaming of Ellen. Maybe I was better off being a crazed junkie in the madhouse of America. You only live once, and it all comes down to shit in the end. O God, where did it all start? How did I ever end up here? I'm seeing the world through a madman's eyes here in the world of limits, when my eyes have already seen far horizons, light-years from this miserable gray hangover limbo. Sometimes I think I can see right through the black hole of the crippled ideology of my fellow idiots and all our futile little human contrivances, and I shed a silent tear for all of us, for myself mostly, as I sit reeling from another terrible dark night of drunken nothingness. Sitting alone at a little bar last night, the rain poured down and mournful ships' horns boomed out over the harbor. No jukebox, nothing, just the old bartender's wife in her sad, lonely nightgown, looking out the window at the Greek sailors chasing after aging hookers, and rusty old taxicabs in the rain. There she stood, waiting in stoic silence for me to finish my drink and leave—a sad, faceless old lady in a ratty, tattered nightgown and big muddy Dostoyevsky boots, just like that. And I did finish my drink and went back to my room to sleep, and that was the end of the night.

JOURNAL ENTRY—Puerto Cortés:

Eyes, so many goddamn probing eyes! I can feel those dull, staring incredulous greasy bovine orbs following me every moment in this shit-forsaken place, piercing, invasive, moronic, idiot insect eyeballs and gaping mouths, and there is no escape, no peace. I duck into a little movie theater, cringing in the midday sun, seeking refuge from the maddening crowd of eyes, to sit watching some boring, idiotic American movie I didn't want to see. I come out to another swarm of pulsing, bulging eyeballs. Walking off down the street, a pair of fat-assed, piss-eyed chicas give me the big stupid stares. It's too much! Silently enraged, I turn back and give the ignorant slobs a look that could kill puppies. Moving on, I hear a heartless uproar of laughter behind me. Probably trying to guess how long my cock is and if it's striped like a barber pole and rotates and glows in the dark. I know their rudeness is just childlike curiosity. But I'm dying of loneliness and alienation and the ever-present paranoia of being a strange bird in a strange tree in this strange, ugly flatline land of Nada, and there's nothing I can do about that but keep trying to find a ship and get the hell out.

JOURNAL ENTRY—PUERTO CORTÉS:

Wandering along the docks this morning, looking for work again, I climbed up the gangplank of a big Italian freighter and got stopped at the top by some power-mad soldier-port-cop who was standing up there, supposedly guarding the ship. But who's guarding the ship from this stupid mummy-lipped mammy-jammer, I'm wondering as he suddenly reaches out and sticks his fucking hand in my pocket, just like that! He starts asking me all kind of idiot questions about who I am and what am I doing and where's my papers. I just dummied up and stared at him, pretending not to understand a word, till he got bored and went back to talking to his cop buddy about soccer, killing time, I guess, till he can go home to eat and get drunk, beat the wife and kids, screw the dog, whatever. You could tell he didn't really give a shit, anyway, so I just wandered off and went up to the first crew member I saw, a big friendly, smiling Italian guy with a thick black mustache, who obviously loved spaghetti and wine and big families. He seemed to sympathize with my predicament and immediately dragged me into the galley (not even asking if I was hungry) and sat me down before a huge black iron skillet full of octopus in garlic and olive oil. He proceeded to talk nonstop, waving big clumsy hands in the air, struggling for the words in English, as if his wild sweeping gestures were way ahead of him and giving him all sorts of trouble. He just kept going, "Aw, well, what de hell, ehh? Eat'a! Eat'a!" He starts telling me about his wife and kids in New York and a brother-in-law who has a grocery store in Brooklyn, and how Greeks are all "shit peoples" and Greek freighters are no good to work on, and how he couldn't believe an "American boy" like me was looking for work on a ship in the first place. "Wassa hoppen? You de American'a boy'a. Gotta plenny good'a job'a fa you at de home'a." He seemed genuinely puzzled, like he really couldn't begin to understand why I would want to work at sea. It made me feel bad and want to apologize for the thousandth time for being born in America. But before I could say anything, he was off on something else, and I could see that this big fumbling character was free of malice and really pure and innocent, like a big crazy goodhearted child. All he wanted was to be back in Mamma Italia, bouncing babies on his knee with a smell of garlic filling the room and big white sheets flapping on a clothesline outside. The man had a lot of soul. But no job. Now his ship is gone, off

to some distant Mediterranean port, and here I am still. Fuck it.
Tomorrow I head back to Mexico and Veracruz.

Cigano stops reading and looks over at Jaco. "So, this is what I'm dealing with here, man." He snorts, shaking his head. "Between these old diaries and all the new stuff I been writing, it's like a big baffling jigsaw puzzle, piecing all the stories together in some kinda order. Sometimes it feels like I'm goin' nuts. . . . "

Turning a page, he pictures himself sitting atop a lumbering cargo truck. A road sign, **VERACRUZ 100 KM,** flashes into his memory as he remembers a pocket-sized comic book borrowed from a fellow traveler in a dusty bus terminal somewhere in northern Mexico. ***El Mutante.*** The Mutant.

Cigano stops to jot down the name in the margin of his notebook. It feels like a fitting description for the young traveler in his mind's eye; a freakish post-modern Frankenstein creation, haphazardly assembled by unseen hands, conjured from dust molecules of the long Mexican road, the jungles, cities, and towns—an endless parade of places, faces, hotel rooms, *cantinas*, roadside eateries, people, and a hundred blurry dreams. A plume of black smoke crowds his vision as he begins to read again. A sputtering truck blasts by in the street below, forming a ghostly soundtrack to his words.

"My memories of the road are a boozy circus riot of imagery," he reads, "where the fuzzy borders between time, space, reality, and dreams all seem to blur together like the pages in a worn little hand-me-down Mexican comic book."

Feeling awkward, the tattoo man pauses. He reaches over the table and takes a long swig from a bottle of sticky, lukewarm orange soda. Staring down at the page again, he clears his throat and reads on.

"By the time I finally reached the port of Veracruz, the road had transformed me into a lusty, hard-drinking, hard-living wandering soul—a seasoned hobo, fluent in Spanish, molded by dust, and riding the wind. The ragged, road-weary vagabond sitting atop a truck that day bore little resemblance to the shy, introverted young *gabacho* who'd set out a dozen months and thousands of miles before. With a wild Zapata mustache framing a crooked yellow smile, my essence had definitively merged with the wayward spirit of an unknown Gypsy grandfather. It was as if there really were two of us now; a pair of devil-may-care drunken road dogs, two sets of hungry eyes flashing in the wind as we lumbered along another winding jungle road together, descending toward the Gulf of Mexico and the mysterious port of Veracruz.

"As my destiny unfolded in sunsets and sunrises over the highways of Mexico, I'd come to count on that unseen spirit companion, whispering in my ear on drunken *cantina* nights, sitting beside me as the wind blew in my face, watching over all my days and nights, a steady reassuring presence, always there, guiding my cockeyed path along that long, lonesome Gypsy pilgrimage."

As Cigano reads on, he pictures the young traveler taking a pull of tequila and passing the bottle to his phantom partner. He remembers how he loved the road with all the fervor of his obscure Romani roots, the fire of his ancestors, a passion for the unknown, riding the wild, uncertain winds that were his only home, his only family, the only place he ever wanted to belong to.

The tattoo man sets his notebook down on the table.

He closes his eyes, envisioning a bright red dot bouncing across a muggy tropical sky. A cross-country truck's monotonous diesel motor sputters in his inner ear as a young traveler looks up, embracing each perfect puffy cotton cloud.

Scanning the sky, the restless camera of his mind's eye zooms in, racking focus on a solitary red balloon floating and dancing in the distance, bouncing across the wild, choppy currents of his aimless, vagabond heart.

19. FREEDOM

Cigano leans back in his chair and lights a cigarette, chuckling. "It's a weird feeling, reading all this old stuff. Kinda like watching some old movie I saw a long time ago, then forgot about."

He shrugs. "I never woulda been able to write any of it if there wasn't always this weird little inner voice, telling me what to say, what to remember, where to go with it. But it's funny. All those years tattooing, ya become used to getting instant gratification from your work, and then, suddenly, this. . . . " He sighs, gesturing at the pile of notebooks cluttering the table.

Cigano takes a deep drag on the smoke and exhales. "I dunno, man. It's like, with the tattooing I always had the dubious comfort of knowing when a job was finished. At least there was always a beginning and an end to it, y'know? Writing, man, this is a whole other kinda deal. It's like ya *never* really know where th' fuck it's all going. And then ya get to feeling like maybe you're lost in the wilderness without a map. I dunno, sometimes it seems like it'll never come together and make any sense, like it'll never fucking end."

Jaco smiles. "But you wrote for the tattoo magazines for years, so you must have some clarity in your writing process, no?"

"Yeah, man, sorta. But that was basically commercial writing, nothing like this kinda big project." He shrugs. "With the tattoo rags, I always had to get a new issue out every month, with deadlines and printer's schedules. No time to think about stuff. With all the editing, and putting articles together, there was always like a foreseeable payoff in sight. And I always had inter-action with people, traveling to the tattoo conventions, interviewing artists, working with publishers, art directors, editors, I was always getting some kinda feedback with that stuff. And when whatever feature I was working on was done, I could just put it down and move on to the next issue or whatever."

Cigano sighs and stubs his cigarette out. "With this shit, it's a whole different kinda challenge, like flying blind, working all by myself here. It's like vivisecting your own fucking soul, without anesthesia." He spreads his hands out. "And then ya just start to trip, wondering what th' fuck you're even doing. . . . "

"It must take a lot of discipline to write a book."

"Yeah, well, more like desperation, in my case." He guffaws. "But I guess there's a certain freedom in it, too, in not ever knowing where you're going, or what th' fuck you'll end up with."

"Freedom?"

"Yeah, man. Freedom from the illusion of being in control. I guess that's the only real freedom, just letting go." He reaches over and lights another cigarette, then falls silent.

An old *pachanga* plays on the radio, blending with the sounds of traffic outside. Jaco's eyes wander to the table behind the tattoo man, taking in the details of his world: his worn leather travel bag, his portable tattoo kit sitting on the table, a weathered leather jacket hanging from a nail on the wall, a battle-scarred motorcycle helmet; all the personal effects of a lifelong traveler's restless soul.

Finally, the kid breaks the silence, looking at his host dead on. "Freedom's always been very important to you, Jonathan Shaw, no?"

Cigano takes a deep drag and emits a long, cloudy sigh. "Freedom?" He seems to contemplate the word. "I dunno, maybe I've been real slow to learn, man. Jeez, it's taken me most of my fuggin' life to grasp the idea that freedom's really an inside job. But traveling used to give me a powerful illusion of being free."

"Illusion?"

He shrugs. "Yeah, man. Illusion. Cuz all I was really doing was running around like a rat in a fuggin' maze." He pauses and scratches his head. "Freedom's a funny word, bro. Means so many different things to different people. For me, nowadays, the only real freedom is learning to trust in a higher order of things. Cuz that's what's in charge, so why fight it?"

He falls silent for a moment and grins. "This whole conversation reminds me of some shit Artie said to me once. . . . "

The tattoo man reaches across the table and picks up another notebook. He leafs through the pages, and begins to read.

"The old man's eyes stared off into a space I couldn't see. They seemed to shine with a weird, otherworldly glint. It's strange. I could never remember what color my father's eyes were. Maybe they're gray. Soon, the old bastard will be dead and gone forever, and then I'll never know. Cold deal. Cold, steel-gray eyes. What does it matter? The man is a stranger to me. Always has been. Always will be."

As he reads on, Cigano's mind travels back to his father's living room, the night Artie finally gave in to weeks of pestering and finally presented him with a copy of his memoir, *The Trouble with Cinderella*.

He remembers handing the old man a pen and asking him to dedicate the book to him—then feeling his heart sink as he read the hastily scribbled words: ***Best wishes. Artie Shaw***. Feeling the limp weight of the book in his lap like a dead rat, Cigano sunk back into the soft beige sofa. He stared at his father, sitting in his big overstuffed easy chair. . . . *Fuck, it's like he's signing an autograph to a fucking fan or something, a stranger. What the fuck is wrong with this guy? Doesn't he give a shit that I'm his fucking son?*

An amber light plays on the old man's pale, waxy face as he sits like a king on a throne in Cigano's memory, pontificating in that familiar, endless loop of cynical, solitary monologue.

"I guess it's all in the way you're brought up. . . . "

"Whaddya mean, Artie?"

"What I mean is that people are victims of their upbringing. . . . " Artie talks on in that same neurotic, high-pitched, quasi-desperate tone. "If it's a choice between following your own inner vision, or sticking around, inflicting misery on a wife and kids, well, the best thing a guy can do, if he wants to do something different, is to just go away!"

Cigano stares at him, his gut stinging like a giant cold sore.

"That's an extreme statement, I know," Artie growls. "But doing something with your life *is* extreme. Most people do nothing. . . . "

An explosion of silence fills the room. Sitting for hours across a book-littered table from his father, listening to the old man's self-serving, arrogant horseshit, Cigano feels that his brain will melt if he sits quietly for another fucking minute. He struggles with an almost overwhelming urge to kick the table over in that pompous, self-righteous, waxy face.

He braces himself as he looks the old man in the eye and finally speaks his mind.

"Jeez, Artie! Maybe not everyone has the talent to be some great artist or philosopher, sitting around speculating about what th' fuck came first, th' chicken or the fuggin' egg. Most people just do the best they can, y'know, go to work? Raise a family? How can ya call that doing nothing, if ya never even tried it?"

Artie looks back across a gulf of time and space, as if noticing his son sitting there for the first time. Quickly, he looks away and slips back into the invisible current of another bitter declaration.

"Argh! I think families are all fucking cannibals!" Artie's voice is the weary old growl of a captive circus lion. "The less family, the better, I say. When relatives come around here, *hah*, I just tell 'em 'go fuck yourselves!'"

20. TIME IS ALL YOU'VE GOT

A radio announcer's hysterical, rapid-fire barrage of words crashes into Cigano's memories. Angry horns blare outside the window like a pack of disturbed dogs barking.

He closes the notebook and looks up at Jaco with a bitter guffaw. "Jeez! 'Go fuck yerself!' th' guy tells me. How do ya like that shit? Those were his last words to his fuggin' son! Nice, huh?"

"Maybe he's a little crazy? You know, an old man like that?"

"Argh, what's the use, man?" Cigano sighs. "He's a piece of *shit!* A fuggin' coward! The great Artie Shaw! Hah! My half-brother Steve and I are his only living relatives. So that 'go fuck yourself' was meant for *us!* The two sons he fathered, then threw away like so much fucking garbage when he couldn't get along with our mothers."

"So you have a brother? What's he like?"

Cigano shrugs. "No idea, man. Haven't seen or heard from the guy in like forty years. I only met him once, when I was around sixteen. He was about ten years older than me. Came around one time, and we were both high on heroin." He laughs. "That's the only time I ever met him. Last I heard from someone who knew about him, they said he'd turned into a bitter old hermit, just like Artie. Far as I know, he never had a relationship with the old man, either. . . . But at least I tried, man. I really did try to get to know Artie, and let him know something about me. He just never wanted to, poor bastard. . . . "

"That must be very sad for you, Jonathan Shaw. I'm sorry."

"Argh, save the drama for your mama, kid." Cigano laughs. "Don't feel sorry for me. I'm good with it. That selfish old son of a bitch was the best father I coulda had. I really know that today. Yeah, it hurts sometimes, sure, but ya get over it. It takes time to heal old wounds like that, but ya find a way if ya really wanna. Real forgiveness only comes with understanding, so I've tried real hard to figure the guy out, y'know. Truth is, he prolly had it a lot worse than I did as a kid. So he's a victim too. We all are, one way or another. The trick is not feeling sorry for yourself. That's pure fuggin' poison. And when ya come to realize we're all in the same boat, it makes the resentments a lot easier to let go of. And what if Artie *had* been a 'good' father? I mighta wound up being some spoiled trust-fund brat, like so many kids I grew up with who died like rats from heroin. Nah, I got no regrets."

Cigano grows quiet, chuckling darkly, then looks up. "They made this movie about the old man once, a portrait of his life and times. The thing even won an Oscar for Best Documentary."

"Really?" Jaco says. "I'd like to see that. . . . "

"Forget it. Ya can't. The movie never got released. Can't find the damn thing anywhere. Artie wound up getting in some kinda big romantic hassle with the lady who directed it, then he tried to sue her. Whole thing ended up in court, and even though he lost the case, the film she worked on for years never saw the light of day. God! She actually buried her own fuggin' project, just to spite the guy! Hell hath no fury! That's what the old man always says. Guess he oughta know."

He laughs. "But that's Artie, always fighting with the ladies. His mom, over and over. The title of the thing was *Artie Shaw—Time is All You've Got.* That's like his brave little motto."

"That's an interesting name for a movie."

Cigano throws back his head and laughs out loud. "Time. Hah! What the fuck is time, anyway? For all his lofty intellectual double-talk, Artie's always been a card-carrying atheist, just like my mother. Mentally superior, spiritually bankrupt. 'Time is all you've got'? Seriously?"

He snorts, as if still arguing with his father. "What the fuck kinda fucked-up philosophy is that, man? Spend yer whole fuggin' life watching the clock? Yeah? That's *slavery*, man! And Artie's always been a slave to his own inflated ego, poor devil. I guess we all are, in a sense. We get so caught up thinking we're nothing but these fake identities, our names and places, the jobs and titles and money. We forget that this life is just a big long fairy tale, a dream, an illusion."

Jaco nods deeply. "Einstein said that reality is an illusion."

"Yeah, but it's a helluva persistent one!" Cigano laughs. "You're a lot wiser than I was when I was your age, bro. Maybe that's what's going on with human evolution, like so many people seem to be getting smarter, more perceptive and intuitive. I dunno, sometimes the human race looks to be getting dumber and more destructive by the day, but on some other level we really might be waking up. Maybe that's why people seem so pissed-off and neurotic, more warlike and ignorant than ever. Cuz they really don't *wanna* wake up. And now it's like they're being forced to, by their own DNA or something. The Apocalypse, 2012, all that New Age stuff? To me, it's not really about the end of the world. Well, maybe there's gonna be that too, way things are going." He shrugs. "But somehow it feels more like a redefinition of linear time, something like that, like some kind of a slow-spreading spiritual wake-up going on. And it's gotta be a really rude awakening for alotta folks. I mean, most people have a lot invested in staying asleep. Just look at my mother and her husband, Len. Poor bastards spent their whole fuggin' lives dreaming about some big Happy Tomorrow. Maybe that's why they call that shit the American Dream. Cuz ya gotta be fast asleep to fall for it." He snorts. "Then, one day, they suddenly realize the whole thing's a big fuggin' nightmare, a lie they wasted their whole lives believing in, working for. And then it's too fuggin' late. That's gotta be a real bitter pill, man. . . . "

Cigano thinks back to his last visit to Los Angeles, standing outside the house with Len, looking at his old gray stepfather in the lengthening afternoon shadows, as his mother lay in her bed inside, drunk, babbling to herself in a dark, stuffy room.

He can almost hear the mournful call of a dove in the distance. He remembers the tragic look of defeat and disappointment on the old man's face as he stood in a weary, defeated slouch.

"I never thought it would all end up like this, Jono," Len moans, staring into space. "All our plans and dreams. . . . I worked all my life for a comfortable retirement. I was planning a round-the-world cruise for us, a second honeymoon. And now. . . " He stands there, a sagging human shrug, gesturing at the house, the silent tragedy behind the neatly manicured hedge—"now this. . . . "

Len's voice cracks like brittle porcelain in Cigano's inner ear as he recalls his old nemesis breaking down and weeping; the harsh, childish sobs of a hopeless, devastated creature.

Cigano just shook his head and hugged the old Nowhere Man he'd hated all his life, the man who'd been a lifelong accomplice to his mother's long, slow alcoholic suicide. What else could be done?

Reaching in his pocket, he handed his stepfather the letter he'd written the night before. Then he got on his motorcycle and rode off.

Dear Len—I don't know when I'll be coming back this way, so I wanted to tell you how sorry I am that we've always been unable to communicate. Especially now that my mother is so weak, I often ask myself what I could have done differently to make things better between us. The answers are hard to find. But I've come to believe we're all better off not blaming each other, or blaming ourselves. I have many regrets, of course, and I'm truly sorry for having been a difficult kid and making your life so difficult. And I'm sorry for all the resentments I harbored against you and my mother. I deeply regret so many of my actions and attitudes. Anything I can do today to make up for my part in the mess this family became, I would gladly do. But all I can really do now is ask your forgiveness, and try to be a better person in the future than I've been in the past. Everything else is a waste of time, and I've already wasted enough time and energy on useless, destructive emotions. As you know, I'm a recovering alcoholic, and a survivor of an alcoholic family, too. I know that subject has always been taboo around here, and I know the odds are stacked against me even now. But in order to have a chance, there are things I must uncover and bring to light. I know today that a lifetime of tiptoeing around the elephant in the living room always put you and me at odds with each other—and for that I am truly sorry for us both. I'm sorry for you for not being able to see that my recovery from the alcoholic scourge that killed most of my family is the best way I can honor my mother's life, and perhaps avenge (if that's the right word) all of our lifelong sufferings at the hands of the alcoholic curse that's plagued us for so long. And I guess I'm a little sorry for myself, too, mostly for not having the satisfaction of knowing that you're proud of me for being the only one of my poor mother's tortured bloodline to ever be winning this battle. Don't get me wrong. I don't expect any medals for staying sober to save my own skin. But I'm working hard to be a different man today, and I'm truly grateful for any chance to speak my truth. I'm just sorry my recovery hasn't been able to heal the scars that remain on all our souls. For that reason, I find it crucial to let go of an ugly past with all the love and compassion I can find in my heart, without blame or regret. Today, I can only look to the future for healing. That's why I'm going back to Brazil now, to find the son I never knew, and try to give him the kind of acknowledgement I never got from my own people. Maybe it's been hard for you to acknowledge my recovery because the very admission of being part of an alcoholic family might stir up a hornet's nest of guilt and shame. So I want to make it very clear that I hold you and my mother absolutely blameless today for whatever happened in the past. I know you both did the best you could, and that you are a good man who would have never deliberately done my mother or me any harm. For what it's worth, I want to tell you I love and respect you. Thank you for your love for my mother, and thank you for trying to be there for me, despite almost impossible obstacles. I want you to know that I admire and appreciate your efforts—more than I've ever been able to express. I'm so sorry we weren't able to be closer all these years. But I know that it wasn't any of our faults. A demonic malady like alcoholism is no respecter of good intentions. In that, we were all victims of the same affliction—perhaps our only real common bond. May we all be forgiven together. Love always, Jono

Cigano snaps out of his musings and looks at the kid. "Sometimes I wonder if it's not really like the dark shadows right before the dawn, this whole End Times thing, like an alcoholic having to hit some kinda hellish bottom before he can start to wake up and get better. That's never easy, man. Who wants to concede defeat? People just aren't wired for surrender. Unless there's no other way out. It's like the whole world's started hitting some kind of big horrible bottom now, a war between our shit-brained primitive survival instincts and our divinity. Spiritual war. It's probably too late for people like my parents. But, I dunno, I guess it doesn't really matter. . . . "

"How so?" Jaco says. "Why do you say it doesn't matter?"

Cigano grins. "Cuz if the whole concept of linear time is an illusion, then so is death, right? So if life goes on, spiritually, beyond time and space, they can just keep battling it out in the next dimension, or wherever they end up after they step out of their miserable old suffering skin suits and leave the mess they made here behind."

He smiles. "Sometimes I think even Artie's been starting to see things a different way. I mean, what th' fuck, the guy's been a philosopher, a truth-seeker, all his life. He even wrote this memoir where he basically pulled the pants off the whole American Dream. He knew it was all bullshit. But, I dunno, it's like, somewhere along the line, he just dropped the ball."

He sighs. "So maybe it's up to me to take over where the old fart left off. It's a weird feeling, 'cause I really have no sense of any emotional connection with my father; but still, there's gotta be something there, some kinda weird spiritual bond, or like a karmic lesson, whatever. . . . "

Jaco nods. "I saw this documentary film about quantum physics, where scientists were doing experiments to prove basic metaphysical principles, things like the Law of Attraction. . . . "

"Yeah, man!" Cigano beams. "I was just thinking about that movie, and then you start talking about it. See? Goes to show ya, everything's connected. And it all happens for a reason. I been reading a lot of stuff like that too lately. . . . "

"I saw the books." Jaco gestures to the piles of spiritual literature stacked on the dresser. "I've read some of them as well."

"Whoa." Cigano throws his hands up, grinning. "See what I mean? There's all these little coincidences, like how I went out to sea when I was just about your age. Just like you, man. I didn't know it at the time, of course, but now I realize I really went out *to see*."

He grins putting a finger to his eye. "To find a way to look inside, to learn about myself, the human experience, destiny and all that. . . . "

"That's deep, Jonathan Shaw," Jaco says with a playful grin.

Feeling a deep wave of kinship with his new friend, Cigano picks up the tattoo machine lying on the table. He buzzes it a couple of times.

"Enough of this idle chatter, kid." He winks. "Back to work. Ya ready for some more pain?"

"No pain, no progress." Jaco shrugs as he positions himself in the chair.

Cigano nods, putting needle to skin.

21. A NEW HOME

Taking a break from the tattoo work, Jaco sits up and stretches.

"You really like it here in Veracruz, Jonathan Shaw, no?"

"Yeah, man. I love this fucking place!"

Standing by the window overlooking the port, Cigano lets out a long sigh, stretching his tired arms over his head. "I been writing a lot about my life here back in the day."

He smiles and gestures outside. "So many memories on those old streets. The place really became like a part of me. I guess cuz it's the first city I ever really felt at home in, so I ended up staying for a long time. I was kinda stuck here anyway, till I could get work on a ship, and, I dunno, it just sorta became a refuge, a home. . . .   I started tattooing here, too. Not professionally or anything, but this is where the first real seeds for the thing got planted in my brain."

As Cigano talks on, his mind travels through the muggy air of the old port, back to another chamber of time.

Like a photograph emerging in a developing tray, details slowly take definition; movements, color, smell, sound. Picking up another notebook, he comes across an old poem he found somewhere, a long time ago. For some reason, it's always reminded him of Veracruz.

There is a place far beyond where the sky meets the sea. I will go and wander there, on the rugged cliffs, high, where wild birds fly and cry. The hunt and the haunt, bereft of time. I know where I am going, and I am going there, where the wild winds blow free. I'll venture out into the storm and bear the thunder and the lightning. A call will come through to me. Ships steer their cargo loaded with spices and ivory white and jade. With a flask of wine. To an unknown paradise. A Gypsy's life for me. I know where I am going, and I am going there.

He stares at the page, lost in the memories, then reads on.

○   ○   ○

My first day in the port was a colorful avalanche of imagery, a vaguely familiar black-and-white movie suddenly sprung to life. As I explored the streets of Veracruz, her magical déjà vu spell wove through my senses like an exotic new drug, leaving indelible imprints on the tattered road map of my soul.

Faded, blurry blue-gray tattoos on weathered brown sailor arms floated by my eyes like hieroglyphics as I wandered past couples strolling the seawall at dusk. Spit-shined Chinese seamen stood huddled together on humid corners, like lost children, eyeing the local girls in their colorful weekend dresses. I marveled at the savage grace of the timeless whores of the port, giggling outside the shadowy dockside *cantinas*, innocent as schoolgirls, and predatory as the ancient white seabirds gliding above the ships. In Veracruz, I fell into a winking, blinking funhouse of life; drunk on that special, whimsical culture shock that comes only at rare and privileged times in this life.

On my second day there, I awakened to sounds of blaring traffic outside an open window. Where was I? What day was it? My blurry eyes scanned a shabby hotel room. My travel bag sat on a nearby table like an accusation as rays of hot afternoon sunlight stabbed at my booze-parched brain.

I lay motionless on the bed, staring at dust particles swirling in the muggy air, piecing together fragments of the night before. I recalled a fight, and drinking with a new friend, before blanking out. Pepe, that was his name. As more details came into focus, a sense of dread tugged at my gut like a rusty nail. I looked around, groaning at the dark recollections, as a loud truck shook the building.

Snapped into action by a loud chattering of boistrous tropical black-birds outside, I pried myself from the sweaty mattress. I staggered across the room to the window and looked out. My friend from the night before was standing down on the sidewalk, talking with some other guys. Wearing a pastel green guayabera and crisp black slacks, he seemed unfazed by any hangover. How did these people do it?

More dark snippets of the night tugged at my conscience. Pepe and I had been drinking with some sailors, I recalled. My nerves quivered as a brutal vision of me beating a would-be mugger half to death came crashing into my brain like a hammer.

I reached for a smoke with a trembling hand, my head pounding with shame and remorse.

Slinking down the hallway to the common shower stall, I saw the friendly hotel manager's young helper standing by an open room talking to the cleaning girl. She cast me a sheepish glance as young Memo (yes, that was his name!) smiled a chipper greeting. I mumbled a passing *buenas tardes* and shuffled off. I could hear the door close behind him, then his muffled voice inside, followed by the maid's girlish whine. *"Aii, no-oo, cabrón!"* More giggling protests, then the kid again, chattering away like a sex-crazed parrot.

I grinned, picturing him grabbing her ass as she bent over a bed to change the sheets. The lukewarm shower water soothed my head as I washed my lonely balls in the dark cubicle. . . . *Aii, no-oo, cabrón!* How long since I'd been with a woman?

Back in my room, I dressed and combed my hair in a timeworn mirror above the sink. Feeling a little better, I reached for my Timex. Almost four. Shit, where had the day gone?

I lit another smoke and headed downstairs, longing for a beer to jumpstart my throbbing brain.

○   ○   ○

Over the next weeks, Pepe and I patrolled the steamy wharves together daily, seeking work on a ship. I soon realized it wasn't going to be as easy as I'd hoped. I didn't care. Those ancient docks stained with a mildewed patina of the sea and the lure of far-off adventures kept calling, spurring me on in silent, exotic, alien codes. Sailors in shabby, sun-bleached uniforms were a constant reminder of the sea, leaning on the hurricane-beaten corners by the port, phantom sentries passing languid joints in the septic Gulf breeze.

Day by day, the essence of Veracruz carved itself into my brain, in a slideshow of indellible mental snapshots: weathered fishermen in tattered straw hats and yellow guayaberas lounging under scruffy white-washed palms like sleepy alligators; wind-beaten faces hovering above lazy domino tables, under slow ceiling fans in bug-stained, blue-tinted barrooms; *mestizo* kids hawking *dulces* and chile-lime *pepitas,* patrolling the plazas and *cantinas* like midget rag dolls of their proud indigenous ancestors; and always the eerie background hum and whir of machinery from the docks, clanging and banging through the hazy sepia sheen of night.

Since leaving home, I'd been living in a state of perpetual momentum, a long, shuffling desperation prayer to the road, always on the move, just a step ahead of the Curse. But, as I settled into a routine in Veracruz, my drinking soon took on a life of its own. The dreaded delirium fevers of my childhood returned in the form of brutal hangovers, casting a surreal pallor over everything.

As the weeks slid by like sands in a surreal hourglass, the old nightmare visions blended with the banging winches from the port in a constant mechanical lament from the musty wombs of the ships; always the ships at dock, humming like phantom cities in a glowing fog of watery night. The deep moan of their horns formed a haunting backdrop to the incessant tinny chatter of a hundred transistor radios as I sat by the seawall at dusk, listening to the strident Salsa beats reaching across the radio waves from old Havana, and watching those great sea-battered freighters stealing away to sea with a persistent sense of longing in my heart.

Sometimes Pepe and I would be invited for lunch on the vessels. One sympathetic Nicaraguan sailor even swiped us a couple of sheets of official stationery from his captain's desk, with the freighter's stamp embossed under a shipping line's authoritative letterhead. I typed up sterling recommendations in English on an old typewriter at the *mercado,* and we took turns practicing florid signatures of a fictitious ship's captain for our forged seaman credentials.

Nights, we would hang around the hotel courtyard, drinking beer and playing cards or dominos with Ramón and his cronies. When we had a little money, we'd go sit at the bars around the lively central plaza, dressed in our best clean clothes; sailors without a ship. Mostly, we kept to the quiet back streets around the hotel. Drinking beer from a corner *mercado* or shooting lazy billiards under the spinning fans of dockside *cantinas,* the languid days and nights all blended together in a dreamlike, tropical daze.

22. THE MOMENT OF CHANGE

"THE MOMENT OF CHANGE IS THE ONLY POEM."

—ADRIENNE RICH

"Late one afternoon, as I stood drinking a beer on the sidewalk," Cigano reads, "Pepe strode up. With a sheepish grin, he reminded me we had to go downtown to buy all the needles and other supplies for making the tattoos we'd spoken of. I'd forgotten all about it, but Pepe's flashing gold-toothed enthusiasm was contagious. . . . "

As the tattoo man reads on, the rust-stained walls of the old *Mercado Hidalgo* at dusk loom over bustling streets of memory.

Vendors sweep the sidewalks by their carts and stalls. Shopkeepers are beginning to roll down noisy metal shutters. Crowds of workers swarm the colorful, battered commuter buses lining up at day's end.

○   ○   ○

I followed Pepe's blurry shadow down the aisles of the sprawling old indoor market. Sweeping through a maze of chaotic details, I felt an ancient excitement stir in my gut. Reminded of breathless trips downtown with my grandmother as a child, I marveled at the kinetic jungle of shimmering cloths and colorful bursts of plastic flowers. There were wedding gowns, maternity dresses, baby clothes, toys, suits, and uniforms; the whole prismatic cycle of Mexican life and death, all lined up under a big, sweaty tin roof.

I stumbled behind as my friend wove through rows of sheets and flowery fabrics, past stalls crammed with shirts, shoes, boots, belts, buckles, beads, and handmade leather sandals. Bins of sun-dried chilies, fruits, nuts, and grains stood among glistening jars of mysterious medicinal herbs, roots, and potions, flanked by the ever-present statues of saints and exotic *Santeria* paraphernalia.

We rounded a corner, into a narrow aisle overflowing with recycled books, magazines, comics, posters, records, and yellowing antique postcards, all stacked from floor to ceiling, before venturing deeper into the darkening space, past mounds of produce, vegetables, boxes, cans, and packages with gaudy, colorful labels.

A sickly-sweet stench of death stabbed at my nostrils as we hurried through the butchers' bloody realm where grotesque gutted pigs dangled from giant metal hooks. Men in blood-soaked white aprons stood holding big sprays of straw, shooing at the angry clouds of fat black flies hovering over their morbid fare. Rows and rows of gamy flesh, hooves, tails, and skinned heads, unseeing white orbs of the dead peering up like ghosts, every massacred creature that walked the land on display at the blood-stained tiled counters.

A pungent odor of fish tore at my nostrils as we skirted another section of long cement stalls bulging with glittering, silvery, slithery undersea wonders and bug-eyed sea monsters; a slippery parade of eels, shrimps, conches, crabs, spiny green lobsters, and big droopy blue octopus tentacles. It was like visiting some weird Jules Verne nether region, a world of mysterious aquatic creatures, all laid out on shiny white tiles.

At the neighboring seafood bars festooned with colorful hand-painted signs of mermaids and sailing ships, wooden stools lined the long marble counters littered with fresh lime halves, bright green slices of a secret seafood code of the tropics. Tinfoil-capped bottles of spicy red *cóctel* sauces crowded the shelves. Sailors in crisp white uniforms sat, elbow to elbow, devouring overflowing portions of shrimp, octopus, oysters, and crabmeat from tall, thick glasses.

The nearby lunch counters were manned by an army of chubby-faced brown women, smiling and beckoning over gleaming pots and pans; good-natured witches, stirring their bubbling cauldrons of stews and sauces. Workers sat like animals at feeding time, stuffing their faces in a riot of unrestrained gluttony, oblivious to the flow of frantic activity around them. A scent of garlic and spices tugged at my nose. I lusted after the fresh *tamales* and steaming bins of shredded meat, beans, rice, and plump *chiles rellenos.*

My mouth was salivating like a hungry dog, urging me toward the piles of greasy tortillas, stone bowls of fresh guacamole, and spicy salsas. But no, not yet. *Vámanos, cabrón,* Pepe nudged my arm as he barreled onward, a human torpedo. Food would have to wait. My friend was on a holy mission.

Turning another corner, clusters of bananas, mangos, pineapples, and ripe red papayas dangled above big glass jars filled with brown sugar, honey, and malt powder. Old-fashioned blenders sat on the bright-blue-tiled counters, festooned with bottles of milky yellow *rompope* and fresh vanilla extract. I quickened my pace as my guide rushed on past the beckoning *licuados.*

The insistent fruit-juice hawkers' invitations faded into the distance as I followed him into another dark maze of mysterious corridors: aisles packed with all sorts of hardware and gleaming instruments, boxes and barrels of screws, nails, nuts, and bolts. Wooden bins overflowed with rusty hinges, clasps, and springs of all sizes and shapes, as the intricate parts and pieces of a million dismantled machines bombarded my senses.

Cross-eyed with sensory overload, I staggered along behind him, past shelves piled high with white straw hats and boots, leather vests, belts, lengths of rope, saddles, and spurs. We powered on through a wide archway and into a crackly new region of dry goods, stationery, sewing supplies, and shiny scraps of glittering complexity. Pepe was a hyperactive shopping machine, stopping here and there to inspect, haggle, and bargain over unfathomable gleaming items too small and intricate to make out in the frenzied blur of his hands as he slowly, methodically filled his plastic mesh shopping bag with supplies.

Finally it was done. He turned with a wide grin. *"A comer!"*

Thank you, Jesus! I followed him to a cramped little seafood stall under a colorful hand-painted mural of a sexy mermaid. We took a seat. The smiling white-haired owner brought us two cool, heaping glass mugs of *cóctels* stuffed with shrimp, octopus, conch, crab meat, and oysters, everything good from the Gulf floating in a deep red tomato sauce topped with chopped onions, cilantro, avocado, chili peppers, and lime juice.

Grinning as he watched us devour the delicious fare, the old man took a seat between us, nodding to Pepe. *"Remember, I e'say ju before, Pepe, I gonna e'show it to ju frieng mis fotos."*

Turning to me, the old man pulled a stack of well-worn black-and-white photographs from the bottom pocket of his faded yellow guayabera. He wiped the countertop with a rag and lovingly set the pictures down, one by one. Taken in ports around Latin America, they showed him as a young sailor. As he and Pepe talked about life at sea, I stared at the faded images from another lifetime.

My eye kept coming back to one picture: a group of young sailors, sitting at an outdoor café under stately royal palms. In the background, tall, white colonial buildings, lush hills, and an old streetcar. It had to be Rio de Janeiro.

The old man nodded, smiling. The snapshot was taken in Rio, he confirmed, right after the Big War. "Rio de bes' place I ever visit! An' so many pretty girl ever'where! Oh jes, I wan' e'stay there, *chavo*, I almos' get off de ship an' go live in dees country *para siempre.*"

"Why you don' e'stay?" Pepe inquired.

The old sailor sighed with a faraway look. *"Pues, tú sabes, mi hermano,* Veracruz de home *puerto."* He pointed at a corner of the old photograph, worn by time and many hands. *"Oye, hijo, ju* see dees mountain over here? Look it. *Aquí, ves?"*

Looking closer, in the background I could make out the famous statue of Christ the Redeemer on a distant mountaintop. I felt my heart swell with nostalgia for a place I'd never been—the one place on earth I knew I would surely call home one day.

As we finished our meal and stood, Pepe reached in his pocket. His friend pushed the money away. He shook my hand and rested his other one on my shoulder, grinning at me like a benevolent old pirate.

"Yo sé que vas a ver Rio de Janeiro muy pronto, mi'jo!"

I know you'll see Rio very soon, my son! With the blessings of an ancient sea dog, I felt my heart swell.

He must have known my mind.

23. PUSHING INK

"THE OLD SAILOR SITS ON THE DOCK, AND HE CURSES AND SPITS IN THE SEA. THERE'S A CIGARETTE PACK IN THE SOCK, AND HIS PANTS ROLLED UP OVER HIS KNEE. THERE'S A GIRL'S FACE TATTOOED ON HIS ARM, AND THE BLUE FADED LIPS SEEM TO CRY, TATTOOS THAT YOU GET WHEN YOU'RE YOUNG STAY ON YOUR ARM TILL YOU DIE. AND THE JUNKIE HE SITS AT HIS SIDE, SAYING, TELL ME SOME TALES OF THE DEEP, AND IS THERE A WAVE I CAN RIDE THAT'LL TAKE ME TO WHERE I CAN SLEEP. BUT HE'S FEELING THAT FIVE O'CLOCK HUNGER, AND IT'S TIME HE WAS MAKIN' A BUY, 'CAUSE THE TATTOOS YOU GET WHEN YOU'RE YOUNG STAY ON YOUR ARM TILL YOU DIE. AND THE WAVES MAKE A SUFFERING SOUND ON THE GRAY CREAKIN' PIER WHERE WE STAND, AND WE'RE WATCHING THE SUN AS IT DROWNS, TALKING OF FARAWAY LANDS. BUT MY TRUE SONG WON'T EVER BE SUNG, AND THE WORDS THAT YOU HEAR ARE A LIE, 'CAUSE THE TATTOOS YOU GET WHEN YOU'RE YOUNG STAY IN YOUR MIND TILL YOU DIE."

—SHEL SILVERSTEIN

Approaching the hotel, I spotted Ramón standing out on the sidewalk, drinking beer with his *compañeros*. He gestured at me, grinning. "If ju gonna mek de tattoo, *guerrero*, ju gotta mek it de good wan. Like dees." He rolled up a sleeve to a naked girl tattoo on his upper arm.

I stared at the crude, hand-poked lines, blurry and thick with age.

"My wife she never like it." Ramón smirked, patting his arm. "I finish with de wife long time, but always I got my lucky *chamaca.*"

Laughing, Pepe and I bounded up the stairs to his room. He switched on all the lights and the radio. Salsa music rattled in the air as he tore open the packages, arranging their contents on the bed.

"*Mira las agujas.*" Pepe pulled out a bundle of gleaming sewing needles and a bottle of India ink. "*Y tinta china.* Now I gonna show ju how ju mek de *tatuaje,* e'same way I learn it from de *chino.*"

He lined up all his purchases, talking all the while about some mysterious Chinaman in Panama. I watched as he punched little holes into beer-bottle caps with a knife. He explained the holes were to keep the needles in place while he fashioned them into little clusters, held together with plumbing epoxy. He squinted at the groups of tiny metal paintbrushes, then carved ditches into some wooden chopsticks. He inserted each of the needles into the improvised little wooden handles. With their points sticking out, they looked like miniature harpoons.

Clearing the table and moving it close to the bed, he laid everything out on a newspaper, a surgeon preparing an operating room.

"*Listo.*" Grabbing a pen and paper, he looked up with a gold-toothed grin. "Now we gonna mek de drawing, *vámonos, cabrón!*"

I watched as he sketched out a crude Popeye anchor. When it was done, he squinted, shaking his head. "Meybe no so good, no, eh?"

He went over and rummaged in a drawer for a little tin anchor medallion. He passed it to me. "Meybe ju draw de one like it?"

I studied the thing for a minute. I took his pen and drew a passable rendition of it onto the paper. I asked him for the scissors. I cut around my rough sketch, making a careful mold of the design.

I held the makeshift stencil up to my arm and grinned. "We can do the same thing on a piece of cardboard, Pepe." I shrugged. "Then we can just trace the design onto your skin with a pen."

"*Órale!*" He nodded.

I watched as he uncapped a bottle of alcohol. There was a sickly-sweet scent of burnt sugar cane. He poured some into a glass and filled the cap with black India ink. He shoveled a gob of Vaseline onto a plate and handed me the little wood-handled needle harpoons. I squinted at the tips. The smallest grouping had just a few needles, pulled tightly together. The biggest looked like a couple of dozen points, in a looser round cluster.

"Mos' important thing, *chavo,* always de needle." He took one from my hand and held it up to the light. "*El chino,* he show it to me like these. If ju mek de needle jus' right, ju gonna mek de good tattoo. Like de one I get from him. *Mira!*"

He hiked up his pant leg to reveal a large fish, jumping out of water. The fish, the waves, and the black-to-gray background shadowing covered his whole outer calf. He grinned with pride. "*Ves?* De chino he mek all these in only one hour."

I couldn't believe my eyes. It was perfect. I ran my hand over it, as if touching the thing could somehow dispel the mystery of its flawless manufacture: the intricate scales, the graceful curve of each wave, the subtle, silvery shading.

I needed to know more about the baffling little miracle. "He didn't use any kind of electric tattoo gun for this, Pepe?"

He shook his head. "*Puro hecho a mano, cabrón!*"

I scrunched up my face like a skeptical monkey. "But how. . . ?"

"*Qué se yo? Asi es, chavo.*" Pepe shrugged. "*Cosa de maestro.* De China peoples mek it de *tatuaje* these way for thousands year."

"And the design?" I looked at him, an insistent kid pestering. "Where'd the picture come from? Where'd he get it?"

He shrugged again. "Donno. He take de pen an' draw on me."

I kept staring, a human question mark.

"*Mira,* Joni," Pepe spoke patiently. "If ju mek it de practice, sure ju gonna learn how." He held up the needles, turning them around in the light. "De *chino* he take de points like these, *así, mira.*" He pushed them back and forth between his fingers fast, like a pool cue. "I try one time for mek it e'same way he do, but I only get de crooked line, like drunk man walking home." He chuckled. "I gonna show ju de good way, gonna be more easier. . . . "

I felt a nervous wave in my gut. I was about to get my first tattoo, then do one on him. What was I getting myself into?

He poured us two glasses of rum. I swallowed mine in one fast gulp. I stood, and Pepe drew the anchor onto my bicep, using the little stencil I'd made. It was time.

He pulled a chair up for me. Positioning himself on the edge of the bed, he took hold of my arm. I made a fist, tensing my muscle.

"No-oo, *pendejo!*" He laughed. "Ju don' gotta hold ju hand hard like that. Jus' relax ju body, *cabrón,* an' I gonna pull de skin."

I nodded and took a deep breath as Pepe grabbed my arm again, stretching the skin taut like a drum. Dipping the needles in the ink, his face was all concentration as he started poking. It stung a bit, at first, like a series of little insect bites. He hardly lifted the needles from my skin between jabs. One, two, three, four, five, six, seven, I counted. Then he stopped, dipped, and went back to pushing the ink in where he'd left off. 1, 2, 3, 4, 5, 6, 7, 8, dipping the needles again, then resuming. 1, 2, 3, 4, 5, 6, 7, stop, dip, jab. 1, 2, 3, 4, 5, 6, stop, dip, jab. 1, 2, 3, 4, 5, 6, 7, 8, stop, dip, jab.

After repeating the process a few more times, he wiped the tattooed section with a tissue, and sat back regarding his handiwork.

I looked down to see where the little insect bites had resulted in a crude line, about an inch long, at the bottom of the design.

"Mira, cabrón!!" Pepe gestured at my arm. "These how ju mek it de line. Is pretty easy, *cierto?* Sometime, meybe ju gotta go back an' do some more, so de line she e'stay e'same, an' when ju finish, ju check it again for de weak place, an' then ju fix up everything."

He picked up the needles and grabbed my arm again. Fascinated, I watched on, slowly getting the hang of it.

24. VAGABOND HEART

"MY VAGABOND HEART WANTS TO HOLD THE WORLD
INSIDE OF ME."

—CAETANO VELOSO

As Pepe poked away at my skin, we drank and talked. I kept asking questions and watching, till finally the hand-jabbed outline was done.

"So that's it? *Listo?*" I asked.

"*Pues, casi. . .*" he mumbled, still holding on to my arm. "Is little more I gotta finish. . . . "

Not looking up, he picked up a larger group of needles, dipped them in the ink, and started filling in the center. This part stung a bit more, but it seemed to be going faster. As I watched, my anchor began to take on a new weight and shape. It was looking like a real tattoo. I was starting to get the mysterious process; but I knew it could only be learned by practice. Questions wouldn't help.

He stopped, washed the tattoo with soapy water, and gave it a gentle wipe with a paper towel. He sat back and lit a cigarette. Grinning through a cloud of smoke, he nodded, gesturing at the dresser mirror.

I got up and stared at the perfect little anchor emblazoned on my bicep. With a rush of elation, I felt a subtle transformation, sealing my bond with all the restless spirits who traveled the seven seas, wearing tattoos like secret badges of honor. It felt right.

"How ju think? Is okey?" Pepe smiled.

"*A huevo, cabrón!*" I beamed. A different person was looking back at me in the mirror; a proud new man with a new beginning. *"Gracias, hermano!"*

○   ○   ○

Before starting on Pepe's tattoo, we decided to go downstairs for some beers to fuel our next session. Descending into the shabby *cantina* on the corner by the hotel, a familiar stench of tequila, vomit, urine, stale beer, and tobacco smoke stabbed my nostrils. The place was packed with the usual babbling drunks, hustlers, trinket vendors, beggars, and street-corner car-washers in their dirty sun-bleached rags. They were all spending their tragic dockside wages on a collective hangover. Groups of men sat slumped over tables littered with empty bottles. Those still conscious shouted over the distorted noise blaring from an ancient jukebox in a beat-up wire cage. More quarrelsome drunks argued in the shadows, barking like sea lions over the music.

Navigating the pissy chaos, I spotted young Memo at a table in the back, drinking among a cluster of drunken stevedores in shabby brown uniforms. A look of relief filled his cherub-like face as he got up to join us.

From the bar, I glanced over at a table where some men were yelling and gesturing wildly. One guy seemed to be defending an unconscious crony. I'd seen the passed-out guy at *cantinas* around the port, always carrying his little wooden box from table to table, clinking a pair of metal tubes together. His job was to encourage drinkers to prove their manhood by clenching the metal tubes in their fists, as he turned up an electrical current with a dial on his contraption, increasing the voltage till the customer would have to let go, cursing to the jeers or congratulations of his friends. These drunken displays of dubious *machismo* earned the box's owner a few pesos.

He must have made enough cash to drink himself into a stupor. Now, the poor bastard was about to get a taste of his own medicine, I realized as a couple of guys snatched his box from the floor and set it down on the table.

Over the protests of his tipsy defender, one of them slipped the wicked metal rods down his pants. Fascinated and horrified, we looked on as a grinning, weasel-faced rascal with beady, close-set black eyes pulled up a chair next to his victim.

Then he reached over and flipped a switch on the box.

"Mira que hijo de puta!" Pepe nudged me, wincing.

At first, nothing happened. As the weasel turned the knob, the sleeper suddenly shot bolt upright from the table. His box and a dozen empty bottles crashed to the floor. He started swinging around blindly, and the whole bar erupted in a free-for-all slugfest! Tables and chairs flew. Bottles exploded onto the cement floor like bombs as the weaselly instigator scampered out the door.

Others tried to restrain the fiery-eyed shock-box man as he stood swinging his beefy fists around like a punch-drunk prizefighter. Bottles were flying through the fetid air. Stools hurtled across the room. A burly, black-bearded bartender emerged from behind the bar, brandishing a nasty length of steel pipe coated with black tape. More bottles crashed. Cowboy hats were flying in the swirling mayhem. Then someone grabbed my arm.

Wincing in pain at the shock to my fresh tattoo, I turned to swing at my aggressor. It was just Memo. He gestured to the door as Pepe edged us out onto the sidewalk.

We dashed across the street and stood watching from the little plaza. Drunks stampeded from the swinging doors like rats from an overturned garbage can. I could still hear bottles crashing inside, and a lot of cursing and yelling. Then two gunshots.

We ducked behind a park bench as a small platoon of black-uniformed soldiers, clutching machine guns and long black batons, came running from the train station across the way.

○   ○   ○

Back in the room, we were still laughing as Pepe handed Memo some money. *"Qué desmadre!* Go de store for beer, *chavo. . . . "*

Memo started for the door, then stopped, asking to see my new tattoo. I rolled up my sleeve. He let out a long, slow whistle.

Pepe came over and put his arm around the kid's shoulder, grinning. "Ju wan' get de nex' one, *chavo?*"

Memo jumped back and bolted out the door.

Pepe laughed, pointing to the chair. "Okey, Joni, ju ready?"

"I guess. . . . " My mouth felt dry. I wanted Memo to hurry back with the beer. Swallowing hard, I nodded. "Where ya want this thing?"

He sat, unbuttoned his shirt, and put his finger above his right nipple. I looked at his little anchor medallion, leaned over, and sketched it onto his chest with a ballpoint, ignoring my stencil idea.

He stood and inspected the drawing in the mirror. He turned to me. "I think meybe is gonna be more good with word. How ju think?"

"What kinda words?"

He smiled. *"Corazón Vagabundo."*

Vagabond Heart. Yeah. *Corazón Vagabundo.* I drew the words in two semicircles, just above and below the anchor.

"Órale! Asi se juega, cabrón!" Pepe grinned.

I nodded. It did look better like that, bold and emblematic like those hypnotic little images I'd seen as a kid. A sense of déjà vu hit me like a premonition. In that moment, somehow I knew I would be a tattoo artist someday, like that skinny, old blue-armed shadow I'd seen carving at a blurry sailor's arm through a dirty window a long time ago.

I thought of Pepe's mysterious Chinaman and my mind flashed back to the shady back alleys of the old Pike amusement park. My heart was stirring with an ancient longing. I could feel a fuzzy, indistinct presence, like a hazy image of the Cyclops Baby in its murky jar at the old Hollywood Weird Museum. Some inner voice was speaking to me, assuring me that I hadn't been running away at all when I'd left home to travel the world. No, I'd just been looking for my purpose, my destiny. *Corazón Vagabundo.*

This was one of those rare, special times, I realized, where everything fell together, and suddenly it all made perfect sense.

25. STEWED, SCREWED, AND TATTOOED

"TATTOOS HAVE A POWER AND MAGIC ALL THEIR OWN. THEY DECORATE THE BODY BUT THEY ALSO ENHANCE THE SOUL."

—MICHELLE DELIO

My thoughts and dreams were on fire as I drew on Pepe's chest, tweaking and fine-tuning the design.

Satisfied at last, I nodded to my friend. He went over to the mirror again and stood in silence, studying my handiwork.

He came back and sat. *"Ándale pues, cabrón."*

"So, what do I do now?"

"Now ju gonna mek it on me de *pinche* tattoo, *pendejo!*"

Grinning, he picked up a medium-sized needle cluster and passed it to me; seven or eight needles pulled together, like the one he'd used on me. He kissed his little gold *Guadalupe* medallion and unclasped it from around his neck.

"Now ju put de needle in de ink an' stick it, dot, dot, an' keep it de little dot close together, *sabes*, follow de line e'same way ju watch me. Ju e'start de bottom an' go de right to left, an' down side to up, so ju don' rub out ju drawing. Put de *vaselina* over de part where ju work, so is more easy for ju see."

I took the little harpoon and dipped the needles in ink. My hand was shaking a bit as I rubbed a light coat of grease over the bottom word, *Vagabundo*. Taking a deep breath, I started with the O, poking the little marks in rapid succession, lightly at first, remembering to stretch the skin with the fingers of my left hand, like I'd seen Pepe do. 1, 2, 3, 4, 5, stop, dip, 1, 2, 3, 4, 5, stop, dip, 1, 2, 3, 4, 5, stop, dip.

As I completed the first letter, I cleaned the small section with a scrap of tissue and checked it out. There were gaps, but it looked passable. Recalling what he'd said about going back to touch it up afterwards, I moved on to the D. After a few more minutes jabbing and dipping, I finished the N, then the U.

Sweating, I realized tattooing required real concentration. The slightest miscalculation could queer the whole deal. For some reason, that concept had a calming effect. A dot at a time, it was getting easier. It was going to be okay. By the time I finished the bottom word, *Vagabundo*, I'd stopped shaking, nodding my head to the radio music. Pepe seemed relaxed, too, as if the whole process was a great comfort to his soul.

Just as I was thinking of a cold beer, Memo appeared at the door. He set the bottles on the table. Pepe nodded to me. Time for a break. He stood and looked in the mirror, as Memo opened one of the big *caguamas* and poured out three glasses.

"*Órale, chingón!*" Pepe grinned. "Ju see how good she look?"

Memo came up to see. "*Qué padre!*" He looked down at his own bare arm, as though just noticing it attached to his body. "Do it hurt?"

"No too much, *chavo*." Pepe grinned. "*Por qué?* Ju ready for get ju *tatuaje* now?"

Memo winced comically and backed away.

I lit a cigarette, and we sat drinking. After a while, Pepe gave me a nod. I picked up the needles and we started back in.

Pretty soon, I was on autopilot. We sat laughing and talking as the tattoo session went on into the night. A cool ritual bond was forming between the three of us, as if the needles were creating something deeper than simple marks on skin. By the time I got to putting on the final touches, we'd fallen into a long, comfortable silence. Pepe seemed half asleep as Memo quietly filled our glasses.

Without looking up, I could sense another presence in the room. From the corner of my eye, I saw Lupe, the hotel girl, standing beside me. I didn't know how long she'd been there.

I turned and nodded. She gave me a sheepish smile, as if noticing me for the first time too. She must have been there a while, watching with those half-drunk sparkling obsidian eyes.

"Me gusta," she breathed, running her lazy brown fingers down my back. Goosebumps swept over my neck.

"Deja que trabaje, pendeja!" Memo scolded her to let me work.

"No! Está bien!" I cut in, a bit too fast. "She's okay, *'mano.*"

Memo moved away. Pepe opened his eyes and winked as I finished the outline. I touched up a few uneven spots, and then we took another break. My friend and I sat back smoking, finishing the beer while Memo stood quietly by the door.

Without a word, the girl came over and sat on my lap, cool as a cat. I slipped a casual arm around her firm, slender waist. As she sat there, drinking, I half expected her to start purring. It was still a few hours before dawn; the first roosters were already crowing in the distance. Pepe stood again and checked out his tattoo in the mirror.

"A huevo, Joni." He yawned. "Is perfect, *'mano!* Don' gotta finish de fill in now. I like even more better these way, meybe."

And so it was done, my first tattoo.

Memo came over and shook my hand, then wandered out the door. Pepe started picking up empty bottles. Lupe slid off my lap as I moved to get up and lend a hand.

"Cansado?" she asked with a sleepy drawl.

I nodded. Yeah, I was pretty tired.

"Yo también. Is okey I come e'sleep ju room?"

"Claro." I nodded without hesitation. I had to wait a minute before standing up to help Pepe put the room in order.

He lit a joint and passed it over. As we smoked, I asked him if the tattoo was really okay. *"O-key?* Is de *bes'* tattoo, *cabrón!* Ju de *campión!* Now get de fock out from here. An' take these one together wit' ju!" He winked, gesturing at the girl.

She turned and flicked a sleepy pink tongue at him, like a naughty schoolgirl, as we made our way to the door.

Down the hall, I let her into my room and went for a good long beer piss. I was still hard.

When I emerged from the toilet, she was passed out, face up on the bed. Her dress was hiked up around her thighs. I stripped and lay down beside her, studying her dark indigenous face like a puzzle.

I hadn't been with a woman in almost two years. She wasn't pretty, but there was a rough, oriental femininity to her, a hot animal sensuality tugging at my loins.

Lying there half-drunk, with that strange primal creature snoring softly beside me, I drank in her age-old Mayan countenance with an age-old longing. Then I leaned over and kissed her.

"Aí no, cabrón," she mumbled. She didn't try to stop me as I explored her open mouth with my tongue, caressing her firm little breasts. She just lay there in a trance, moaning *"aiií, pára, cabrón."* I pulled off her red cotton shorts, exposing her plump, golden-brown nakedness. *"Aí no, para—"* she protested weakly as I mounted her and climaxed right away. She began snoring again.

Still rock hard inside her, my dick was a slumbering monster, awakened after years of hibernation. I pumped it a few times and came again. Then, a hungry beast at a sumptuous banquet, I started for another round as she snored on.

Gorging on her inert body, my appetite seemed to be increasing with each new release. She never moved as I had my way with her, pouring my desperate seed again and again into her hot, wet Mayan hole. Between spasms, I lay astride her, sweating, nibbling at her slack-jawed, yellow-toothed mouth, studying each detail of that savage, fascinating, indigenous face. I was an archaeologist beholding some strange and terrible primitive work of art, drinking in the smooth, cool image of her fine jet-black hair, the tight pore-less skin of her high-cheeked brown face—like one of the ancient Mayan wall carvings at the Tomb of the Inscriptions. Sacred. I was a dirty dog of a bloodthirsty *conquistador*, my dick a brutal battering ram, as I humped away, desperate to shoot another breathless spark of life into those dark, secret depths.

I shuddered and gasped as my flaccid sex lunged out a final, lusty dry heave. With the light of dawn, I rolled off her sweat-drenched, snoring pre-Columbian vessel at last.

Panting like an exhausted mongrel, I dropped into a deep, dreamless slumber; dark and untroubled as the cavernous chambers of the great, abandoned, jungle-encrusted pyramids of the mysterious Mayan lowlands.

○   ○   ○

I awakened in the afternoon, a loud truck exhaust rattling the windows, shaking me out of a deep sleep stupor. Angry flies darted over my sweaty carcass as I blinked in the dusty heat, alone on the bed.

The girl had departed, as stealthily as she'd appeared the night before, the only trace of her a sickly-sweet female stench on my skin.

My gut quivered with a wave of hot revulsion. I lay still, conjuring an image of those dirty yellow teeth, that slack, bovine mouth, moaning *"aiií, no, cabrón"* as I plundered her vanquished cunt like a Spanish armada.

I rose up and stared at the semen-stained sheet, an autopsy doctor trying to unravel some hideous, violent crime. It was marked with spots of dried blood and ink from my fresh tattoo.

I felt oddly tainted and elated at once, as if I'd broken through some intangible barrier. The vague sense of accomplishment was as real and permanent as the stinging little anchor emblazoned on my right bicep.

I thought of the words on Pepe's tattoo, *Corazón Vagabundo,* and I knew they described me perfectly in that special moment; a vagabond heart lying all alone in a hot, noisy little fly-infested room; stewed, screwed, and tattooed forever in the dusty Mexican afternoon.

Another truck rumbled by outside the window. A ship's horn boomed a long deep soulful lament. I lay back and closed my eyes again, dreaming of faraway lands.

Sleep came to me at once, like a trusted old friend.

26. SHARING THE WEALTH

The following weeks passed in a lazy time warp as I hung around the hotel with my friends. The Indian girl went about her daily chores. Bearing the brunt of their dirty little comments, she remained silent and demure as a ghost of her fallen ancestors.

Then, one hot Saturday afternoon, around siesta time, I was crossing the tracks by the port entrance when a bright-eyed old mulatto woman called out, gesturing to an assortment of colorful trinkets, candy bars, and cigarettes spread out on a cloth beside her taco cart. I stepped up and asked her for a pack of unfiltered Delicados.

The woman frowned. Why would a foreign sailor want to smoke that cheap Mexican crap? She handed me a pack of Dunhills.

I wagged my finger. *"Eso no. Delicados Sin Filtro, por favor."*

"Tú, de donde vienes, güero?" With a wry commical grimace, she demanded to know where I was from.

"El Norte," I mumbled vaguely, adding that I was looking for work on a ship.

Her eyes lit up. "Many good e'sheep in de Puerto de Veracruz. Ju gon' find de good *chamba* here soon, *chavo,* plenty good chance. I gon' pray for ju to de *Virgin Guadalupe.*"

With that, she reached into her canvas bag and handed me the pack of Dunhills again. I shrugged and emptied my pocket, handing her my last twenty pesos.

She waved the money away. "No! Dees *cigarillo* de *regalo* for ju, *amigo. Por suerte, sabes?*" The kindly old vendor smiled. "When ju luck she arrive, den ju pay me back, *vá?*"

I thanked her and walked away, grinning. There it was again, that humble, humanitarian, light-hearted Mexican generosity. Her shining brown eyes fixed in my memory as she turned back to her broom and water bucket.

I strolled along the docks, dodging the shouting port workers in darting forklifts. Navy blue pickups filled with official mustaches in crisp tan uniforms rolled by. There was always an urgent, frantic energy in the air of that other city. I could feel its special kinetic heat as I wandered the busy wharves, looking up at the ships' big straining winches. Thick metal cables hummed with grinding gears, as palettes descended into the crowds of swarthy brown hands outstretched in mute supplication from the docks, a riot of dirty white shorts, sandals, straw hats, and tattered brown shirts.

I looked up, scanning the ports of origin of the great seagoing hulks. Hamburg, Panama, Liverpool, Monrovia, Copenhagen, Lima, Caracas, Buenos Aires; strange, exotic words in Greek emblazoned on big rusty hulls, and a gigantic white Russian freighter, with a large red hammer and sickle on its gleaming white smokestack. Spotless white-clad Soviet sailors peered down from its deck like stoic military dolls.

Spying a Brazilian freighter, *Nossa Senhora da Paz—Rio De Janeiro*, my heart beat fast as I stepped closer. Peering up at the deck, I half expected to see Orfeu dancing down the gangplank, a gang of colorful Carnaval revelers in tow.

Instead, a group of amused-looking mulattos stood watching me squint up into the harsh noonday sun.

Someone called down, gesturing an invitation to come aboard. Without hesitation, I started up the long gangplank, trying to act casual, like I'd been boarding ships all my life.

Every eye seemed to be following my unsure steps. No lighthearted dreams of romantic adventure in faraway places now. This was real. Could this ship be my ticket to Rio?

As I reached the top, a graying mulatto sailor greeted me like an old friend. With a wide, childlike smile, he inquired in soft accented Spanish what ship I was on.

Before I could think, the words left my mouth. *"El Rey del Caribe,"* I lied, recalling a Panamanian freighter I'd seen in port the day before.

I regretted it instantly as I saw his eyes widen and his mouth fall open like a surprised cartoon character.

"Porr-rra, rapaz. . ." he drawled.

It sounded serious.

I cast furtive glances around at his shipmates. Another sailor stepped up and explained in English. "Shoo sheep. . . " he looked me over with a sad, downcast air ". . . she go sail-it away de morning."

The solemn look on his face and that hilarious Portuguese accent conspired with my near panic attack on the gangplank. I broke out in a fit of nervous laughter. To my horror, I couldn't stop. Realizing how ridiculous I looked just made me laugh harder. My eyes went teary as I stood there, convulsing and cackling, a drooling idiot.

Catching my breath, I looked at the first guy. He was gesturing to the others as if to say "was it something I said?"

One of his shipmates shrugged, drawing an index finger in circles around his ear. *"Sei la! O bichinho ficou maluco. . . ."*

Oh, shit! They thought I was nuts. I started laughing again, harder than before. What could I say? What could I do to get out of this mess?

After a helpless, drooling, snickering, nervous eternity, I held up my hand. Some of them were laughing now, too. Then, suddenly, we were all bent over, howling like a gang of drunken schoolboys.

A gray-bearded white officer in a crisp tan uniform peered down from an upper deck. *"Más que diablo?"* he growled. *What the devil?* We all looked up. Someone guffawed, and the hilarity raged on.

Taking pity on me, my new friends pulled me into the galley, where a stout Negro chef sat me down and fed me a delicious meal of black bean *feijoada* stew with garlic-studded greens, and a big plate of gleaming white rice.

As we sat there, eating, talking, and drinking frosty Brazilian beer, one of the sailors inquired how I could have been so careless as to get myself stranded in a strange port.

There was no way out now but to continue the charade. "I dunno," I lied. "I went out drinking with some guys from the ship last night, then they went off and left me in a bar with some *chicas* and, I dunno, I was pretty drunk, I guess. Those damn whores musta slipped something in my drink, cuz that's the last I remember. I woke up in a hotel room with a bad headache." I massaged my temples dramatically. "Then I came back here, looking for my ship." I shrugged.

As the Spanish-speaking sailor translated for his mates, I prayed my tale sounded convincing. I only got a bit of their florid Portuguese conversation, but their sympathetic looks made me feel like a heel.

One of them asked if I had any money. He looked truly concerned. There was no answer. I told him the *putas* had left me skinned. How could I admit to having money after the elaborate fib I'd just spun?

I could see from their serious faces that my plight was their worst nightmare as sailors; waylaid, stranded in a faraway land, abandoned by shipmates, broke, and far from home. As they spoke among each other, debating how to help me out, I wanted to cry. Their concern for a total stranger was heartbreaking.

It got worse. My dejected look of shame was taken as despondency. The first guy put a big hand on my shoulder. "Don' worry, *amigo*. We gonna get de help for shoo, an' give to shoo de money for e'stay here an' make de phone calls home to shoo peoples."

When I tried to refuse his generosity, it was waved away as a show of bravado. What a mess! The more I assured them I'd be fine, the stronger their resolve to help.

I cringed as they all stood up and began to disperse about the ship, running back and forth from cabins to galley with clothes, whiskey, cigarettes, and—worst of all—money. They'd gone as far as soliciting contributions from other sailors around the big freighter to help a stranded fellow seaman.

As they showered me with their good-hearted charity, I felt sick to my stomach. I was in fact broke, didn't even know how I'd pay my hotel bill. Still, I felt like a louse for inspiring such a display of generosity, by deceit. It was all wrong. I hadn't come looking for a handout, and now I was staring at a jackpot of whiskey, cigarettes, and cash—all on false pretexts. Story of my fucking life.

But it wasn't over. One of them said he'd go ask a ship's officer to send a wire to my ship, explaining my dilemma, and requesting they contact the shipping agent in Veracruz to arrange my plane fare to the ship's next port of call.

Panic! Think fast! I nearly puked.

"No, por favor!" I begged. "That would be too much! I'll deal with the agents here myself. You must go to no more trouble for me! You've been far too generous already. Please!"

The kindly sailor insisted it would be no trouble at all.

"No!" I croaked like a cornered rodent. *"Por favor!* I'll be fine here, I swear! Truth is, I want nothing more to do with that damn bucket. I was already planning to get paid off soon and look for work on another ship. Now, thanks to your kindness, I can stay here till I find a better job. With luck, the next vessel I sail on will be blessed with a crew half as good as yourselves!"

I was laying it on thick as I jumped up and embraced each one of those kind souls with real gratitude. I gathered up my ill-gotten gains in the large shopping bags they'd brought and said good-bye.

Beating a hasty retreat, I slithered back down that endless gangplank, feeling like a tapeworm crawling out of a wharf rat's ass.

I scampered off toward the port gate, my dark burden of guilt lightening with every step. As I turned a corner, I felt a sudden flash of elation, realizing I suddenly had enough money now to live for weeks.

My dwindling finances had been gnawing at my gut since coming to Veracruz, but I'd kept telling myself something would come along soon. And now it had. Who was I to refuse a stroke of good fortune? After all, I hadn't set out to hustle anyone, had I? I'd have done the same for somebody else in my position, wouldn't I?

My good cheer began to wane again as I remembered that my "position" was a fucking lie.

That guilty thought must have had wings. As I approached the street, a bored-looking soldier stepped out of his guard post and whistled, motioning me over.

"Oye güero! An' where ju going outside de *puerto* with so much *taxable* merchandise, heh?" His bushy mustache jumped like a greedy caterpillar as he spoke, poking a baton at one of the bulging bags.

"Just some presents for my *amigos* in Veracruz." I shrugged.

"Ah, qué bueno!" The soldier grinned like a lottery winner, as he fished around and plucked a bottle of Johnny Walker from a bag. *"Gracias. . . 'amigo'!"*

One bottle lighter, I hurried out past the gate, hugging my shameful haul to my chest.

Approaching the kindly old lady's taco stand again, I reached in one of the bags and handed her a full carton of Dunhills.

Her wide, gold-toothed grin shone on me like the sun. "De Virgin Mother always generous to her childrens!"

The warmth of that sweet smile followed me as I crossed the tracks. It was a good feeling. Sharing the wealth, that's what it's all about, I thought to myself as I hurried toward the hotel.

Ramón raised a curious eyebrow as I set my contraband treasure down on the counter. He peeked in the bags and looked up with a slow whistle. Pepe knew a guy at the *Mercado Hidalgo*, he whispered, who would buy all that stuff for good money.

Bingo! I was flush! And it was Saturday night—a perfect time to share the wealth with my friend. I grabbed my bags and took the stairs up to Pepe's room, two at a time.

27. EL GRAN BAILE

"*Que suerte, mi hermano!* *Bonito! Bonito! Pura vida!*"

Pepe leaped off his bed and paced the room, gesturing and chattering like a joyful parrot. We had to go out to celebrate, right now, let's go, go, go. Bustling around the little space, pulling out his best shirt and shoes, my friend was all animated movement and good cheer.

"*Sábado! Si-iíí Señór!*" He sang and did a playful little rhumba dance. "Gonna be de big *fiesta baile* in Villa del Mar tonight," he announced, parroting the radio ads that had been playing all week. "*Este Sábado! La Internationa-allll, Sonora Santanera-aa. . . .*"

It was time for a new adventure, and now we had cash. The famous dance orchestra *Sonora Santanera* was playing at the big ballroom on the long seaside stretch of scruffy, windswept beaches where locals gathered on weekends to eat and drink rum from coconuts in straw-roofed *palapas*.

As Pepe rattled on about the upcoming *baile*, his joy was contagious. "I so much wan' we go dees *baile!* But when ju no got de money, ju no can tek de *e'sheet*. No buy even de toilet paper, ho ho! I don' wan' go e'stand in de street like a farmer, more better for jus' e'stay home."

His face broke into a wide grin. "*Pero ahora sí!* We gonna get de mo-ney, *chingón*, ya-ass, go sit at de table like big shot. Gonna be lotta pretty girl, *wey!*

Oye, ju know how for dance? *Ai, cabrón,* we gonna have goo-ood time tonight! *Chicas!* Take de pretty girl an' spen' de night *chingando,* ya-ass, fucka fucka fucka, ho ho, an' we go e'swim tomorrow in de *playa,* too, ya-ass, e'same like de rich *turista. Oye,* ju wan' wear my e'special jacket? Try it now, *vamos!*"

I put on the jacket. It fit.

He nodded. *"Asi se juega, chingón!* Ju de big lady-killer *gato* now. Big dance tonight, oh *jess-sss!*" He slapped on some cheap cologne as we stumbled around the little room, primping like matadors.

We rushed out to get downtown before the *mercado* closed. After a quick transaction with Pepe's acquaintances, the weight of cash in my long-empty pocket felt thrilling. We bopped along the busy sidewalk, grinning and strutting, a pair of prosperous men.

Not bothering to wait for a lowly bus, we jumped in a taxi and sped off through the scruffy downtown streets, which suddenly looked different and new.

A circus feeling was in the air as we rolled up to the busy seaside ballroom. Barefoot Indian children scurried around, selling candies and loose cigarettes. People were milling about, most of them too poor to buy tickets, just wanting to be close to the action. Poor people have to make their own fun any way they can—and in Mexico, the poorer people are, the more fun they insist on making.

Behind a line of run down blue taxis, I could see the *orquestra's* big streamlined chrome-paneled bus. I pictured that shiny vessel streaming like a freighter through the sea of night, traveling from small *pueblos* to big cities across the land to bring a few hours of excitement and musical gaiety to the people: common working folks, whose simple lives those musicians would touch and then be gone again, off to the next port of call. They were a special kind of sailors.

Winding our way through the crowd, I pictured the shadowy figure of my father, thinking of the years he'd spent traveling with his band, moving from town to town to deliver a sweet, melodic cargo to anony- mous fans and admirers: people whose names he would never know, faces seen only as a blurry stream of scenery, drab and monotonous as the sleeping hamlets glimpsed from a rolling porthole in the long, hazy jazz night.

o   o   o

As the tattoo man reads on, his mind travels back to his father's living room and another of Artie's long, rambling monologues.

"One day a guy came around and rang the gate." Artie guffaws. "Said he came all the way from Switzerland to see me. So what?"

Cigano looks at the old man. "So what happened, Artie?"

His father scoffs. "I didn't let him in, that's what happened. Hah. But he kept insisting he wanted to meet me. So I went out and said 'Well, look, man, I don't want strangers coming to my door, ringing my bell here.' He said 'But I came all the way from Switzerland to meet you.' And I told him 'Well, I'm sorry, but whaddya want me to say?' He said 'I brought you some chocolate.' I told him to put it through the gate. Jesus! Just kill me, why don'tcha. I can't eat that fucking stuff! And then he went away, thank God. People just don't seem to realize, you know, they don't understand there's only one of you, and hundreds of thousands of them. I mean, I sold over a million fucking records, man. That was a real lot of exposure back in those days. So a lot of people out there, they still know my name, and, you know, they wanna talk to me. That doesn't mean I want to talk to any of them! Jesus! Most people have nothing to say that interests me. Idiots! I don't get these guys who just gotta have your autograph. I asked one of 'em once: 'Whaddya do when ya get home? Take it out and look at it?'"

Cigano shakes his head, laughing as he turns a page and reads on.

◦ ◦ ◦

Watching the band lugging their heavy black cases into the ballroom through a side door, it hit me again that my own father had been a radio-wave legend, just like these guys: musicians traveling in beat-up long-distance buses, sailing the highways to bring a touch of poetry and romance to the common people, the ones who cleaned the toilets and cooked the food and built the bridges, who worked the factories and watered the soil of the Empire with their blood and sweat, never asking why. Waiting in line, I remembered the little traveling circus I'd met on the road, and I suddenly felt a strong bond with the father I'd never known: the same affinity I'd felt for those road-weary Mexican carnies. I realized that was the call of the big shadowy freighters for me. I knew I would always feel that deep connection with all the wandering armies of the road, stretching out forever before our restless, vagabond hearts.

As we stepped up to the *billeteria*, I could hear big booming strains of music from within; a swinging tropical blend of horns and congas, and a crooning amplified singer whose voice I recognized from the radio. Festive, kinetic electricity trembled in the air as we edged in with the crowd. Machine-gun–toting soldiers stood guard at the doors. A couple of older guys in shiny black suits scrutinized our tickets and tore them in half. A few steps farther, a group of uniformed guards patted us down. A smartly dressed young lady held her purse open for inspection, while another cop frisked her date.

Inside the big cavernous dance hall, the orchestra was up on stage. Looking larger than life, they lumbered through a swinging Salsa like a well-oiled machine. They were all dressed like mariachis, in matching brown uniforms and crisp white shirts. Their black ties were dotted with white music notes and treble clefs—a touch of class.

The crowd was an eclectic mix, from well-dressed older couples sitting at expensive tables near the front to young people in casual street clothes. The dance floor was a democratic cross-section of locals, too. Nattily attired young guys showed off their snappy rhumba steps, leading their pretty dates across the floor in precise, graceful swirls. Other couples just shuffled around, happy to hold each other tight. A fat guy who'd obviously had too much to drink dragged an exhausted partner around the dance floor like a sack of beans, bumping into other couples who just danced on, unconcerned.

This wasn't some snooty high-class event, I realized, but a simple *fiesta popular*, where common people came to simply have fun. Veracruz had its own unique character and rhythm, distinct from the brooding, melancholy North of Mexico, and nothing like the sullen indigenous states of Oaxaca, the jungles of Chiapas, or even the bustling, neo-colonial megalopolis of Mexico City. Here the atmosphere was relaxed, laid back, and just shabby enough for no one to care much about appearances.

In Veracruz, life's edges were softer, the details clearer than anyplace else I'd ever been. There was always that sweet casual *jarocho* attitude riding the soft sea breezes that seemed to sing *"Tonight, another fiesta, and life goes on. All week we work and toil. Now we dance and drink, laugh and celebrate, because soon our lives will be over."* It seemed like a smart way to live.

Watching people dance, I realized you could tell a lot about them: which ones were on their first dates, their shy steps awkward and tentative—so different from the older couples moving together as one. Nobody paid much attention to anyone else. Each pair just moved in their own self-contained little circles, oblivious to the others. And at the same time, they all seemed bound together by some larger purpose: music. I watched as the orchestra played on with indifferent mechanical precision. They seemed almost insignificant to the crowd swaying at their feet like a vibrant, moving underwater forest.

As we backed against a wall, Pepe shouted to me over the music. "Too much peoples here, *'mano*. All de table full up. *Vamos.*"

We pushed through a crowd thick as tortilla dough and out into the cool night air, where people sat at a special VIP patio overlooking the sea. A few steps down toward the beach, more tables.

A warped plywood dance floor was laid across the sand, enclosed by a flimsy makeshift barrier manned by lazy guards. The long corrugated tin fence also served as a convenient urinal. From time to time, a ragged street urchin would clamber over, boosted by *compañeros* on the other side. As the intruder landed right in the waiting arms of the bouncers, they would extract a few coins from him to let him stay. Quite a few people entered like that, providing extra income for the amused-looking guards. Only a few, too broke for the payoff, were led back out by the scruff of their pants.

"Ya-asss! Is okey here!" Pepe flashed a gold-toothed grin. "*Ven*, Joni. We tek a seat on these side, *vámonos.*"

I followed him over to an abandoned table littered with empty bottles, fly-infested shrimp heads, peelings, and browning lime slices.

As we went to sit, a couple of guys lounging by the piss fence stepped up. A heavyset mustache grabbed the chair away from me, growling. "*Oye*, de table she reserve for us!"

Pepe smiled. "*Ah, perdón, jefe.* We think meybe someone finish here already. Wan' give us a chance?"

"Meybe." The guy rubbed his chin. "But we pay for de table."

A friendly payoff was in order. Pepe smiled back. "*Cuánto?*"

"Fifty pesos!" the other cut in, fast. "Is what we pay."

I could see a hint of desperation in his face. He and his pal had obviously blown all their cash on booze. Now they were drunk and broke, in a foul, moneyless, restless, womanless way. They wanted out.

"Twenty!" I cut in. "It's all we got." I shrugged, then turned to walk away, silently counting. . . *uno, dos, tres, qua.* . . .

I felt a hand on my shoulder. I turned and saw the big drunk standing there, beefy palm extended. *"Dámelo!"* He grunted.

As he snatched the cash like a crocodile, I saw his whole attitude brighten. The belligerent bully was our amicable host now. He and his *compadre* swept their rubble from the table. They even pulled the chairs out for us to sit.

"Unbeatable!" I beamed at Pepe as a white-jacketed waiter hurried over to take our order.

Sitting back sipping a cold can of Tecate, my eyes wandered the patio. Clusters of girls stood by a wall, like a high-school dance. Once in a while, a guy would wander over and ask one for a dance. The girl would shake her head, and the guy would disappear.

After watching the odd ritual for a while, I turned to Pepe. "What's up with these *chicas?* They stand around all dressed up, looking all sexy, but when guys ask 'em to dance, they just keep standing there. What th' fuck are they doing?"

Pepe winked. "They only wait for de real *caballero* invite them for drink at de e'special table, *cabrón!"* He stood up, patting the tabletop like the hood of a fancy car. "Ju just gotta know for talk good."

I watched as he strolled over to a pair of girls standing in a corner like shy birds. With an exaggerated bow, he chatted with the bird-like creatures, pointing at our table. They looked over. I waved, feeling kind of stupid. Pepe kept talking.

To my relief, they smiled demurely, shaking their heads. No dice. Scared little birds. He kissed both their hands, and with a low, comical bow, he turned and sauntered back.

Pulling up his chair, he flashed a sheepish grin. "Meybe ju wan' try wit' de nex' ones?"

"Forget it!" I laughed. "I'm no good at that kinda shit."

He shot me a quizzical look.

"Look, Pepe," I sighed, "I don't get these chicks. Where I'm from, the girls are, well, it's just a different kinda deal, I dunno." I shrugged.

"What kinda deals?"

"If a chick likes ya, they just fuck yer brains out, y'know?"

"Pues, sí, chingón!" His eyes lit up like a cartoon wolf. "They got de girl like these one here too. But ju gotta *pay!"* He rubbed his fingers together.

I looked at him. "Yea-ah? How much?"

"No too bery much. Meybe like, ehh, twenny peso."

I smiled. Now he was on to something.

He grinned and went on. "*Mira!* If we don' got no lucky chance in here, we go an' visit de *putas* downtown, ho ho, ya-ass?"

I glanced over at all the sexy little birds lined up at the wall again. Sounded okay to me. A fuck was a fuck.

We sat back again, drinking our beers.

As I watched the little wooden dance floor, one older couple stood out; a stocky man in his mid-fifties in spotless white pants and a blinding white guayabera. His wife was a cheerful-looking woman of similar age and girth. They were having big fun. I sighed. How happy they seemed together, just an old married couple on their night out. I watched them sway among the other dancers, circling each other, moving their feet and hips in perfect unity, without ever missing a beat. At times they danced precise, complex counter-rhythms to the music, at others they picked up on themes that were inaudible to me until expressed visually in their dancing.

I knew they'd probably been doing those same dance steps together since they were teenagers; a simple ease and harmony I'd never known with a partner. I felt a sudden wave of sadness cover me like a clammy shroud. I sipped at my beer and watched them, suddenly feeling very lonely.

Before I could slip into full-scale boozy brooding, Pepe snapped me out of it. "Come, Joni! *Vamos!*" He grinned, steering me by the arm. "Let's go an' walk inside, check it out these *pinche baile.*"

After circling around for a while, we managed to find a couple of chubby girls to dance with. It was kind of fun, but after a half-hearted attempt to invite them for a drink, even those good-natured, dog-faced creatures demurred.

The band took a break between sets, and we went back to our table. As people began to fill the patio, Pepe spotted someone he knew. He whistled, gesturing for them to join us.

Antonio and Vera were a good-natured "modern" Mexican couple in their mid-twenties. We shook hands, and they sat. I recognized them from the pool hall near the fish market, a lively after-hours gambling spot they managed. Vera was high-spirited and outgoing for a Mexican woman, nothing like those timid little birds huddled by the wall. Antonio had an overly friendly, slightly shifty manner, but he seemed pretty cool.

"*Oye,* Joni!" He winked, slapping me on the back like an old pal. "I see ju mek de good tattoo on Pepe! I wan' mek one like these too."

"Well, I'm not really a tattoo artist. . . . " I mumbled.

"*Mira,*" Antonio went on. "Ju know our bar, we got lotta peoples over there wan' mek tattoo. Ju can get de good money *güero.* I introduce ju all de *muchachos.*" He rubbed his fingers together. "Ju can mek to us a little contribution, meybe like ten percent, an' den ju gonna keep de rest. An' ju mek one free tattoo for me, *que tal?*"

"Sounds okay, but I'm not really a professional tattoo guy."

"An' who de professional tattoo guy around here?" He shrugged.

As my companions sat drinking and talking, a light bulb lit up in my head. I'd only done one little hand-poked anchor, and just vaguely pondered the idea of tattooing professionally; now I already had people wanting ink! What next?

As my dreams took flight, I envisioned myself traveling the world, working as a real tattooist in distant ports, seeing new places, earning a living, and meeting all kinds of people—a boss of my destiny. I thought of those musicians again with their big long-distance bus, sailing the roads, connecting with people wherever they went. Yeah, maybe I was on to something. Tattooing was a lifestyle well suited to the road. As I took another drink, I conjured a picture of my new self, like some old Humphrey Bogart character, a tattooed underworld shaman sitting at a back table of a faraway *cantina,* carving on a sailor's arm as palm trees swayed in a tropical breeze.

Then my dreams came in for a crash landing, as I tasted the bitter truth. I had no fucking idea what I was doing. How would I even start? Where could I learn? My heart sank like a defeated pirate schooner as I recalled the complex, colorful tattoos I'd seen on foreign sailors. It seemed an impossible goal to learn the secrets of that mysterious practice. But, on the other hand, one thing I'd learned in my travels was that anything was possible. I felt a wave of hope. My future would unfold somehow, someday, if only I just believed. I didn't know how, but that would come too. I smiled to myself, downing another beer.

After a while, the orchestra began playing a strident *cumbia.* Vera and Antonio rose up to go dance. As we all shook hands, he grinned. "Don' forget it what I e'say ju, *güero,* we gonna mek de good *negocio.* Ju come an' visit, okey?"

As they moved off, Pepe called for more beers. "Her *familia* load up with de money," he whispered. "*Muy importante* peoples in de Veracruz e'society. She like a black e'sheep in de family, with these pool hall an' de crazy boyfrien'. But ju know what he e'say ju about de tattooing? Is no so bad idea, eh? Meybe we go an' check it out, mek de little tattoos party. Lotta peoples from the *puerto* go for drink over there, *chavo*. They all got too much money. An' ju know, ever'body love it de *tatuaje*."

Pepe was right. Everybody loved tattoos.

I beamed at my optimistic friend. He made it all sound so easy, I had to smile. Attitude. That's what it was about Pepe. He had Attitude. There was no stopping his highflying dreams.

"What about the real *artistas*, Pepe?" I stared at him like a curious child, remembering the tattoo parlors I'd peeked into as a kid. "You know, those professional tattoo guys? They got special tricks, all those colors, some kinda fancy electric needle guns, right?"

He got a faraway look in his eye. "*Pues, sí.* I 'member I go one time with de e'sheep to Puerto Rico. We go over an' visit de old *boricua*, El Indio. Got de big place in *Calle Luna* where he mek de tattoo with electric ma-cheen, she go *zzzzzz, como dentista.* He can do it one big tattoo in meybe ten minute only, whole thing finish. . . . But, I dunno, meybe it don' look so good."

There it was. A clue. It wasn't the tools, but the artist that made a difference. I thought back to tattooing Pepe, starting out with slow, plodding baby steps. If I could make a passable tattoo my first time by hand, I could surely learn. I might even get the electric tools and become a real tattoo artist someday. It was all about believing. Attitude.

I sat back, drinking, thinking how good it would be to learn a craft and get good at it; to travel the world with a talent and a trade. I'd been living off my wits my whole life, and I'd been pretty lucky so far. This tattoo thing was becoming an obsession. Now there was even a pool hall full of paying guinea pigs. An omen?

And there was always the lure of the port, the big ships. I sensed the answer lay at sea. Maybe Rio, maybe Hong Kong, who knew? But that was the beauty of it. Life was a random roll of the dice. Anything could happen. I had prospects. I had dreams, and I didn't care to know the future. Looking across the table at Pepe, it just felt good to be alive, with a little money in my pocket, with a friend and a drink and a dream.

We fell into an easy silence, sipping our beers and watching the dancers sway to the music.

After a while, the melodies began slowing down. The lively crowd started to thin. Then, abruptly, bright outdoor lights came on.

Pepe stood. I followed him into the ballroom. The place was already almost empty. The last few people were straggling out toward the exit. The musicians were packing up their gear on the empty stage. A few men were standing around chatting near the bandstand as we walked past.

On impulse, I strode over to where the bandleader stood to one side, talking with an older guy in a suit jacket.

"*Con permiso.* Excuse me for bothering you." I smiled. "I just wanted to tell you, I really enjoyed the music. Thank you for coming to Veracruz to play."

He smiled back, automatically, but warmly. "*Muchas gracias, amigo!*" He shook my hand. "I am bery happy ju like de show."

That was it. I walked away, still thinking of my father, how many hands of anonymous fans he must have had to shake like that.

Pepe put his arm around my shoulder. "Wha' ju e'say him?"

What did I say? Nothing. I went over because it was the right thing to do, to compliment an artist. I suspected most people didn't bother. "I just thanked him for the music, Pepe, that's all."

"Yea-aah? An' wha' he e'say ju?"

"*Nada.*" I shrugged. "He just said 'thank you,' *pendejo!*"

Pepe looked back with mock outrage. "*Cómo?* He call ju a *pendejo?*"

"No!" I laughed. "I called *you* '*pendejo,*' *pendejo!* He just said '*gracias.*'"

"So he thank ju for call me a '*pendejo*'? These focking *pendejo!*"

As we stood joking around, I imagined the bandleader watching us. Just another pair of obnoxious drunks. Maybe he'd think we were making fun of him, calling him a *pendejo.* Maybe it was incidents like this that had turned my father sour on music.

"We better get outta here before they throw us out." I laughed.

"Pssssh! Hah! I gonna kick their assssh, ho ho!" Pepe slurred, imitating a drunken sailor.

"I'll kick your asshhh!" I laughed. "Right in the asshh, *pendejo!*"

People stared at us as we hit the street, cackling like schoolboys.

28. RED-LIGHT NIGHT

A mild tropical breeze was blowing in off the gulf as we stood by the seawall outside the dance hall, watching the young couples stroll past, arm in arm.

"So much de pretty *chicas* here." Pepe grinned. "Mek me feel, how ju e'say? Horny. Yass-ss! I am in de mood for *love*, ho ho. *Oye*, Joni, let's go now an' rent some poo'sy! *Vámonos!*"

I liked the way it sounded. Nice and easy, like renting a car or something. I snickered at a surreal mental image of us walking into a rent-a-car place. . . . *Um, yes, ah, we'd like to rent some pussy tonight? Something without a lot of mileage.*

I was still grinning as we jumped in a waiting cab and sped off into the night. I'd seen the ever-present "girl bars" in my travels around Mexico. I'd even gone into one once, drinking with some prosperous farmers I'd hitched a ride with near Guadalajara. But the girls there had all been too fat, too old, or too ugly for me.

I thought of the street corners littered with *putas* around the seedy hotels I'd stayed in. I'd never been with a hooker, though. Not that I didn't want to. It just never happened. I'd always been too broke, too shy, or just too intimidated by the whole confusing process of paying for a fuck. But I always knew I'd have to embrace all the ways of my adopted culture. And whorehouses were a fact of Mexican life. "Good girls" didn't "do it" like back home. Sex commerce was open and easy in Mexico, no big drama. Guys went to whores without shame or disgrace to fragile male egos. It was simply a way of life.

I stared out the window as the cab sped through the sleepy downtown streets, thinking of our upcoming adventure. I felt excited, and a little nervous, wondering what kind of place we were headed to.

As if reading my mind, Pepe leaned over, grinning like a kid on his way to an amusement park. "*Oye, Joni!* These *cabaret* got plenty pretty girl. Music, drinking, an' dancing. *Pura vida, chavo!*"

Rolling into the mysterious red-light zone, I suddenly recognized the area. We were right by the downtown marketplace. But now, late at night, everything was changed. There was that weird Mexican duality; a sense of hidden worlds just beneath the surface.

The familiar neighborhood was another city now, a winking, blinking, nocturnal metropolis with another sort of merchandise; a flip side to the *mercado's* normal daytime incarnation of crowded eateries and busy alleys bustling with activity and commerce. This was the seedy side. And I liked it.

We paid the cabby and got out. The usual bustling shops and market stalls were all locked down. Little hotels I'd never noticed before were all lit up with glowing red neon. Girls in miniskirts and heels lined the corners around busy taco carts. A smell of grilled onions, chiles, lime, roasting meat, and cilantro filled the humid air in great billows of smoke. On a corner by a little open-air eatery, people crowded around a food counter. Others sat at plastic tables on the sidewalk, eating, drinking, and talking. Salsa music blasted from a pair of big radio speakers.

"*Aquí!*" Pepe led the way. We sat down at an empty table. A girl came over and we ordered *tortas* and beers.

I sat watching the street as Pepe talked. In the *zona*, he explained, there were certain unwritten codes. This place was a sort of neutral ground. The lines were clearly defined, I noticed, but they seemed to blur a little, too. I sensed a loosely controlled chaos around us; that odd sense of shadowy double meanings and unspoken customs lurking in the trembling night air. There was a subtle order to the place, where cops and other shady characters mixed comfortably with the drinkers and whores.

A small army of strolling musicians and peddlers selling the usual assortment of flowers, cigarettes, and trinkets vied for space with the omnipresent Indian kids with their little wooden boxes of hard candy and Chiclets. The most striking thing was the total absence of any sort of tension. Everything was as calm and good-natured as an afternoon at the market. I felt right at home, like on that train from Nogales, where an invisible veil was lifted and I saw a new world revealed. I smiled at Pepe, knowing I'd be spending a lot more time in places like this.

As if reading my thoughts, my friend nodded toward a red neon doorway across the way. "See it de *cabaret* there? Got too much pretty young *chicas* inside. You go an' drink, talk with de girl, ju know? Is, how e'say, de all-night girl. Girl cost more mo-ney, bar charge more commission to girl. Girl charge more to ju. Or meybe ju jus' wan' go with de e'street *chica. Más fácil tal vez. . . .* "

I followed his eye across the street. One of the "easy" street girls lined up in front of a cheap hotel was looking pretty good to me.

"Ju like de one there?" Pepe winked. "These *chamacas* lot more cheaper than *cabaret* girl. No drink, no talk, just pay twenny peso an' go upstair. *Boom boom!* But no tek too much time, *chingón*, cuz she only for de short-time *boom-boom*, fifteen minute an' Game Over, she back outside, wait nex' guy."

It appealed to me. Quick, easy: wham, bam, thank you, ma'am. I grinned. "You gonna go too, Pepe? I already see one for me."

"No, *'mano*, is okey. I wait ju here. When ju finish, meybe we go de next bar for drink. *Ándale chingón!*"

Sounded good to me. I was up for a nice easy fuck, without all the mind-bending complex emotional rituals I'd grown up with in the "Free Love" sixties. If those fucking flower children had been Mexican, they'd have called it "Free Sex." What the fuck did love have to do with it? I'd had plenty of free sex back home. But love, well, that part had never been free. Not with all the drama, heartache, and gnashing of teeth that came with it. My fondest adolescent sex memories were of many one-night stands. Love had not been kind to me. The girls I'd been closest to had either disgusted me or betrayed me, like Silvia and Suzanna, or died on me, like Ellen. I looked forward to just getting laid and walking off into the night a free man, without a knife in my fucking heart.

I downed my beer. Pepe slapped me on the back as I stood up, eyeing a slender teenage girl in a tight black miniskirt and shiny black boots. I crossed the street, feeling like a horny cartoon wolf, focused on her short skirt and knee-high boots. All I had to do was walk over and in a minute I'd be fucking her. Just like that. No polite conversation, no foreplay, no bullshit; just instant sex, like a wet dream. Easy.

I ambled up and grinned, nodding to the hotel. *"Vámonos?"*

Her eyes darted away as a girlish voice floated over my head in a bored, mechanical drone. *"Veinte. Por adelantado."* Twenty. Up front.

No mincing words. Kind of bitchy. I liked that.

As I reached in my pocket her hand came up like a stop sign. *"Aquí no!"* She scowled. *"Ju pay upstair. Sígueme."*

She strode over to the door and went in. I followed that bouncing ass up a short flight of stairs. As we reached the top, I was already hard.

She stopped at a desk where a fat man sat reading a comic. He glanced up with an air of boredom and handed her a towel and a tiny bar of soap. He scribbled something into a ledger and went back to his comic. Without a word, she clip-clopped down a hallway and opened a flimsy little wooden door.

Inside, she set the soap and towel on a table by a sink. *"Veinte."* She held her hand out, palm up. No purse.

She took the twenty-peso note, folded it in half, and slipped it in her boot. Then she sat on the edge of the bed and motioned me over.

"Quítate los pantalones." She ordered me to take my pants off, casual as a barber. Feeling a little self-conscious, I left my shorts on.

Without ceremony, she yanked them down and inspected me for sores. Her hands were cold as she gave it a couple of businesslike squeezes. After the perfunctory prick-check, she sat back on the bed and hiked up her skirt. No underwear.

As I stood there with my dick in my hand, our eyes met for the first time. She looked away quickly and stared at the wall. She settled back against the headboard, spreading her legs, her boot heels resting on the bedspread. My cock led the way, an eager dog straining at a leash as I knelt on the bed, looking into her unsmiling eyes.

Without a word, she reached down and put it in. The cunt felt good, tighter than the hotel girl's, harder—in a blank sort of way.

As I started working it in and out, she stared over my shoulders at the ceiling fan. Then she let out a cold, mechanical "sexy" moan. *"Aí, papi. Así me gusta. Dámelo!"*

It sounded so ridiculous, so insincere and corny, I almost burst out laughing. I tried to kiss her, mostly to shut her up.

Her body tensed up. She turned her head. "*No! Besos no!* No kiss! An' don' touch me!"

Oops! I must have violated some unwritten whore code. I backed off and she relaxed. She didn't speak again, so I put it in deeper. Looking down at her skinny boot-clad legs spread-eagled against the bedspread, the absurdity of it struck me; this bitchy little whore, bullying me with a cold, professional manner, as if to keep the upper hand somehow by limiting my movements—the only power she had.

It was crazy, a young girl lying on a bed, getting screwed by a total stranger for the price of a burrito, but still acting like she was in charge. There it was again—that weird Mexican duality. No matter what she said or did to minimize it, she was getting fucked—the ultimate submission.

It was unlike any sex I'd had before, essential and raw, stripped of all the hypocrisy of courting, all the sad, shameful little head games, whispered cries and lies, eternal vows and broken promises of that great four-letter word, Love. All those pathetic little romantic mating rituals were suddenly reduced to dust in the cold, stony totem glare of this stark act of benign violence.

That's why the short-time girl didn't want to be kissed or touched, I realized, only fucked, as if to say: *Let's get it straight. This is a simple business transaction. Love is something else. You can rent my pussy, but that's all you get for your twenty pesos. I get no pleasure from you. I find you neither attractive nor repulsive. This is my job, and these are my boundaries.*

I respected her honesty—all but one thing: that mechanical *"aí, papi!"* That tainted the whole thing. Why the lame pretense?

For all her businesslike straightforwardness, the short-time girl was a hypocrite, too. She was no better than anyone else. How could a simple animal act like fucking mean so many fucked-up, confusing things to so many fucked-up, confused people?

Humping away like a happy dog, I checked my Timex. Fourteen minutes. Showtime. I deposited a long, emotionless load deep inside that confusing little rented snatch, and rolled off.

She leapt up and moved to the sink. As she stood washing my lonesome seed from her crotch, I reached for my pants. She turned with a toneless *"adiós"* and was gone. Before I had my socks on, her clacking high heels were echoing off down the hallway.

As I sat back down at the table, Pepe checked his watch. *"Veinte minutos."* He grinned. *"Campión de la chingada!* Prize: One beer!" He shoved a fresh Superior across to me, raising his bottle in a toast to the girls lined up across the way. My girl was already back at her post, leaning against the wall with the others.

We finished our beers and walked off.

As we passed, I glanced at the short-time girl, wondering if I should nod or smile or something.

She just stared straight ahead, like a storefront dummy.

29. DREAMS

The *cabaret* was a whole different deal: A loud, festive whorehouse. After paying ten pesos each, we were frisked by a burly thug in a crisp black suit. Another hefty bouncer held the door open.

Inside, thatched palm fronds covered the roof. Red neon tubes ran along walls strung with blinking lights, tinsel, and colorful paper flowers. Couples and groups of men sat at little round bar tables littered with bottles. Pretty young *chicas* outnumbered the men, three to one.

A small combo was grinding out a jumping *merengue* on a tiny dance floor where a few very drunk guys dragged their rented dates around. Everyone seemed to be having a pretty good time.

We sat at an empty table in the middle of the room, right next to a larger table of giggling *chicas*. We called for beers and settled back in our seats. Girls, girls, girls! I looked around, grinning like a kid on a Ferris wheel.

Pepe poked me. *"Eii, Joni, check de girls on de next table, de two chamacas sitting together there, que tal?"*

I glanced over at the two young chicks. They were big-boned and squat, like most Mexican girls. But they had friendly, girlish faces, and they weren't ugly. I gauged their ages to be somewhere between sixteen and twenty-five—probably closer to sixteen. It was hard to tell, as they were covered in makeup, and both had that ephemeral, ageless whore quality. They seemed friendly enough, in contrast to the grumpy little short-time girl. If this was going to be an all-night party, either one would do. I nodded.

"*Órale!*" Pepe smiled. "I gonna tell de *mesero* we wan' buy de two a drink, okey? Then he gonna bring 'em over for sit with us."

As I nodded and grinned, a big glassy-eyed drunk in a cowboy hat who'd been eyeing us from across the room strode up to our table.

He stood over me, glowering. "Hey, ju, *pinche gabacho!* Wha' ju wan' in here, ehh?"

The obnoxious prick had obviously worn out his welcome with the girls. Now he was looking to pick a fight. Great. I hated being called *gabacho* or *gringo*. It was the worst insult you could hit me with. Sure, I was a foreigner, but I always tried not to look or act like one, and I wasn't in the mood for some drunken farmer's bullying insults.

Half in the bag myself, I let him know all about it.

"*Gabacho es quien chingó tu puta madre, hijo de puta!*" I growled, rising to my feet before Pepe could stop me.

Hearing me call his mother a whore in flawless Mexican slang must have taken the cowboy by surprise. A shadow of hesitation flashed across his dull-witted face.

I shot him a fast, hard right hook to the belly. As he doubled over his beer-inflated gut, I grabbed his shoulders and shot my knee into his face, knocking him backwards, flat on his ass. I moved in and kicked him once in the ribs, short and hard, for good measure.

A couple of bouncers rushed over and grabbed me from behind. Another pair of stocky guys in suits hustled my victim out the door as a heated debate ensued between Pepe and the others.

The guy holding me let me loose and spun me around, snarling in my face. "*Ya basta!* Ju gonna behave now, eh?"

Pepe was pleading with the well-dressed one. "*Mira, jefe, no hay problema.* We only come in here for fun, no wan' any troubles. *Ese pinche pendejo. . . .* " He pointed to the door. "He come over here an' insult my frien', *así fue todo!*"

"It's the truth!" I cut in. "I'm sorry for the trouble, boss."

The bouncer rubbed his chin. Pepe sealed the deal, handing him a fifty-peso note and even inviting him for a drink. Attitude.

The boss pocketed the cash and laughed. They shook hands, and the other bouncers drifted off. "Just keep one eye on ju *compañero*." He turned, gesturing at me.

Pepe grinned and we sat again. "*Por favor!*" He whistled to a waiter and handed him a few pesos. The guy smiled, nodded, and went over to speak to the two giggling girls at the next table.

My friend turned to me, resting a gentle hand on my shoulder. "Joni, ju got too much *huevos*, but ju gotta tek it easy. Hold ju temper, cuz one day she gonna make to ju some *problema, sabes?*"

"Whatever." I shrugged. "That fat pig had it comin'! I wasn't bothering nobody. Who told him to start some shit with me?"

Pepe gave me a patient look. "*Mira*, Joni, I don' care wha' ju do. I e'say to ju these as de frieng. You no gotta all de time fight de peoples, so tek it easy, maing. *Pendejo* like these guy in every bar. Why only ju de *cabrón* wan' get up an' fight? For why? Some e'stupid *pendejo boracho?* Get wise, 'mano. De life she too e'short. Why ju wan' mek even more shorter, eh? Maybe e'stupid *pendejo* wan' come back wit' de big cowboy gun an' shoot ju, *bum!* Then ju dead! Game over! Then ju finish, like de short-time *puta*. You wan' dead in some *pinche burdel? Para qué?*"

I knew he was right, but I couldn't leave it. "That *pendejo* couldn't afford a drink!" I sucked my teeth. "Let alone a gun!"

"*Y qué?*" Pepe rolled his eyes. "These no my point, *hermano*."

I nodded, backing down. "You're right, brother. *Me perdóna*."

"You don' got apologize for me, Joni." He shook his head. "Meybe I do e'same like ju, *quién sabe?* But I watch ju sometime, an' I think ju too much e'smart for fight all de time wit' de peoples. Ju think about it, *va?* Save ju balls for more better thing."

He flashed a big grin at the two chicks standing by our table with the waiter now, snickering like naughty schoolgirls on a blind date.

Pepe pulled up chairs, and they sat. "We watch ju beat that *pendejo!*" The girl planted a humid little kiss on my cheek. "*Bien hecho!* Ees good t'ing they put dees *cabrón* out. All de night, him bother every girl, an' never buy no drinks for us, *pinche maricón!*"

The other girl was already snuggling up beside Pepe as he slipped an arm around her. We had a couple of drinks, then got up for a slow dance. My date pressed close to me on the dance floor.

Nice. Nothing like the hostile little short-time girl.

Finally, we called for a bottle of Bacardi and some soda waters. To go. Now, Pepe winked, we'd take the party to a hotel. My girl slid up against me. I wrapped my arm around her waist, and off we went.

○   ○   ○

The shabby-looking little fuck hotel turned out to be a modern, clean oasis inside. The air conditioning was already going full blast as we stepped into our room. It was a lot bigger than the ratty little short-time hovel, with two large beds, a color television, and a radio with speakers built into the wall. Luxury by the hour.

I kicked off my boots and looked out a big picture window overlooking the darkened *mercado* as our dates disappeared into the bathroom together, giggling.

Pepe busied himself pouring out glasses of rum and Coke, and I dimmed the lights and turned on the radio. Lighting cigarettes from a fresh pack of Dunhills, we sat back on our beds like millionaire playboys, sipping our drinks.

The girls came out, still giggling. Pepe led his date to the bed. He handed her a drink. She kicked off her heels and cozied up beside him. I saw him taking her shirt off. I leaned over and kissed my date. Working my tongue around in her willing mouth, I fumbled to remove her skimpy clothes. This was more like it.

The room filled with the sounds of sex, as the low TV dialogue blended with the radio music and the steady hum of the air conditioner. As I pushed it deep inside my girl, I glanced over at Pepe and his date in the next bed. It was like some weird syncopated mirror image.

The sex was easy and fun, if not sensational. But sex was like food, I figured. Even if it's not the greatest meal, it's still pretty good when you're hungry. And I'd been hungry for a long time.

The girl hung in like she was born for it. After getting my money's worth for an hour or so, I could feel her pussy drying up. Pepe and his date were already passed out in a twisted jumble of bedclothes as I shot my second load of the night into my obliging little partner. I curled up beside her like a cat, listening to her breathing as it turned to a light snore, luring me down, down, into a hazy, air-conditioned sleep.

The dreams were overpowering and surreal. Recalling my old childhood delirium nightmares, they were visions from a chilling other dimension, a haunting, missing piece from a bizarre jigsaw puzzle.

о   о   о

I dreamt I was sitting in the hotel's courtyard with Pepe, Ramón, Memo, and some others. It was late at night. A group of strangers had just arrived by train. Through a dusty haze, I spotted a big well I'd never seen before, right in the center of the courtyard.

As I walked over, a tiny demon scurried out of the gaping pit. The ominous little creature was black and shiny, all covered in a dark prehistoric oily sheen. No one seemed to notice the silent figure rising from below, a somber, haunted, tormented being.

The hairs stood up on my neck as it shot into the hazy air above. I looked up, and the night sky was swarming with bat-like clusters of howling, malevolent entities.

Someone was shouting. "*Los demonios!* Don't look!"

Horrified, I turned to the people. "Does anybody have a Bible?"

One of the strangers motioned me over to the hotel's front desk. It was suddenly the ticket counter of the dusty old train station in Nogales, where I'd first begun my journey into Mexico.

The man handed me an ancient, dusty tome. He grabbed my arm, staring into my eyes. "Look to this book as a bible, *guerrero!* It's the only thing you will ever need to expel the demons."

I opened the book and flipped through its brittle yellow parchment. Staring at the unfamiliar type on the pages, I realized it was a dictionary, filled with unfamiliar words in an unknown language.

Baffled, I turned back to the courtyard. A small group of people had gathered in a corner. I pushed through the crowd to see what they were all looking at.

Some terrible operation was being performed on someone by one of the strangers, a scruffy longhaired pirate I hadn't noticed before. His gaunt, shirtless torso was covered in odd occult tattoo marks. The waxy figure was a leather-draped, animated skeleton, reminiscent of the dusty human mummies I'd seen in cavernous catacombs in northern Mexico. He moved with mechanical slow-motion precision, as if underwater, as he tattooed one of the other strangers. In place of needles, though, he wielded a worn wood-handled knife, like the ones used by shoemakers at the *mercado*. With practiced motions, he began gouging out big chunks of the other's bloodless flesh, and carefully inserting polished turquoise gemstones into the gaping holes.

As he sat carving into the other's body in that haunting primal rite, I pictured a vulture, rending carrion from a rotting corpse. Watching the morbid ritual, fascinated and repulsed, I was unable to look away, just like in the terrible nightmares of my childhood.

○   ○   ○

Coming awake with a start, I sat up in the hotel bed, shaking in a cold sweat. Reaching over the girl's sleeping form, I lit a cigarette and sat smoking in the air-conditioned darkness, surrounded by the snoring bodies of my companions.

After a while, I staggered over to the window and watched a distant pink dawn forming over the gray, tomb-like edifices of the deserted marketplace.

As I stood there, stupefied, contemplating my dream, it began to take on the portent of an epiphany; a prelude to what I suddenly knew with great certainty would be the course of my life. The conviction was like a ship floating on uncharted waters beyond the horizon, a firm knowing of what waited for me out there: a sure, true, inflexible destiny. Try as I might to dodge it, the only exorcism from the demons of my past would be via the written word. And just as surely, I realized, tattooing would be the vehicle by which my path would be shaped, as precisely as the hand of that animated mummified pirate carving codes of mystery and magic into the other stranger's inanimate flesh.

Shaken, perplexed, and groggy, I craved sleep like a drug. I dropped the cigarette into an empty Coke bottle and settled into the bed beside the sleeping girl. Her warm body felt solid and alive. I pressed my back against hers, taking comfort in the closeness of the sleeping naked stranger. I pulled the sheets up over my head.

Feeling safe from those dark, oily, fitful demons, I dropped off the ledge of consciousness into a deep, dreamless slumber.

30. THE MORNING AFTER

I awakened to the sound of Pepe singing in the shower. Paralyzed by waves of nausea, I turned in the bed. The girl was gone. I lay still under the rumpled sheet, gauging the degree of my hangover, not daring to move. As waking life took shape, I stared at a patch of sunlight on a wall, dumbly piecing together the night's events. Feeling like a rusty bucket of cold, trembling worms, my brain slithered into a familiar morning-after paranoia. Shadows of dread marched like storm troopers across the bloody battlefield of my mind.

With my friend's cheerful voice echoing from the open bathroom door, some merciful trick of gravity pried my aching carcass from the bed. Feeling raw and nervous, I crept over to the window and parted the curtains, a tissue-thin veil to a sickly empire of fear. I stood in my underwear, staring out at the silent streets. Through the cool tinted glass, everything looked bleak and deserted out there, surreal.

My gut was an empty pit of horror, my mouth dry and bitter as I surveyed the shabby landscape of a devastated war zone. I had a sudden overwhelming impression that a sinister curse was upon the earth. It was like some terrible extension of the night's creepy dream, projected onto the outside world. Every sordid detail of those empty, desolate streets troubled my soul. Nothing moved, not a car, a cat, or a solitary human figure, none of the usual bustling activity of those lively, chaotic downtown streets. Nothing. It was too quiet!

A deathly little jumping bean of panic was rattling around in my gut. Something wasn't right! *Oh, God!* Another wave of terror gripped my heart in a madman's clutch. My nightmares had come to life! Everything was filth and poverty, stagnant dirt and decay. I could feel the Curse breathing down my neck.

I lit another cigarette with trembling fingers and stood there, smoking, staring out the window, a miserable, condemned soul. My stomach was squirming like a dying rodent as I watched a flock of dirty rat-gray pigeons alight on the roof of the deserted *mercado*. My eyes followed a tangle of bare electrical wires down the walls of the weathered old structure—a hellish mirror of my psychic landscape. Bleak. Confusing. Ugly. Dreadful. Wrong.

Pepe's singing snapped me out of it. My trembling breath relaxed as I suddenly realized that, *shit*, it was just another Sunday morning! That's all, the *mercado* was closed for the Sabbath, God's official day of rest. The world hadn't ended!

Thank Christ! Just another sleepy Sunday in sleepy old Veracruz. I was going to make it! *Thank you, Jesus!*

I slid open the big double windows. A warm, septic wind engulfed me like a giant mouth. As the shabby tropical heat of the living world penetrated my frigid bones, the familiar smell of rotting garbage, raw sewage, and dust was an alluring perfume.

Just then, Pepe emerged from the bathroom grinning, a towel wrapped around his waist. His voice filled the room with his big-hearted exuberance. *"Buenos días, cabrón!* Ju pass out like cadaver all de morning. *Aí, que noche!* Is lucky t'ing we no rich mans, *chingón*, or we gonna be finish in one month!"

"What happened to the *chicas?*"

"'Mano, they talking so loud, I wake up fast an' give 'em de money so they can go. An' ju e'stay all de time e'sleep like a mummy."

I shuddered inwardly at his ironic choice of words, remembering my dream as the hangover tugged at my guts again.

I forced a painful smile. "Shit, Pepe, I didn't know what day it was till a minute ago."

"Wha' day? Ha! Is de beautiful sunny Sunday, *'manito!*" He howled. "Now we gonna go de *playa*, e'sleep in de big chair by de *piscina*, get de beer an' e'shrimp *cóctel*, an' e'swim in de sea, *que tal?*"

Despite my pounding head, I found myself nodding, grinning back at the most positive person I'd ever known.

"Okey!" Pepe was bustling around the room, taking charge again, booting me out of my stupor. "Ju go e'shower now, wash de old pussy from ju balls, ho ho. *Vuelve a la vida, cabrón!* Come back to de life now. *Vamos, ándale, chingón!*"

I knew better than to argue with Pepe. Pepe was life.

The lukewarm sulfury shower water flowed over my head, a vital healing elixir.

We were going to the beach, and that was that.

◦ ◦ ◦

As the rickety old taxi rattled through the dusty backstreets of the old Negro *barrio*, La Huaca, I stared out the window. How I loved Veracruz, I mused as we passed a row of tin-roofed wooden shacks. Those houses seemed to embody a special intangible poetry. Something ethereal and magical lay embedded in their humble weatherbeaten façades, their faded blue and green paint plastered with rusty advertising signs. One strong wind would blow those meek little dwellings right down into the banana trees clustered around them.

It seemed as if we were passing through a dream. I could feel tears welling up in my eyes. Or maybe it was just the hangover.

As we turned onto the seaside boulevard and rolled along the sparkling waters of the Gulf, I marveled at the passing scenery. I'd known from my first day in Veracruz that this heroic old port would be a gateway to the far-off places I'd long dreamed of. There was always a strange unseen connection to mystical other dimensions just beyond my perception. Veracruz was a true port; a portal, a magical time warp of extrasensory glimpses into hidden realms, where ghosts of Mother Africa and the Caribbean dwelled in her ethereal shadows. I could feel that familiar longing for the fabled cities and jungles of South America, the fertile green hills and sparkling blue waters of Rio.

"Mira, cabrón!" Pepe's voice crashed into my daydreams. "They already e'start de *preparos* for de *Carnaval.*"

He gestured out the window, reminding me that in less than a week visitors from all over Mexico and Central America would be sitting right there, enjoying the colorful Carnaval parades of Salsa bands and Afro-Cuban drum sections.

All along the scruffy beachfront road, ragged workers in straw hats labored under the blazing sun; men, women, and children, unloading planks of rough-cut lumber from sagging pickups and mule-drawn carts. Gearing up for the coming festivities, onlookers sat drinking at makeshift tables on the sidewalks, as an army of carpenters hammered at platforms and bleachers, climbing rickety wooden ladders and stringing lights around the shabby whitewashed coconut palms.

The car pulled to a stop at an intersection, where a small crowd was dancing to a rehearsing samba band. The spirit of *Carnaval* was in the air. Drums pounded as people spilled out into the street, shuffling their sandy, thong-clad feet to the rhythms.

I took a deep breath and closed my watery eyes, propelled through time and space to visions of Rio de Janeiro, a sparkling dreamscape of mystical intrigue. I pictured Orfeu, descending a lush green tropical hillside, surrounded by costumed revelers.

Hypnotized by the drumbeats, I could feel the spontaneous joy of ordinary people celebrating the marvelous treasure of life through the sensuous miracle of *Carnaval,* a vibrant triumph of the human spirit, where for one brief week, maybe even I might be able to forget the oily jet-black demons haunting the dark hallways of my mind.

31. BLACKBIRDS

"BLACKBIRD SINGING IN THE DEAD OF NIGHT, TAKE THESE BROKEN WINGS AND LEARN TO FLY."

—PAUL MCCARTNEY

We sped around twists and turns of deserted road, through coconut groves, and down onto a tree-lined gravel path leading to the shabby old beach club of Mocambo. Arriving at a ramshackle wooden gate, we got out of the taxi and strolled around.

The overgrown grounds were dominated by a gigantic blue swimming pool, peppered with little concrete islands. Worn fiberglass beach chairs and creaky wooden tables sat, mostly empty, under white-washed palms. Weedy footpaths led to a palm-thatched bar, where locals sat eating shrimp dishes under slow-moving ceiling fans. White-jacketed waiters bustled around, carrying drinks and food to the poolside tables.

Out by the choppy Gulf waters, *músicos* in worn straw hats patrolled the beach like scruffy angels, lugging their big wooden harps. Underwear-clad families lolled in the dark sands littered with dead fish, coconut husks, beer bottles, and fly-infested shrimp carcasses. Sad-faced horses and burros shuffled along the murky brown foam as their ragged owners hawked greasy snacks and drinks.

We handed a few coins to a bored-looking woman with rough indigenous features. She pointed us to a run down locker room where we stripped to our underwear. Emerging like weary gladiators, we wandered the grounds some more. Finally we took a couple of beach chairs in a quiet, shady spot by the pool facing the sea, where the warm sea breeze lulled me into a comfortable stupor.

As I lay back like a lizard on a rock, sweating out the demons, I thought how a guy could easily doze his life away in a spot like that. Maybe that was all I needed, I mused, a tropical poolside retreat, a cool drink, and a long, lazy season in the sun to heal my road-battered soul.

Drifting in and out of that languid dream state, oblivious to everything but the heat and the oneness of the moment, I fell into a deep, peaceful, dreamless slumber.

An hour later, I awakened, covered in sweat. After a cooling plunge in the deep blue pool, I went back to the chair. Pepe and I sat in silence for the rest of the day, drinking rum from chilled coconuts, peeling bright red shrimps, and drifting in and out of a glorious stupor, lulled by the distant, birdlike screams of splashing children.

As shadows from the blackbird-chattering palms grew long, I rose up and stretched in the golden late-afternoon light. The noisy families were all gone, packed like cattle into their broken-down cars. I watched the cocky little black scavenger birds picking at scraps on abandoned tables and flying to the pool in a great swarming flash of fluttering wings. Their lusty chatter shifted from wolf whistles to baby cries as they mimicked cats, unmuffled cars, and even the crackling rustle of wind in the palms. All the sounds of Veracruz came alive in their sweet, haunting birdsongs.

I sat back and smiled, hypnotized by the frantic beating of their sleek shiny black wings against the water. I'd always loved those crazy little blackbirds. Nobody else seemed to notice their melodic chattering whistles calling out in the tropical winds. To me, they were the perfect soundtrack to the tropics, living extensions of their lush weatherbeaten home. I wondered if their magical birdsong was one of the indescribable little Somethings that made that old sailor at the *mercado* tell Pepe that Veracruz would always be his home port. I wondered if he missed them when he was away at sea, even as the lure of Rio beckoned. I wondered if others longed for their ethereal chatter after they left Veracruz. I knew I would.

At day's end, we strolled over to the restaurant for a final beer. The tables were mostly empty now. The waiters stood in the back, listening to a soccer match on a little radio.

I noticed a group of distinguished, rail-thin old mulattos sitting at a neighboring table, wearing the traditional guayaberas of the tropics. The cool ease of their presence struck a fond chord in my heart. There was something timeless and mystical in their proud, regal bearing. They looked otherworldly, like spirits. Somehow I sensed they were musicians, from Cuba.

I needed to know more. *"Son cubanos?"* I whispered.

Pepe nodded. I kept staring. They had an air of royalty about them, cool and classy.

"Músicos?" I wondered aloud.

"Salseros, sí, claro. Prob'ly they come for play in de Carnaval dance. *Los jarochos aquí son locos por la pachanga cubana."*

La pachanga cubana. At his mention of that exotic rhythmic blend of primal African beats, cool Iberian melody, and lively *latino* swing, I felt the lure of Cuba. I'd always longed to visit that nearby island country, so shrouded in legend, mystery, and history.

I took a deep breath, suddenly feeling very small and ignorant. How did Veracruz come to feel so much like I imagined her fabled sister city, Havana? What made her so different from the rest of Mexico? What gave her people their unique, jaunty Caribbean rhythm? Her mysteries haunted, baffled, and enchanted me, like the magical songs of her lively little tropical blackbirds.

My eyes drifted to where the *cubanos* sat like Mafia dons, and my mind flashed back to a long-ago night, standing in the back of a dark little jazz club with O'Connell, tripping on acid and watching, spellbound, as John Coltrane's quartet wove their supernatural musical spells, like magicians, carrying me away to another dimension. That had been a milestone moment, I knew, where an invisible veil had been pulled from my eyes, giving me a glimpse of pure magic.

One of the old Cubans noticed me staring. As our eyes met, he smiled like the sun. I stood up, walked over, and shook his cool, leathery hand. The others rose and shook my hand in turn. Meeting those guys was a déjà vu vision of some mystical other world to which there was no definition, no explanation, no conclusion.

Without a word, I returned to our table and sat. Pepe got up and walked over. No questions, no conversation, just a respectful handshake and another quick exchange of smiles.

As we stood to leave, I thought of their vibrant Caribbean rhythms, a backdrop to revolutions, poverty, hard times, and hope. Stepping into the courtyard where a couple of taxis waited in the shade, I could still hear the echo of shiny mulatto fingertips drumming on the tabletop as they sat arranging their soft Caribbean spells, an inscrutable language of steamy tropical night.

As we got in the cab, their ghostly Cuban Spanish blended with the sweet silvery chatter of the blackbirds.

o   o   o

"My mentors when I was a young player were these old black cats up in Harlem." Artie sits back in his chair, reminiscing. "Those were the guys I always looked up to in music, the ones who gave me my respect for jazz. A bunch of old black players. I wasn't cut out for the business end of it, though. I respected the music, but I couldn't stand the fucking public, man. . . . "

Cigano stares at his father. "Why's that, Artie?"

"Because they sabotage your fucking career by not allowing you to do what you need to do artistically. That's why I got out of the band business. The audience would not allow me to do what I wanted, and I sure as hell wasn't gonna do what *they* wanted me to do. I could give 'em a little of that, sure. I kept playing 'Begin the Beguine' and 'Stardust' for 'em in order to pay the rent. But I wanted to do other things, innovative stuff. And they just wouldn't have it. So I split."

"It's funny." Cigano rubs his chin. "That's probably the same reason I'm thinking I gotta get out of the tattoo business. . . . "

"No question about it," Artie nods.

"Sometimes I wish these people could leave me a hunk of skin overnight, and just lemme do some really great artwork on it, then come pick it up in the morning, like a dry-cleaner or something."

"Well, the logical thing would be to paint on canvas."

"I do, Artie!" Cigano glares at the old man, feeling a stab of irritation. "I been painting for years, just to keep my sanity. God knows ya can't make a living at it. That's why I've hadda stay with the tattooing. Most of these tattoo people don't know shit from real art, they just want their colorful little ego trophies. It's all about feeding people's vanity, that's what pays the rent." He snorts.

"But I never painted for money. I do it for the freedom of just being able to make my own art without a bunch of ignorant jimooks breathing down my fuggin' neck. . . .   I had that big art gallery show a few months ago, remember? You were invited, y'know. . . . " He frowns, remembering how his father had never even bothered to go.

"Well, I was *busy* that night, Jonathan!" Artie growls. "Jesus! Whaddya want from me?"

"Nothing, Artie." Cigano sighs. "I don't want anything. Just thought ya might be curious to see my work, that's all."

"Yeah, well, do what ya gotta do, kid, but you can't ever get away from it, no matter how many galleries you show at, see? 'Cause you're a tattoo artist. You're already labeled as that. That's what you're known for. That's all they want. You can't change it. Too late."

"Well, I've had some success with tattooing, sure, but that don't mean I can't start over and do just as good at something else. I'm more interested in writing these days. I been working on a book, y'know——"

"Doing good, hah!" His father cuts him off. "What's the point? Too much success will ruin you." Artie sneers. "I keep telling people that. But failure's a hard thing for people to live with. We live in a society that puts a dishonorable connotation on what it sees as failure."

"Well, I think it's cause this culture measures success by the size of your bank account, not the integrity of your work."

"Yeah, well, people need to get rid of all these hang-ups they've been taught. They hammer it into you since you're a kid! What are you gonna 'be' when you grow up? That wonderful line in *The Graduate,* when the kid comes out of college. This businessman, he comes to the kid's graduation, he says, 'I just want to say one word to you: Plastics.' So that's your life, man. Plastic. Make a lot of money and get a big house, buy a big car, and have a lot of kids who come home from the dentist with good checkups. That's American life, man. Toothpaste. We're based on this shit. And we buy it. All those cars out there on that freeway." The old man gestures toward the window. "Ya know why they all don't just run amok and kill each other out there?"

"Why? Tell me, Artie. Why don't they kill each other?"

"'Cause they don't wanna dent their fucking fenders, that's why."

Cigano laughs so hard, he begins to cry.

32. LA PARROQUIA

Back at the hotel, lukewarm water washed over my head as I showered, getting ready for the next adventure. I hurried into clean clothes and rushed downstairs, excited at Pepe's idea of going to the stately old landmark coffee house, La Parroquia. My friend was already waiting out on the sidewalk, dressed for the occasion in a navy blue guayabera and white loafers. Attitude.

La Parroquia. I'd passed the bustling air-conditioned gathering place almost daily now for months. But, knowing a cup of coffee there would cost more than a good meal at the *mercado,* I'd never dared to venture inside. Now, with enough money to live on for weeks, and feeling confident I'd finally be going off to sea soon, it was time to experience another side of Veracruz.

Approaching the seawall, the outdoor tables were jammed with foreign sailors, upscale locals, and a few Mexican tourists drinking *café lechero* from tall, thick glasses. Strolling musicians and loud marimba bands shared the sidewalk with wandering vendors as we stepped past the crowds and into another world.

The shiny yellow-tiled walls of the big café were buzzing with animated conversations, punctuated by a constant tinkling symphony of spoons on glasses. The melodic *clink-clink* of old men signaling for refills echoed like a hundred tiny church bells, an otherworldly backdrop to the luxurious chaos as we sat at a table.

Taking our order, an ancient waiter told us of a streetcar conductor who always rang his trolley's bell as he approached, announcing that he'd be stopping in for a coffee. When his casket passed on the trolley one day, the café's regulars all clinked their glasses in his honor. After that, it became a local tradition.

I sat back, looking around, watching the busboys distributing coffee and steaming milk from giant aluminum kettles, as white-jacketed waiters bustled back and forth with military precision. A battalion of other workers scurried around, cleaning ashtrays and filling glasses with ice water.

A proud altar of antique coffee machines graced a long marble counter at the rear. The whole place seemed a perfect microcosm of Veracruz's special melting-pot culture, where African slaves had worked the cane fields and shipyards, together with Italian and Cuban immigrants to the thriving old port, creating the exotic, hybrid race of modern-day *jarochos*. The very walls seemed to vibrate with a special patina of history. I gawked at the antique photographs of the old port, gateway to colonial Cuba and Spain, where flotillas of pirates had once patrolled the lazy green waters.

I grinned. "It's like a crazy little time warp in this place, all these old guys sitting around in their Sunday best. Gives you a feel of what the port musta looked like a hundred years ago."

Pepe's eyes were all lit up like a kid seeing snow for the first time. La Parroquia was the soul of another old Mexico, that odd duality lurking just beneath the surface again. Spirits of the past seemed to whisper in hushed undertones behind the busy din. History, and tales of bold under-takings, floated in the air with echoes of ghostly pirate voices as I pictured long-gone writers, poets, and intellectuals scribbling their passionate impressions of the Mexican night, smoking big Cuban cigars, and drinking strong, pungent coffee from those same antique espresso machines.

This was nothing like the rough *pueblos* and humble language of the big-hearted Mexican life I'd come to love in my travels; the quiet dignity of the tragicomic working-class *mestizo*, for whom a rough, short existence was one's only tangible earthly possession—a fleeting gift which one misplaced word or deed might extinguish like a fragile candlelight. This was another world; another facet of the complex, fascinating puzzle of Mexico.

The attentive white-haired waiter returned with our *café lecheros* on battered aluminum saucers. We sat back, drinking from the heavy glasses. Ah, Veracruz! My heart filled with an indefinable ache.

Maybe it was something in the humid rotting tropical air, or the haunting song of her bold little blackbirds that bonded me to this magical port. Perhaps it was the sense of having finally found a home here, after so many long, solitary months on the road, of knowing people and making friends, that endeared it to my soul.

As I sat there, a familiar darkness crept over my whimsical musings. Maybe I was just another restless lost soul, living a useless pipe dream, like some tragic little character from a Eugene O'Neill drama. I suddenly felt like one of his old Bowery drunks, with all my childish notions of ships and travel, writing and tattooing. Maybe all those big plans and schemes were just another pathetic fantasy, lulling me into a useless life of wandering mediocrity.

Still, I was glad for that special moment; thankful to have Pepe there, spurring me on, rattling the cage of my inertia, and reminding me that life was here and now, not some shuffling barroom dream. I knew I could easily fall into that kind of pit. But so had O'Neill, and he'd gone on to become a great playwright. Could he have ever created the compelling stories and characters he'd brought to life without having lived with the drunken pipe-dreamers of the Bowery?

I wondered if he, too, had been plagued with confusion and insecurity. Had he been stalked by dark, oily demons, like me? Maybe, I mused, but he'd faced them down and fought them off, somehow, and gone on to leave behind a legacy. Maybe I would too, someday.

I sighed, thinking back over my life, all the people I'd known. Some, I mused, were destined to win against the odds; and others, like Malcolm and Ellen, weren't. O'Neill must've seen that odd duality in things, too, I thought, remembering his words: *It was a great mistake, my being born a man. I would have been much more successful as a seagull or a fish. As it is, I will always be a stranger who never feels at home, who does not really want and is not wanted, who can never belong, who must be a little in love with death!*

I thought of how O'Neill had been born in a hotel room. After traveling the world by sea, prospecting for gold in the malarial jungles of Honduras, and challenging his spirit to produce a magnificent body of brilliant, groundbreaking work, he'd finally died in another anonymous hotel room.

Well, maybe I would too. What did it matter? The question that haunted me now was, would I ever manage to do anything worthwhile with my life?

As if reading my somber thoughts, Pepe reached across the table and poked me on the arm, grinning. "*Oye,* Joni, listen de idea I having. We go tomorrow morning, tek de bus to Mexico City, eh, *que tal?*"

Surprised, I stared at my friend. What now?

"Okey, *mira!*" Like a general mapping a strategic attack, he spread his hands out on the table. "Firs' t'ing, we gonna go visit de *chicas* I know over there, ho ho, bery good girl. Now we got some money, *cabrón,* we gonna go see ever'thing, have de good times over there, then come tek de bus back to de big *Carnaval* week in Veracruz. How ju think? Is good plan?"

"*Órale pues!*" I grinned back, feeling a great love and kinship for my joyful *compadre.* "*Vámonos!* Let's do it, Pepe!"

What else could I say? Pepe was a doer, not a talker. A ringleader. Like me, he'd come to Veracruz with nothing but dreams and an unstoppable enthusiasm—destination unknown. His wits, good humor, and drive, his life-affirming fervor, those were his only possessions: an undying faith in his innate ability to make things happen. Maybe that's why we were friends. It was always through people like Pepe and Paul that I affirmed my own nebulous faith in some positive outcome.

Pepe and I were survivors. People like us would always land on our feet and hit the ground running, facing life like warriors. I looked across the table at my wizened *compañero,* knowing he could afford no pipe dreams. For Pepe, life was for keeps.

I hoped I could face my own path with the same bold, fearless spirit, and not end up like so many I'd watched eat shit and die a thousand deaths. From the day I'd set out on the road, I'd embraced magic, and a living resolve not to be bogged down by the horrors of my past. Sitting in that lively café, to the tinkling of glasses and animated conversations, I thought of my old friend Paul, saying a silent prayer that he would find a way to tame his demons, somehow, before they dragged him into the gaping abyss of another tragic junkie demise.

With hopeful notions dancing in my head, Pepe and I toasted the last of our *café lecheros,* got up, and walked out into a humid rush of hot, fetid air. Dodging through the sweaty crowds of scruffy street urchins swarming the patio like frantic tropical insects, we crossed the street and wandered out along the seawall.

The ships loomed out there beyond the breakwater like sleeping behemoths, calling to me from the dark, mysterious waters.

33. IMPENDING DOOM

—ORSON WELLES

Cigano stops reading and sets his book on the table.

Lighting a cigarette, he gets up, moves to the window, and stands looking out over the port.

"Like I told ya, man, I been writing a lot about this place." He flicks an ash onto the shiny tiled floor. "Some real life-changing stuff happened for me here back in th' day. . . ."

○　○　○

As we approached the central plaza of *Los Portales*, the muggy night air was trembling with loud mariachi and marimba bands. Strolling harp players and vendors flittered through the crowds, persistent as horseflies, under the fluorescent glare of the tall colonial arches. At the far end, facing the port, the cheaper low-end bars were packed with the usual fishermen, stevedores, and assorted dregs of the port.

We took an outdoor table across from a dingy alley, where the whores stood in shadows, eternal, stoic sentries of the night. Inside, drunks sat passed out at bottle-littered tables like moribund sea lions. Under a lazy ceiling fan, the cracked tiled walls and flyspecked light bulbs were a dingy backdrop to a gang of dilapidated transvestites wearing more makeup than circus clowns. Stumbling around a battered jukebox, their wizened exuberance and ability to remain vertical seemed to transcend the laws of physics.

A familiar waiter came out with two cold beers, and we toasted our upcoming trip. "It's pretty busy out here tonight, for a Sunday, huh?" I looked across at Pepe, glancing at my cheap watch.

"*Claro!*" He grinned. "De Carnaval soon come."

"Man, I been dreaming of Carnaval in Rio forever."

"Rio!" Pepe grinned. "I wan' see these place too,"

"You will. When ya get there, you can stay with me, *hermano.*"

Pepe's smile lit up the night. "I already see it, *cabrón!* Ju gonna mek de real professional tattooing e'studio there."

I gawked at my optimistic friend. "Yeah, maybe, someday."

"Forget it de meybe someday, Joni. What ju put it inside ju mind for do, ju always gonna mek it happen. *No es cierto?*"

I nodded at Pepe. Attitude.

Sitting back, watching the night, I could sense a subtle dark edge in the humid evening air. Aside from the usual local vendors, drinkers, and street urchins crisscrossing the crowded plaza, there seemed to be more druggies and delinquent types than usual. Packs of wild-eyed coked-up wanderers, heavily armed soldiers, and clusters of ominous-looking guys in suits. A vague feeling of barely controlled anarchy and impending mayhem.

All of a sudden, the lights dimmed and the bar's steel gates were pulled down halfway—a signal to patrons at the outside tables to drink up and leave, or move inside.

We were finishing our beers when a crowded neighboring table burst into a chair-throwing, bottle-crashing free-for-all, and a pair of aging hookers tore into each other in a hair-pulling, shrieking drunken frenzy. The waiters rushed over to break it up, too late. A dozen uniformed cops and plainclothesmen led the savage whores off in headlocks. The men went back to their drinks. The barmen killed the lights. Things were getting ugly. Pepe nodded to me and I downed the last of my beer. Time to call it a night.

Walking across the plaza, an evil feeling lingered in the heavy air. Last-gasp drunks and furtive street people gathered in shadows under the watchful eyes of tense-looking cops.

We were cutting through an alley, a shortcut to the hotel, when I heard footsteps rushing up behind us. Before I could turn, a gang of black uniforms grabbed us from behind in rough armlocks. Shadowed by two burly plainclothesmen, they led us off by the seat of our pants.

"Vámonos, vámonos!" a squat, evil-looking bastard in a riot helmet and bulletproof vest growled as his colleagues shoved us forward.

"Qué pasó, jefe?" Pepe asked. His answer was a solid leather-gloved backhand to the face from one of the uniforms. *"Cállate, hijo de puta!* Shut up, asshole, an' keep walking!"

The uniformed thugs seemed overeager to impress their bored-looking plainclothes overseers, who both stayed ominously silent as we marched along. Turning a corner, we were pushed through a doorway and into an shabby, nondescript colonial building, where two cops in full black military riot gear stood guard with shotguns.

They herded us up a flight of stairs and through a big room, where more uniforms sat drinking beer and watching a soccer match on a black-and-white television set.

A scruffy kid lay sobbing quietly on the ground in a corner, handcuffed to a steel bench bolted to the floor. His longish hair was matted with blood, his left eye blackened and swollen shut, his torn white shirt soaked red. Over the television's blare, I could hear muted cries of animal pain from an unseen recess of the building.

Nobody looked up as we were pushed down a hallway. We came to an open door, where a graying suit and tie with a bushy mustache sat at a desk. The two silent plainclothesmen nodded to him, and he gestured them inside. They shut the door behind them. The uniforms led us off in separate directions. Pepe disappeared around a corner.

I was shoved into a small, windowless chamber. Standing at the ancient steel door, the cop pointed to the cement floor. "Sit!" he barked, and the door banged shut. As the bolt clanked into place, I could hear another anguished cry from somewhere nearby.

Welcome to Hell.

A sour taste flooded my mouth. My throat went dry. What was going on? Did this have something to do with that scuffle at the bar? Had any of my dealings in the port gone wrong, somehow?

I sat like a trapped coyote, looking around. The cell reeked of piss, blood, and excrement. Those cops must've known we were "locals," or they never would've grabbed us like that, since foreign sailors were pretty much off-limits to the regular police. I racked my mind for some clue to this mess. Suddenly feeling painfully sober, I sank down in the corner under a stark fluorescent glare.

Waiting was a blank, empty eternity, punctuated only by the blood-chilling screams from the depths of that terrible cement tomb. My thoughts flew around in all sorts of unhappy speculations. Had Pepe gotten involved in more than the usual low-key hustles? Had the cops been watching us for weeks? Was this some kind of setup, or just part of a routine roundup of "suspicious" characters in the frantic, pre-Carnaval activity that'd taken over the lethargic port?

As my mind flipped the brittle pages, I began to feel some hope. It was probably just some routine cop business, I decided. It would all soon be resolved. Worse came to worst, we could always buy ourselves out with the rest of my cash.

I settled back and waited. The act of waiting soon came to represent an act of faith. But, after over an hour, the beers were catching up with my bladder. I stood up and paced, contemplating my latest dilemma. Looking around the stark toilet-less little cell, I could picture those guards whipping me like a bad puppy if I dared to piss on the floor. What to do?

Just as I started to worry again, I heard footsteps, then the sound of the heavy bolt sliding. The door swung wide, and one of the plain-clothesmen looked in. *"Vámonos!"*

He gestured for me to follow, leading the way in eerie silence. A uniformed cop stepped up from behind and escorted us down the hall, prodding me along with a short black shotgun. My mind began to race again. Were they going to cut us loose? Had Pepe paid somebody off?

As we came to the office where the bushy gray mustache sat behind his desk, the uniformed cop placed his hand on my shoulder for me to stop. The mustache looked up from a pile of papers and nodded. Plain-clothes shoved me forward and shut the door.

"Documentos!" Mustache intoned, not looking up.

I fumbled in my pocket and handed him my passport.

"Norteamericano?" He looked up at me, raising a curious eyebrow.

He leafed through the little green book. Stopping at the page where the friendly immigration officer in Chetumal had stamped my new tourist visa, he nodded and handed it back. *"Se puede marchar."*

That was all. *You can go.* No explanation. He was already looking at his paperwork again as the other cop put a hand on my shoulder to lead me out.

"Y mi amigo. . . ?" I ventured.

"Ilegal." The mustache grunted, still not looking up. *"Él permanece detenido para deportación."*

Deported. Fuck! Pepe was going to be sent back to Nicaragua!

"Y no hay otra. . . solución?" I tried again.

At my subtle hint of a possible bribe, both cops smiled. The mustache shook his head, sadly this time. *"Lamentablemente, no."* He frowned, still rifling through his paperwork, avoiding my eyes. *"Lo siento, pero la Policia Federal* is very strict on *ilegales* now. Is out of our hands, a matter for de *políticos."* This last word, politicians, he mumbled with an air of weary distaste.

That was it. Pepe was screwed. There was nothing to be done.

34. SITTING IN LIMBO

"ALL OF US FELT AT TIMES THAT WE WERE REGAINING CONTROL, BUT SUCH INTERVALS—USUALLY BRIEF—WERE INEVITABLY FOLLOWED BY STILL LESS CONTROL, WHICH LED IN TIME TO PITIFUL, INCOMPREHENSIBLE DEMORALIZATION."

—ALCOHOLICS ANONYMOUS

***Carnaval* passed uneventfully,** a depressing drunken whimper. With Pepe gone, Veracruz quickly lost its flavor.

A cold, barren loneliness descended over my days like a greasy shroud. The long, tedious, humid nights were the worst as my life became a slow, soggy, protracted hangover. As clammy shadows of solitude enveloped my heart, I realized I'd stayed in one place for too long. The Curse had caught up to me again.

Before arriving in the old port, I'd spent countless months drifting the roads of Mexico. Always alone, those aimless days and nights of travel all blurred together in a comfortable blanket of isolation. My brief encounters with other people were always happy and life-affirming. Solitary self-reliance had been a good and faithful friend, fortifying me with a blessed sense of freedom from the past.

Then I'd found a home in Veracruz, defined by laughter and camaraderie. But up until Pepe's arrest, I hadn't fully understood what a crucial part of that happy home our friendship had been: an anchor. With that vital tie broken, I felt myself adrift on dark, uncharted seas again. Were there storms ahead? Land? I knew Veracruz would never be the same for me as the Sickness came back to haunt me with a cold, empty pit in my gut.

Walking the familiar streets of night, I felt like a spinning top that would soon lose its weak momentum and topple over, defeated. I tried to occupy the long, solitary days visiting the ships, looking for work or roaming the chaotic afternoon streets by the *mercado*, in a vain attempt to draw some comfort from the frantic energy of its familiar colors, smells, and sounds. But there was something missing now, a nameless, annoying flatness to my surroundings.

At *siesta* time, I'd retire to my room for a cool shower and a nap, then go sit around the radio in the courtyard with Ramón and Memo in the cooling shadows of day's end. The haunting light of the old hotel filled my soul with a vague, ephemeral longing, deep and moving as the smell of fresh orchids, conjuring bittersweet memories of the lazy afternoons I'd spent there with Pepe, lounging on rickety chairs out on the dusty sidewalk and watching the world go by.

Those ancient walls, stained with the patina of generations, still stirred up a fleeting fond flicker in my heart at dusk. But, as the shadows lengthened, the rumbling human traffic began to thin. Darkness fell over the railroad yards by the docks, and, one by one, my companions would move off to their rooms, their worlds, their sleep. Life was winding down for them. Their days were done, and then I'd be sitting all alone like a vampire, brooding, watching, and waiting for the night. That's when the dirty old desperation would come, that ancient, lonesome, restless longing for something unknown and unknowable, a slow, simmering ache, an itch that couldn't be scratched.

As night beckoned to me like a ragged, snaggletoothed old whore, I would seep out into the shadows again, searching, wandering, longing. *Shit!* Why couldn't I just go to my room to sleep or read or jerk off like the others? What was this dreadful, cancerous, black-hearted compulsion pulling me out into those dark, steamy streets like a zombie? I was a shipwrecked sailor, and without even a goddamned ship! I'd always been a loner, and there it was again, that old, restless restlessness, shuttling my vagabond soul back to the solitary nocturnal wanderings of my adolescence, always bumming around from place to place, with no destination, wandering the streets of Los Angeles, San Francisco, New York, New Orleans, wherever, looking for whatever; but always alone, forever trying to fill the empty hole in my gut with something, anything, lost in the sparkling, enigmatic matrix of night, a homeless, rambling shadow, haunted by the Curse, stalking dark, empty streets like a nervous ghost, without even a house to haunt.

Lacking the cheerful, reassuring presence of Pepe, the port became a very different place, a strange and unhappy one. As a crippling sense of paranoia engulfed my heart, it seemed as if people could smell some deathly, contagious virus on me, making them instinctively shun me like a leper—all but the decrepit transvestite hookers and beggars of the port. Those kindred beings could certainly sense the madness in my soul, drawing us together in some dark, unholy psychic bond.

Like them, I was but a phantom, a memory, an invisible stranger drifting through streets of music and laughter, past groups of carefree locals sitting at lively café tables, eating, drinking, talking, laughing.

Moving past lovers sitting on benches by the sea, the sights and sounds of Veracruz were all dead to me now. I was invisible, untouchable, set apart from humanity; half predator, half prey, a solitary, forlorn shadow shuffling along by remote control, drawn to darkness and attracting only darkness to myself from the clutches of some nameless, malevolent spiritual sinkhole.

Like a sinister photonegative image of my frantic daytime incarnation, the night would enfold me in dark, leathery batwings. I could feel some terrible "something" coming down upon me. The Jabberwock. The Terror. The Curse. Powerless to stop its rapacious advance, I tried walking it off, wandering ever deeper into night's clammy spell, drinking alone at seedy dockside bars with other lost souls, hoping to dull the edge of an invisible knife to my throat. But I could smell a stench of demons surrounding me; dark, oily, shapeless things, a frightful nightmare presence come to life.

Even the giant cockroaches patrolling the hotel corridors seemed to avoid me now; until one afternoon when I came to, sweaty and hungover, trembling with the habitual waking dread.

Unable to bear the stink of decay around me any longer, I reached into a corner of the room to gather up my dirty laundry—as if by so doing I could somehow rinse away the filth of my existence. Suddenly, dozens of giant roaches came scurrying out of the pile, indignant at my intrusion into the dark, clandestine world where they'd laid nesting in my moldy socks and underwear.

That did it. I sat down on the bed and cried. Holding my head in my hands, a throbbing, broken thing, I was all done in. My inner decay was reproducing itself in the creepy landscape of my surroundings. It was everywhere I turned now, everything I saw.

Those were the worst of times. I would sit for hours by the seawall, friendless, hopeless, penniless, and alone, watching the big lumbering freighters stealing out to sea. As those massive phantom shapes moved past, a terrible longing filled my heart.

I knew it was finally time to say good-bye to Veracruz. More desperate than ever to get to Rio, I was only praying for a chance.

35. FOND ANTICIPATION

A few weeks after Pepe's arrest, I was drinking away my last few pesos downtown when suddenly everything changed.

It was a hot, muggy evening. The bars were packed with the usual sweaty crowds of drunken men sitting at noisy tables cluttered with bottles, boasting their tipsy prowess, telling their boozy Mexican lies, and eyeing the passing whores. Vendors in battered straw hats navigated the clammy chaos, carrying handwoven baskets of shiny white farm cheese wrapped in dark-green banana leaves.

I sat at a dark corner of a low-end bar on the outskirts, watching the familiar parade of life and listening to the cries of children hawking colorful trinkets. Now and again, a small kid would stagger through the tables, hauling a big handmade wooden ship on his shoulder, like some black-eyed worker ant lugging a leaf ten times its size.

A group of neatly dressed guys at the next table—obviously foreigners, but without the ungraceful, lost-child slouch of gringo tourists—entered into negotiations with a worker ant over one of the giant mementos. An older boy appeared, then another, and then the serious haggling began.

I watched as one of the sailors debated with the oldest boy in awkward Spanish. His shipmates seemed to be egging him on in their native tongue—Greek, I guessed, or maybe Russian.

One of the seamen grinned and nodded to me, pointing at his mate with a derisive snort. "This one here, big spender, think he American tourist, always buy every stupid shit! *Malaka!*"

As I grinned back, another stocky sailor with blurry anchor tattoos on both forearms poked his partner in the ribs, saying something. They both laughed.

The first guy nodded to me. "He say this thing more bigger than the guy cabin, and now he gonna finish all his pay. You watch him now." He snickered as their friend peeled off two twenty-dollar bills from a dwindling roll and handed them to the kid, with the air of a man who'd just made an important purchase. The urchins moved off, leaving the ship sitting beside the table. We all laughed.

The first guy turned to me again. "What ship you work on, friend?"

I told him I wasn't with any ship yet, that I was hanging around Veracruz, hoping to find work soon.

They both nodded. The big tattooed guy wrinkled his bushy black eyebrows, as if consoling a distant relative over some tragic loss.

"Okay, never mind the work now." He motioned me over, pulling up a chair. "Tonight we drink together, tomorrow you come my ship and meet our captain. We good vessel, maybe need one more deck hand. I talk for you. Come! Sit!"

With a grateful smile, I moved over and joined them.

As the evening wore on, the laughter faded and the bottle dwindled. The good-natured banter of my new companions ran to mundane topics. Watching the faces around the table, it hit me that this was all a familiar routine to these guys.

I could feel an old cynicism creeping into my blood, even as I despised myself for it. The mythical, poetic sailor's life I'd long romanticized was nowhere to be seen here. Where were those heroic figures from faraway lands I'd always envisioned? These were just a bunch of guys blowing off steam after a hard day's work; might as well be factory workers. It was a letdown.

As they talked among themselves in Greek, I brooded. What little these sailors had seen of the world seemed filtered through the limited vision of their own culture, always sticking close to their ship and their own kind. They appeared to have no real curiosity about the places they visited, and little but a perfunctory relationship with the people they met. And those people, too, were locked in their own little self-made cultural cages, with no interests beyond their dreary day-to-day reality. *Fuck!* The rum burned my guts as I fell into a dark, boozy funk.

I could feel that treacherous old sense of futility, a deathly inbred despair. I wanted to weep for myself and for the world. What good could ever lay ahead for someone like me, with my naïve, childish ideas? I suddenly envisioned Malcolm lying on his deathbed.

Thankfully, my gloom went unnoticed by my half-drunk friends. Finally, the big guy called for the bill, waving away my handful of crumpled pesos. Again, he told me to come to their ship tomorrow. We would eat some "real food" in the galley, he said, and then talk to the captain about a job for me. We all said good night. They headed back toward the port gate, and I set off alone.

Feeling a little more hopeful, I took a couple of turns around the plaza and then wandered out along the long whitewashed seawall.

Looking out over the dark, choppy waters of the Gulf, I could feel the unseen presence of Brazil out there in the vast unknown. The elated, drunken longing of my twenty short years in this strange and confusing world gave way to a familiar burning need to fit in somewhere, to do something, anything.

Maybe I'd just been alone too long. I spat into the water and thought of Pepe, locked up like a dog in the pound, awaiting deportation to his war-torn home in Nicaragua. But I knew he'd be fine. Nothing could keep someone like him down. People and places came and went for guys like us; sailors of the road, just passing through, never forming lasting bonds, interacting with this one or that before moving on to the next port of call.

But, unlike Pepe, I felt useless. A fisherman goes to sea to harvest its fruits. My harvest could only be life, experience, knowledge, worldliness. Or something more, I mused, something indefinable. Probably something quite futile. *Shit!*

I cursed and spat in the water again. What the fuck was wrong with me? Why could I never be satisfied? Even a mundane purpose would do for most people, like those sailors; a simple job at sea, saving money for a few years, then returning home to settle down among old friends and family, becoming part of a community somewhere. Why not? Anything would be better than what I had to look forward to. I had nothing. No past. No future. No home. No family. No friends. I was truly nobody. *Shit.*

As a great aching melancholy longing filled my heart again, I pictured the wretched limbo of my insignificant existence stretching out before me like a vast ocean of nothingness, a depressing void of endless black futility. Waves of sadness and solitude struck me again and again, like the breakers hitting the seawall and jumping up in the wind to wet my face with sobering blasts of salty spray; crocodile tears from the dark, indifferent depths of the sea.

I thought how simple it must be for those guys, just going home and settling down. But for me, no such luck. I'd been a lone wolf all my life, unable to fit in where I came from. Now there was no home to return to. No big happy family awaiting my triumphant return.

Whatever friends I'd left behind would soon be dead of drugs, inertia, and the crushing disappointment of their own shattered dreams. Those who survived would just grow old, bitter, and dull, defeated by life like their parents before them. *Shit.*

Staring out over the Gulf, I knew there had to be a place for me out there somewhere beyond those dark, mysterious waters. Only the sea could be as deep and unfathomable as the recesses of my self-imposed solitude.

Then, as I reflected on the chance of finally shipping out, a sneaky little smile began to cross my face, at last, like a drunken clown tiptoeing out of an empty circus tent in the dead of night.

Shrugging off that fuzzy shroud of creeping futility, I shot to my feet and trotted back to the hotel, surfing a giddy wave of fond anticipation for the next phase of my life—whatever it might be.

36. SEVEN SEAS AT LAST

—EUGENE HUTZ

The next afternoon, having been hired on the M/V *Argoland*, I hurried back to my room and packed my bag. After warm embraces with Memo and Ramón, I headed straight to the docks. My friends in Veracruz would remain behind, like Paul and all the others before.

Whistling to myself, I strode through the port with an old, inherited Gypsy flourish, a blessing and a curse, a talent. A way. The crooked gold-toothed smile I'd acquired at a cheap downtown dentist in honor of Pepe flashed in the morning sunlight as I sauntered along the wharves, breathing in a nostalgic, fishy blend of machine oil, paint, fried meat, and something indistinct. Expectation.

Another ending. Another new beginning. Nothing more to think about. I was already gone. If I was ever good at one thing, I mused, it was leaving people and places behind, and moving on alone.

As I stood on the familiar bustling dock, looking up at the ship that would soon take me away from Veracruz, the muggy gulf air danced in my nostrils like a powerful drug, imprinting the smells of the old port in my senses forever. Then, with the cool practice of the Gypsy's crooked DNA, I started up the long metal ramp. As it shook and bounced beneath my weight, by the time I reached the top, Veracruz was but another cherished memory.

○ ○ ○

My new home was a rusty mid-sized freighter, sailing under the flag of Liberia—a country I'd never heard of before stepping aboard.

The big tattooed Greek sailor greeted me on deck and led me into the galley, where a motly group of seamen sat drinking beer and playing cards. Central American boys, West Indies Negroes, Greeks, and a few rugged Dutchmen were all talking at once in different versions of English. Officers sat at another table, eating canned cashews, cheese, and olives from South America.

Down below were the humble seaman's quarters. I set my bag on a narrow bottom bunk, feeling strangely at home. As the ship lumbered out of the breakwater, the steady hum of its huge machinery dulled all earthly concerns. I lay back and fell into a deep, peaceful slumber, secure and safe against the warm, vibrating metal bulkhead.

The next months would be the happiest time of my life, engulfed in a placid, solitary calmness at sea—reminiscent of the euphoric comfort of heroin, before addiction opened the gates to Hell.

But, unlike that long fuzzy drug stupor, I was wide awake and fully aware now, alive and participating in a real world of vital new experience. That good salt-sprayed existence of healthy manual labor on the waves brought me a deep and abiding sense of peace—and without having to stick a spike in my arm to get it.

Rocking over the dark blue waters, I knew I'd been born for that sacred calling; sailing away forever—destination unknown. Life became a timeless watery spell of rhythmic, mechanical chipping and sanding at rust on the ship's metal railings. Rust on walls, portholes, stairs, doors, floors. Rust that never slept. I spent the long days hard at work defending the ship's bobbing infrastructure from the constant corrosive onslaught of time and ocean breeze, salt, sun, rain, and motion. The ceaseless poetry of that watery momentum was always followed by blessed tranquil hours at day's end, spent writing in my solitary notebooks at the ship's prow, curled up like a cat in a comfortable nest of thick salty rope. Looking up from the pages crowded with sketches and poetry, I'd sit staring out over the water as the ship cut its churning wake through a dark, undulating blanket of sea, cruising into spectacular unearthly sunsets.

After dark, I'd stand out on the empty deck as night slowly engulfed my shadow. Descending into the vessel's warm, welcoming bowels at last, I'd sit drinking beer and playing cards in the galley, enjoying the easygoing fraternity of my shipmates at the end of another long day. Ensconced late at night in the comfort of my warm vibrating bunk, I'd write myself to sleep in my journal—my heart's secret home in a long, silent, floating dream.

Sweating belowdecks in the oily sauna of the engine room one afternoon, I saw the compelling vision that would come to define my whole life's path in one simple, timeless image. As I handed a wrench to the ship's chief mechanic, my eye focused in on a fuzzy tattoo on the stalwart Dutchman's weathered forearm. A faded blue-gray sailing ship with a flowing banner beneath it, highlighting two simple words: *HOMEWARD BOUND.* To me, the design evoked visions of a long life at sea—all the ports, barrooms, and whorehouses, the fleeting interactions with people in strange exotic places, the elemental journey of a solitary, restless vagabond spirit traversing the seven seas.

I spent countless hours ensconced in the shadowy sanctuary of my bunk at night, enveloped in the steady hum of the darkened ship in motion, sketching different versions of the design over and over in my notebook—conjuring, contemplating, and perfecting the lines, curves, and details; obsessed with the haunting phrase: Homeward Bound.

By the time we made port in Panama, I felt I'd known those two magical words as a metaphor for my life forever.

Now I was ready to commit the journey to my skin.

HOMEWARD
BOUND
Oliver
Pecker

37. HOMEWARD BOUND

Thrilled with my first shore leave in weeks, I rode along the windswept tropical outskirts of Panama City in a dilapidated taxi.

As I stared out the window, details of the Caribbean carved themselves into my soul; deserted streets shimmering under a burning midday sun, scrawny dogs sleeping in the shade. Insect-like human figures drifted along rutted dirt side streets as the car sped along past groups of scruffy brown kids playing barefoot soccer in the dust.

The air reeked of a special melancholy poetry, a pungent odor of raw sewage, grilled meat, and an indefinable sickly-sweet fishy scent hanging in the humid ocean breeze. Shabby, whitewashed palms leaned at crazy angles in a surreal collage of mental snapshots tattooing themselves on my brain. Weathered Negroes loitered on windswept corners, eternal phantom statues standing by their crooked tin-roofed shacks peeking out from the lush tropical vegetation. A moody whispering intrigue was calling to me in a dreamlike haze, where past, present, and future all seemed to merge under the steamy weight of those green-brown, wind-chopped waters.

The taxi let me off on a quiet downtown corner of streamlined art-deco edifices facing the sea. With their nautical porthole windows and chipped green glass-block façades, those buildings seemed to have been designed for dreaming of far-off lands. Boisterous green parrots screeched from wooden perches on weathered old Spanish tiled balconies as I walked the streets in a purposeful trance.

Hours later, in a shady, rain-swept back alley, I came across the destination I'd secretly been seeking. I stopped and peered in a foggy window. Then, with a mixture of awe, elation, and trepidation, I grabbed the door handle.

A brass bell attached to the dark wooden doorway announced my arrival with an otherworldly tinkle. The cramped little space was cluttered with mysterious objects and mementos, tattoo art covering every inch of the dim cubbyhole's walls. Shelves in a darkened corner overflowed with books in strange, unknown languages. Hundreds of scraps of translucent paper covered in sketches dangled overhead like dried butterflies, fluttering in the breeze of a slow metal ceiling fan.

My mind raced back to the first time I'd peeked into a mysterious cave of tattoo dreams, a lifetime ago. And then I saw it. The schooner tattoo, that banner with the same familiar words: Homeward Bound.

There it was, on a colorful section of wall under a wooden staircase that creaked and moaned with footsteps of sailors and whores trudging up to a run down by-the-hour hotel.

Homeward Bound. The haunting little image was calling to me from the depths of a timeless, hazy vision, shining like an all-seeing eye, drawing me closer, closer.

I bent down and squinted at the glowing talisman. It evoked unlived memories of adventures in faraway lands, carrying my imagination away on an ancient pirate schooner cutting a colorful wake through a sea of paint and ink, sailing away forever, with no known destination or port of call.

The monotonous hum of a tattoo machine spiked my senses as I heard a strangely familiar voice from across the little room.

Jesús Wong, Pepe's fabled Chinaman, was an ageless, skeletal figure with jet-black hair tied in a long, skinny braid, like some old-time Charlie Chan movie character. I looked over to where he sat under an old brass desk lamp in a cramped workspace, etching an elaborate, colorful dragon tattoo onto a sailor's arm.

My eyes drifted down the wall again, studying my little ship of dreams, sailing through an endless ocean of panthers and tigers, dragons, roses, hearts, anchors, and voluptuous smiling pinup girls. I studied my bare right arm, then my left, then right again. I rolled up my sleeve, inspecting the virgin skin below my little handmade anchor.

My vision fixed on the compelling icon again, as if it had been waiting for me there forever.

Taking a deep breath, I wandered over and stood quietly watching the tattoo man at work. He was talking to his client in a soft, low monotone blending with the rhythmic, hypnotic buzz of that mysterious little tool, mumbling special words in a secret language only for the initiated: the tattooed, those who knew that shadowy rite of passage, those who wore the Mark etched into their skin in a painful mystical bloodletting ritual as ancient as time. And I knew right then that there was no turning back. I, too, would soon have to wear the Mark.

I went back to the wall and studied the design some more. Waves of anticipation and nervous excitement jiggled my gut as invisible insect shadows stirred inside me. Time stood still. I felt like a diver standing on a cliff, looking over a dark blue pool stretching out forever over a glowing horizon.

Then, I sensed a presence sliding up beside me, cool and graceful, inscrutable as a Siamese cat.

"So, sailor, ju mek de trip back to ju home port now, eh?"

I turned to look into a pair of catlike, almond-shaped eyes. Friendly, smiling eyes—but oddly aloof, the mysterious black orbs of a spaceman.

"Uh, no," I stammered. "I dunno, I guess I'm just starting out."

"So now ju has de lo-ong journey ahead of ju." The wizened tattoo man seemed to look right through me. With that mysterious alien smile, his voice rang out clear as a temple bell, unhesitating and distinct, warm as the lush musty air of the tropics. Still, it told nothing.

I heard a ship's horn calling long and low from the port, the voice of night reaching into that dim space where invisible shadows stirred.

Jesus seemed to read my thoughts as he spoke again. "De tattoo ju chooses, sailor, she always gots to come from inside he-ah. . . . " He fell silent with a Zen master's patience, touching a finger to his chest in a ghostly, delicate sweep.

I stared at his weathered hand, like a silver spider landing on the smooth tattooed skin beneath his silk shirt. A simple jade pendant dangled from a thin golden chain, frozen in space, an eternal question mark. I cocked my head like a curious dog as he went on with that serene, knowing smile.

". . . Even when ju thinks she come from inside he-aaah." The skinny old Chinaman pointed a long, elegant manicured finger to his jet-black-framed head, then cackled like a playful jungle monkey sitting on a lost statue of the Buddha.

I followed Jesus Wong over to his cluttered workspace. I took a seat across from the wizened old tattoo man, watching intently as a straight razor swept across my skin like a cool metallic lizard.

Surrendering to the master's practiced hands, I winced, dreaming of faraway ports as the dancing needles began to pierce my flesh, uniting body and soul at last.

38. TRUE NORTH

I spent my twenty-first birthday at sea, proudly wearing my first real professional tattoo. Homeward Bound.

Those two words, would soon take on a deeper portent for me as I came to understand that, all along the long, lonesome road, I'd been slowly piecing together an identity. From random scraps of experience gathered on an endless, haphazard journey, I'd stealthily, methodically been scavenging a character for myself, a road map to a life—just as old Bukowski had told me to do.

And a part of me had inevitably perished along the way, in order to be reborn. Like a lost bird of prey on the run from its own extinction, I was a refugee from some forgotten endangered species, wandering the earth by land and sea, searching, always longing for a home that didn't exist. And that simple tattoo would become a master link to a great, baffling puzzle—an anchor to the world. Something far more significant to me than just a mark on skin, my new tattoo was an emblem of initiation into an elite fraternity of hard-living, seagoing men; a secret fellowship of outcasts and outsiders living on society's mismatched margins—wandering, homeless, rootless vagabond spirits, united by a common allegiance to the road; some running from, others running to, and others, like myself, simply running. Running down the long, solitary path to nowhere. Running by virtue of our very nature. Running for the sake of the run.

A long booming wail sounded in my ears as the ship's horn reverberated over a thick green sea of jungle. As day faded to night, I stood out on deck, watching the low, flat landmass of Central America disappear into the distance. I was a random passenger in space again, surrounded by dark unknown waters, a ghost in search of a home. My hand absently caressed the patch of raw tattooed skin throbbing below my shirtsleeve, securing me, at last, to something solid and real.

With a crooked smile, I stared up into an infinity of winking stars. As the ship cut through the darkness, I studied the graceful little sailing ship on my arm. Shuttling through time and space that night, under the intricate tapestry of cosmos, my heart swelled with the lofty weight of a sudden, comforting epiphany: that we're all just passengers on an errant little dust ball in space, and nothing really matters.

Maybe that's why I'd always felt such a mad, burning lust binding me to the journey itself, rather than any real concept of destination. Weeks passed in a blur of sparkling blue sea and fleeting ports, and nothing mattered. Traversing that endless limbo of water, sea, sun, moon, and stars, the constant movement of the giant, lumbering vessel covered me in a comforting blanket of peace.

Then one day the rusty metal hulk emerged from that long watery limbo. Cruising along the lush green northern coast of South America, approaching the wide mouth of a massive river, I stared out at the steamy, mysterious continent materializing before me. My heart was beating like a jungle drum.

o   o   o

We made port at sundown, gliding in over silent brown waters to a scent of rain and dark red mud. Burning anticipation stirred in my center as a jumble of shacks and low-lying buildings came into focus through the haze. Rust-colored tin roofs dotted an endless, verdant expanse of banana plantations hissing in the humid twilight.

As the ship's steady rocking motion gave way to an eerie new stillness, my water-bound home plodded through a wide estuary, and into another surreal dream, where my feet would first touch South American land in the improbable port of Paramaribo.

Paramaribo, the capital city of Suriname—formerly Dutch Guyana— was an antique outpost of obsolete history, a murky mildewed pirate backwater, lost to time and the modern world; a phantom nether zone of brooding African shadows whispering a moody Creole patois into the stagnant jungle air. Anticipating my upcoming shore leave, I breathed in its otherworldly aura with the fervor of a kid on his first visit to a mysterious all-night carnival, all lit up with bright winking colored lights of adventure.

Descending the gangplank under glowing moonlight, I felt like a swaggering pirate captain, proudly sporting a loose-fitting Hong Kong silk shirt—a gift to myself bought with my last pay in Panama—the sleeves rolled up just enough to reveal a hint of my new tattoo.

As I moved along the dock, I thought back to getting the clap on another boozy cathouse night in another strange port. I winced, remembering a Cuban shipping agent's doctor coming aboard in Havana, and sticking a glass tube up the shaft of my pecker, slowly, painfully filling my bladder with a terrible, burning purple liquid. I felt as if I was pissing fire in reverse as my shipmates stood around in the galley, hollering like unruly monkeys at my shameful agony.

Walking another dusty dirt road, a scent of cheap cologne haunting my nose, phantom memories of lives unlived stirred in the humid evening shadows. I slowed my gait, sweating in the stagnant, mosquito-laden air, drunk with the awareness that my arrival in that odd obscure backwater had brought me one crucial step closer to my goal in neighboring Brazil.

Baptized by weeks of sun, rain, and salty sea spray, my new tattoo had finally healed and settled into my flesh; an essential part of my being peeking out under my shirtsleeve, it felt empowering, like a gun tucked in my belt.

But there was no gun. Only a little tattooed sailing ship and the simple words: Homeward Bound—a shield of protection, an anchor, a talisman, a compass, rudder, and mainstay. My own True North.

39. MAN'S RUIN

Wooden fishing boats bobbed in the muddy water of the tiny port, rocking like toys in the shadows of a few looming freighters at dock.

Whooping shouts in an unintelligible Creole patois stabbed at the sweaty night air in a weird blend of Spanish, Portuguese, Dutch, French, Chinese, Javanese, Hindi, and indecipherable, grunting African dialects. A jukebox was playing a boisterous Calypso as I moved along through the jingle-jangle dockside crowds of blue-black stevedores, sailors, and whores.

Paramaribo was a world's end colonial jungle frontier, a languid stew of unlikely civilizations thrown together on the humid margins of nowhere. Haunting rhythms blew like a dreamlike breeze through that surreal tropical garden of mismatched souls. No one seemed to notice me as I navigated a squalid jumble of tin-roofed wooden shacks and open-air bars, where muddled shapes moved to hypnotic tropical beats.

I was invisible again, and I liked it.

Feeling comfortable in a cloud of ghostly anonymity, I stopped at a crossroads and put my back to a wall, looking on as two burly fishermen with coarse African features broke into a loud quarrel. A small crowd gathered. Suddenly, one of the Negroes reached to the small of his back. Quick as a rattlesnake, he slashed his adversary across the arm with a short, rusty blade. Dripping blood, the wounded man ran into an alley, barking guttural curses behind him. I could feel the curious heat of the crowd as I moved on past the knife-wielding victor, who was already arguing with another man.

Standing outside a cramped dirt-floored barroom shack, I peered at the animated shadows moving around inside. Drunken men and half-naked mulatto girls gyrated to blaring music under frantic, blinking whorehouse lights.

I lit a cigarette, and stepped into the dark, twinkling sex arcade. A chaotic, crashing cacophony of two competing jukeboxes shook the crowded little space. Scrawny, shirtless brown bodies glistened in the sweaty piss-tainted air. Girls were dancing around, grinding supernatural asses to the jumbled tropical beats like wild machines in a fantastic factory of raw animal abandon. Grinning faces flashed with life, feral young whores shouting and gyrating in a mad traffic-jam of eyes and pearly white teeth, shining spook-house skeleton masks in a pounding blast furnace of lust.

As I leaned against the bar, my eyes fixed on a cherub-faced young mulatta swaying before a battered jukebox. Glowing in the pulsing lights, she was a crazed, flashing obsidian fuck-shrine.

Transfixed, I marveled before her lanky long-bodied yellow shadow. Beneath a crotch-hugging miniskirt, a peek of blood-red panties lured me closer to where she wobbled outrageously on impossibly high heels, grinding a hypnotic cobra snake's ass-chant into the vibrating wall of sound.

I stood watching that lethal man-eating creature of low-down crazy-bones night, my eyes riveted to a perfect holy altar of ass. I swallowed a glass of treacherous white rum that tasted of gasoline, and the thirsty spirits of the Curse began a mad voodoo hell-dance in my blood. As I leaned back against the bar, drooling like a horny cartoon jackal, she slithered up toward me, weaving a Special Delivery sex-spell on my lonely, waterlogged sailor's dick.

I should have known I would never stand a chance against the Devil's own perfect laughing, dancing muse. That one should have been marked with a skull and crossbones: Poison. Danger. Man's Ruin.

Another drink went down as she chattered at me in the ridiculous language of that godforsaken place. I understood nothing; but whatever she was saying, it was fine by me, didn't matter. I was already gone, lost, drowning like a pig at sea in those crazy green Whore of Babylon eyes, hypnotized by every movement of her gleaming baby-doll lips.

The night dissolved into a frenzied blur of bottles and shacks, overgrown muddy dirt paths, lanterns, candles, mumbled words, and frantic whorehouse negotiations in that oddball world-end dialect I didn't need to understand. She led me to a shack on a dark path of dirt and wild tropical foliage. The air was heavy with a smell of the sea, of rain, jungle, and raw sewage, and nothing mattered.

As I lay on a hard little mattress with her, there was nothing but the beacon of those mad dancing green eyes and that perfect doll-faced mouth twisted into a childlike grin of lusty mischief and delight.

I grabbed her ass in a desperation death grip with one hand and her kinky golden brown hair with the other, ramming myself deep into the dizzy cosmos of her being. If that little whore had been a slot machine, her cunt would have spit gold pirate doubloons out onto the sheet as I kissed her neck, running my tongue along her silky golden brown skin, feasting on those crazy pink lips, licking the perfect pearl necklace of shiny white teeth, nibbling at her cheek like a baby wolf.

Frantic as a dying beast, I chewed her tongue, drinking in the wild intoxicating liquor of her musky jungle-bunny saliva, inhaling her hot Creole breath like a deep hit of strong red-dirt marijuana. The last thing I remembered was the primal roller-coaster ride of those full, healthy adolescent hips, creeping up-up-up to the top of a drunken amusement-park morning. . . ***click-click-click-click-click.*** . . then, bang! ***wheeeeeeeeeeeeee***, flying down, down, dowwwwnnnn, with science-fiction G-force death-throe abandon, coming, climaxing, dizzy as a glue-addled zombie ghost, shooting out spaceship-white sparks of my desperate seed into her insane, savage, impossible core, again and again, dying forever in the mad velocity of that perfect eternal pristine moment. A long wailing scream tore out from somewhere deep in my being, and it was done.

Quick as a shape-shifting alien, she was on her feet again. In a blur of jerky mechanical movements, she slithered back into her party rags and began going through my pants pockets, a hideous scavenging jungle buzzard.

I lay back, drunk, sweating, paralyzed, panting like a roadkill dog on that dirty mattress in the ass-backward ass crack of nowhere, suddenly realizing, *fuck-fuck-fuck, I've been drugged, bitch slipped me a fucking mickey, and I don't care, don't care, fuck-fuck-fuck,* as a dark blanket of sleep descended over me like a gang of unseen thugs.

40. THE MORNING AFTER

"SOME OF US SOUGHT OUT SORDID PLACES, HOPING TO FIND UNDERSTANDING, COMPANIONSHIP, AND APPROVAL. MOMENTARILY WE DID—THEN WOULD COME OBLIVION AND THE AWFUL AWAKENING TO FACE THE HIDEOUS FOUR HORSEMEN—TERROR, BEWILDERMENT, FRUSTRATION, DESPAIR."

—ALCOHOLICS ANONYMOUS

Morning came in a burning spear of white heat, cutting through a crack in a rough wooden wall. Where was I? What happened last night?

A rude ray of sunlight pierced my tortured retina like an ice pick. A cement sledgehammer of pain was pounding at my head, engulfing my senses, right down to my spine. A foul taste of outhouse stench permeated my cotton-dry mouth, a harsh chemical whiff boring into my sinuses, my eyes, my soul, as my brain crawled back to the surface of consciousness like a drowing possum.

Groggy and stunned, a condemned soul praying for mercy, I was a helpless sacrifice to the Mother Goddess of Ruin. A sharp lightning bolt of pain shot through my vision as I rose up on the thin mattress. The saggy wooden bed frame creaked and groaned. I looked over to see an elderly white-haired naked Negress snoring and gurgling obscenely beside me. *Oh, God!* I looked to my watch for the time. It was gone. *God, oh, shit, oh, God, where am I, how did I get here, what day, what time, what the fuck? Oh, shit!*

I leapt off the bed like a frog from a cook pot, moaning in agony. A sinking cloud of doom filled my gut in a flood of fetid sewage as I struggled into my clothes. In a stumbling flurry of blind panic, I scrambled around looking for the door, banging my head on a hellish symphony of battered black pots and pans dangling from the low tin ceiling and knocking over a bucket of foul-smelling sludge on the packed dirt floor. *Fuck fuck fuck! Get me out of here! Out!*

Slivers of sunlight jabbed like knife blades through the crumpled corrugated roof. Spider webs of shadowy horror were all I could see as I scampered around the dim little hovel, a frantic rat in a maze.

As I stumbled out the door, a flash of brutal equatorial sun hit me like a hammer blow. Momentarily blinded, I tripped over a massive gray pig foraging in the mud. Struggling to my feet, dripping pig shit and debasement, I turned and ran, tension grabbing at my heart like a whining beggar.

Groping my way through a ragged warren of tin-roofed shacks, insect-buzzing weeds, banana trees, and huge green elephant-ear foliage, I hurried along past barking mutts, Aunt Jemima washer-women, and naked Indian children. Laughing Negroes sitting gambling in the shade looked up and whistled, jeering in that odd guttural language as I rushed past. The whole world was mocking me as I followed my crippled senses back to the port.

Arriving, breathless, to the pier where my ship had been docked, a dull thud of realization fell like a tiny cadaver in the dirt at my feet. A dead pit of dismay consumed my stricken entrails as I stood on the empty quay, frozen in place, watching my only home for the past several months steaming out to sea. Without me!

Oh, fuck! No!

The sun beat down on my throbbing skull like an accusing searchlight as I cast a final shamefaced look at the departing vessel, shaking my head in bitter defeat. *Shit shit!*

Saliva filled my mouth. I leaned over and puked my poisoned guts out into the dark red South American mud.

That horrible gray moment was an eternity as my stomach sunk like a forlorn turd to the bottom of the sea. Everything was bleak and hopeless again as I stood sweating under the harsh noonday sun.

Stinking like an outhouse, covered in weird bruises and insect bites, my head was pounding as the reality of my plight descended like a cold, squirming net of eels. I was stranded in some god-forgotten third-world shitwater limbo where I didn't speak the language. I wanted to sit down in the dirt and slit my throat.

Shaking my head in hateful surrender, I turned and walked away.

41. PARADISE LOST

For hours, I wandered the bustling morning streets of Paramaribo, a bizarre, melancholy tropical dream world forsaken by time and logic. Feeling myself lost in an old *National Geographic* magazine, I marveled at the surreal mix of obsolete cultures and peoples from the four lost corners of Hell.

Then I remembered: I still had my passport and some cash. A spark of hope lit in my heart as I flashed back on the three crisp new hundred-dollar bills I'd had sewn into the cuff of my jeans by a dockside tailor in Nicaragua. Recalling the old *mestizo's* rambling accounts of a massive lake filled with mutant man-eating fresh-water sharks, random images flickered across my mind like distant lightning: whispered tales of hapless political prisoners being thrown out into the deadly waters from military helicopters.

Drifting along on a boozy cloud of memory, I thought back to my life in Veracruz. It all seemed a million years ago.

Maybe, I mused, memory is more in the way we see the weird dream-like visions we bring to life than any actual "reality" of people, places, and events. Haunted by glimpses of the crooked road map that had brought me to that desolate, distant crossroads, the recollections seemed like old phonograph records now—warped, worn, scratched, distorted by time and distance. And as the creator of those memories, I was like a drunken illusionist conjuring spirits from a bottle in some dusty roadside freak show.

Lumbering on in a foggy, hungover stupor, I ducked into a shady space between two ancient wooden buildings. I looked around. Seeing no one watching, I made a quick incision in the seam of my jeans with my knife, extracting a life-changing hundred. After exchanging the banknote for a handful of oversized Dutch guilders with a fat man in a shabby suit by the port, I downed a bottle of beer at a little dockside bar. Surfing a fuzzy new wave of beery momentum, I wandered back out into the blazing afternoon heat.

I came to another honky-tonk oasis, where a dark round-faced Hindu was selling fried conch patties and beer. The big green bottle was labeled with an unpronounceable Dutch name, resembling the hellish gurgle of my guts as I'd retched black chemical bile into the dirt that morning. The recurring image of my ship sailing off without me bit at my conscience like a vengeful badger as I gulped down the beer—my fourth since coming to.

Slowly, the waves of panic began to subside.

As I drifted the streets of Paramaribo like a ghost, I could hear a rumble of approaching thunder. I looked up at the steamy black storm clouds gathering in the darkening jungle sky as the first big drops began to fall. Taking shelter in a large, bustling indoor market, I stumbled around in the musty shadows of the ancient colonial structure, staring up at the ornate gray steel beams overhead. The whole building seemed to be perspiring inside, as a sudden heavy downpour banged at the giant metal roof, booming like cannon fire from unseen pirate ships.

Navigating the shadowy indoor bazaar, I came upon a group of half-naked Amazonian tribesmen. Covered in intricate primitive tattoo patterns, they sat huddled together on the packed dirt floor, brushing flies from a pile of silvery-golden *piranha* fish laid out on a mat of banana leaves. As I stood staring down at the gaping aquatic mouths of needle-like teeth cocked open in frozen death gasps, a bulky Negress in a flowery housedress and the darkest skin I'd ever seen appeared in an animated rustle of flowery fabric. She began haggling with the natives in that weird hybrid patois. In a flash of bare skin peeking beneath her colorful garment, I saw a dizzying pattern of intricate scarification markings crisscrossing her entire upper back. Later, I would learn from a Brazilian sailor that the woman was descended from a tribe of escaped slaves who'd set up villages deep in the jungle upriver. Still living by their ancient African tribal customs, they were known in Suriname simply as the Bush Negroes.

Moving on, I came to a little wooden lunch counter. I pointed to a cooler in that universal language of the bottle. The swarthy vendor handed me a lukewarm beer before resuming his animated dialogue with a group of Oriental-looking men. One stocky fellow in a Hindu turban had a faded blue dagger tattooed on his hand. Captivated by the lilting rhythm of that odd language, a mix of exotic worlds and sub-worlds, I stood drinking. As the familiar warm golden glow lit up in my blood like lights in a flashing pinball arcade, I smiled, watching a wiry Negro boy racing along the gauntlet of market stalls, shouldering a huge burden of green plantains. Each African man he passed reached out to pat him on his fuzzy little head.

That simple, poignant gesture was one of those rare, random moments that carve themselves into your soul forever, like a tattoo.

42. SOMEWHERE ELSE

In a cheap hotel room by the port, I slept for over twelve hours.

I awakened the next morning feeling better. After a lukewarm shower and a quick wakeup beer, I ventured out to explore the curious world of Paramaribo again.

Wandering crooked streets of antique two- and three-story wood frame colonial buildings, I was lost in a moving tapestry of details from a bygone era. Crude handmade tattoos on the weathered brown arms of fishermen poked at my eyes like blurry hieroglyphics in a foggy old slow-motion movie. Suddenly, that strange world seemed alive with promise. In the light of the new day, I could sense the presence of impending great events lurking around each mysterious corner.

As the long sweaty afternoon wore on, a cooling wind blew in across the muddy river at last, kicking up a wild flurry of debris. Taking refuge from another late-afternoon thunderstorm, I ducked into the musty shadows of the marketplace again. The winds raged outside. Pounding thunder and apocalyptic lightning claps shook the building, a furious hailstorm pounding on its high metal roof like a bombing raid, filling the world with echoes of raging spirit warfare from above and blasting the humid red earth below to smithereens. Then, after an hour, an abrupt ceasefire.

Out on the street again, the crisp, shimmering sparkle in the air seemed especially pregnant with possibility. I trudged on through the soggy town like a refugee. Then, just before nightfall, I found myself standing on a decrepit wooden wharf on the outskirts of the port, staring out over the wide muddy river, where fishermen stood like phantoms on the rain-beaten earth by decaying shacks.

A whiff of marijuana smoke burned in the humid jungle air; a sickly sweet rotting secret in some forgotten language, emerging from the dark red clay of that dull unforgiving land. Yearning for the soothing deep-sea motion of travel, like a junkie craving a fix, my heart longed for Brazil. But how? There was no overland route.

Just then, my eyes focused in on a small wooden boat bobbing in the rust-colored water, reading the hand-painted words on its prow: ***SÃO JORGE GUERREIRO–BELÉM DO PARÁ, BRASIL.*** Dozens of rusty bicycles cluttered the deck like mechanical exoskeletons of some doomed race of giant insects.

From a dilapidated pickup parked in the mud, three dark-skinned men were loading the scruffy red-and-white vessel with wooden crates filled with cigarettes, whiskey, and small electrical appliances.

Hearing them speaking among themselves in Portuguese, a cool wave of excitement stirred in my gut, conjuring memories I'd never had. A fine mist enveloped my senses with a nostalgic taste of the sea, and I knew I would soon be there at last. *Brasil!* The hissing jungle seemed to come alive with the word *Brasil,* again and again, *Brasil, Brasil,* like a million electric cats.

I shuffled over and greeted one of the men in Spanish, *hola, por favor, para donde va este barco?* which he seemed to sort of understand. His reply came in Portuguese, which I could sort of get but not really speak. With smiles, laughter, and comical sign-language, we came to an agreement: I needed to get to Brazil, and they could use an extra hand unloading their goods at points between Paramaribo and their Brazilian home port, Belém, near the mouth of the Amazon.

Leo, the captain, a thin, weathered mulatto smuggler with an easy smile and a crude hand-poked anchor tattooed on his forearm, pocketed my handful of withered Dutch guilders. With a smiling thumbs-up, he studied the sailing ship tattoo on my arm. We were good.

He shouted out to his crew, gesturing for me to go help them finish loading. I strode over to the boat, unbuttoning my shirt.

We'd hug the coast of French Guyana, one of the sailors explained, then cross the wide Amazon basin to the port of Belém do Pará, Brazil's northernmost shipping port.

I grinned like an escaped convict. Homeward Bound again.

43. MOVING ON

"PERHAPS HE KNEW . . . HE HAD BEFORE HIM AN IMMENSE JOURNEY. PERHAPS THE SAME REALIZATION HAUNTS THOSE WHO LEAVE A CROWDED DINNER PARTY TO STEP OUT INTO THE COLD NIGHT AIR AND LOOK UP AT THE STARS."

—LOREN EISELEY

We set off just after nightfall, chugging into the dark, murky waters under a huge red rising moon. As the boat's wooden hull slapped at the rippling tides, we glided through the silence like a shadow. Vague contours of the somber landmass to our right glowed in the eerie moonlight. Occasional lights flickered on a darkened shore, unimaginable sparks of life on the ragged edge of nowhere.

As we skirted that savage coastline, I stared at the endless expanse of jungle. I had a sudden disturbing vision of eels; an unseen world of ugly jet-black beings writhing and slithering around in the depths beneath my feet. The gruesome image froze my heart with a shadow of dread as a cool ocean wind slapped at my face.

I turned and stared at my companions huddled on deck, drinking from a bottle of Johnny Walker. Leo must have known my mind. He motioned me over and I sat with them, smoking and drinking. As the bottle went around, that sacred elixir began to still my troubled thoughts. Lulled by the boat's steady movement and their soft, easy Portuguese banter, I sat back and dropped into the watery depths of a calm, dreamless sleep.

At dawn, a subtle change in the boat's steady rhythm awakened me. As I stood at the edge of the deck, pissing into the dark blue water, ghostly shapes appeared on the dim horizon. A red pinprick of sun was emerging like a cigarette burning through a dirty curtain as some distant islands grew distinct in the gray expanse.

One of the sailors, a large Negro named Baiano, spoke to me in a melodic mix of Spanish and Portuguese, pointing to one of the islands. "You see dat place deh, *amigo?*"

I squinted and nodded.

"French country dat, *rapaz*. Ol' prison. Debil Island, dem call it."

Devil's Island! I took a deep breath and stared at the infamous French penal colony, thinking of the legendary prisoner, Papillon. My mind flashed back over the pages of his story, a survivor's tale of super-human cunningness, strength, hope, and endurance.

Baiano's voice broke into my musings with a husky chuckle. "Hah! Imagine de place deh, fo' dem mek so evil de name, eh?"

Captain Leo steered a sharp turn toward another nearby atoll, a little closer to the coast. It was a strange destination—a leper colony.

I never knew such places actually existed, apart from in old black-and-white movies I'd seen as a kid. Standing on deck as we approached, I could make out a group of low-lying buildings.

Drawing closer, I spied a small wooden dock and rows of neat wooden dwellings with rust-colored tin roofs. Under bent coconut palms with whitewashed trunks, a black dog ran in circles, barking. As the boat chugged alongside, a group of men seemed to appear from nowhere. The tallest one was a lanky European priest with a thick mane of snow-white hair. Standing behind him were three grotesquely disfigured brown-skinned lepers.

The Negro Baiano threw a rope. With the practiced movements of an old sailor, the priest caught it and tied us off to a wooden piling. Leo jumped onto the dock. The two men shook hands like old friends as some of the lepers helped us unload boxes.

Seeing them up close like that was a shock. I'd never seen anyone with leprosy. Staring at those disease-ravaged faces and bodies, I realized they weren't like any cripples I'd ever known. But as I grew accustomed to their appearance, it was hard to escape the idea that they were pretty much the same as anybody else, maybe better off than many—because their deformity was out on the surface for all to see.

The world I came from was full of people falling apart, disguising it on the outside, hiding their hobbling afflictions behind spotless white walls of sanitized lies and respectable appearances. Where I was from, all the decay and abnormality was kept well hidden, tucked away behind closed doors, cloaked by dull plastic happy-masks of practiced propriety. All my life, I'd been an outcast—a social leper—and I'd always had to go it alone. At least these lepers had a community, I mused, a colony, a family. And they had a God.

I didn't know what I had, but the road had taken me as far away as possible now from the world I'd left behind. I figured those lepers were the lucky ones. Unlike me, they'd found their quiet place in the bright sunshine. They had a home.

44. A PIRATE'S LIFE

Staring out over a sparkling sunlit sea the next day, far from sight of land, I noticed the others standing together on deck, pointing at the horizon. I went over to check out what appeared to be a flare, some sort of distant distress signal. Searching the water through Leo's binoculars, I could make out a shimmering white shape in the distance. As we drew closer, I saw it was a large luxury yacht. An American flag hung like a soggy eagle over the shiny gilded gold letters at the stern: *LUCKY DAWG—Ft. Lauderdale.*

Pulling alongside, my mates tied off to the big unlikely vessel as I gawked at another unexpected sight: a pair of chubby bikini-clad blond-haired Barbies lounging on deck, cool as cats, sipping brightly colored drinks from dainty champagne glasses with little pink umbrellas. I followed Leo onboard.

A ruddy-faced guy with a crew cut, Bermuda shorts and a loud Hawaiian shirt greeted us. The archetypical Ugly American. "Hey, buenas dios, amigos! We got a li'l pro-blem-o." He held up an empty cocktail glass. "We done ran fresh outta ice. Ice-o. Compren-day?"

I blinked. Was I tripping? Leo stared at the incongruous gringo as the others waited for me to decipher his alien words.

I turned to Leo and stammered in Spanish. "He says, uh, he needs. . . ice. . . . " I shrugged, feeling kind of embarrassed.

Leo gawked. "They put up the emergency flare. . . for that?"

I shrugged. "That's it, Captain. Guess they really want ice. . . . "

"*Porra!* De gringo gots de very serious crisis on de high sea." Leo threw back his head and guffawed. "*Que merda! Eu hein. . . . *"

Baiano called back in Portuguese, chuckling from his ample belly, and we all snickered in unison.

"Does somebody wanna t-t-tell me w-what th' hell's so goddamn funny hea-ah?" The Ugly American was sputtering like a broken lawnmower, his ruddy red face growing redder.

On a cabin door, I spied a familiar sticker: **AMERICA—LOVE IT OR LEAVE IT!** Laughing a little harder than the others, I snuffed my cigarette butt out on the shiny wooden deck.

That did it. The Ugly American turned uglier. Picking up his flare gun, he leveled the stubby wide barrel at my chest, shouting. "HEY, BOY!! I SHOT MEN OVER IN 'NAM FOR LESS'N THAT!! THAT THERE'S A GODDAMN TEAKWOOD DECK, GODDAMMIT!! WORTH MORE'N YER WETBACK LIFE, YA LI'L PECKERWOOD!!'"

I stared back at the angry redneck, making no sign of understanding a word he uttered. My companions appeared more baffled than ever.

"I think it's time fer y'all ta git th' hell back on yer g-goddamn b-b-beaner-bucket there!" He scowled with the face of an angry toad— if toads were pink and obnoxiously stupid.

Suddenly another half-drunk gringo appeared from below, clutching a spear gun. "Hey, Bubba, what th' hell's goin' on up here?" He took one look at us and leveled the weapon in our direction.

"*Que porra, Joni?*" Leo looked between the gringos and me.

"*Son piratas, Leo.*" I heard myself whispering a bullshit warning. "Pirates! These guys wanna take your boat, *hermano!*"

Just then, the Barbies called out from the stern. "*Bubba! Hey, Bubba-aa. . . . *" Distracted, the Ugly American turned.

Leo seized the moment, putting his long fishing knife to Bubba's pudgy throat. As Leo struggled to disarm him, the signal gun went off, sending a flaming orange flare scuttling across the deck into a corner.

Nobody moved.

"BUBBA, HEY, BUBBA, THEY GOT ANY ICE?" The Barbies were hollering like alley cats in heat, oblivious to the standoff on deck.

As Leo pressed the knife harder into the redneck's Adam's apple, Bubba called out to his friend. "Uh, I think ya b-better p-put that thang down thare, Luke."

Luke lowered his spear gun. I snatched it and flipped it around, leveling the sharp point at Bubba's ugly blue-gray eyeball. I could see terror in his dull-witted toad face. I liked it.

I grinned, flashing a pirate's gold tooth. *What's worth more'n my fucking life now, shit-for-brains?*

"*Piratas, hein?*" Baiano barked, stepping aboard brandishing a long machete. I shoved the other redneck toward the big Negro, poking the spear into his face and drawing a spot of blood as Baiano held his sharp steel blade under his chin.

As I turned to open the cabin door, the bumper sticker caught my eye again. A wave of hatred clutched at my gut as I tore through cabinets and drawers with a purpose, filling duffel bags with cameras, radios, watches, wallets, money, and jewelry.

Grinning, I threw the bulging bags out on deck. Leo was holding his own wood-handled sawed-off shotgun now.

"HEY, AMIGO!" Bubba was stuttering like Elmer Fudd. ***"YA WON'T G-GIT AWAY WITH IT! D-D-DO YA KNOW WHO I AM?"***

Leo slid up beside me, whispering in Portuguese. "I cut their fuel line. They don' gonna follow. *'Bora!*"

Throwing a final smirk at the hapless gringos, I withdrew from the unlucky ***LUCKY DAWG*** as they scrambled to put out the flames.

45. BETHLEHEM ON THE AMAZON

"And so it went that, once upon a time at sea, I officially became a fuggin' pirate." Cigano laughs.

Jaco stares at him, dumbfounded.

"Don't get me wrong, man." The tattoo smiles with a faraway look. "During my time at sea I heard some really hair-raising tales of real pirates in those waters. The sailors used to refer to the murderous scumbags as 'water rats.' That's another story. But, believe me, contrary to popular Hollywood fairy tales in the movies and so on, real-life pirates are not fuggin' cool. Not at all."

He flips a page and reads on.

○   ○   ○

Days later, late at night, I spied our final destination emerging on the horizon. Holding my breath, I marveled at the sparkling lights of Brazil's northernmost outpost, Belém do Pará, Gateway to the Amazon.

Gliding closer over a still, silent estuary, the musty colonial frontier lay spread across the water like a lazy old whore. Holding a small leather satchel stuffed with my share of the confiscated gringo booty in my lap as we drew into the port, I sat out on deck with the others, writing in my journal till a fine rainy mist bogged the pen down like a truck spinning its wheels in dark jungle mud.

After tying the boat off at a deserted wharf on the outskirts of the strange new city, my companions and I jumped in a dockside taxi. They dropped me off in a sleepy downtown area.

Wandering the quiet night streets of Belém, I stopped at a little *boteco*. I had a few shots of *cachaça*, then walked around some more.

Feeling excited and somewhat disoriented, I stopped and sat awhile in a deserted plaza, smoking a stolen pirate cigar and imagining earth-bound spirits of the dead dancing in the smoke. I didn't know what year it was anymore, and I didn't care.

Finally, I rose up and walked on, feeling my way like a blind man through the rain-slick streets of the sleeping old river port, vaguely searching for a place to stay the night.

JOURNAL ENTRY—BELÉM DO PARÁ, BRAZIL:

Midnight taxi scuttling over sleeping streets of mud, wood shacks, tin roofs, dirt, whitewashed palms and hissing banana plants. Faceless zombie shadows lurking on dim yellow corners. Distorted scraps of eerie tropical music float in the pregnant night air like tattered newspaper moths. In the shadows of the sleeping port, I float along on tipsy feet, past schools of crooked piranha girls lining murky corners, a lazy snarl of treacherous red lips mumbling at waterlogged ghosts of washed-up sailors, swallowing their boozy dreams like deep-sea suckerfish. I pass a hole-in-the-wall bar where tipsy samba dancers stagger around to a hazy chorus. A fiery-eyed mulatto girl twists and spins around and around, a mad Gypsy spirit of humid night, a skinny brown man bent like a beggar at her satin knees. Twenty hungry dockworkers watch from the soggy shadows in a silent prayer for shining junkyard angels to descend from the cloudy heavens of fine yellow rain and make this sad, rum-soaked tropical existence whole and sacred and new.

Later, feeling restless in a cheap hotel room overlooking the dark downtown streets, I gave up on sleep. The ghosts of ages were groaning and banging in night's empty tomb as I rose from the creaking wooden bed and descended an ancient marble staircase stained with dried-gum-spotted memories. I wandered along the wide, deserted Avenida Rio Branco till I came to a ragged plaza with a charming old outdoor café under a baroque looking kiosk. Among crooked tables populated by aging whores, my eyes fixed on a lively-looking girl sitting with a group of drunks.

Our eyes met, just like they're supposed to in a dream. Slouching into my somnambulant vision, she drifted over and took me by the hand. Without a word we moved to an empty table. I signaled to a skinny old waiter, and it was on.

Just like in a dream, we drank beer and *cachaça* rum, and I knew I wasn't alone anymore. She talked at me in panting frantic bursts like a rabid dog imitating Faye Dunaway, and I learned of her life. She was thirty years old, she said, a native of that humid downbeat dreamscape. A salty seasoned street hooker of the lethargic old port, she had written a book once, or was writing one, or would like to write one, something like that, from what I could understand of her garbled, frenetic patois. Her words glided between English, Portuguese, and Spanish, and I didn't really understand, and it really didn't matter as I watched her mad pink lips moving like fabulous dancing spirits.

She told me she lived alone in a wooden shack by a muggy brown canal surrounded by fruit trees with strange names. She was the ex-wife of Belém's Great Bohemian Poet, or something like that. As a girl she had been a promising ballet dancer, performing for local dignitaries in the stately old *Teatro Municipal* she pointed to across the way, where she had whirled and pirouetted with such staggering force of abandon she spun and twirled her long youthful limbs right off the stage, out the door, down the stairs, across the road, and into the park, and she didn't stop till she landed face up in this shabby little rotunda, where she had been holding nightly court ever since, delighting sailors and traveling men of the night for twenty Brazilian cruzeiros a whirl.

As she leaned against me like a purring alley cat, I felt grateful for her company. She smoked cheap filterless cigarettes and dirt-brown marijuana rolled in thin paper bar napkins. She drank *cachaça* like a stevedore, chattering gaily into the pre-dawn silence, words in many languages falling on my ears like a relentless tropical rain.

She came back to my room at first light and, with a body hard as the ancient cobbled streets of Belém, she fucked me to sleep, taking flight with the dawn like some noisy jungle scavenger bird.

I might have easily stayed on forever in Belém with her, writing mildewed poetry in a shack by a brown canal in a cloud of sticky brown Amazon marijuana smoke as the jungle swallowed my dreams like quicksand. But in the harsh light of dawn I saw that her nipples were ringed with strange monkey-like hairs. A large, sinister lump protruded from her armpit. Her feet were crooked and dirty as witch's claws, her eyes desperate as a suicide note.

After she left, my sleep was jumpy and crowded with dark rambling phantom shapes, like the hulks of the looming riverboats silently plying the murky brown river basin outside the dirty rain-streaked hotel window.

46. THE LONG AFTERNOON

"WITH NOTHING TO DO BUT EXPECT THE HOUR OF SETTING OFF, THE AFTERNOON WAS LONG."

—JANE AUSTEN

At daybreak, the noisy movement of the chaotic downtown streets below my room roused me early. After a quick lukewarm rinse in a mildewed shower stall, I staggered out to join a raging current of swirling, blaring humanity.

In the glaring light of day, the buzzing outdoor marketplaces of Belém were a colorful riot of frenzied activity—all circulating around the dozens of dirty white wooden riverboats moored at the crowded street-side docks. I stared up at those big cargo-laden vessels: floating microcosms of a boundless green jungle expanse upriver whose only links with the outside world were the great wide waterways of the fabled Amazon territories.

A burning equatorial sun blasted the world with white-hot intensity in a surreal, frenzied dockside carnival of life, imprinting indelible snapshots on my retina: A grizzled Indian walking the crowded dock with a purpose, carrying a small spotted jungle cat cub on a short rope. A brown-skinned boy holding a shrunken head in his grubby little hands. I gawked at the grotesque mummified human doll face, its dark, leathery lips perforated with tiny shafts of wood, and I wondered if the girl from the night before might have slipped some weird hallucinogen into my drinks.

A nervous sweat began troubling at my flesh like a tic. I needed a drink. My soul craved darkness, shade, shelter from that merciless daylight glare. My eyes darted around like nervous goldfish, watching the crooked wooden boats crowding together in the murky brown water. Big sputtering flatbed cargo trucks rumbled over the sagging wharves as stubby brown men in khaki shorts and high rubber boots shouted and scampered around in a dizzying blur, offloading oversized straw baskets bulging with colorful tropical fruits. I could feel myself breaking into a cold sweat. My hands trembled. My empty stomach twitched as the whirlwind of clamorous motion all around me pounded a million tiny hammers into my hungover nerves.

I spotted an ornate ironwork entrance to a big indoor *mercado*. Seeking refuge, I crossed the street, sidestepping a rumbling olive-green military transport packed with bored-looking young soldiers, and ducked inside.

Birds roosted in the lofty dark rafters. A pungent stench invaded my nostrils. My mouth filled with saliva, my guts churning like a garbage truck. My innards trembled in a high-pitched discordant symphony of nausea as I moved through a sickening display of gigantic gutted fish. Feeling about to puke, I stepped up my pace and marched onward through a sweaty gauntlet of strange religious icons.

Charms, medallions, necklaces, potions, glittering portraits of saints and odd, otherworldly voodoo entities crowded the endless, crooked spook-house aisles. Feeling increasingly faint and dizzy, my bloodshot eyes zeroed in on a little *boteco* where bottles of sweet, colorful rum-based liquids with fruits and herbs beckoned from dark wooden shelves. I staggered up to the counter and pointed at the only medicine for what ailed me.

A gap-toothed old mulatto filled a water glass with cloudy green liquid, and I gulped it down. Feeling immediate relief as the sour tangy fire of *cachaça* hit my core, I motioned for another shot, from an orange bottle this time, and then another. Red bottle. Chasing the bittersweet elixirs down, one by one, with a large bottle of beer, I sighed and leaned back against the timeworn wooden counter. Feeling restored, I busied myself studying the beer bottle's ornate label as my spirit slowly slipped back into my body, blending into sync with my colorful new surroundings.

At once, life was in perfect divine order. I was in Brazil at last, I mused! Yes! I wanted to jump up and shout with joy. Grinning, I lit a triumphant cigarette, and through a boozy haze, my memories drifted back over the long, arduous voyage that had brought me there, across deserts and mountains, jungles and ports, a dizzying mental blur of villages, towns, and cities of Mexico and the humid, rum-soaked vistas of Central America.

I downed another glass, and my thoughts continued shuttling backward in slow-motion detail, by thumb, train, truck, bus, and motorcycle, by highway, road, and jungle trail, ship, boat, and foot, through islands, rivers, and sparkling green seas.

Coming clearer with each new drink, I envisioned all the people, places, and events of my travels. And I knew the road had changed me deep inside forever. Its strange, unspoken codes had slowly woven themselves into my cells with all the meals I'd eaten, the meat, vegetables, and fruits of the gritty mystical Mesoamerican lands whose spicy-lipped, brown-eyed daughters I'd slept with and kissed, mixing my saliva and breath with their musky indigenous thoughts and dreams; it had all become an essential part of my being now.

How profoundly the bumps and grooves of that long lonesome highway had subtly, inexorably rewired my very genetic codes, giving birth to a whole new man: a solitary Gypsy warrior. And all along, the road had been my teacher, molding and training me in a benevolent boot camp of life, schooling me in all new ways, manners, mannerisms, customs, habits, languages, and gestures, slowly, patiently indoctrinating me into this blessed new reality, a marvelous new existence that a hungry American kid could never have dreamed in his wildest acid trips or delirious opiate stupors.

All the road dirt and dust I'd swallowed had nourished and created this rough rootless being whose scars, memories, tattoos, and dreams now made up an abundant new baggage of experience, a totality of crazy life, honing my instincts and survival skills, hammering my mind, body, and spirit like a samurai sword being tempered and sharpened, readied for unknown battles of strange and mystical portent. For me, there would be no end to the road.

Sitting at that dark little market counter, drinking in the afternoon heat of those sad, evocative tropics, I wanted to weep with gratitude. I could feel my heart swell like a red balloon, bursting with fear, excitement, and a sudden absolute certainty that my long, crucial love affair with the road had only just begun.

I downed another beer and staggered off, floating onward in a swirling, sensory kaleidoscope. As the ground melted under my feet, each step was a euphoric perfumed revelation, delighting my senses like a child seeing magic for the first time.

Yes, the booze had given me wings to fly away to magical worlds of romance, poetry, and adventure, opening my soul to a mystical union with each new perfect moment. I was deeply obliged to the Spirits for rescuing me from a long, hopeless heroin stupor that had nearly ended my short, troubled life; for lending me the courage to finally get out and search for my rightful place in the world. And, all along that long crooked road, the kindly Spirits of the bottle had carried me on golden wings of peace, comfort, and hope.

◌   ◌   ◌

"It's funny." Cigano grunts, looking up from his reading. "When I finally sobered up, for a long time I thought my big problem was always the booze. If I could just find a way to live without it, who knows? Maybe things would get better for me, somehow. . . . "

Jaco looks at him, saying nothing.

The tattoo man shakes his head. "But after a few years living with myself sober and eventually relapsing cuz I couldn't live without the sense of ease and comfort it provided, I realized the alcohol had never been my problem. Not at all." He sighs. "It took me a long fuggin' time to figure out my only real problem was always *me*. Drinking was my solution, my medicine. When the liquor finally stopped working for me, that's when my whole mental outlook *really* started turning to shit. Sober. . . .   Stark raving sober. . . . "

He stops and stares at his words on the page again. *I was deeply obliged to the Spirits. The booze gave me wings to fly.*

"This next part kinda sums it up." He shrugs, falling silent. He stares at the page for a moment. Then he begins to read again.

"Little did I know that those soothing, benevolent spirits would someday take away the very sky, dashing me onto a cold clammy rock with broken wings, like Prometheus; singed, frazzled, and melted from flying too close to the sun."

He takes a deep breath, then reads the rest.

"But I was still on a long, happy honeymoon with the Spirits. Alcohol was still my sacred elixir, a mystical time machine on a mad magic-carpet ride to nowhere. The Spirits were still my only friends and allies, the only companionship I thought I would ever need."

o   o   o

For the rest of the afternoon, I staggered around the streets of Belém, like a heat-crazed, rabid dog on the prowl. My brain tingled with the fuzzy visions of a feral child on a wild and dangerous funhouse ride. Stupefied with a driving lust for motion, and lost in a restless maze of bottomless hunger, I walked on, looking, seeking, searching, craving, wanting; always wanting more of some mysterious, unattainable Something. My plodding boots propelled me forward like a pair of tipsy guides as I trudged lopsided shantytown paths, past ragtag eateries where sailors gathered at wobbly wooden tables in the dirt, playing cards and drinking with wild-eyed *caboclos*, their leather-sheathed machetes strapped to muscular brown legs.

Coming to a wide wooden shack teetering over the water on rickety gray stilts, I paused. Drawn to a blaring Calypso beat from within, I edged closer, peering into the shadowy space. Amid shimmering, blinking whorehouse lights, men sat drinking among groups of half-naked teenage girls with jet-black hair and fabulous indigenous features.

I stepped in the door, a weary gunslinger stepping into a Wild West saloon. A lanky Negro sat alone at the bar, shaking toothpicks from a plastic container, making a sound like a rattlesnake. I signaled to a thin mulatto barman in mirrored sunglasses. He handed me a full glass of *cachaça* and a beer. Time plodded by like the murky brown river beneath the sagging wooden floor.

After several drinks, I got up and wandered off down the deserted sunbaked street by the riverside again, a sleepwalker lost in a boozy waking dream. The day wore on in a fuzzy blur of swaying patterns of light and shadow, pockmarked with the ever-present olive-green Jeeps packed with faceless teenage soldiers.

Indistinct human figures lurked in the humid shadows, waiting for nothing. I lumbered on into a labyrinth of ramshackle shacks and little outdoor market stalls. A group of fishermen was standing around a rough-hewn wooden table near a boat, pointing at the enormous carcass of an alien-looking fish. They were arguing like soccer fans in grunting regional Portuguese, speaking of mermaids and terrible storms at sea. Chuckling to myself, I shuffled off.

Coming to a tattered map of Brazil on a weathered wooden wall, I stopped and stared. My finger absently traced its way down the crooked, mysterious lines of that vast country, over curves and shapes, traveling unknown highways and borders, across states with strange, unpronounceable names, and cities of wild promise and adventure, over thousands of kilometers of empty green Amazon territories, then following a long, jagged blue coastline, down, down, like a well seeking water, to a familiar little ditch along the distant southern coast, and the magical words: Rio de Janeiro.

Thinking of that fabled city of dreams, I turned and drifted on again. Rough wooden piers jutted out over the muddy water. Lopsided riverboats chugged past in the distance, plying the river like lost fragments of time's forgotten memory. Finally, sweaty and tired, I stopped to rest in an overgrown plaza.

That's where I saw the Thing.

Laid out on the ground between a pair of mismatched stone benches sat a chunk of raw meat carved into the shape of a man. The bizarre apparition was surrounded by a dozen burning red candles. Etched in the dirt around the disturbing little meat effigy, I could make out a primitive stick figure in a dusty frame of cryptic, esoteric symbols. The surreal voodoo offering was swarming with flies, like some ghastly living thing.

I wanted to look away from the macabre spectacle, even as I sensed a dark, morbid switch being thrown in some forgotten corner of my being. As it crept over me in waves of insidious epiphany, I knew I'd suddenly crossed some hideous occult frontier, stepping into a sinister nether-realm from which I sensed there would be no turning back. And in that moment, a grotesque seed was planted like a time bomb, deep in my psychic hard drive—programmed to grow and take on its own savage self-perpetuating life form, something far beyond my ability to grasp or control or escape.

The Curse had caught up with me.

My shirt was a steamy bog of drunken misery as I moved to a crumbling cement railing, swatting at mosquitoes and staring out over the river. A nagging pit of dread was growing in my center as I watched an indolent dung-colored canoe gliding along the water's edge. Four bare-chested tribesmen rowed in silence. Wearing only loincloths, their giant *National Geographic* lips protruded from stoic painted faces. My eyes focused in on an old man sitting at the helm. A black and yellow cap with the words *CAT* shadowed the gaunt face staring straight ahead behind a pair of Ray-Bans. Across the road from where I stood, another drab olive-green truck rumbled by; a blurry vision of blank-faced soldiers clutching sinister black rifles.

Startled by a pair of weird little cartoonish voices, I looked up to see a pair of feathery missiles: two giant blue macaws alighting on a nearby branch. I could see the shiny black buttons of their eyes, a dash of bright blood-red plumage around their dark gray squabbling beaks. Their childlike chatter shook me from my torpor as they took to the air again, clowns rolling out of the Big Top, making way for lions and tigers, elephants and bears.

My skin tingled and twitched like a cat as I turned and walked away from that accursed plaza. But, deep inside, I knew there would be no walking away from whatever dark, hellish forces that creepy vortex in the dirt had released. I was fucked.

Wandering down the road in the dim dusk light, I could feel the troubled spirits of an ancient Curse joining me again, lodging themselves on the outskirts of my soul like an encampment of restless phantom parasites.

47. THE RIVER OF SOULS

The next day, in an impromptu gathering of shady merchants at the sprawling *Ver-o-Peso* marketplace, I sold off the Ugly American's purloined possessions. Flush with enough cash to move on again, I quickly secured passage on one of the big white wooden boats.

As the drab embarkation plodded its way upriver, my brain oozed into the heart of Amazonia, lulling me into a long, monotonous stupor. Chug-chug-chugging an endless expanse of still brown waters, the boat slowly became a reflection of my deteriorating psychic landscape—a sluggish phantom shape plying my dreams and merging with the pungent smoke of jungle fires dotting the distant shorelines.

Staring off into space from the humid cocoon of my hammock on deck, I opened my journal. My pen stood poised over the paper like a hesitant diver. But the words wouldn't come. Lost in the plodding blank waterlogged nether-zone of the boat, the days and nights all blended together in damp, greasy, indistinct smudges on my spirit.

Like a slack-jawed prisoner whose cell becomes his only world, I grinned stupidly as the smell of wet earth filled my head like a sick-house balloon. I would find myself suddenly giggling over nothing in that lingering muddy stew without name, without time or space or definition.

At day's end, the river would swallow the sun in a murky, mosquito-humming mist. Flashes of lightning, thunder, and rain defined my existence, as I became a heat-crazed, shell-shocked ghost, wandering a tangled labyrinth of hammocks crowding the slippery wooden deck.

All the clammy spirits of mankind, past, present, and future, living, dead, and unborn, seemed to be murmuring together in a mad, voiceless cacophony of anguish as the storms marched across the jungle floor like angry giants, followed by a long weary steam, their echoes lingering on in every aching cell and molecule of my being, and then slowly merging into the next interminable round of apathetic, empty-minded tedium.

The brain-melting boredom of the long, soggy voyage was broken only by infrequent stops at faceless muddy little jungle outposts at the watery edges of nowhere. Spectacular sunsets, sunrises, and booming displays of thunder and lightning heralded the constant comings and goings of a bizarre cast of characters parading before my weary eyes in a surreal slideshow of watery mental snapshots: A group of Argentine boys chattering like drunken parrots. Indigenous families bundled together in their hammocks across the deck, cowering before the elements under clammy gray blankets, like alien pods on a sleeping monster's back.

A coppery brown kid with a sunken tubercular chest and eyes black as the night stood at the railing for hours, a small monkey with a long tiger-striped tail perched on his bony shoulder, picking lice from his hair. As the boy turned to stare at a bare-chested Indian girl breast-feeding a baby no larger than the monkey, the attentive creature's head pivoted around like a surveillance camera, eyeing me with suspicious little monkey eyes.

I sat back in my hammock, exhausted, dreaming an invalid's dreams, lost in feverish visions of past lives in other strange, humid lands. And all the while, I drank mechanically from an endless succession of bottles of cheap sickbed rum—a sweet, useless medicine for that dreary, plodding malady without name or cure—as I wondered, always wondering, what did those people think about? What was this place, this stark unfathomable replication of a world? Who were these oddly familiar human creatures all around me, these weird vagabond beings with faces like monkeys and minds I would never know?

Stuck in a tedious replay whirlpool of memory and random contemplation, drained of all energy but aimless thought, my mind drifted back to a fifty-cent hotel room on the Mosquito Coast of British Honduras, long, lazy nights spent under the stars there smoking stupefying marijuana cigars on a rickety wooden boat dock with a group of Negro boys who had never seen the world beyond their tiny fishing village, and probably never would.

Fueled by that surreal slideshow of recollections, the days floated by like the river. From time to time, I'd sit up, rubbing at my unshaven chin and studying the other forlorn passengers: A gaunt, toothless white man with a cross crudely tattooed across his ageless granite face who boarded at the last muddy river port. Demented-looking and agitated, the ghost-like stranger spent his days pacing back and forth on the deck like a mangy old circus tiger, his shirtless bony sun-ravaged torso marked with a long, vicious Frankenstein scar. Would that be me in twenty years? No way, I mused, I'd surely never live that long.

Another sunset, another day gone by. Mosquitoes humming at my ears at the start of another long faceless night on the river, another listless, godless, boring mist of eternal nothingness. My sweat-soaked shirt stayed wrapped around my head like a dirty turban. My unhappy somnambulant eyes snapped open and shut, twin camera shutters registering the drabness of another dusk or dawn or whatever over those murky waters covering the earth's afflicted surface like a moldy tuburcular blanket.

Under an oppressive low cloud cover blocking the sky in an awful milky stew, the smallest details seemed to take on massive proportions, carving themselves like graffiti onto the walls of my brain, my memory, my dreams.

A dead cow floating past, a bloated, grimacing leather balloon, its four lifeless brown legs sticking straight up, pointing obscenely at the impotent, drizzly, uncaring gray heavens.

48. A SAILOR'S GRAVE

By the time the boat reached its final port of call—a nameless village in the middle of the jungle—I'd traveled hundreds of miles upriver.

Staggering off that accursed floating purgatory, drained beyond exhaustion, I felt as if the steamy flatline eternity on the river had eaten into my brain like an infestation of tiny jungle termites. My legs were jelly as I stumbled onto a bustling wooden dock crowded with boxes and bundles, with pigs, chickens, and people, all clamoring around like hungry insects.

Teetering down a short wobbly ramp like a zombie, I wandered away from the chaotic little landing, swatting at a living cloud of mosquitoes. They seemed to intensify in ferocity with every agonizing step, as my feet guided me like a soggy human compass through the desolate muddy streets. Dirty and sweating, I lurched forward without direction or destination, waving an impotent hand at the alien hum of invisible predators battling one another for my blood.

As day slipped into night, a drowning man's dying gurgle, a mad, overpowering dirge of insects buzzed in the vast, twittering jungle— millions of bugs, billions, trillions, more insects than all the grains of sand of all the deserts on all the godless planets in a hellish, malevolent universe; all bleating and rattling, chirping, singing, and trilling away in a maddening bloodthirsty riot, a hopeless cacophony of infinite malarial swamps surrounding that godforsaken flyspot on a moldy map of Hell's forgotten regions.

Too tired to curse or complain, I was a broken war-battered refugee limping along a step at a time, past empty-looking thatched-roof huts where hollow human eyes peered from the shadows like blunt arrowheads. Coming to a decrepit wooden shack displaying a rusty tin Coca-Cola sign—the only trace of any commerce—I gravitated to its half-open door, desperate for a bottle of rum, a beer, something, anything to fuel some semblance of salvation for my trembling hungover soul.

An ancient geezer leaning on a wooden post in the dirt gaped at me with forlorn unblinking eyes, expressionless as a cow: awful emotionless sunken orbs staring out from under a silver-dollar-sized birthmark dominating a scab-covered balding skull.

What could the old cow possibly be thinking? I stood at the door, waiting. No one came. The loitering dirt-toad said nothing. Nothing; only those ugly, persistent, bloodshot, shit-colored cow eyes boring into my soul. Shrinking under his unbearable gaze, I wandered off, muttering under my breath. I could feel that indolent bovine stare at my back, following me down the muddy road like a persistent beggar's loathsome shadow.

I walked on, as if I even knew where the fuck I was headed. But, right from the start, walking had always taken me wherever I needed to get to. As my plodding boots sank into the dark muddy soil, I knew that red-clay dirt knew my sadness and despair. It knew my interminable irritation, frustration, and unease as it reached up from the ground, silently guiding me, propelling me through an undignified molecular frenzy of scrawny mutts barking behind rusty barbed-wire fences where skinny chickens ran around in dusty circles of futility, like tiny lost space aliens.

Gangs of naked brown children gathered and gaped, pointing and giggling, snickering hordes of demon runts pursuing me down the road. Their numbers swelled as I trudged onward, a pissed-off, plague-ridden runaway sideshow freak. Groups of dull-eyed locals gawked and stared. I was a spaceman, an alien, a miserable wandering public curiosity.

Finally, I came to what passed for a town square, a shabby mudhole of weedy ruin only distinguishable from its desolate surroundings by a crumbling cement monument to some ignoble-looking military honcho. A group of ancient Indians sitting in the dirt didn't even seem to notice my presence as I wandered past. I was invisible again, at last, a wandering ghost of the night.

Spotting a weatherbeaten hotel sign under a weak bare lightbulb surrounded by a swarm of huge flying insects, I ducked into the ramshackle wooden structure, as if it might fade away like a mirage if I hesitated.

A wrinkled toothless hag took some limp bills from my hand and passed me a hammock, a stiff cotton towel, and a tiny slab of soft white coconut soap. Handing me a key, she pointed a skeletal finger toward an unpainted wooden corridor. I could hear her grunting something behind me as I staggered off down the hall, too tired to turn around.

Fitting the key into a worn brass padlock in a galvanized metal hasp on a flimsy plywood door, I stepped into a dark, humid little cubicle. My hand felt its way along the wall like a crab till it found a switch. A dim bare bulb lit the windowless coffin: four wooden walls, tin ceiling, cement floor. No furniture. No sink. A hammock hook on each of the walls. Water closet at the end the hall. Maybe I'd even find a toilet there, rather than a hole in the floor to squat over like on that shit-forsaken riverboat.

I stepped inside. A massive brown insect was dragging itself across the floor. Scrunching up my face, I nudged it out into the hallway with the tip of my boot. I slammed the door shut behind me and threw the latch. It didn't match the hole in the doorjamb. *Shit!* I bent down, cursing, and pulled the door up from the bottom with one hand, aligning the lock and the hole.

There was still a gap between the floor and the bottom of the door— plenty of space for that hell-spawned creature to crawl back in. *Fuck.* I ventured out into the hall. The bug sat there buzzing, a miniature alien spacecraft. I kicked it with the side of my boot and watched it scuttle off down the hallway. Then I stepped back inside and closed the door, feeling a sudden head rush.

Dizzy, exhausted, sweating, I was shivering with cold, despite the stifling heat. As if watching an old slow-motion movie, I saw myself pick up the hammock, then drop it again.

I sunk down to the floor and fell sideways, the hard cool cement pressing against my feverish skin. At eye level now with the crack under the door, I suddenly pictured a battalion of bugs lurking in the hallway, just waiting for me to pass out so they could come and devour my burning carcass.

Shit! Painfully, I rose to my feet. Somehow I managed to hang the hammock. Mosquitoes were humming in my ear. I raised my hand to shoo them away, almost blacking out from the effort.

Easing down into the clammy net, testing the hooks, the balance, I sighed as the hammock grew taut. I was barely able to kick off my muddy boots. I tried to sit up and lower my pants. It was all too much effort. Trembling all over, I fell back into the hammock like a scuba diver dropping off a boat as a creeping stupor enveloped my brain, dragging me down, down, down. . . .

Down, down the underwater camera eye drops. Consciousness descends like a heavy anchor, emerging in a murky green-brown haze of sadness. The dreamer can taste a bloody stench of raw liver. Heavy fog surrounds an indistinct faraway shape emerging across a dark rolling body of water—the familiar form of an old-time sailing ship. The words HOMEWARD BOUND appear in the dreamer's mind. His sight focuses in on a weird telescopic vision of the ship's hull bobbing in dark blue waters. He spies a blurry shape in the water beside the vessel. Squinting, straining to see something moving around in quick mechanical patterns, the vision becomes distinct. A sailor has fallen overboard. Horrified, he watches the man fighting, struggling and splashing in the water. A gigantic blue-gray snout is pushing him around the surface like a frenzied toy. A shark is about to eat the unfortunate mariner, maneuvering to sink its powerful toothy grip into his frantic body. The dreamer tries to look away but his eyes are paralyzed, riveted on the terrible spectacle. As the desperate seaman twists and turns in a mad acrobatic effort to survive, the creature bites him in half in one fast, sleek sweep of slashing jaws. The thrashing blue water turns red and the sailor is torn to pieces in a tragic bloody ballet of primal feeding. The vision shifts, and the dreamer is standing on a barnacle-covered rock jutting out of the ocean. Waves wash over his unfeeling translucent feet. Feeling sick and dizzy, he realizes he is the ghost of a dead sailor whose ship has run aground and sunk. A familiar inner voice urges him to go below the sea to search for his place, and then he is walking on the bottom. As his eyes scan the ocean floor, he sees the thick wooden mast of his ship settling into a silent cloud of sand. He can feel the words A LONG TIME AGO forming in his awareness as he moves toward the looming underwater graveyard. Deep in the wreckage he comes across a body. The lifeless face stares up through the indifferent fishes darting around. Feeling a deep sense of longing, the dreamer reaches out to touch the waterlogged corpse. Suddenly, a disembodied spirit flashes from its mouth and shoots skyward in a blinding silver burst of light, and then he is back standing on the rocks again. Shaking his head, he looks out over the sea. "I may as well be dead," he *sighs. Muttering and complaining, he sits down on the cold wet rock of ages, a stranded earthbound ghost. "Wait! **I am** dead," he cries. The feeble words seem to emerge from a distant valley. It's hard to comprehend that it is he who uttered them. As he scuttles along the slippery rock like a crab, searching for something he's forgotten in the world of the living, a mosquito's high-pitched hum begins boring into his disembodied ear. Growing louder, louder, the sound is soon buzzing like a power-saw, reminding him of an animated old-time cartoon shark's gleaming teeth. Different noises join the buzz, growing into an ascending cacophony of booming, pounding infernal machinery. He loses his footing, and then he's slipping, sliding down the rock. Everything is melting in a jumble of prehistoric lava, slithering down, down, descending into a raging, undulating sea of mud. His delirious sweat-stained bodiless body is floating on the surface, suspended, trapped, naked but for a dirty hand-hewn cotton loincloth. A cloud of cartoon mosquitoes descends over him and begins tattooing him all over with bites, and the monotonous buzzing drone continues to rise in volume. He lies prone, immobile, paralyzed, unable to cry out or move, like in little Jono's recurring nightmares. Recalling the horrible voodoo effigy in Belém, he sees himself morphing into that helpless, soulless little meat puppet, and now he is a hunk of lifeless dark fetid raw meat lying on a bed of shiny green banana leaves, surrounded by burning black and red candles. The disembodied dreamer watches, helpless, as a swarm of blue-black flies descends over his featureless face. The insects shift around all over him, covering his body, reminding him of the magnetic shavings in an old puzzle game he'd had as a child. They begin to take form in primitive tribal tattoo patterns, bold intertwining designs like the ones covering the body of his teenage comic book alter-ego, Captain Cringe. A muddy fog of sadness invades his soul as he struggles to remember. Peering through the haze like a deep-sea diver, he enters a cave-like chamber bathed in an eerie amber light. He can make out the petrified figures of two ancient pirates with dark, weathered parchment-like skin. One begins moving in the slow, jerky robotic waves of a silent movie, something from another time, another life, another place, another dream, a long time ago. The mummified pirate and the dreamer are one as he takes a rusty knife with a worn wooden handle and begins carving into the waxy flesh of the other. Then he turns the blade on himself. Making a deep incision in his own cold lifeless gut, he removes a shiny gemstone. The jewel is pulsing with life, shifting from blue to red to a deep purple amethyst. With slow, careful movements, he implants the living stone into the pale flesh of the other's chest. The mummified figure opens its eyes. It begins to speak to him in an unintelligible ancient language. The muddy livery-tasting veil of mourning grows across the vision like a fungus, and the dreamer is drifting away on a turbulent sea of pounding machinery, a throbbing wall of drumming sound like the giant insistent heartbeats of some monstrous, unseen creature, coming closer and closer as he surrenders to his death, again and again and again.*

49. GONE WITH THE WIND

Leafing through another notebook, Cigano pulls out a yellowed scrap of paper and reads out loud.

Malaria is a vector-borne infectious disease, widespread in tropical parts of the Americas. It is the greatest selected pressure on the human genome in history. Symptoms include fever, shivering, vomiting, anemia, and convulsions.

With a wry grin, the tattoo man folds the clipping and inserts it back into his journal. "Yeah, and I got hit with all of the above, man, some real ultra-violent fever hallucinations, seriously fucked-up nightmare visions."

He sighs as he flips a page and reads on.

o o o

I'd already been shitting blood for months from all the cheap rotgut rum. Now malaria joined the ravages of full-blown alcoholism, befuddling my senses and blotting out all fuzzy borders between dimensions, warping my perceptions into a chronic, chaotic delirious haze. Then, somewhere near Porto Velho, Brazil—a small river port on the Madeira River, a tributary of the Amazon near the Bolivian border—the journey became one long, surreal, foggy blur.

My feverish hallucinations were invaded by a steady mechanical booming as I came to one day, finding myself sitting in a very weird place. I opened my eyes to a strange slow-motion vision of shadows moving around in the peripheries of a moldy green metal fuselage. Not knowing where I was or how I'd ended up there, everything appeared as a rambling phantom reflection of a world that was once real—a place of ephemeral cutout people blowing on a tattered clothesline in an ill beggar's wind.

I blinked and looked around. . . . *This must be how a baby sees things. Or a dying person. Or an earthbound ghost.*

The pounding mental fog gave way to sounds and indistinct patterns. Had I died? Was this the Underworld? Hearing a whirring of landing gears, I suddenly realized I was sitting in the darkened bowels of an old WWII-vintage military airplane, surrounded by olive-clad teenage soldiers. Their stoic faces formed an animated still life of weird statue-people. *What the fuck? Where am I?* Panic jerked at my gut. . . . *Forget it! You're dead! A hundred and sixty pounds of dead-meat-cargo!* My hand felt at the lump sewn into the seam of my pants. . . . *Wait! Money. Passport. Good. Awake. Not dead. Okay. . . . But where the fuck* **am** *I? What's going on?*

Then I remembered. I was in Brazil. That much seemed certain. I reached out for my bag. It was sitting right beside me. *Good.* A young soldier was chattering at me, talking real fast in Portuguese, gesturing to my chest. I stared at him and he pointed to a strap bolted to the metal fuselage. As I struggled into the rough canvas harness, I looked down and saw a crude new tattoo mark on my forearm, right below the elbow. The vision slammed into my brain like a bird of prey crashing through a window. It was that same weird stick-figure symbol I'd seen carved in the sand beside the creepy meat doll in Belém!

I looked again. There it was, etched into my flesh! *What the fuck? How did that get there?* It was real.

I could feel a throbbing burn like a firecracker wound on my inner forearm as I stared at the baffling little mark. It was really there! *Fuck!* As the realization hit me with the force of a maniac breaking free from his restraints, I battled an onslaught of incoherent thoughts, struggling to recall how the hell I'd acquired that ugly occult blemish. Then I fell back, surrendering to the paralyzing knowledge that reality had suddenly shifted, and things would never be the same.

The soldier was speaking to me again, saying something over and over, the same senseless phrase, again and again, till I was dizzy with it. I looked up, confused. Then my vision went funny and I passed out.

The dreamer looks down at himself as young Jonathan's eyes roll back in his head like the fruits in a slot machine, and then he is floating in deep water, shape-shifting into a school of tiny fish at the bottom of the sea. Up ahead, a wrecked ship. He feels himself morphing into the school of fish, and then into a man, then a meat doll, then a ghost in another dream. Someone is speaking, repeating the same fuzzy phrase over and over, words he knows must mean something. But what? It's hard to hear without ears. Hearing as a school of fish, the sounds are an incomprehensible muddle of jumbled words, shifting in and out of focus like a television with a broken antenna. He strains to understand the words, words, words he knows from before somewhere, a long time ago. "Frankly, my dear, I don't give a damn!" The phrase blends with the sound of pounding machinery. Other voices join in, growing louder and louder, a senseless, garbled mantra of angry voices, yelling, shouting, cursing, spitting out insults, incantations, and demonic drunken cackling. He strains to hear through the noise, but the sounds keep fading in and out, in and out. Then only a long, toneless, monotonous ringing sound, and he realizes he is deaf! He puts his hand to the side of his head and grabs his ear. It feels wobbly, unstable. He tries to adjust it like an antenna. It comes off in his hand! Oh, God! Why? This shouldn't be happening! OH, GOD, I'VE BECOME A LEPER! He's a rotting human carcass, a drowned, impotent, earless meat-puppet! He struggles to attach the ear back to the side of his skull, but it won't stay. It keeps coming off in his hand like a broken battery cover to a transistor radio. He tries to snap it back into place, pressing down harder with his fingers, pushing at the wobbly, unstable thing with all his might. A nauseating sound lands like a rubber hammer in the pit of him. Startled silver fishes dart around in his gut as his fingers give way, one by one, breaking off his hand! OH GOD, OH SHIT, NO, PLEASE GOD NO-OO!! The dreamer tries to scream but no sound comes. As he opens his mouth to yell again, he can feel his jaw unhinging and dropping away from his face, a dull, lifeless hunk of clay! He tries to catch it but everything is happening in slow motion and he can't move fast enough underwater. The detached jaw begins falling down, down, down. He reaches out to grab it but it's incredibly heavy, like a slow-moving bowling ball. It takes both of his hands off at the wrists, and then everything goes down, down, down, and he's drowning in a crowded fistfight of pounding machinery and angry voices. A crowd gathers, a shifting sea of bored, gawking monkey-people staring at him accusingly. He can make out the vague faces of kids who used to tease him at school. An ascending mechanical chorus of mad, hateful voices is shouting, swearing, cursing him for his deformity. Then his mother emerges from the crowd, red-faced, hysterical, yelling. "Lepers! Outlaws! Scum! Those are somebody's children?" As her voice becomes swallowed up in the pounding, shouting din, he hears his father's voice joining in, rising in volume, growing louder and louder, until it's all he can hear. "Frankly, my dear, I don't give a damn!" The same hellish mantra is repeated over and over, again and again, before disappearing into the jumbled, vibrating wall of noise. Emerging from the chaos, the dreamer is a familiar leathery pirate, slowly, mechanically implanting a throbbing gemstone into the flesh of another mummy-like figure. It's Pepe. In the background, he sees Lupe, the hotel girl in Veracruz, as she emerges from the crowd and edges toward him. Tugging at his arm, pestering, insisting, demanding his attention, she keeps trying to tell him something. "Not now! I'm busy, can't you see?" he snarls and pushes her away, and then he is Jonathan's father, and the knife he holds is a clarinet. A haunting music plays over the other noise as Lupe becomes Jonathan's mother, cursing, raging, screaming. "Scum! Outlaws! Tramps!" He can feel his own lips moving now, repeating the same words, over and over. . . . "Frankly, my dear, I don't give a damn. . . . " He wants to stop saying the words, wants her to go away. He wants to scream "shut up, ya fuckin' bitch!" but he can't stop parroting the same obnoxious phrase, again and again. His mouth is not his own. All he can do with it is repeat that monotonous incantation, over and over, a mechanical recording croaking from a marionette's cold, stiff, painted wooden lips. His mother shape-shifts into a shining, satin-robed Virgin de Guadalupe, bathed in a shimmering golden light glowing fiercely from within. The Virgin Mother is holding a baby wrapped in a shiny green blanket. She hands it to him, but he pushes it away, trying not to look. From the corner of his eye, he sees her set the bundle down on a table. She begins unwrapping the blanket, and then he sees the horror. It's not a baby! It's the meat doll! The Virgin Mother looks up at him with the opaque, glassy eyes of a fish, staring right through him as she begins pulling off strips from the tragic little creature. He can hear its flesh tear, an amplified rending of beef jerky. Its horrific screams pierce his soul. Agonized, piercing wails of terror bombard his ears as she starts to eat it, piece by squirming, suffering piece. The crowd of angry voices grows quiet and everyone starts to cry. He feels a deep shame cover his soul. A taste of sulfury water begins falling from the sky. His mouth is still moving against his will, a cold, stiff, wooden puppet's lips, clacking, wood to wood, clattering, repeating the same senseless words, over and over, as stinging salt water tears flow from his hard, leathery eyes. "Frankly, my dear, I don't give a damn. . . . "

50. THE GREAT MOTHER ROAD

After hitching a ride out of the heart of the Amazon on a shadowy military transport plane I didn't remember getting on, the following weeks crept by like a tedious line of worker ants. Traveling on, I roamed the back roads of northern Brazil, following the setting sun to the next nameless, faceless village; the next drink of rum, the next glowing pink cigarette point burning in the darkness of those long, desolate nights on the road.

Always on the move, forever waiting for a ride to the next unknown destination, I inched along, one plodding day at a time, down the long, lonesome road toward Rio.

As I sit sifting through hazy mental snapshots of those harsh threadbare travels, phantom images jump onto the page in a surreal spook-house parade. Like an archaeologist squinting at dusty artifacts, I stare at a fuzzy vision of myself sitting at a crooked table somewhere, surrounded by a parched, starving landscape of forlorn dirt and despair. I'm watching a gang of rag-doll children battle a pack of scrawny dogs, fighting over a pile of leftover bones. Yelling and throwing rocks, snarling and barking, ferocious, tenacious and desperate with raw animal hunger, the kids fight as savagely as the bony feral mutts.

As my pen guides me through the musty tunnels of these recollections, random faces appear out of the darkness; ghosts of solitude and despair in the desolate, heartless backlands of the arid Brazilian *sertão*. Moving on, I was a scrawny, desperate alley cat clawing through its nine allotted lives, chased by a fevered demon and thirsty for a fading dream of Rio. As my money ran out like sand in a cracked hourglass, any unfortunate Guardian Angel watching over my travels must have been left behind in a ditch somewhere, murdered by the merciless punishments I continually heaped on myself in my obsessive pilgrimage.

Trudging past giant potholes on a deserted lunar landscape of ruined blacktop in the middle of nowhere, waiting for a ride, an incessant din of insects hummed from the surrounding walls of cane fields. Too exhausted to take another step in the intense midday heat, I stopped. Gaunt, hungry, desperate as a red-eyed rat in a sickening maze of endless nothingness, fed up with the sight of my own outstretched thumb and that ugly occult tattoo scar burned into my forearm like an angry fever blister, I slumped down by the roadside. A crooked parade of cane-laden trucks lumbered past, rickety mechanical beasts of burden, interspersed by the occasional booming steel procession of speeding trucks, angry behemoths rumbling through time and space in a hellish metallic river of dust and diesel fumes.

No one stopped.

Sitting among the debris of squashed, burnt sugarcane husks littering the rutted asphalt, I knew the road was my mother, my only home and family. And she was slowly, persistently schooling me in the ancient art of waiting; instructing me to look within for the courage, faith, and patience to surrender to the laborious uncertainty of the journey; teaching me to sit stoically again, waiting for another ride, another drink, another change of scenery. Soon enough, I knew, the great Mother Road would provide me with all that I required to survive another day, just as she had always done before.

Finally, after a dull, thirsty eternity, a shiny black Ford with black-and-yellow São Paulo plates appeared—a surreal apparition in that deserted place with no name. Hoping against hope, I watched as it pulled to a stop. I opened the back door and slid into the strange air-conditioned world of two young white guys with dark longish hair. Without a word to me, they sped off down the highway, tossing their empty beer bottles out onto the roadside, and jabbering at each other as if I wasn't even there.

After a while, the passenger turned and passed me a beer. As the bubbly, cool sting hit my parched throat, I sat back, feeling a sudden fresh wave of peace. I stared out the window, watching the barren countryside speeding by in a blur of industrial-strength horsepower, surrendering, once again, to the mad velocity and motion of the great Mother Road.

Many miles later, we came to a stop at a primitive roadside hamlet of dilapidated straw huts. I looked out at those toothless impoverished faces of the land, selling whatever they had to sell. Tattered ghosts of hunger from the dried-out desolate backlands of nowhere, gaunt, stoic faces floated before me, offering up broken empty hands to the merciless gods of starvation; holding out withered baskets with the meager fruits of their poor landless lives, beseeching the strange white-skinned aliens from a distant concrete dream they would never know.

A dusty Negro boy approached, carrying a pair of bright green parrots in a crude handmade wooden cage. The driver bought some bags of fried stuff from him. He didn't buy the birds. As the two men conferred with each other in Portuguese, I leaned forward, listening, moving my lips in silence behind each odd musical phrase, learning, feeling the sounds and intonations of the swooshy dialect. It sounded enough like Spanish for me to make out the general meaning of things, but it was also distinctly different.

Staring at the parrots, I could feel my cells rearranging themselves again, shifting, mutating, changing, growing and knowing on some deep molecular level of non-understanding, bonding like a parrot with each new word and inflection. I remained silent as the language of my new land slowly imprinted itself, taking residence in the dusty back rooms of my being.

I looked up as the driver gunned the big motor and rolled some fifty meters down the road. Slowing to a stop by another group of humble thatched-roof dwellings, he gestured to another barefooted boy standing in the road. Wearing only a pair of dirty white underpants, the kid was holding a monkey by a length of kite string, clutching it with grubby little hands.

The driver leaned out the window, whistled him over, and said something. The youngster handed him the monkey, still holding on to the string. The driver passed it to his friend. It sat in the passenger's lap, looking intelligent, like that was its job. Its owner stood in the dirt waiting. The passenger whispered something to the driver. The driver nodded back, grinning. Suddenly, the car lurched forward in a roar of big American thunder. They sped off down the road, leaving the boy in a cloud of dust.

The men seemed delighted with themselves. The phrase "Born to Lose" leaped into my mind with a sudden vision of Richard Speck; those portentous words tattooed on a big murderous forearm. The two men laughed, playing with their stolen monkey, talking in their Big City Portuguese, throwing empty bottles out the window as the thundering vehicle ate up the ruined blacktop, all the way to the coast.

Hours later, on the outskirts of the seaport of Fortaleza, the big car pulled over to the side of the highway. I thanked them for the ride, clutching my bag under my arm so they wouldn't drive off with it.

I departed their heartless white man's world, the little monkey watching me from the dashboard with intelligent human eyes. As they roared off, I felt relieved to be out of that car at last; glad to be somewhere, anywhere away from the hot, dusty road and the two unfathomable big-city monkey thieves.

I stood by the highway, looking around for a moment. Then I wandered off into a ragged neighborhood of crooked tin-roofed shacks—an enticing new world at the shabby edge of a magnificent palm-studded tropical coastline.

51. TRAGIC TROPICS

The squalid ghettos of Fortaleza were like oozing open sores on the virgin face of the tropics. But on some deep instinctual level, I knew I'd traveled long and far enough to break from the road and its brutal demands for a spell. And Fortaleza seemed as good a place as any.

Once again, it was time to stop and resume the familiar task of constructing a new person in another new place: another new character for another incarnation with a brand-new past, a vital new future, a hopeful new psychic road map to all the details clicking past my eyes in the moving slideshow of life on the road.

I marched along the crooked cobblestone streets of the sunbaked equatorial metropolis for hours, searching, seeking, wandering like an empty-bellied beggar, alert for any little scrap of history, for straws and crumbs of imagery and sensory stimulation from which to build a new nest for my wandering vagabond soul.

Ambling through hot unfamiliar neighborhoods crowded with strange flat-headed people, the tragic poetry of those scruffy tropics blasted my senses as I traversed the winding septic alleys of a seaside purgatory; a lost netherworld of squat-bodied humanoid beings milling around in the dust; a baffling lost civilization of stunted grunting diminutive monkey-people, marching round and round in desperate little circles of sun-bleached dereliction.

As the afternoon wore on, I came to a shady overgrown plaza near the port. Slouching among broken-down benches populated by groups of hollow-eyed teenage hookers and weary dock workers, one girl stood out of the ragged human stew. She looked to be about fifteen. She was dressed like a normal teenaged chick in a short denim skirt and tennis shoes, but I knew why she was there.

Fearing she might disappear before my eyes if I waited, I strode up and asked her how much. My cash was almost done but it seemed a worthwhile expense.

She was cheap—even for a short-time hooker in a ratty little plaza. She grinned and took me by the hand. But, instead of taking me to one of the usual short-time fuck hotels, she led me to a run down shack in a slummy cluster of drab little shacks facing the sea, where she lived with an elderly mother.

After a long friendly shag, we sat up on the bed, smoking and talking. Her name was Simone.

"You got a girlfrien'?" Simone spoke in a slow, languid Portuguese growl, which I suddenly understood perfectly.

"Nah." I shrugged.

"I use to got de regular man. He buy for me de pretty clothes an' thing. But den he go 'way. I wait, think maybe he gon' come back, but he no come, an' den I go work in de *praça*, maybe fin' de new man."

I said nothing. She poked me on the arm, staring at me with intense, bright green eyes. I blinked.

"Eehh, you wan' be my boyfrien'?"

"Sure," I heard my penis reply.

I'd been married to the road for so long, I was lonely and horny as a weary young traveler could be. Simone had perfect dime-sized pink nipples, and bright shiny eyes as green as the choppy sea outside her door. She liked to talk and drink, and we talked and drank, staring out at the lazy white seabirds gliding past in the muggy air.

Happy as a piss clam at high tide, I languished the weeks away in that melancholy tropical refuge. Sheltered from the road and its monstrous demands and captivated by an irresistible animal attraction to Simone, I felt a connection I hadn't known with a chick since Ellen.

After our long sweaty afternoon fuck sessions, I'd collapse beside her, lost in her musky animal scent, studying the fine contours of her feral childlike face, her perfect adolescent body vibrating with primal sex-energy, drawing me closer, luring me in again. And then, like a pair of remote-control hump-puppets, we'd be at it again.

Those dick-crippling, pot-smokey, rum-soaked days oozed by in a long languid sex spell, sliding like a dirty mop across the damp stone floor by the churning green sea. Awakening at noon to a sound of scissors snipping at fabric, I'd sit up in my hammock, massaging my eyes, wondering how long I'd been there. There was no telling. I'd lie back again, half-asleep, watching Simone's mother at work across the room as the gray-faced old woman tinkered endlessly at an ancient sewing machine, making baby clothes to sell at a local street market.

And so, time rolled by in a dull procession of dead-end life, the mother snipping away and humming to herself, her daughter lying suspended in the other hammock, a bundle of undulating dust snoring off another hangover. As I faded in and out of sleep in that languid limbo zone, the steady drone of the television was the only string of conversation between us. Nobody seemed to talk in that odd netherworld, where survival was its own reward and its own seething curse.

Brief snakebite stabs of brutal passion in our dark nights of careless lovemaking filled the gaps as Simone's mother slept. The sound of the old woman's lazy broom and a pair of cheap rubber sandals scraping at the hot cement was our alarm clock, the music of those eternal fading afternoons making cellular imprints on my soul in the random noises of Simone's world: cars and machines, a truck's sputtering motor, a jumbled babble of radios and motorbikes, crying babies and barking dogs.

Suspended in limbo, lost in the foggy dreamlike haze of long aimless afternoons, the furtive shadow of a cat tips through my mind's vision of those humid days in Fortaleza; a phantom shape skirting a wall above my sweaty head suspended in a creaking hammock like a departing soul sailing the sky. As Simone's mother puttered in the background, an ever-present purposeful ghost, the echo of dogs and cats barking and meowing ushered in long murky nights of fuzzy dream-shapes stalking invisible things in the darkness on my long solitary walks through forlorn windswept streets where the passage of time was defined by cheap wooden coffins standing on a corner by a sleeping church, waiting to be filled.

Oblivion was our religion. Simone drank cheap *cachaça* like a steve-dore when not out turning tricks or sniffing glue. We spent most of our time together drinking, fucking, and fighting in mute eruptions of hateful fury and frustration, breaking glass, grunts and spittle, dark sex and tender violence; the savage complicity of two lost souls locked together in random fits of mortal combat, love, hate, and mindless zombie passions.

After finally being kicked out by her stone-faced mother after an especially obnoxious nocturnal duel, we migrated to another shack in a neighboring shantytown. If refraining from murdering each other for weeks on end there was a measure of our complicity, I suppose we did pretty well—until one day, driven by the usual restless, pot-befuddled, rum-soaked boredom, Simone brought another girl home.

I was still half-drunk from the night before, snoring off a hangover, when she came in with a lanky wild-faced glue-crazed mulatta with the eyes of an alley cat in heat. Without a word, the new chick shed her clothes. Simone grinned and nodded as I threw her friend down onto the bed and stuck it in. It was a good fit. Tight and frenetic. Kind of like riding a bucking bronco on cocaine. Then Simone joined in. It was all good, till the glue-head started running her mouth.

I was deep kissing Simone while hammering the other girl to the mattress, trying to ignore her incessant chatter, when the chick's husky tone became shrill and insistent. Something about drugs and the *policia* and money. Simone had robbed her or tricked her out of some cash, apparently. Getting her money back must have been the pretext for our little grunt-fest, and it was quickly plummeting south. She kept babbling about cash and the cops. It was annoying. Finally my dick went soft and slunk out of her trembling twat like a whipped mutt. I rolled off, panting and sweating rum.

Sitting back, I watched them thrashing around on the bed like a pair of punch-drunk Mexican wrestlers. Finally, they got bored and started quarreling over money again. Still stoned enough to find it all mildly amusing, I was already starting to get worked up for another stab at that frantic pussy when, suddenly, the crazy bitch jumped up and started throwing all our stuff around the room. Baffled, I sat on the edge of the bed, holding my dick in my hand like a wounded bird.

Then, out of nowhere, the little maniac came flying across the room and leaped on me in a blur of hissing teeth and flashing pink finger-nails. As if by its own accord, my fist flew up and caught her square on the chin. Lights out. A sudden dull silence, then in a flash Simone was coming at me too. Baring her teeth like a baby shark, she produced a big rusty fishing knife. In a savage sweep, it slashed into my arm! As she raised the blade to strike again, I got ahold of her wrist and twisted her hand back. The knife clattered to the floor. She struggled and screeched, fighting back like a wild animal. With blood streaming from my wounded limb, I dropped her with two sharp head butts to the face, knocking her out like a bad dream.

Good night, Cinderella.

As the savage cunts lay passed out on the floor like a pair of broken dolls, I packed my bag and quickly cleaned out their purses.

Now they could really fight over money.

Stepping over the two unconscious bodies, I beat it out the door and hurried off down the narrow dirt path. I'd been disloyal to the Great Mother Road, and this had been my punishment. Repentant, I climbed onto a rickety local bus and rode it to the outskirts of town.

I got off at a crossroads and stuck my thumb out on the busy highway, quickly getting a ride in a beat-up pickup.

I sat in the back with some fishermen, drinking sweet *cachaça* from a cloudy brown bottle, laughing and talking about soccer and whores and the sea.

52. THE ROAD TO NOWHERE

—LAURENCE PETER

Fortaleza turned out to be a flat tire on the road to Rio. Desperate to get there, I contemplated my progress. So far, I'd traveled only seven hundred miles in Brazil as the crow flies. God only knew how far I'd actually gone in that twisted land-air-river trajectory. And the fucking crow still had well over a thousand miles to fly.

On the move once more, I was awaiting a sign again, a word, a gesture, a falling leaf, a smoke signal from somewhere; something, anything. Like a newborn baby waiting for a slap on the ass, I wandered on, always watching and witnessing; waiting for the nameless King of Whatever to point his crooked, capricious finger down the great Mother Road to nowhere.

JOURNAL ENTRY—João Pessoa, Paraíba, Brazil:

Rode into town on a hot air current of sudden camaraderie and laughter, drinking strong white rum with a truckload of toothless fishermen in battered straw hats. Another day, another blazing afternoon sun imprinting another new city on my eyes, I wander the crumbling colonial wreckage of this lethargic old dreamscape. Like

*every downtown worth a shit, this one has obviously seen better days.
After spending hours in shadowy places where faceless men congregate
to drink, I checked into an ancient hotel, home to many ghosts, where
soothing waves of silence engulfed my weary brain in a welcome
wave of peaceful, solitary quietude. After weeks of drunken battles
with Simone, I luxuriated in the simple freedom of a quiet hotel room
all to myself. Standing in my underwear like a prince overseeing his
domain, brain buzzing on cachaça, all alone on a faded–blue-tiled
colonial balcony, I surveyed the archaic plaza below, peopled with
moneychangers in shabby suits and blackbirds calling out from an
ancient mango tree, leaves rustling in a murky warm sea breeze.
Drifting in and out of sleep after cool showers in a phantom dark-tiled
shower stall, I followed the hallway to a beat-up old water cooler,
then back to dream more short-circuited dreams, cross-wired with more
ghostly shadows, lingering phantom imprints of long-gone immigrants
from other times and places in this crumbling building's silent spirit
memory. Woke up in the late afternoon to a hypnotic pulse, like the
sound of pounding machinery. I looked out the window, then hurried
out, following vague distant zombie drumbeats down to the edge of
the water. Staring into the dull gray eyes of the choppy sea, I followed
the shore to a place where two skinny brown kids were kicking a ball
around in the dirty sand. Nearby, a crooked-legged black dog scavenged
for scraps. Fishermen cast their nets into the ocean on the twilight
horizon, stick-like silhouettes against a setting sun inching its way to
a new sunrise across the wide, dark sea, where shiny, blue-skinned
Negros wander under cool ocean breezes of Mother Africa, awaiting
a mirror-image palm-studded dawn. My thoughts time-travel along
the deserted shoreline, thinking of old friends and lovers in another
life, another incarnation, another place, another dream. I picture my
mother and her henpecked hostage sitting in their stark white tomb back
home, prisoners of a dingy little whirlpool of fearful rituals; a long,
dreary, self-imposed nightmare of habitual angst; a colorless stew of
whitewashed mediocrity. Do they know they're missing this magnificent
sunset? Would they even care? The crippled black dog clumps by.
Does he know he's crippled? Like my people, a race of hobbled lost
souls, he's just limping along, doing the best he can. At the end of this
monkey-bin life, that's probably the best anyone can ever hope for. I
sit at a lopsided wooden table in the sand, surrounded by threadbare*

*human scarecrows drinking their day's-end cachaça. A plate of
miraculous lobsters is set before me by the hands of an ancient Negress
with a white cloth tied tight around her skull. I squirt the crustaceans
with the juice of bright green lime halves, soaking them till they vibrate
in the silent moonlight. Wresting the glowing white meat from its shiny
red cocoon, I stare out over the water as the last tiny orange speck of
sun disappears over the horizon like an extension of the intense redness
of the lobsters on my plate. Beans, rice, and fresh white meat. I eat
with a gusto and fervor I cannot recall knowing in a long while. When
I look up again, the sea is flat and dark, and the absurd feast of
equatorial night has begun.*

JOURNAL ENTRY—

*Walked along the seaside after dinner, smoking a pale white
cigarette. Met a lanky teenage girl with stunning features, a mad mix
of races running hot like an exotic tropical stew in yearning young
veins. She brought me home to the slummy rat-shit squalor of a shack
by the sea; two of us walking hand-in-hand down a dark dirt road,
past rows of murderous ghetto eyes. She handed her sleeping mother a
few coins and a short bottle of rum to let us use the bed. As she shed
her clothes, I saw a crooked tapestry of blurry blue/black handmade
tattoos all across her ass, calves and back; proprietary brand-marks,
coarse, angry souvenirs of the random comings and goings of brutal
neighborhood thugs who came to take the only thing she had of value
before moving on, leaving her with scars and tattoos and babies she
can't sustain, and a bovine, gum-chewing, cynical aversion to sex—
other than as a quick, mindless means to survive another day in a
savage world not made for the curse of her haunting beauty. I felt bad
for her, and maybe even worse for myself, when I split at dawn, putting
a few crumpled banknotes into her elegant hand. She kissed me on the
cheek with the heartbreaking words: "vai com Deus, meu amor."*

JOURNAL ENTRY—

*Back in my little room late at night, a fearless cockroach the size
of a mouse scampered across the floor. I held the door open for him,
like a departing guest, and he obligingly ran out into the hall. I stood
in my underwear, smoking my last cigarette on the cool Portuguese-tiled
veranda overlooking an eerie vista of shadows and ghosts. The last*

image of the night was a shirtless teenage goon taking a mechanical blowjob at knifepoint from a skeletal transvestite in the deserted plaza under a tragic piss-yellow streetlight's flickering glow. I fell asleep thinking of tomorrow; a new day when I shall run like the damned back onto the long road south to Rio de Janeiro. I dreamed with the dead, their lonesome, wayward spirits colliding with mine in the sagging hotel bed.

JOURNAL ENTRY—Feira de Santana, Bahia, Brazil:

After a brief stay in the old seaside city of João Pessoa, I surrender to the highway again, waiting in nameless dim enclaves for the next bumpy ride in a mad flurry of rusty roadside barrooms, eternal waiting rooms of hollow-eyed, motherless, restless spirits of the road fallen around me like the bloody overripe mangos splattered from lush old trees by the riverside. Fallen in sunny boneyards and plazas, across quiet streets and highways of waiting, we all sit, waiting, waiting, wilting hungry dogs of extinction drowning in brown waters of time and endless rounds of pissy white rum. The only thing that's kept me going these last few weeks is the foul gasoline-tasting cachaça; that and something fixed and focused in my befuddled brain—a vague, shaky vision of Rio. After Fortaleza, the weeks passed like spider-web shadows crawling along in a listless parade of beggars and whores and howling barroom babblings; days and nights falling like blackbirds shot from a telephone wire along this dry, dusty old road stretching into cloudy restless nights of nothing. My forlorn comrades of the road are with me in all broken battlefields of tooth-shattering desperation and drunken fistfights, shouting for the blood of this ravaged, forsaken land so very far from heaven, on hot, broken streets that all look alike. And so my crab-like shadow crawls into another dingy barroom of arguing restless lost souls at the edge of the road, waiting for a ride that never comes; another three days of heat and tension in stagnant air filled with dusty moving shadows, a procession of scattered snippets, a tedious tapestry at world's end; a rusty brown riverside limbo, where lost-eyed toothless men congregate, sad human meat puppets hanging by rusty hooks, plagued by angry flies. A radio preacher recites a drab, incomprehensible litany of our many sins in a droning mechanical voice competing with football matches and meaningless weather reports from the bottomless pit of humanity's great misunderstanding. Unseen mine explosions detonate somewhere out in the darkness, and then all is quiet again in the stifling heat of these killing days of fugitive monkey dreams. I walk along another empty stretch of road, staring at heaps of impossibly huge green bananas and colorful tropical fruits, bursting like drunken fireworks on the gray wooden dock of another tiny river port without name, without hope or escape; a forgotten world of sleeping men and giant black urubu buzzards hopping like crippled beggars in the garbage by a muddy riverbank. From a sandy plaza of one-armed fishermen, a church bell tolls in the pale haze. I make another wordless pact with the Great Mother Road as I stand before another metal time machine of trucks rolling south from this abandoned corner of Hell, hoping against hope to crawl another few inches on the tattered road map of this life toward Rio—away from these broken roadside bars of horror-show eyes, where people sit around and around, on and into forever, emptying their souls into thirsty brown bottles of sullen, nameless despair.

53. OVER THE MOUNTAINS

Dripping sweat, I ran toward the stopped truck. I climbed in, smiled at the driver, then settled back in the hot, vibrating cab as the rusty old contraption hissed and groaned and rumbled off into the night.

The chatty smiling trucker's name was João Batista, John the Baptist—and yes, he was headed to Rio. We passed a bottle of *cachaça* as he maneuvered through the darkness, telling me stories and lies neither of us must have believed.

A day and a half into the ride, I looked on in gut-sinking horror as a Negro boy crossing the highway was swallowed under the wheels of another truck and spit out onto the roadside, a mangled human meat puppet. A deep sickness welled up in my throat as the next gulp of rum washed my revulsion down, down, deep into the darkness of my being. It was all a crazy movie now, where life was cheap. The road was my mother, teaching me the randomness of this earthly existence.

Time and space flickered by in a long rolling dream of motion and mystery. Then, just before dawn on day three or four, I felt a subtle change in climate, dust blowing around us in big gasping breaths of wind. Lush green rain forests appeared as we flashed downhill, past huge granite rocks jutting out of razor mountain curves.

Descending in a symphony of grinding gears and hissing brakes, a battered green road sign, **Rio de Janeiro**, flickered past my eye like an afterthought. The truck kept winding downhill, down, down, past a series of glowing yellow lights: *macumba* candles dotting the roadside—voodoo offerings to the spirits I knew had finally brought me to my destination.

But the sights seen through the cracked lens of an old truck window bore no resemblance at all to the Rio I'd long fantasized—just as I had little in common with a dying junkie kid who'd dreamed of it in a delirious heroin daze back in another lifetime, a long time ago.

JOURNAL ENTRY—Rio de Janeiro:

Death in the afternoon, followed by a long, slow descent into the unknown killing fields of an impossible nightmare vision. A sour stench of raw sewage invades my senses as I awaken at dawn to a blurry mix of horns and grinding gears, my head pounding from the night's cachaça, sweet-sickly rum scent oozing from my pores mixing with diesel fumes, humid jungle air, and strong black tobacco smoke, I blink sleep from my eyes and look around in a fog as the driver rattles on like a dull radio announcer. He must have been talking the whole time I slept, I realize, and he's still going in that monotonous, singsong Portuguese slang. A steady road rhythm welcomes me to Rio as João Batista maneuvers his nasal Benzedrine monologue around wild hairpin turns over impossible mountain roads, and down, down into the hazy dawn of dusty blue-gray flatlands, a swampy industrial shantytown sprawl of crawling rat-shit squalor. I squint into an animated morning dream world as my nose drinks in a septic, mildewed odor of raw sewage and factory fumes, smoke, rain, and fecund tropical rot. So this is Rio de Janeiro. After long years of anticipation, imagining, and expectation, it's all a murky, crashing anticlimax. Columns of black smoke rise like a witch's spindly fingers, beckoning across endless acres of miserable gray tin-roofed hovels dotted with soot-blackened brick buildings: smoke clouds billowing up from crooked smokestacks into flat, insolent skies of circling vultures; ramshackle factories sinking into the barren red mud like broken teeth in a corpse's gaping mouth. These infernal wastelands look nothing like the Rio de Janeiro of my frivolous junkie dreams: that wistful home of Orfeu Negro, with its lush, verdant mountain vistas and smiling samba-dancing mulatto girls. Where are the cinematic, sparkling waters and sun-drenched tropical vistas of Rio? This poverty-ridden horror show is a depraved massacre of the soul. Gray garbage fires burn at the roadside like belching farts from a thousand dying assholes; shirtless, skeletal men, anthill souls of the damned, stand hoisting impossible burdens on defeated leathery backs onto limping lines of smoke-spewing, idling trucks; scrawny mutts slashing savage red fangs at each other in vicious little circles on the tortured sod of a freakish nightmare, a filthy, foul-smelling Purgatory of drab shit-colored brick dwellings reminiscent of the terrible Infernos of Dante. Maybe I'd died somewhere in the malarial fevers of buzzing jungle wastelands between Mexico and here? Could I have descended straight to Hell? Am I just another restless ghost now? And if this is indeed Hell, surely there's a place for me here, I think, as we're swallowed into a grim urban whirlpool of morning traffic, a rusty swarm of creeping, jittery jalopies, all different hues of speckled rust and decay, cutting in and out of trucks and rumbling buses packed with scrambling masses of doomed, eternally damned sinners. What have they done to Rio? I want my fucking money back! Where the fuck is Rio de Janeiro? I wonder as I sit choking on an acrid Hell-stench of sulfur, fire, and brimstone, poisonous black fumes spurting in thick clouds of jagged, muffler-less flatulence, a rotten doomsday vision enveloped in a toxic light-gray drizzly mist, descending into a shitty swamp of drab, oppressive foreboding, trouble and strife, somewhere on the lost, forgotten outskirts of nowhere.

54. THE MARVELOUS CITY

The friendly trucker dropped me off on a shady side street by the port. With a thumbs-up and a wide carefree *carioca* grin, he threw the big machine into gear and rumbled off down the greasy cobblestones.

I wandered through an ancient red-light district by the dockyards. It kind of reminded me of Veracruz. The whole place seemed to be shrugging off a massive hangover as I moved along the crooked streets, sweating, staggering down dizzy morning sidewalks of chaotic hawker commerce. A boisterous morning flow of human activity spewed from the teeming shanty-town *favelas*, labyrinthine paths winding up into the bursting hillside slums. I walked along, slowly taking it all into my senses like a shot of some powerful new mind-altering drug.

JOURNAL ENTRY—RIO DE JANEIRO:

Spent my first day in Rio wandering the shadows of its looming old downtown colonial buildings, their once-grand ornate façades now crisscrossed with tangled clotheslines; littered, dilapidated courtyards crowded with chattering hordes of naked brown children. Weeds growing into small trees jutted from abandoned stone palaces, where crumbling statues of angels and saints peered down from ancient rooftop perches with lifeless yellowed marble eyes. And so this was finally Rio de Janeiro. My brain was melting under a stupendous sun's burning shadows as I walked the chaotic urban labyrinth, my perceptions exploding in rhythmic paths of samba sound and crazed vibrations echoing from a jumbled mix of blaring ghetto mazes; intoxicating scents of smoking meats on sidewalk grills, garlic and roasting sardines, spilled beer, sweat, piss, and exhaust fumes, all crowding together in my senses in the pregnant, pounding pre-Lenten summer air. Whole families stood crowded in the shadows of ancient doorways, staring out with eyes dull as bullets. Hot zigzagging shadows of kamikaze motorcycle boys ruled the streets, horns blasting, engines screaming, sounds of a crazy new world drilling into my ears in a cacophony of drumbeats, firecrackers, and shouts; unseen voices from jukeboxes spitting out music; radios blaring soccer games in frantic Portuguese to a dull electrical background hum of traffic, shouts, and rawboned, noisy life. My little travel bag weighed heavy at my shoulder as I passed the ubiquitous macumba candles flickering beside bottles of cheap cachaça, plates of food, flowers, and cigarettes laid out on the ground at a crossroads; offerings to spirits, unearthly entities I know with a great and final certainty have always been mingling around me in silence, nudging me on toward this crucial time and place. Being here now, at last, I realize I'd forever felt the subtle presence of those lusty unseen spirits, whispering, whistling across wormholes and gulfs of time and space, clamoring from other dimensions, calling out to me over the years from their tangled underworld webs. I could almost see them moving around me as I walked the streets of Rio; dancing, laughing, silently mocking and driving my desires through the sprawling septic favelas, rolling hills, and cracked industrial wastelands, slums, buildings, beaches, and barrooms in a shadowy blanket of life; a subliminal parallel existence, a World Unknown; a steady Presence in this indefinable, arcane energy field subtly vibrating behind the faces popping up all around me, showering these strange, laughing people with a special grace; an industrial-strength ironclad humor, charity and style; twisting their weak tragic mortal flesh into a bulletproof armor of courage and fortitude as they run through their lives here, robbing and killing, fucking and loving, cheating and lying, living and dying, dancing madly in a strange, unforgettable collective human symphony of hideous beauty, decadent opulence, crawling rat-shit squalor, stench, and crazed, hungry raw passionate life; a perverse and enigmatic race of people among whom I shall now, at last, have to find my own crooked little place and purpose.

My first impressions of Rio de Janeiro were a world apart from the sparkling expectations engraved in my mind a long time ago. At a casual glance, it looked like any other big Latin American city. But, as the days flashed by like the pages of a very weird storybook, I could feel an intangible undercurrent of Fate lurking behind the wild shouts and smiles of its crude, comical, childlike inhabitants.

I didn't know it at the time, of course, but my first weeks in that strange and magical city would come to mark the beginning of a new life for me, and a new career as a tattoo artist—the prelude to a perplexing confluence of circumstances and ongoing events which would come to shape my destiny, subtly, dramatically rearranging my perception of this complex, baffling planet and its complex, baffling inhabitants.

I'd always dreamed that my arrival in Rio would be the end of the road for me. In truth, the most significant part of my long, cockeyed journey had only just begun.

○   ○   ○

The tattoo man stops reading. He gathers up his notebooks and carries them over to his traveling bag. He stacks them carefully and puts them away. Sitting down across from his young confessor again, he begins setting up his tattoo gear.

"It's amazing."

"That's what she said last night, kid," Cigano scoffs.

"The storytelling, Jonathan Shaw." Jaco frowns. "Seriously. I've never heard such a short depiction of a city that says so much. Your descriptions are like a painting! You've captured the deepest essence of Rio with such evocative, poetic language. . . and it's even more impressive that this was written about the city I grew up in by a foreigner just seeing it for the first time. . . . "

"Yeah, well, thanks, man." Cigano falls silent.

"I mean it. Thank *you*, Jonathan Shaw."

After a long contemplative pause, the tattoo man's eyes light up. "Y'know, maybe sometimes it takes an outsider's eyes to see past all the day-to-day bullshit and get to the real soul of a place. In that sense, I guess I been pretty lucky."

"Lucky? How?"

Cigano rubs his chin. "I dunno, maybe cuz I always felt like such an outsider, a foreigner, far back as I can remember. Especially in the place where I came from." He chuckles. "So I guess growing up all dazed and confused like that musta gave me a certain point of view."

He shrugs. "Who knows? Maybe all the fucked-up character flaws that always made it so hard for me to live in the world are finally comin' in handy for me with this writing thing. . . . "

"No doubt. Have you written more about it?"

"About Rio?"

Jaco nods.

"Well, yeah, man. How not?" Cigano shrugs. "I mean, I wound up living there most of my life, on and off, so God knows I got volumes to write about the place, and all the crazy shit I lived through there. Lotta wild adventures, seriously formative stuff went down for me in Rio back in the day. And more recently, too. . . . " He sighs. "But that's all for another story, another book, maybe even a few more books, if I ever finish writing this big fuggin' desperation derby." He sucks his teeth and spits a tiny scrap of food onto the floor.

"So what's going to be in your next books?"

"Well, Rio's where I first got my start as a tattooer, so I guess I'll have to get into a pretty deep examination of how all that went down. That, and all kinda other weird stuff that happened there. Then, there's all the years I spent tattooing in New York, and all these other places, traveling all over the world, meeting a lotta crazy characters. A whole fuggin' lifetime of *vida loca*." He pauses, scratching his head.

"I dunno, man. Who th' fuck knows where the whole thing's gonna take me? There's plenty more to write about, though, for sure. Probably more than I'll ever know what th' fuck to do with, should I live long enough to finish. . . if there's such a thing as ever being finished. . . . "

"Sounds like you've got a lot of work ahead of you."

"Yeah, right?" Cigano snorts. "Shit, man, I probably shoulda started writing this whole fuggin' saga a *long* time ago. . . . "

"I think you actually did, Jonathan Shaw. Maybe you just didn't realize that's what you were doing at the time."

Cigano laughs. "Guess you're right, bro. I was prolly just too busy trying to survive the whole fucked-up deal."

With a sneaky little grin, he picks up his battered brass tattoo machine and buzzes it twice, signaling the start of another day's work.

TO BE CONTINUED. . . .

AFTERWORD

TRUE ARTIST

BY ALESSANDRA DE BENEDETTI

Just as it's difficult to discuss modern jazz without Artie Shaw's name coming up, it's nearly impossible to talk of modern tattooing without conjuring the name of the legendary jazzman's unlikely offspring, Jonathan.

A traveler of the Seven Seas, tattooist to Johnny Depp and celebrities galore, confidant to the rich and famous, the dark and infamous, and the original inspiration—alongside Keith Richards—for Depp's famous pirate Jack Sparrow, Jonathan Shaw has been a lowbrow cultural icon for decades, wearing many hats: Underground entrepreneur. Gonzo journalist. Producer. Director. Poet. Novelist. Screenwriter. Painter. Creator. Curator and collector of lowbrow art and memorabilia. Lowlife. Underworld celebrity. Wheeler. Dealer. Hustler. Healer. Psychic. Psycho. Pirate and pimp. Roving reporter. Contributor and editor-in-chief to cutting-edge art culture publications. And, last but not least, the eccentric, eclectic, world-famous founder, owner, and operator of the legendary avant-garde New York City landmark, Fun City Tattoo Studio. While Jonathan has long left Fun City and the tattoo scene behind for new challenges on happier horizons as a full-time writer, his legacy is forever carved into New York City's collective conscience—not to mention a thriving tattoo culture he begrudgingly admits to having spawned.

When I first met Jonathan Shaw, he spoke to me about such diverse topics as the spirit world, exorcism, metaphysics, science, anthropology, history, political conspiracy, quantum physics, art, literature, and God; everything, in fact, *but* tattooing. He talked for hours, describing with disarming openness his fifty-something years of hard living, sex, drugs, and rock & roll, burning up the road to Hell. Stories of pain and suffering. Experience, strength, and hope. Fame and fortune. Success, failure, and ruin. Pitiful, incomprehensible demoralization. Major-league insanity, eventually giving way to his many hard-earned years of solid recovery from alcoholism and drug addiction, the curses of a long and colorful life.

"There's a lotta water gone under that bridge, sailor. Shit, man, I was in Baghdad when you were in Dad's bag." He winked at me through a cloud of cigarette smoke, the ever-present cheap filterless Mexican cigarette dangling from his lips, dancing as he talked, his gold teeth flashing in the smoggy shadows of another Hollywood night in exile from his home in Rio de Janeiro. "My motto used to be: *'Live fast, die young, and leave a pretty corpse.'* Well, it's too late for all that now, so I guess all I can do is just keep living the best I can. But, hey, I got no regrets. Every day above ground's a good day for me." He threw back his head and laughed out loud.

This statement seems to underscore a newfound peace and simplicity after a long absence from the world of tattooing, a world he was once passionately involved with. After a week-long nighttime montage of motorcycle rides between Hollywood coffee shops and late-night taco stands, I was beginning to understand the essence of the man sitting in front of me: Jonathan Shaw, the infamous cult figure, lowbrow author and underground journalist; a walking, talking, living encyclopedia, embodying vast experience and knowledge of all my budding interests; the enigmatic tattoo master who, over the last three decades, spawned an industry—before disappearing into thin air; the outlaw visionary with whom I would soon find myself consorting on much deeper levels. As his longtime editor, part-time personal assistant, and full-time sounding board, I have to say that Jonathan is not an easy being to keep up with. Still as demanding of quality from those he works with as he has always been of himself, he's forever pushing the envelope—often to his own consternation. A true artist, an old-school craftsman and one-man creative enterprise, he's a perfectionist who breaks balls to get things done. And he does get things done. Naturally. After all, he is the Captain; he calls the shots and that's that; he's been there and done that for decades in all of his various endeavors and incarnations.

On a recent trip to New York, freshly clad in a brand-new sleeve and back piece from JS (one of his last major tattoo works), I got to hear many firsthand accounts of some of his more colorful personality traits. Traits that, happily, I have never seen myself. His old character: the control freak, the boss-man, the ne'er-do-well playboy, coked-up drunk and junkie—the world-class asshole; the trendsetting artist and dangerous maniac who carried two pistols and a ball-peen hammer in his many pockets, which he wouldn't hesitate to use on any poor devil who stepped out of line as he conducted his nefarious outlaw business with thieves, derelicts, outcasts, criminals, and other dregs of society. JS was always out there, making it happen in an aggressive, edgy, authentic way, among bloody, bone-breaking rumbles, gunplay, chaos, and good old garden-variety drunken punch-ups.

Most of the people I talked to were decorated in Jonathan's surreal abstract black and gray neo-tribal work. All of them made it abundantly clear that he was boldly pioneering the style long before it reached a mass-market phenomenon to become the meat-and-potatoes, status-quo staple of today's tattoo industry. That was, to my understanding, around the time when the Captain finally abandoned ship, the beginning of the end of an era, an era in which tattooing was still edgy and antisocial and, well. . . hip.

JS, like the song goes, was "Country When Country Wasn't Cool." And, talking to him, I got the impression that he'd known for years that he'd somehow created a monster. Continuing to go through the motions after losing his fervor for tattooing, he described himself like a ghost haunting a house long after its death. Ghosts are haunted, too, by memories and regrets about their previous lives.

With a sigh, he shrugs. "What can I tell ya? If I had it all to do over again today, I'd do a lot of things different. I was an insane person back in those days, simple as that, a pissed-off alcoholic who couldn't drink anymore and didn't give a fuck about my own life or anybody else's. What they call a 'dry drunk,' restless, irritable, a ticking time bomb. In a word: miserable. People didn't even have to do anything most of the time to piss me off. I was already pissed off. I just came that way. Unfortunately, I was in the position where I came into contact with a whole lot of really irritating people." He breaks out a sheepish, gold-toothed grin. "Bad news. Guess I might owe a few apologies here and there. . . . "

After years of white-knuckled abstinence from booze and drugs, predictably, he eventually relapsed and began another steady descent into a slow, drug-addled alcoholic suicide. But divine intervention was at hand. Just after the apocalyptic events of September 11, he had something of a spiritual awakening. Realizing once and for all that he was tired of living a life he'd come to hate, being a "brand name" with diminishing returns, Jonathan Shaw soured on being a parody of himself, chasing his tail for money and acclaim. The tattoo world had finally lost all sparkle or appeal to an artistic spirit in desperate need of redemption. The time had come to begin working in earnest on his many long-ne-glected literary projects.

Long story short: he sobered up. Then, after one last swan-song tattoo tour of Yakuza family business in Japan, without fanfare or comment, he quietly retired from tattooing. He was heard to remark to a friend at the time: "Old tattooers are kinda like old tattoos. They never die. They just sorta faa-aade away."

A lot of the stories I heard about his "dry drunken" years tattooing in New York City seemed blown far out of proportion, like long-held urban myths: incredible, cinematic anecdotes of a mysterious gun-packing psychopath who would go off on anybody for just about any reason—or no reason at all. Strangely, though, most of these lurid accounts ended in breathless, almost reverent accolades. "What a great artist!" was a common theme heard from friends and detractors alike.

Alfred Albrizio, owner of another legendary downtown business, the landmark C'est Magnifique jewelry store, a fixture on Macdougal Street for decades, was a close friend on the scene back in the early days of Jonathan's World Famous Fun City Tattoo. He recounts the time when a local wannabe tattooist, who'd managed to build up a prosperous clien-tele by operating in Jonathan's shadow, one day fizzled out and quit after a short, lackluster career.

According to Alfred: "Jonny was kind of offended this guy didn't bother to tell him he was going out of business, maybe give him some referrals and so on, especially after he'd been generous to the guy with his time and experience. Tattooing was an old-school, underground thing in the city back then, real shady and competitive. Nobody ever told nobody their trade secrets. And Jonathan had been good to the guy, gave him a lot of good advice and so on. He never said nothing about it, though; he just went and called the phone company, pretending to be the guy. Ha! He had the guy's old number transferred over to Fun City, so whenever customers called, Jonny or one of his workers would tell 'em, 'Yeah, sure, so-and-so just stepped out for a minute. We're at a new location. Come on over and we'll take care of you.'

"Jonny was always pulling funny shit like that!" Alfred laughed. "The other guy found out about it and yelled at Jonathan's wife on the street. Real tough guy. I guess he didn't have the balls to face JS in person. He's lucky to still be alive and not crippled, I'll tell ya, the way JS used to carry on. Thank the good Lord he's got religion now."

Another old friend and Fun City customer, Vinnie Sorentino, got a faraway look in his eye, remembering the enigmatic tattooist. "It's true, he used to have a pretty bad temper. But it was usually well-placed. His victims always had it coming, one way or another. A lot of people thought he was just a straight-up lunatic. But he was really a pretty crafty businessman. He just had his own whacked-out code of honor. JS was a product of the streets; a Gypsy, y'know; he always had a million crazy tricks and scams going on. Nobody could keep up with him, though, as an artist. He was always way ahead of his time, but at the same time he was a real balls-out, no-bullshit, old-school tattoo man, not some egghead, college educated, art-fag artiste like ya got around here nowadays. We miss him, hot temper, blunt objects and all. New York won't be the same without Shaw."

I listened to these bizarre, disquieting tales, all chillingly alike. Story after creepy story of dirty tricks, bloody beatings, death threats, rumbles, hostile takeovers, urban piracy, and all sorts of shady under-world dementia, all taking place in a decrepit nether-landscape: a burned-out, pre-Giuliani, thug-controlled Lower East Side operating on the same streets I grew up on, decades before I was born. It sounded like something out of *Gangs of New York*. I was confused and amused by these epic accounts. It seemed that my soft-spoken friend and kindly mentor Jonathan, the kitten-loving, girl-chasing, hopelessly romantic, *generous-beyond-measure* dude I'd come to know and love, had been the stuff of legends back in the day.

"Teddy Roosevelt said, '*Speak softly and carry a big stick,*' right?" says a longtime friend, Hollywood screenwriter Kenneth Shiffrin. With him, Jonathan wrote a screenplay, along with Hubert Selby Jr., based on his ongoing *Scab Vendor* memoir series. "Well, Jonathan used to speak loudly and carry a really big stick too. But he has a big heart. And he's really a much nicer dude now. No doubt about that."

Even today, mellowed down, chilled out, living a new incarnation as a sober, reflective man of letters who spends a good deal of his time trying to help and inspire other people, Jonathan, hard as he tries, is still just not terribly tactful. Suffice it to say he doesn't suffer fools gladly. No doubt a tricky personality trait for a tattoo artist to have possessed and still survived, even thrived, in a world of raging egos, frantic greed, undisguised vanity, and ugly, unprincipled ambition. Truth is, he's much better suited to being a solitary writer than a tattoo artist in constant contact with John Q. Public. As he himself has allowed repeatedly, Jonathan is not much of a "people person." But in his well-documented New York tattoo persona he had been, by all accounts, a real hard-ass, albeit a colorful one. That's the Jonathan Shaw who was once described in a blurb for his first novel, *Narcisa—Our Lady of Ashes*, as "the great nightmare anti-hero of the new age" by rock legend Iggy Pop. Why am I not surprised? Perhaps because I know him personally to be one of the most eccentric and unpredictable human beings I've ever met.

On a recent trip together to his home base in Rio de Janeiro, we schmoozed at high-society cocktail parties with one of his many weirdly diverse groups of friends: movie directors, captains of industry, architects, artists, and musicians. Then, a heart-stopping motorcycle ride later, bobbing and weaving through road-warrior traffic and midnight military police roadblocks, we were hanging out in a teeming, decrepit shantytown-world of foul-smelling third-world favelas, eating *feijoada* with hairy cooked pork snouts peeking out through bowls of beans while coked-up, gun-toting twelve-year-old drug-soldiers and pregnant teenage whores crowded around Jonathan, shooting the shit and gawking at his full bodysuit of tattoos.

This exemplifies that same weird duality that always made him stand out from the herd: a singular cross-pollination of diverse worlds and unlikely cultural orientations. Grinning crookedly at his own off-color jokes, flashing his diamond-studded gold teeth, putting out his hand with the dollar sign tattooed on his palm. Jonathan was always more than just a tattoo artist, more than even a living legend. He's a bloody pirate! He's been around the world a hundred times and has enough stories to tell for days on end, speaking with uncanny authority on subjects ranging from art and literature to the Hidden Hand in global politics; from philosophy and anthropology to obscure underworld history, to the occult.

In his penthouse office and home away from home in a landmark gothic building overlooking Hollywood's glittering lights, hanging above his desk where I worked for years, editing his literary efforts while he was off writing and traveling the world, are framed portraits of him drawn by old friends: well-known artists like R. Crumb, Joe Coleman, Robert Williams, and Johnny Depp. The Depp portrait bears a portentous inscription:

"To my brother JS – Captain Jack the Pirate."

Oh, my God! Jonathan was the original Captain Jack! So *that's* where Johnny Depp got so much of that character from: the gold teeth, that cynical, mischievous half-drunk swagger. I knew I'd seen all that somewhere before. "You know, you remind me of someone," I'd told Jonathan when we first met. But it wasn't until I read that inscription (penned many years ago, before Captain Jack the Pirate was a gleam in a Hollywood screenwriter's eye) that it all clicked into focus.

Still, it's just another brief episode in Jonathan's long, colorful life. He likes to reminisce about the old New York, reminding me that I never experienced its glory days; that by the time I was born, I had missed the '70s and '80s completely, spending most of the '90s learning how to ride a bike and write in cursive. He talks about his original tattoo studio just off the Bowery—years before the acclaimed Fun City—in an innocuous basement on a shabby street peopled with beggars, drunks, and junkies. The Bowery. That name conjured up images for me. The birthplace of Electric Tattooing, and the end of the line for armies of lost souls—including Jonathan's own grandfather, "an alcoholic Lithuanian Gypsy who died in the gutter before I was born," as Jonathan describes his unlucky progenitor. It's weirdly prophetic that Jonathan would have conducted his own shady business in the shadows of the Bowery two generations later, as if he'd been led back to the scene of ancestral crimes by some bizarre DNA strand.

"It was a really dodgy, dangerous underground scene down there," says Luke Miller, a customer and helper at the original Bowery location. "I used to answer the phones, wrangle customers for them, stuff like that," he tells. "It was crazy. Super secretive. That's the way Jonathan wanted things. This was before cell phones. We used to tell people to go to the corner and call us from a pay phone. Nobody knew where the place actually was." He laughs. "After the secret call, JS or one of us would walk up there and check them out from across the street. If they looked all right, we'd go up and introduce ourselves, then walk 'em back over to the studio. The place was real low-key, just a boarded-up little storefront, no sign, nothing to indicate a tattoo shop in there. It was a violent, hardcore environment to do business. He used to get all kinds of death threats and stuff, mostly from other tattoo artists over in Jersey and other places. I guess they didn't like the idea of competition from some upstart Brazilian Gypsy tattoo guy running a busy illegal shop right in their back yard. Jonathan was pretty paranoid back then. I guess he had good reason to be. He didn't even go out for smokes without packing at least one gun."

Jonathan laughs about it today. "Yeah, well, like Lenny Bruce said, *'I may have been paranoid, but there really were people out to get me.'*"

Characteristically, he persisted, slowly, stealthily building an underground art empire in the shadows of the great city, working from an anonymous basement studio covered from floor to ceiling in original antique tattoo-design flash sheets. These were priceless folk-art archives collected over years of travel and adventure in his insatiable hunger for scraps of knowledge and obscure tattoo history. An antique wooden case above his work area displayed real South American shrunken heads. The walls were covered with pictures, exotic mementos, original artwork and paintings by friends and frequent visitors, underground art icons like Robert Crumb, Joe Coleman, Robert Williams, S. Clay Wilson, and Kim Deitch. These artists were Jonathan's true peers, since he never really felt at home among other tattooists—save for a select few, such as tattoo legend Filip Leu, who often worked from the secretive appointment-only studio, tattooing side by side with Jonathan. Influential old-time New York hipsters like Jim Jarmusch, Dee Dee Ramone, Vincent Gallo, John "Bloodclot" Joseph, Steve Bonge, Clayton Patterson, Jonas Mekas, Ronnie Cutrone, Carlo McCormick, Larry "Ratso" Sloman, Lydia Lunch, Jean-Michel Basquiat, and Kembra Pfahler would stop by to hang out. The Maysles brothers, filmmakers of *Gimme Shelter* fame, filmed the proceedings, while Pulitzer Prize-winning artist Art Spiegelman sat in a corner sketching a portrait of Jonathan at work for the cover of *the New Yorker* magazine.

What? A tattoo artist on the cover of the stately old New Yorker? All in a day's work for Jonathan Shaw. The paintings that once hung in that fabled studio now decorate his homes in Hollywood and Rio de Janeiro.

Paintings that I gawk at in amazement, because I know they really belong in a museum. But his houses, like the shops he used to run, are a lot more like museums than homes, filled with rare, eclectic works of art and littered with random tchotchkes from around the world.

"Jonathan was always a step ahead of the rest; he intuitively knew what was cutting edge, way before it ever became popular," says Clayton Patterson, Gonzo historian and president of the seminal but now-defunct *New York Tattoo Society*. "But he was never what you'd call kitsch. The culture he cultivated was completely uncommon. All of Jonathan's art collection, including his own paintings and tattoo works, are testimonials and souvenirs from a lifetime of exploration, all showing some side of his very special weirdness and coolness."

As graffiti artist Angel Ortiz took Keith Haring's crawling baby and barking dog and made them into pop art by filling them in with bright colors, Jonathan did something similar with traditional "tribal" art. By adding his own original design spin of color, finesse, obscurity, flavor, and creativity, he made each piece individual and unique, something that would be enthusiastically embraced by an American counterculture always craving something novel and fresh. The difference between Angel Ortiz and Jonathan Shaw, though, is that Ortiz did not have the wherewithal to sustain the spotlight, nor the inspiration and savvy to continue to grow as an artist, remaining stuck in the familiar realms of his brief success. No one-trick pony, Jonathan did, and has continued to evolve and grow creatively. And that represents another aspect of his artistic success: his innate ability to float like a butterfly and sting like a bee, to adapt and excel in everything he ever put his hand to in whatever field of endeavor.

He spent decades traveling the world, working alone by appointment, as well as alongside other notorious tattoo legends like Spider Webb, Crazy Ace, Zeke Owen, Bob Shaw, Colonel Todd, Gil Montie, and Filip Leu. Then, in the mid-'80s, Jonathan Shaw's World Famous Fun City Tattoo was born, flaunting—for the first time ever—an archaic law banning the practice within the city of New York. Spawned out of the original clandestine Bowery basement location, it landed one day like a flying saucer at 94 St. Mark's Place, smack dab in an astonished public eye, blowing minds and turning heads. Tattooing was still illegal in New York City. The bold new studio emerged as New York City's first legitimate walk-in tattoo shop since the decades-long official prohibition was enacted in the early 1960's.

Fun City Tattoo became the impetus for the legalization of tattooing in New York City, eventually becoming "the" East Coast landmark tattoo parlor, synonymous with the highest standards of tattooing the world over. The same antique flash from around the world covered the walls. Other décor: classic handwritten signs like "If assholes could fly, this place would be an airport," and the rusty meat cleaver that hung under a plaque reading **TATTOO REMOVER**. A pistol was duct-taped under Jonathan's chair—just in case. A dead fly was crucified on the wall with a tattoo needle by tattoo legend Zeke Owen, and it stayed there for years. You could not sit in the place for an hour without learning volumes about tattoo lore, just by looking at the walls. And if you spent weeks or months in there and thought you had seen everything, you could walk in one day and suddenly notice something completely new.

"Jonathan drilled tattoo history into us all day long," says Elvis Crocker, one of the scores of seasoned tattoo artists who worked at Fun City over the years. "I'm so grateful for that now."

The studio wasn't just a prominent landmark because of its well-earned reputation in the trade, but also a bold testament to the Lower East Side's own oddball collective personality. The first time I set foot in there, I remember being overwhelmed, and not just because I was a stoned-out fourteen-year-old punk rocker, but because I couldn't believe how much stuff was everywhere. It was astonishing! By all accounts, Jonathan loved that place like a baby. He made it, watched it grow, and when it passed its prime, beginning a slow, steady descent into decadence—largely marked by his increasing disinterest and absence from the scene—he let it go gracefully, selling out to an ambitious local operator, even as St. Mark's Place not-so-gracefully suffered its own gentrified, globalized transformation into a youth-oriented version of Fifth Avenue.

Today, like the neighborhood, the shop is different: clean and sterile, devoid of much of its old air of mystery and danger, reflecting a "safe" and sanitary new New York, stripped of its once-terrible and fantastic aura of history, mystery, and tradition. Gone are the walls and ceilings oozing the deranged mystique of its former owner and his colorful cronies. The place retains only the notorious Fun City name now to distinguish it from the dozens of other neat, modern, cookie-cutter tattoo places that sprang up like a crop of plastic mushrooms in the creeping wake of respectability and post-Giuliani homogenization.

"In all fairness to the new kids on the block," Jonathan explains with a sheepish grin, "Fun City had really degenerated into a filthy, morally bankrupt, toxic old shithole over the years. Kinda like me; a nasty old dinosaur." He chuckles sheepishly. "Toward the end, I was just too soul-sick and burnt-out on liquor and drugs to even give a shit. My heart wasn't in the thing anymore. I ended up with a bunch of crack- heads and junkies running the joint while I kept my distance from the scene. I was already gone, living back in South America getting sober, and the place just sorta went to rats and ruin. Oh, well." He shrugs. "The people who bought it off me did a big fancy renovation there, spent a shitload of daddy's dough fixing it up. They just pulled the wicked old plant out by its roots and built a whole new fancy shop in its place. All that remained was the name. The old Fun City was long dead and gone. Good riddance, I figured. One of the guys who used to work for me ended up buying it from them later. Last I saw, he was doing a really good job blending the old school with the new, turning it into a really nice environment with a deep respect for tradition, but more in keeping with modern times."

"Working under Jonathan back then was really cool and immersed me with some of the best artists in the industry" says Steve Pedone, Fun City's current owner. "There was definitely a wild cast of characters, but I couldn't have asked for a better place to start."

After a long, reflective silence, Jonathan laughs, not without irony. "Yeah, well, tattooing has become a respectable gig nowadays, ya know. No place in the modern 'tattoo industry' for a crusty old dump like that. Whatever, I'm just glad to be done with the whole nasty mess. By the time I sold the place and split from tattooing, it was like waking up from some long, terrible, bloody nightmare. Getting out was a relief. Done. Next?"

Before the Lower East Side of Manhattan underwent the mass urban "yuppification" Jonathan describes, it was essentially a small tight-knit community where Fun City Tattoo played its own unique role. Everyone on the block knew the notorious tattoo man well and always had his back. He did business with everyone. The cops would drive by as he stood in the middle of the street with his size-twelve motorcycle boot on someone's face and wave to him without stopping. Everyone was on his side. I listened to another day-in-the-life account where Jonathan had gotten into a bloody rumble with some bridge-and-tunnel "jimooks" because some guy had been harassing one of his girlfriends, and a gang of Dominican drug dealers on the corner jumped in to help him settle the beef. Business as usual on St. Mark's Place. There was drama every day on that street. I was able to see a little of it firsthand myself, having spent half of my teenage years lurking in front of Tompkins Square Park. There was always a whole vibe over at Fun City, kids hanging around outside drinking beer, smoking, laughing, breaking bottles, and talking shit. Everyone seemed to get along, though, living harmoniously in a splendidly dysfunctional downtown ecosystem of artists, freaks, and weirdos.

Jonathan knew those mean streets well and respected them equally. But when people wanted to fuck with him, he was ready. Shaking his head, he reminisces. "Yeah, man, over there, if ya fucked around, ya laid around real fast. We had bloodstains all over the walls in that shop, and most of it wasn't from tattooing." More than a few times he is said to have pulled baseball bats, sawed-off shotguns, and other blunt objects, gleefully inflicting insult and injury on would-be tough guys who came in with attitude. As I've learned, Jonathan Shaw meant business. He'd even had a peephole on the diamond-plate-armored front door of the original Bowery studio specially fitted so the barrel of his AK-47 could fit through it.

Like so many visionary artists, Jonathan's binge drinking, massive drug habits, and unrestrained fast-lane lifestyle eventually took its toll, shuttling him out of a mundane world he didn't relate to and burying him alive in a hellish parallel dimension of bloody warring fragments and surreal nightmare visions, all raging away in his own battle-scarred, increasingly deranged mind. St. Mark's Place had become like a Vietnam minefield. No limbs went missing there, though. They were just marked indelibly by complex, angry-looking tattoo marks: weird dreamlike hiero-glyphics of an underworld landscape that Jonathan's singular perspective personified for a whole generation of New Yorkers.

Through it all, Jonathan always maintained his own special brand of streetwise diplomacy, a certain something that might best be summed up by a sign, a half-hearted reminder to himself, perhaps, that hung above his work station, among the clutter:

TACT—THE ABILITY TO TELL A MAN TO GO TO HELL AND MAKE HIM FEEL HAPPY TO BE ON HIS WAY.

"He was really fucking nuts, and I don't mean that lightly. He just didn't give a fuck. I think Jonathan was basically always more afraid of living a half-assed life of quiet desperation than he was to die," says longtime friend Billy Leroy, an antique dealer, kickboxer, reality show star, actor, and outlaw biker, referring to an incident that occurred when some big drunk guy changed his mind about getting a tattoo. After paying up front, the would-be bully backed out, demanding a refund after Jonathan already spent time working up a design. According to Billy, who was there at the time, "He told the guy there were these carrier pigeons at the window and that the birds flew over to a place in Brooklyn with all the shop's money, so he couldn't give him his money back. Carrier pigeons? Where'd he come up with that?! He just stood up and looked this big bruiser right in the eye and turned out his empty pockets like he didn't have a penny to his name. What balls! The look on his face, you hadda be there! The guy just shrugged and walked out scratching his head. Played by the master. Carrier pigeons! Shit, JS probably had a grand tucked in his boot. What a beautiful maniac." Billy laughs.

As Fun City became "the" staple NYC tattoo parlor in the early '90s, it began to grow an even bigger name for itself. "Jonathan ruled that shop with an iron fist," says Marcus Epstein, who wears one of the last great full-body pieces that Jonathan completed before retiring. The master's swan song was an innovative neo-tribal style masterpiece that won every award going at tattoo conventions all over the world. "He used to say to me, 'Damn it, Marcus, I wish you could just drop your arm off, then come back and pick it up in the morning.' Later, after he got sober, he told me he was massively strung out on heroin the whole time he was doing all that brilliant work on me. How he managed to pull off that quality of tattooing stoned out of his mind seems to defy the laws of nature. But there it was. He was a genius. Nothing could stop that. And we were working five nights a week for months."

Fun City was well-named. It was a notorious bohemian gathering place and hectic underground Mecca packed to the rafters with all the crazed flora and fauna of the still-vibrant counterculture neighborhood: beautiful losers, visionaries, street thugs, cops, mobsters, artists, tourists, bikers, hipsters, high rollers, stock brokers, junkies, strippers, and movie stars. Long days and late nights were just a part of Fun City's surreal everyday dynamics. It stayed open until four a.m. or later, depending on street traffic, visiting friends, hot chicks, the combination of liquor and drugs flowing through Jonathan's veins, or the number of Hells Angels bikes lined up out front. Over time, the clientele got larger and more demanding, eventually growing into a wild feeding frenzy of major proportions. The spot became a timeless twenty-four hour netherworld time warp of vital art and local flavor. Busy all the time now, Jonathan was right in his element, casually banging out pieces that would end up changing the tattoo world forever, without even realizing it. His combination of old-school technique (taught to him directly by the old-time tattoo masters, tattoo legends like Bob Shaw and Colonel Todd), blended nicely with an innovative neo-tribal primitive graffiti spin, producing his ever-present colorful abstract neo-cubist style. His growing body of groundbreaking tattoo work was turning heads all over town, putting him in charge as a true leader in what by then had evolved into a fledgling industry. And with this trailblazing work, he was also building a more demanding, sophisticated, and affluent clientele. By the mid-'90s, he had become the world's Numero Uno celebrity tattoo artist.

"You could tell the difference right away between his work and anyone else's," said a heavily tattooed guy I talked to in Tompkins Square Park. "Just the way he dragged his tattoo needles across the skin, it was a whole different technique. Nobody around here had ever seen that kind of thing before. I've been tattooed by a lot of different people over the years, but Shaw really had a special touch."

And that "special touch" let him create unique works of art, employing a traditional technique that was unusually old-school and simplistic for such intricate masterpieces. He puts ink in with a heavy hand, and I do mean heavy. It stays. JS makes three-hundred-pound tough guys cry, just to say he did. And despite his cold-blooded bedside manner, those of us who have been tattooed by him reap big benefits. They never need a touchup. You can't tell if a tattoo is ten months or ten years old. Musician, and longtime friend of Jonathan's, Ricky Beck knows from experience. Over dinner recently, I asked him about his first tattoo. He lifted his sleeve to reveal a colorful, intricate piece by Jonathan. Over twenty years old, the thing looked like it had been done a month ago. Then he pointed to a fuzzy blue mark on his upper arm, laughing. "See that dot there? That's really my first tattoo. Jonathan did it back in 1982. I asked him 'Does that hurt?' while he was tattooing my friend. We were all coked up and drinking hard. He didn't say nothin'. All of a sudden he just picks up another tattoo gun and stabs me with the fuckin' needle. He goes: 'Well, tough guy, whaddya think? Did *that* hurt?'"

This kind of unorthodox weirdness went on throughout his entire career, I would learn as I pieced together the fuzzy shadow of the old Jonathan Shaw. Secretive bordering on paranoid, as protective of his craft secrets as the old-timers who schooled him, he became like one of the Mulberry Street wiseguys he tattooed. Jonathan never liked to be asked too many questions about his business. So it was particularly ironic when, in the mid-'90s, he made his first appearance on the *David Letterman Show*: the first and only tattooist ever to do so at the time. And so, he began building another kind of reputation, now not only in the insular tattoo community, but suddenly in the general public eye. As Fun City's advertisement said, it was "Where the Tattoo Elite Meet," and this was fast becoming the stuff of legend. The names "Fun City" and "Jonathan Shaw" were known in the celebrity crowd as the Where and Who to go to for tattoo work. But, to his consternation, he was coming to be known publicly more for his high-profile clientele than for his actual tattoo skills. All of a sudden, the very taboo mystique that had once enticed the entertainment world was becoming a sort of fly in the shaman's ointment.

Sucking his teeth with a wry shrug, Jonathan reminisces. "It wasn't what I wanted when I first started tattooing. Never, man! I mean, yeah, the business was good and all that, but then it all just started getting kinda stupid, ya know. Hordes of all these real squaresville types coming in from all over the place, and they weren't even coming for the quality of the work anymore, but just because I was the guy who tattooed all these famous people. It coulda been anybody, for all they cared. The good old herd mentality. Most of these fuckers didn't know enough about tattooing to care, they just wanted the status of that whole 'I got tattooed by the famous guy who did so-and-so's shit.'"

"So and so" indeed: Iggy Pop, Johnny Depp, The Cure, Shane MacGowan, The Ramones, The Velvet Underground, Marilyn Manson, Jim Jarmusch, Johnny Winter, Kate Moss, Orlando Bloom, Kathy Acker, Tupac Shakur and all his bitches. The VIP list goes on. Even Vanilla Ice was lining up for an appointment, much to Shaw's embarrassment. Everyone who was anyone—or thought they were—was clamoring for ink from the Master. While fellow tattoo pioneer Ed Hardy was tapping into the fine art world on the West Coast, JS was doing the same in New York. But Jonathan was also creating a durable personal myth with his own colorful, weirdo, edgy flare.

In 1991, he curated a high profile exhibition of tattoo flash art at

New York's cutting-edge Psychedelic Solution Gallery. One of the first mainstream tattoo-related public events, the show was a huge success. Jonathan laughs. "We were totally shocked and unprepared for the kind of crowds it drew. They had to set up police barricades around the whole block to keep order on the night of the opening. It was insane. The press came out in droves, newspapers, TV, the works. That's when I first began to see the kind of power this stuff had to bring people out of the woodwork. Up till then, the whole thing was still pretty underground. The next show I did was about a year later on the West Coast, at this big gallery in Hollywood. Same thundering crowds, same mad interest. You had all these big movie stars and rock stars lining up to gawk at the artwork. After that, it all just kinda snowballed into a scene."

Jonathan became one of the first tattooists to successfully cross the fine-art line with a high-profile style, and all in public view, as he continued working tirelessly to legitimize the art through the numerous gallery shows he subsequently curated and/or participated in as a painter. There were also the scores of TV, MTV, radio, and news media appearances he made, both locally and internationally. Jonathan Shaw was always in the spotlight, later taking it to the next level yet again—this time with his very own magazine, *International Tattoo Art*.

After cutting his teeth as a regular contributor to *Outlaw Biker*, a motorcycle mag with a section devoted to tattooing, and being the creative driving force behind the short-lived, seminal *Art Alternatives* (predecessor and original role-model for today's highly successful *Juxtapoz* magazine), Jonathan was approached by market-conscious rival publishers with the idea of starting a brand-new publication, one that would be dedicated exclusively to tattoo art. He snapped at the bait, and so it was that *International Tattoo Art* magazine was founded in 1991, christened with an article by Jonathan Shaw, Founder and Managing Editor. With worldwide distribution, it was the perfect opportunity to raise the bar another notch for tattooing, and right at the height of its new novelty status with an increasingly receptive public. Jonathan ran with it in style, engineering a magazine that was the very first of its kind. His brainchild and obsessive new creative project, *ITA* took the common grassroots tattoo-rag format and elevated it to the level of a legitimate art magazine, changing forever the way the public would perceive tattooing. To that end, Jonathan's *ITA* focused greatly on tattoo history, ensuring that priceless folklore, information, and archives were not kept hidden away to be hoarded by a few elitist folk-art collectors. *ITA* created and maintained the highest standards for the emerging worldwide tattoo industry by showcasing world-class works of art. These included many of Jonathan's own revolutionary pieces: his neo-tribal work and detailed abstract back pieces, his first-of-a-kind tattoos of world-class underground art paintings, copied immaculately in loving tribute to his old friends and art peers. Each tattoo looked just like the oil painting from which it was derived. All this had been totally unseen before his time, much to the chagrin of the growing legions of Jonathan's increasingly envious competitors. Via his in-depth interviews with legendary artists from around the world, some of the art world's most respected players—household names today, like Joe Coleman and Robert Williams—were first introduced to a tattoo audience. Through Jonathan's groundbreaking historical articles, the long-neglected exposure he felt was due to his own tattoo heroes, mentors, and old friends was now a reality. Legendary tattooists like Bob Shaw, Jack Dracula, Coney Island Freddy, Colonel Todd, Crazy Ace, Japan's Horiyoshi and the Leu Family, to name just a few, were finally getting their props. Jonathan had brought tattoos into the mainstream by creating a magazine that was centered in tattoo culture and packed with vital information and history in every issue. A whole generation of new tattooists came up weaned on Jonathan's sophisticated, cutting-edge articles and editorials. And he was cool. Mysterious and attractive, well-spoken with a hip, bad-boy charisma, he was an A-list mover and shaker who knew everybody worth knowing. Essentially, he was propelling himself beyond the confines of his own neo-celebrity status, something unheard of at the time. A super- star tattoo artist? No way! Yes, way.

"JS took the role of being a tattoo artist to a whole new level," says Clay Decker of True Tattoo in Hollywood, one of the now-famous Kat Von D's early mentors. "He was completely tapped into all these different worlds, and long, long before anyone else, especially after he started the magazine. Jonathan paved the runway for all these so-called 'celebrity tattoo artists' to glide in and take a bow."

Jonathan laughs. "Oh, man, when that fuckin' rag hit the newsstands, the haters came out of the woodwork like a swarm of locusts. I remember when I was first breaking into the business, Bob Shaw always warned me, 'These tattoo people are like a bunch of jealous old whores.' I didn't know what he was talking about at the time but I sure found out after I started the magazine. Suddenly everybody in the tattoo business wanted to be my best friend. Most of 'em wanted to knife me in the back at the same time."

Indisputably, when Jonathan was running *ITA*, it was at its best. It personified not only a vibe and aesthetic that people were into, but, more important, perhaps, the essence of Jonathan Shaw himself: his coolness and sophistication, his dark sense of humor, his ruggedness, his outspoken opinion and no-bullshit outlook. All that along with a neo-traditional view of tattooing and underground culture across the board. Knowing full well that he was kicking up the level at which tattoo culture would be held forevermore, he painstakingly compiled every piece of information for every issue, personally. At a time when the art form was still largely frowned upon and misunderstood, Jonathan Shaw raised the standard higher than most had ever thought to push it before. To do so, he made his classic big demands on contributors. He wanted research, humor, detail, depth, drama, and art. And he got it.

"*ITA* proposes to edify, educate, and entertain its readers," he stated in the first edition's Editor's Note. In the hundreds of pieces he wrote for subsequent issues, he always gave the reader a feeling of intimate familiarity with his interview subjects, putting you in a place and time so accurately described and well documented that it was almost eerie. An accomplished and well-read writer, Jonathan lovingly devoted his vision and talent to detail, poetic phrase, and description. Many of his articles in *ITA* are the only accurate pieces of written history on many legendary tattoo figures. Needless to say, *ITA* was a contribution beyond measure to the art form, and Jonathan finally gained well-deserved—if short-lasting—worldwide respect for it. That was despite a growing feeling of sour grapes from within the tattoo community.

He shakes his head sadly and reflects. "Even though I lived and breathed tattooing back then, on some levels there was always this perverse part of me that never let me feel I fit in with the crowd. Any crowd. It was no different with the so-called tattoo world I suddenly found myself in the center of. And it would eventually be my undoing, especially where the magazine work was concerned."

It's an inherent reality that he was born into a level of sophistication that set him apart in any crowd. Jonathan's mother, Doris Dowling, was a glamorous Hollywood film star. His father was Artie Shaw, the legendary jazzman and bandleader. But his mother was an alcoholic, and Artie left her when Jonathan was just a baby. As a teenager, Jonathan rebelled against his parents' American Dream values, dodging school and sticking to the streets, later traveling the world for years as a merchant sailor, bartender, and jack-of-all-trades. Nonetheless, a certain artful maturity of vision and taste must have been tattooed into his DNA, always shining through whatever he created in every area of his schizophrenic, multi-faceted world.

"Yeah." He shrugs. "I was pretty much orphaned by the violent alcoholism in my family of origin, so I was kinda raised by wolves, running the streets of Hollywood and New York City, hitchhiking around the country, getting high and living on the edge. Eventually, I took off on the road. I wound up living in Mexico and South America, and never really looked back. I was pretty much on my own from about the age of twelve, so my real family and school were always the streets, bikers, beatniks, winos, weirdos, druggies, hustlers, criminals, and whores. Those good people taught me the art of survival. I didn't come to tattooing so much for the art as I did because of the outsider lifestyle that surrounded the whole deal. For me, the artistic part came later. Much later. Eventually, it all just jumbled together and took over my life, like some kinda fucked-up Frankenstein creation."

Nonetheless, Jonathan seems to have been raised with an inherent affinity for the finer things in life, his rough-hewn personal grace and charm tempered by a very real, streetwise worldview. Sometimes, when I pester him and ask stupid questions, he looks up from whatever he's doing and snarls like a medieval warlord, scaring me half to death. Yet when he walks into the realm of high society, he is somehow immediately respected and accepted as an equal. Jonathan Shaw simply carries an aura of tarnished nobility, some invisible "something" that people in positions of power and prestige seem to smell on him like an exotic cologne—even as he scavenges their fancy buffet tables like he hasn't eaten in weeks.

Maybe his ability to pull this off comes from the rare success he has enjoyed in a diverse multitude of fields. As a writer, he hung out with Charles Bukowski, their first meeting ending in a drunken punch-up, hilariously recounted in the pages of this first volume of his ongoing *Scab Vendor* saga. As a tattoo artist, he apprenticed with tattoo legend Bob Shaw, who taught him the basics of the craft and much respect for the game over countless hours and months of practice on drunken sailors up and down the fabled tattoo factory of the Long Beach Pike. As a screenwriter, he collaborated with the great Hubert Selby Jr. As an aspiring independent filmmaker, he was coached and encouraged by the likes of Johnny Depp and Jim Jarmusch. As an actor, he played the part of a stereotypical tattooed thug in a feature-length Hollywood movie, sharing a scene with none other than Clint Eastwood. As a lifelong biker, he is old friends with many respected Hells Angels. As an editor, he founded and ran the first widely recognized top-shelf tattoo magazine. The list goes on and on. A "Renaissance Lowlife," as he was dubbed by legendary New York author Larry "Ratso" Sloman, Jonathan has an uncanny capacity to carry the most intense levels of perfectionism and sophistication into whatever he chooses to do.

But it was with his innovative, trendsetting, abstract freehand tattoo work that Jonathan Shaw would eventually change the face of popular modern art. When I first came to him for a tattoo, he was already long retired. I used my dubious feminine charms to persuade him to tattoo me—even though I still had no idea what the hell I wanted. That ended up working in my favor. He told me it would have to be the "artist's choice" if he was going to do it. It was his way or the highway. I consented. I just wanted something beautiful and flowing. And I got it, beyond my wildest expectations. Like me, over the decades legions of clients came to Jonathan with nothing specific in mind, only a blank canvas of skin for him to do his bold, original work on. It was easy for me to see why he became so famous for his ability to casually bang out masterpieces, right off the top of his head.

Jonathan Shaw is also notorious for his nomadic lifestyle and his mysterious disappearing acts, which have been going on for the last forty years. He is an enigmatic, spontaneous creature of many faces, a real-life, low-life Indiana Jones, speaking several languages fluently despite his lack of any formal education. Whenever I see someone who knows Jonathan, they always seem to ask "How is he? *Where* is he?" Every time. They name a list of cities and countries he may currently be inhabiting. For decades, as a resourceful, functional maniac forever seeking a geographic cure for his own baffling restlessness, whenever he grew tired of wherever he was living, he would simply "vaporize," then effortlessly build a whole new world for himself elsewhere; only to destroy it and move on again. This rootless Gypsy lifestyle went on ad infinitum until eventually Jonathan came to see himself like a dog chasing its tail, always seeking the next place of imagined sanctuary and never finding it. After many years of frantic travel, finally he found the road itself to be his only real home; more, perhaps, than any of the homes he built, then fled from like a fugitive. Maybe it's the Romany blood in him—being the grandson of a Lithuanian Gypsy on his mother's side. Whatever its roots, this practice has earned him a multitude of homes, pretty much anywhere in the world he happens to be. This all started back in the '70s, when he jumped ship in an Amazon port town in Brazil and began hitchhiking his way across South America. Making crude tattoos for money to survive, he eventually ended up in Rio de Janeiro, the one place in the world he truly considers his spiritual home; and where he is still known by many only as "Cigano" (Gypsy). Maybe that's because, to this day, he still comes and goes so often. But Rio is not the only place he has laid down deep roots. The product of a lifetime of travels, Jonathan literally has odd home bases all over the world, peopled with thriving tribes of friends and family, history and memory. He's equally at home in Bangkok, Buenos Aires, Bombay, Mexico City, Veracruz, Asunción, Porto Alegre, New York, Los Angeles, New Orleans, Miami, Paris, Tokyo, Rio de Janeiro, and a dozen other places. And like an actor on the stage of his own strange, confusing life, it seems he gets to be all the things he is, different sides of a shattered, multifaceted personality naturally coming out to play in all these divergent settings.

During the course of his travels, Jonathan met and studied with tattoo masters from far-flung cultures and traditions. After tattooing in Mexico, British Honduras, Brazil, California, Texas, and New Orleans, he eventually ended up in New York, the city of his birth. Having grown tired of working on sailors in sleazy port towns, he concluded that New York would be a new challenge—one he was born for. His first stint in the Big Apple found him teamed up with old friend and early mentor Spider Webb. He worked side by side with the legendary "Webbo" for years in a midtown Manhattan studio before going off on his own.

Jonathan smiles widely at the memories. "Boy, it was never a dull moment working with old Spider. What a guy! I fucking love that man! He taught me stuff nobody else coulda." He laughs, shaking his head. "We both liked liquor and drugs, and pretty girls. Wooo! We were like a pair of outlaw rock stars without a band, living in this surreal, no-limits world of underground art. It was like Andy Warhol meets *Easy Rider* on DMT. Warhol actually showed up there one time. It was a magical, anything-goes kinda creative situation, y'know? Dinkins was mayor. New

York was like in that movie *The Warriors*. This was all back in the day when Times Square was still Times Square, not fucking Disneyland. We worked in this big loft upstairs from a whorehouse. Man, it was total mayhem."

This was all way before mass-marketed tattoo equipment was readily available. It required real perseverance and determination to break into the game. The handful of professional tattooers in the world back then were a secretive lot: closedmouthed, inbred, and fiercely protective of their mysterious "trade secrets." But persistent to the bone, Jonathan did learn. The hard way. And to this day he carries that old-school way to all who come around him. In keeping with his reverence for tradition, Jonathan has, over the decades, had major tattoo history carved onto his own body. With Ed Hardy's only full-scale black-and-gray oriental dragon back-pieces, done back in the late '70s, a chest-piece by famed underground cartoonist-turned-tattooist Greg Irons, and a miscellaneous collection from legendary artists like Bob Shaw, Crazy Ace, Coney Island Freddy, Zeke Owen, Filip Leu, Spider Webb, and even Johnny Depp, his body is a colorful road map of his many diverse lives, adventures, friendships, love affairs, and dreams, all etched into his skin over count-less journeys around the world.

Maybe because Jonathan was taught by the original masters of old-school tattooing, he always ran his business like they had, keeping it painstakingly traditional, authentic, and down-to-earth. He tried to teach all those who worked for him the meaning of respect, carrying on those old-time carny codes of honor, credos that barely survive in today's tattoo world.

"Yeah! He's a real two-fisted, old-school tattoo man," Baba, of Vintage Tattoo in Los Angeles, says of Jonathan. "He learned the tricks of the trade straight from the old-timers, and he has always honored them, all through his career. Old school is who he is, where he comes from, what he does."

"He's exactly what he says he is, which is rare," says punk-rock icon Howie Pyro. "He's an old-school tattoo gangster with true respect for those roots, not some newfangled goon trying to play Picasso."

And Jonathan was always an astute hustler when it came to the business. By all accounts, he really knew how to sell a tattoo. His over-the-top personality and dark charisma were always a gift in the tattoo shops he worked in before going off on his own. "If ya can't dazzle 'em with brilliance, baffle 'em with bullshit," Bob Shaw once told him. And he mastered that trick of the trade, the whole show-business, carnival aspect of the game. With his slicked-back hair, gold teeth, and gold Rolex, he always looked his best when he went out to meet the public. He possesses the mysterious qualities of any good salesman: that special magnetism that makes people nervous and at the same time excited for whatever's in store. Jonathan was notorious for making customers wait outside for outrageously long periods of time. No one was ever allowed backstage while he set up—even if he was just sitting inside drinking and bullshitting with friends, rock stars, maybe some neighborhood kids, or the guys who worked for him. People knew his tattoos were worth the wait. Jonathan always knew how to keep 'em smiling and keep 'em coming back for more. And although his contributions to tattooing over the most important decades of its evolution have been immeasurable, from his point of view he was just in the right place at the right time, making a buck doing what he liked, and sharing his love for it with the world. For his efforts, he won all sorts of industry awards over the years, most of them recognizing his trademark freehand work. When asked about the accolades, though, he just scowls and waves his hand dismissively. "It's a lot of nonsense, man. Smoke and mirrors. Cheap tricks to impress the thundering herds of 'tattoo fans.' Award-winning this, award-winning that. Shit, man, those fucking trophies were the first thing to hit the dumpster when I sold the shop."

That statement seems to paraphrase his view of the emerging tattoo industry: a lot of meaningless garbage. A jaded view, but one he has certainly earned. Without a doubt, he has a great deal more respect for those who came before him than for many of those who emerged in his wake. Jonathan always saw himself as a craftsman rather than an entertainer. In today's industrialized post-Shaw tattoo world, however, the two have collided, often with surreal results—as seen on TV. Like a handful of other old-school veterans, Jonathan watched, with a somewhat amused, often perplexed, attitude, the humble craft that crawled its way out of the old low-rent bucket shops on the Bowery explode into a worldwide "industry." "Industry!? Really?" He howls with laughter. "Jeez! Some people take this whole thing a little too serious, doncha think? I mean, c'mon, man, all these big-name scab slingers ain't exactly curing cancer, y'know! Seriously. Let's face it, for a lot of these new folks, it's all about the cash and prizes, right?"

He makes a good point. Sadly, in an increasingly globalized, homogenized, media-driven marketplace, tattooing has become a fast track to easy money for many who seem to care little about its real history and essence. To many tattoo artists of Jonathan's generation, this trend seems incomprehensible. And, as much as he tries to downplay any lasting bitterness, that aspect of its evolution clearly disgusts him—even as it may be argued that he was among the first to steer the art form in that direction. In his defense, however, history will prove that if he unwittingly unleashed a monster by helping to legitimize tattooing, Jonathan was always working to promote the art itself, rather than merely exploiting it for personal gain. Nonetheless, a faceless media machine soon discovered and milked tattoo culture in a big way, eventually converting the once-venerable and ancient art into a trendy fast-food phenomenon—and usually without giving anything back. TV has turned tattooing into little more than another facile commercial commodity in the public eye, a source of prime-time ratings, something hip and groovy and young, while neglecting its true potential and ignoring the subject's uncharted depths. The art of tattooing, for all the great technological and artistic advances it's achieved in its long-awaited renaissance, has likewise been cheapened and largely degraded to the level of sitcom culture, catering to a formulaic bottom line. And the focus has rarely been on any of its true pioneers. Joe Dante, a downtown Manhattan resident who was on the scene back in the day, had this to say: "We lived a much more interesting life on the Lower East Side during the '80s and '90s than any of those supposed 'Reality Stars.' Real reality never makes it to the boob tube. The more 'reality' shows they make, the less real they get. The things that went down at Fun City before tattooing got legalized was the stuff of legend. You just can't make that kinda shit up!"

Ironically, right before the advent of the current wave of tattoo-based "reality" shows, Jonathan was approached by a producer for a first shot at the television market. Just having gotten out of tattooing, however, he was committed to his newfound freedom and happiness, living a simpler life in South America, traveling and writing books. Without thinking twice, he turned the offer down flat. When I ask him how come he missed the boat, he scoffs. "Missed *what* boat? Are you kidding? I didn't wanna be on that fucking boat. For me, it was like being offered a luxury stateroom on the *Titanic*. No way was I gonna waste any more of my life pandering to the lowest common denominator of public taste. The public is a shit-eating monster. Just look at what they're putting out in the media these days! And the fuckers just eat it up! It's pathetic. Shit, man, that's why I quit tattooing in the first place, to get away from public taste. Let somebody else do that shit."

I had to wonder how many times JS used to roll his eyes when some dumb chick would come in asking for a ladybug on her hip, really small so her mom wouldn't see it. Or some lame-ass hair-moussed goon asking for a tattoo of a *Looney Toons* character. When I got my first tattoo, I remember I wanted it real, real low, so my parents wouldn't see it. The artist—if one could call him that—didn't roll his eyes. He didn't even check my ID (good thing, 'cause I was only thirteen). He obviously didn't give a shit about the art. He wanted the cash. He took my money, slapped on the stencil and did the thing in about twenty seconds. I guess the joke's on me, though, since I'm the one stuck with a blurry, scarred-up, lopsided star that looks like a crippled spider sitting in the middle of my crotch. As a relative newcomer to the world of tattoo myself, I'm really glad to have gotten a glimpse of its radical transformation, if not firsthand, then through the eyes of someone who has been there and done it all.

Tattoo artists like Jonathan are a rarity nowadays, a dying breed. He came in with the old school and is a direct link to those who fought a bloody, unpopular battle to clear the runway for future generations. Jonathan Shaw is a living witness to tattooing coming of age, and then turning into the worldwide cultural phenomenon it is today. And like a true survivor, he lived it to the fullest and got out intact, with no regrets. Despite his cynical cracks about the burgeoning "industry," he was right at the forefront of modern tattooing's most important technological, ideological, and artistic advances. And, whether he likes to admit it or not, his contributions were a huge impetus for much of that growth. He was one of the first high-profile artists who always kept tattooing original and artful, while others were working just as hard to contribute to its mediocrity. And through his writing, he has helped keep its artistic soul alive—no small accomplishment in a time when unprincipled greed is taking over the world, the youth, the arts, and the quality of human endeavors in general. With the growth of international tattoo conventions to fuel the fire, the tattoo world has become a ready-made cash cow for new generations of hacks to jump into. It seems to be a sign of the times. Just look at what's become of rock & roll, unrecognizable today from the badass outlaw grassroots art form it once was. For better or worse, it's thanks largely to Jonathan Shaw's decades of hard work and dedication that we now have the glossy tattoo magazine, the explosion of "tribal" tattoos, the tattoo-oriented reality shows, and acceptance of the craft the world over—a world in which every other young person seems to be wearing one or more.

Since retiring from full-time tattooing in 2001, Jonathan has mostly split his time between his homes in Rio de Janeiro and Hollywood, where he continues working on a number of literary and tattoo-related projects. Those include the next several volumes of this meticulously detailed, blow-by-blow personal memoir; several books of poetry and fiction; screenplays; and, last but not least his *Vintage Tattoo Flash*, a series of, a magnificent coffee-table art books with an accompanying traveling gallery show featuring the huge collection of antique tattoo design sheets he amassed over his decades working with the old-school tattoo masters.

In 2010, on a visit to New York City, Jonathan Shaw once again made headline news. This time it was for being arrested while cleaning out a storage locker containing the remnants of the life he'd long left behind there. Under pressure by a publicity-hungry New York District Attorney, he was indicted by a Grand Jury and charged with eighty-nine felony counts of illegal weapons possession. Released from jail on a quarter-million-dollar bail and facing the rest of his life in prison, Jonathan had his Brazilian passport confiscated, pending the outcome of an ensuing four-year legal battle. Like the cat with nine lives, Jonathan was cleared of all charges in 2014. With a smile on his face and a prayer of gratitude in his heart, he moved back to Brazil to continue his writing. The rest is history.

No matter where he goes from here, Jonathan's artistic legacy will always remain fresh. His work lives on forever, tattooed on hearts and minds around the world. He is a revolutionary. His contributions have changed Western pop culture. His knowledge, skill, and ideology have been passed on to emerging generations of upcoming artists, many of whom are likewise committed to maintaining tattooing's sacred traditions. The doors of the future of tattooing that Jonathan Shaw first kicked open are open today for good.

And with that began a new chapter in his long, crazy, multifaceted creative life: an unarmed one-man pirate attack on the world of letters. With one widely acclaimed, non-tattoo-related work of fiction under his belt, Jonathan Shaw, the writer, has labored over a lifetime on the book you're holding in your hands. In its pages, he takes the reader deep, not only into the recesses of his extraordinary mind and life, but also into the strange and magical process of memoir-writing itself. If truth is indeed stranger than fiction, then, like his old friend and literary mentor Charles Bukowski once told him, much of the contents of this book would have to be lived before it could be written. In that sense, *Homeward Bound* and *Scab Vendor: Confessions of a Tattoo Artist* are much more than a fascinating memoir of a popular artist's creative evolution. They are installments in an ongoing, multicolored, cinematic, modern-day *Odyssey*, written in blood, ink, and tears—a multifaceted, visionary road map to the journey of the human soul.

GRATITUDE LIST

First, I must give all thanks and praises to Almighty God, and to all of the ascended beings of the celestial court, for their divine inspiration, wisdom, teachings, patience, love and protection over the crooked course of the life that gave birth to this ongoing multi-volume book series. Any success I may have attained as a humble creative channel is far greater evidence of their success than of my own.

Secondly, I want to thank my dear brother-by-another-mother, Johnny Depp, for his invaluable encouragement and support. From the day he first read the original rough outlines of the *Scab Vendor* book series (in the form of a screenplay written at his kind suggestion) and told me of his desire to make this ongoing saga into a movie, the spark of hope he lit in my heart was often the only earthly light guiding me through the daunting process of beginning work on this challenging, and often painful, memoir saga. Sharing his home, heart, and patronage with a struggling writer at a challenging juncture in my creative journey, Johnny was like a modern-day Medici, an old-school benefactor to the underground, the underdog, and the dispossessed. For those angelic, soulful qualities, and for his loyal friendship, vision, generosity, love, and undying belief in my humble efforts, I remain eternally in his debt.

It would be almost impossible to express the depths of my gratefulness to the legendary American artist, Robert Crumb, not only for his generosity in gifting me with the amazing cover art for the first volume of this series, *Scab Vendor, Confessions of a Tattoo Artist,* but also for his inspired editorial advice during the writing process. R. Crumb's massive contribution to our culture over the decades has long served as a guiding light of inspiration to generations of artists like myself.

My longtime colleague Lydia Lunch is also at the top of my gratitude list for writing the inspired introduction to my first published novel, *Narcisa: Our Lady of Ashes.* I'll never forget her loving encouragement and support right from the beginning of my long and winding literary journey.

A special shout out to three of my closest and dearest old friends and brother artists, the great visionary painter, Joe Coleman, the legendary filmmaker, Jim Jarmusch, and our badass spiritual godfather and muse, Iggy Pop. Without these guys' loyal friendship, inspiration, example, encouragement, and moral support, this journey wouldn't be half the fun.

My deepest appreciation to Todd Bottorff, Stephanie Beard, Jon O'Neal, Heather Howell, and Maddie Cothren of Turner Publishing for their diligent efforts in the production, promotion, and publication of all the books in the *Scab Vendor* series. Without the hard work and persistent competent efforts of a great publishing house, and all the wonderful hardworking people who make it great, this ongoing memoir project would still be but a fond intention.

Heartfelt thanks to the great American film director, Orson Oblowitz, for introducing me to a real literary agent who cares, my dear friend, the persistent and attentive Mark Gottlieb of Trident Media Group.

Change this to read:

Many thanks to the great Mexican illustrator Miguel Angel Maese Valdes, and to my multi-talented fellow scab vendor, the inimitable Oliver Peck, for their generous collaboration with me on the cover art and interior art for this book. Miguel Angel is a sensational muti-talented artist well worthy of his angelic name. Oliver is a world-class working class hero, a modern-day tattoo superstar with a deep and abiding old school respect for those who went before him. No thanks to Oliver would be complete, however, without also expressing major gratitude to his longtime collaborator and business guru, my dear friend, Aaron Finnin.

Massive gratitude to the masterful, hardworking production team of the *Scab Vendor* documentary: its co-directors and co-producers Mariana Thomé and Lucas Barros; producers Enrique Aular, Sebastián Arrechedera, Juan Bernardo González, Christian Jurgensen, and Arturo Pereyra; and the sleepless, dedicated editors and production assistants Paula Ferro Neves, Carolina Aular, Keven Sean McCray, Dane Davidson, and Tomas Diaz. Special thanks to La Maraca Films, and a respectful 'gracias' to the brilliant world-renowned film editor Luis Carballar for lending his singular talent and vision to the project.

Major thanks also to my dear friend Peter Antico, for his tireless efforts to see my work represented on the Silver Screen. Bom trabalho, brother!

Muchas gracias as well to all the good people from my fantastic Mexican publisher, Sexto Piso–and especially to its visionary editor-in-chief, Eduardo Rebassa, for having the courage to bring ingenious bulletproof translations of my books to the Spanish-speaking audience so close to my heart.

Mil gracias also to my great amigo, Enrique Marquez, head of the Departamento de Publicaciones y Bibleotecas - Instituto Veracruzano de la Cultura, for his generous and loyal support.

Loving kudos upon my dear friend and longtime editorial consultant, Alessandra De Benedetti—who wrote the marathon afterword to the first volume of the *Scab Vendor* series—for her loyalty, patience, and indispensable input and advice through the long, daunting task of bringing these stories to life.

Eternal loving gratitude to my dear friend, criminal defense attorney extraordinaire and fearless legal warrior, Stacy Richman, who rescued my life from the malevolent jaws of the American justice system.

Special posthumous thanks to the iconic American authors Charles Bukowski and Hubert Selby Jr., who both took time from their brilliant careers to share generous wisdom and advice with an unknown writer. They are both unforgettable examples of how this whole deal works. Another deep tip of the Cigano hat goes out to the late, great American writer, my dear friend Dan Fante, whose love, support, and example have been a constant inspiration.

A significant round of grateful applause to my many other gifted fellow writer friends: Dan Depp, Jerry Stahl, Lisa Douglas, Peter Antico, Jillian Lauren, Legs McNeil, Leon Ichaso, Paulo Lins, Kenneth Shiffrin, Harlan Ellison, Carlo McComrick, Jeff Ward, Justin Smith,

Angie Wang, Anisa Irwin, Amy Fields, Larry "Ratso" Sloman, Rex Wiener, Ida Maria, Alex Orbison, Harold Schechter, Kelly Cutrone, Eugene Hutz, Matthew Bishop, Mayra Dias Gomes, Michelle Delio, Nick Wong, Noah Levine, Paul Gerard, Saira Viola, Herbert Reichert, Salete Andrade, Joe Ryan, Tom Nolan, Denis Fahey, Chris Davis, and Chris Campion. Thank you all for your invaluable input, inspiration, example, advice, friendship, solidarity, encouragement, and support.

Last, but not least, an expression of eternal gratitude to my brilliant muse and partner, the kind and beautiful Genevieve Altamirano—to whom this book is lovingly dedicated.

There are many other good people, entities, and institutions to whom I owe a deep debt of thanks as well, for their help, inspiration, and guidance. Many of them have been with me constantly throughout the writing process. Other supporters came along later in the game, kindly offering advice and moral sustenance. Others have simply lent a quick suggestion or a kind word of encouragement along the way. Still others, whose names and contributions have been misplaced in the anonymous mist of my own forgetfulness, will nonetheless linger forever, somewhere deep in my heart of gratitude.

Principally, I would also like to thank:

Adult Children of Alcoholics, Al-Anon Family Groups, Alcoholics Anonymous, Tonico Monteiro de Carvalho, Marilyn Manson, Alex Bregyan, Alex Gottlieb, Alfred Albrizio, Ana Paula Mendes, The Augustine Fellowship, Ariel Electron, Baba Austin, Bara Byrns, Basil Pologianis, Billy Shire, Bob Anderson and Primetime Recovery, Bronislav Dolgopya, Bruce Paly, Bob Shaw, Jack Dracula, Coney Island Freddy, Colonel Todd, Crazy Ace, Captain Kirk McFadden, The Leu Family Iron, Cheyenne Crowe, China Kong, Chris Garver, Chris Lohnes, Christa and Samantha Fuller, Christi Dembrowski, Christine Natanael, Henry Rollins, Clayton Patterson, Dr. Dave Ores, David Tors, Debbie Harry, Familia Vacite and the União Cigana do Brasil, Gibson Hayes, Heidi Day, Hidalgo Neira, Howie Pyro, Isaac Baruch, Izara García Rodriguez, Izzy Zay, Jacob Reiss, Jason Black, Jerome Ali, Jimena Gueso Tenorio, John Jardine, John Joseph, Johnny Brenner, Johnny Carco, Jorge Flores-Oliver, Jose Angel Baez Albarracin, Julia Cameron, Justin Clark, Justin and Brigitte Smith, Kembra Pfahler, Michael Kortez, Kyle Tonniges, Lance Gold, Leslie Westbrook, Lia Fanelli, Lizzy Cline, Lluisa Matarrodona, Lucas de Barros, Luiz Alfaya, Luiz Segatto, Luke Miller, Big Steve Pedone, Big Paul Williams, Mãe Iansá, Marcelo e Georgia Queroz, Meredith

Miller, Mestre Ireneu, Michelle Cushing, Miguel Filippowitch, Nuria Ocaña, Paulo Roberto de Souza, Padrinho Sebastião, Paí Ogum, Paloma Butcher, Pascal Perich, Paul Williams, Pavlo Pushkar, Peter Kuhn, Philip Sitbon, Publishers Weekly, Rolling Stone, New York Times Book Review, Revista Semana, Rane Jäntti, Richard O'Connell, Rob Pistella, Robert Kerian, Robert and Suzanne Williams, Ron Turner, Rosemary Hochschild, Salvador Preciado, Sami Yaffa, Santa Sara, Santo Daime, Saturnino Brito de Nascimento, Snake Eyes, Stefani Kong-Uhler, Steve Bonge, Steve Mora, Steve Wiener, Tanya Mayberry, Tessa Hughes-Freeland, Theo and Andrez Castilho, Toiskallio Kaisu-Maria, Tony Fried, Vera Perrone, Victoria Talbot, Vovó Catarina de Angola, Walter Gregory, Wayne Henlis, Whitney Ward, and Zoe Romero Miranda.

ABOUT THE AUTHOR

Jonathan Shaw may be best known for his long, star-studded career as a world renowned globetrotting tattoo master. Since embarking on a decades-long hiatus from the skin trade, he has worked exclusively as a full-time writer, publishing several critically acclaimed works of fiction, poetry, and memoir, as well as a widely popular series of lushly illustrated museum-quality art books on tattoo history.

Shaw's work has been featured in countless international publications, translated into several languages, and optioned for film by Leonardo DiCaprio.

A new line of designer fashion clothing featuring Jonathan Shaw's unique, innovative tattoo-related artwork and personal brand is currently being launched worldwide.

When not traveling the world, he splits his time between homes in Rio de Janeiro, New York City, Veracruz, Mexico, and Los Angeles— where a feature-length documentary about his life and times is currently in post-production.

His motto: "Comforting the disturbed and disturbing the comfortable—since 1953"

For readings, book signing events, speaking engagements, and exclusive tattoo appointments, Jonathan Shaw can be reached at: jsfuncity@gmail.com